Hapworth cut him off, his voice higher, more agitated. "I know your name, but who the hell *are* you? Who do you work for? My opponent?" He tried to reason it out, but he only became more confused.

Gorman took another sip of whiskey and felt the warmth spread through his mind. He only smiled at Hapworth.

A note of hysteria crept into Hapworth's voice. "What do I have to do to keep you quiet? To keep you from ruining me?"

Gorman leaned forward and faced the Congressman. "Ruin you? On the contrary, Hap." He played his trump card. "The people I'm associated with aren't going to ruin you. They're giving you the chance of a lifetime. In just two years, we're going to make you President of the United States."

THE MIRAMAR SEDUCTION

KEELING JORDAN

A Division of Charter Communications Inc.
A GROSSET & DUNLAP COMPANY
51 Madison Avenue
New York, New York 10010

THE MIRAMAR SEDUCTION

All characters in this book are fictitious. Any resemblance to actual persons, living or dead, is purely coincidental.

Published by arrangement with The New American Library, Inc.

First Ace Charter Printing September 1981
Published simultaneously in Canada
Manufactured in the United States of America

2 4 6 8 0 9 7 5 3 1

To Wanda, who helped me make it happen . . .
and to Judy, who helped me see through.

THE MIRAMAR SEDUCTION

Part I

Chapter 1

The Gulfstream lifted off the runway, and Hunter could feel the powerful turbofans propelling it upward, higher and higher until finally the backswept wings penetrated the brilliant blue atmosphere of the Pacific.

Below, the late November sun accentuated the golden glow of the southern California shore. The blue and white of the surf was in marked contrast to the sand. Farther out, Hunter noted absently, the colors of the ocean gave way to the deeper grays and greens of the turbulent waves.

Hunter saw it all from the rear of the cabin where he sprawled on one of the leather swivel chairs in the aircraft's conference center. He saw it, but he gave it no more attention than he had the takeoff. He had the look of detached boredom of one who has witnessed the coastlines of the world and found each, in turn, as tedious as the last.

Then before him he saw the rocky outline of Dana Point, and he remembered the man he had so recently left. An uncharacteristic feeling of compassion came over him, and his hand reached out for the intercom switch.

"Turn around and go back over San Clemente. Give him the customary salute. He'll be expecting it."

A reply wasn't necessary, but the pilot's voice spoke through the intercom, obedient, compliant. "Yes, Mr. Hunter."

He'll be expecting it. Hunter's own words echoed back through his mind. Yes, he *would* be expecting it. Pomp and ceremony still mean a lot to him, even after all this time. After the world has stopped observing the formalities. After the protocol has gone down the drain with everything else.

The plane was following his command now, and as the altitude decreased the ground below him took on shape and substance. The small community of San Clemente formed itself and shortly gave way to the sprawling mansions of the movie actors and retired industrialists on Cyprus Shores.

And then the concrete wall, looking strangely flattened and impotent from this altitude. The eight-foot barrier that had provided the answer to his almost psychotic need for protection. And later, after their return, the answer to an even more desperate need—privacy. Privacy from the public, privacy even from the prying eyes of the other millionaires of Cyprus Shores.

The shape of La Casa Pacifica appeared. The office compound. The golf course, its lush putting greens overgrown with weeds. The house, its peaceful serenity soon to be abandoned in favor of a frenetic new life in the East.

On the beach, behind the house, a solitary figure walked briskly up the sunny stretch of sand.

The plane swooped down toward the compound, dipping one wing in salute, and far below the figure stopped and drew itself to attention. One hand extended toward the sky to return the salute and then, for no reason at all, the other hand reached into the air. The man stood there, his arms stretched upward in the victorious gesture that had become, in happier times, his trademark.

Hunter stared at the figure below him, recognizing the characteristic gesture but not understanding it. A wave of irritation wiped away the brief moment of sympathy he had felt earlier.

The damned fool, he thought to himself. He still sees himself as a winner. And until today, Hunter thought soberly, he had seen himself as a winner who could make a comeback. Until today. A wintry smile tempered the angry look on his face. But after today he knows it's finally over. He knows that, just like all the others so many months ago, The Miramar Corporation has no further use for him, that Miramar has found itself a new boy.

Shrugging the thoughts from his mind, Hunter put out his hand again for the intercom. "Resume your course, Cochran."

He reached across to the seat opposite him, took his business case, and snapped it open. Removing a stack of file folders from the case, he directed his attention to them.

But his mind would not focus on the reports in front of him. His thoughts kept returning to the lone figure on the beach.

The man *had* been a winner. A natural winner, tough and determined. He knew the importance of winning and he had let nothing stand in his way, neither the conventions of society nor manmade laws. But he had known something even more important: how to create the illusion of winning. And he had made himself out to be a winner even in defeat. He had molded a tough image that appealed to the American public, from the hard hats who built the skyscrapers of the world to the silk hats who financed them.

Hunter remembered the early days, remembered the man's emergence as a growing political power. Hunter had recognized the qualities early—Hunter and a few others—and eventually he had placed a vast communications empire at the man's disposal. He had watched with fascination as the man slowly and methodically convinced the country that he knew what was best.

Hunter considered. He *had* known what was best for America. And so had Hunter and the tight coterie of advisors who had dictated the course of events. They had known that governing a world power was not a democratic process. People had to be led, persuaded, even manipulated into doing what was best for them.

As Hunter sighed, his face compressed itself into a look of intentness, his jaw set firmly, his mouth a tight, straight line. The folders lay unnoticed on his lap.

It was unfortunate that the man had fallen from power. Unfortunate that he had *allowed* himself to be deposed because of the stupid mistakes of others, because too many of the people around him knew too much. And because of his own inherent weakness—a weakness that even Hunter had not recognized: the need to be loved and admired.

Above all, Hunter thought, it was unfortunate that the techniques of persuasion had not been perfected in the early seventies. Because today Hunter could have helped him sweep the whole dirty mess under a quick-to-be-forgotten rug. Hunter could have persuaded the public to overlook the lies, the indiscretions. He could have made the man one of the most beloved of American leaders.

He could have given complete power. Absolute, everlasting, infinite.

But now Hunter would realize those things, because he held the key. The key to the subconscious mind of America.

He was prepared to use it, carefully and methodically and without emotion. And the people he had chosen to assist him were equally prepared. This time, he assured himself, there would be no weak links, no screw-ups.

He took the folders from his lap, studying the names typed neatly on the tabs.

Andrew Martin . . . Anthony Hapworth . . . John J. Collins . . . Richard J. Craig.

All key figures in his plan. But one of them more essential, more urgent than the rest. He singled out the folder labeled "Andrew Martin" and riffled through the contents, reading the pages briefly, placing the data in context in his mind. He nodded to himself and reached for the intercom again.

"Cochran, send the steward back. I want to send a wire." He paused, then added, "And I'd like a drink."

Hunter busied himself scribbling a brief message and the name and address of the recipient. Having reread the words, he ripped the page from the pad, extending it to the approaching steward.

"Happy Turkey Day, sir," the steward said to him, holding forth a tray with a bottle of champagne and a glass.

The man's words and the unexpected bottle caught Hunter by surprise, and he scowled up at him.

"What? What did you say?"

The steward was addled by Hunter's terse rejoinder and for a moment only grinned stupidly at his employer. Finally he replied. "It's Thanksgiving, sir. Today, I mean. Today is Thanksgiving Day. I thought you might prefer champagne."

Hunter stared at him, trying to comprehend this obvious frivolity. As the meaning gradually seeped into his preoccupation, he reached out to take the glass. But midway he stopped. Involuntarily he shook his head.

"No, just bring me a Scotch."

Not today, he said to himself as the man departed. There's no reason to celebrate. Not yet. But maybe soon.

Chapter 2

On the other side of the continent a small boat floundered through turbulent waters, trying to make port on the darkened island. The sea all along the Carolina coast had already been victimized by winter, and it responded with dark, urgent heavings and white-capped waves.

Finally, lurching into the relative calm of a small cove, the boat edged its way through the blackness toward the dim light that marked the weathered wooden dock.

After it was secure, an old man stepped to shore. The night was moonless, and the premature winter storm spit snowflakes into the air. The solitary figure picked out a path amidst the great forest of sea pines and cedar trees and disappeared into its tunnel-like opening.

Some minutes later he trudged up to a large stone structure, its windows marked by bright shafts of light cutting into the stormy night. He climbed the worn stone steps to a porch, taking such shelter as he could inside the lighted alcove that partially shielded the entrance from the frigid blasts.

His hand reached out with a stubby finger and jabbed at the bell. The movement seemed to intensify his chill and an uncontrollable tremor shook his body. Impatiently he rang again.

A woman in a white clinical jacket appeared and, recognizing the visitor, threw the broad door open and pulled him inside. He mumbled a few words to her and a look of doubt spread over her face. But he spoke again and she searched his weather-beaten countenance and finally nodded, leading him down a long hallway and pausing at the end of the corridor in front of a closed door.

She tapped quietly and then, without waiting for a reply, turned the knob and opened the door.

"Doctor?" Her voice cut through a silence broken only by the crackling of the burning wood in the fireplace. "Doctor?" she repeated. "It's John, from the mainland. He says he has an urgent message for you."

Across the room a desk lamp spotlighted the silver hair of the man sitting behind the desk, engrossed in the words he had been writing in a large leatherbound journal.

The age of the two men was a common denominator, but the commonality ended there. John was short and thick and wrinkled like the bark of one of the venerable sea pines. The other man was tall and lean. His face was virtually without wrinkles, almost as smooth as a man of thirty. But his face bore a florid look, its unhealthy color seeming to come to focus on an enlarged, slightly mottled nose. His long white jacket covered a white button-down shirt and a neatly patterned tie.

He looked up sharply, his concentration distracted by the voice of the nurse and the movement at the doorway. One hand pulled off the heavy horn-rimmed eyeglasses and automatically the other hand reached up to smooth his long, silvery hair.

"John!" Surprise was mirrored on his face. "What in God's name brings you out to the island on a night like this?" He cocked his head toward one of the large windows beside him and listened briefly to the sound of tiny pellets striking the pane. "Good God, man, it's sleeting. And the water must have been worse than a roller-coaster."

The old man was fumbling under the outsized yellow slicker he wore, struggling to remove something from his pocket. Finally he succeeded and brought forth a crumpled yellow envelope and thrust it forward.

"It's a telegram for you, Doctor," he said simply.

"Goddamnit, John, I can see that it's a telegram." The doctor took the message as he spoke, laying it aside. He moved around the desk and started unbuttoning the heavy slicker and pulling it from the old man's shoulders. "But nothing could be important enough to take you out on the water on a night like this!"

He stripped the coat away and led John to the fireplace ablaze with crackling logs. "Why in hell didn't you just open it and read it to me over the telephone?"

John looked at him ingenuously. "It's from Mr. Hunter, Doctor," he said softly.

"To hell with Mr. Hunter," the doctor replied. "Nothing is worth your catching pneumonia—"

"It says, 'Confidential.' " The old man cut him off. "I wouldn't have dared open a confidential telegram from Mr. Hunter, no matter what." Alarm began to register in his voice at such an unthinkable action. "Mr. Hunter wouldn't tolerate such a thing. Not even from me."

The doctor met his eyes, understanding the old man's concern. He turned back to his desk and took the yellow envelope, partly to mollify old John, partly out of curiosity. Ripping it open, he scanned the message and grimaced, staring at the words. With a grunt he looked up at the others.

"Annie." He addressed the woman who had escorted the old caretaker into the office and who still stood, guardianlike, in the doorway. "Take John to the kitchen and get him something hot to drink. And some of our

Thanksgiving turkey. And tell Macomb to make him a place to sleep in one of the Observation Rooms." He raised his hand as the old man started to protest. "You can call your wife and tell her, John. I'm not going to let you go back to the mainland on a night like this. You might kill yourself."

The doctor stood motionless as the two figures departed. But after the door had closed behind them he walked to the fireplace and read again the words on the telegram he still held in his hand.

FINAL EVALUATION OF UTAH EXPERIMENT ESSENTIAL TO SUCCESS OF PROJECT JUPITER. PROCEED WITHOUT DELAY. INFORM ME BY RETURN WIRE OF TIME AND DAY OF EVALUATION PROCESS AND SEND VIDEOTAPE TRANSCRIPT TO NEW YORK OFFICE EARLIEST.

He stared into the flames for a moment, his mind turning from the telegram to the man who had sent it.

The bastard, he thought. The pompous bastard. I know more about the Utah Experiment than he could even comprehend.

A frown formed on his face as he looked again at the request in the telegram. To hell with him, he thought. To hell with Maxwell Hunter.

Slowly and contemptuously he crumpled the sheet of paper and tossed it into the fire. He watched the ball of paper ignite and transform itself into charred blackness. Then, as if the disappearance of the paper had removed an unsavory thought from his mind, he turned away from the fire and addressed his thoughts to the matters at hand.

Tonight, he realized with mounting excitement, he stood on the verge of a medical breakthrough. If tonight's final evaluation of the patient proved successful, the most ambitious research project ever attempted on the human brain would take its place in the annals of medical science. The Utah Experiment.

And tonight, if his evaluation proved successful, he would help launch a project of breathtaking magnitude. The control of human behavior through the subconscious mind. Not of a single mind, but of millions of minds . . .

The doctor pulled his thoughts back to reality. He smoothed the wrinkles from his white coat and walked back to the desk. In a moment he was absorbed in the meticulous handwriting in the journal before him, preparing himself one final time for the procedure that lay before him.

He flipped the pages back, looking for the original entry, but a loud knock on the door disrupted his concentration and he looked up in irritation as Annie abruptly entered the room.

"Walter Cronkite's doing a piece about Drew Martin on the news," she reported excitedly. "I thought you'd want to see it."

He opened his mouth to protest, but the woman had already reached the small television set across from him. Before he could speak, the commentator's voice swept through the room.

"As millions of Americans celebrated the Thanksgiving holiday, officials of the State Crime Bureau of Utah report no new leads on the whereabouts of Andrew Martin, a key figure in the tragic wave of religious riots that has shaken the campuses of that state's three largest universities and, indeed, the Mormon Church itself."

The grayness of the screen had given way to the vivid colors of the network newsroom and the familiar countenance of the commentator filled the screen. Behind him a brightly colored map highlighted western America and then the state of Utah, its principal cities pinpointed.

The commentator continued. *"Drew Martin, a recognized campus and church leader and a football star at*

Brigham Young, has been missing since his alleged participation in the 'Mormon Massacre,' a twenty-four-hour siege of rioting and violence that ended with the death of a fellow student who was not a member of the Mormon faith."

The brilliance of the maps gave way to the black-and-white tones of a photograph, and a handsome, youthful face beamed out at the television audience from behind the announcer's head. Accentuated by a broad grin, the face looked wholesome and boyish. Quickly his visage was replaced with another, this time showing a look of fierce determination as Drew Martin pulled an arm back to pass a football.

"State officials and members of the governing body of the Church of Jesus Christ of Latter-day Saints are still at a loss to explain why the normally tranquil campuses erupted in violence. According to University sources, tensions have been building throughout the fall. First outward signs appeared less than a month ago when, on Hallowe'en, hooded and robed bands appeared on the Brigham Young campus proclaiming Mormon supremacy."

Drew Martin's face gave way to a bank of masked figures, reminiscent of the hooded Klansmen of another time, another place. The figures moved slowly in a processional, their robes eerily illuminated by the flickering torches they carried. And then that scene, too, was supplanted by the filmed coverage of the weekend of rioting, the hooded figures grappling with denim-clad college youths.

The newsman told the story. *"Mormon students became uncharacteristically belligerent, seeking revenge from the 'Gentiles,' as they called non-Mormon students, for the Massacre at Haun's Mill, a violent attack perpetrated in 1838 in Missouri on Joseph Smith and his followers.*

"The final violence broke out on Monday night, climaxing in gunplay and death. Drew Martin was the only 'Marauder' identified by bystanders, when he was unmasked during the melee in a dormitory after the appearance on campus of the rock singer Barry Starr.

"Tonight, an uneasy peace has returned to Utah campuses, but authorities fear that violence may have befallen young Martin himself.

"Andrew Martin was recognized by faculty and students alike as an unquestioned leader among . . ."

The commentator's voice droned on and again Drew Martin's smiling face peered out at the audience. With a gesture of irritation, the doctor stood and walked impatiently across the room. His hand stilled the voice, sent the image on the screen back into the anonymity of grayness.

"That's enough," he announced with finality.

Annie Parkinson jerked her head toward him in surprise, then jumped to her feet to turn the television on again. "There's more to come," she said, as her hand reached out and touched the switch. The sound again flooded through the room, and the doctor again silenced the television, finally.

"I said that's enough, Miss Parkinson!"

She looked at him, shock evident on her face. "But he wasn't through with the report. They were showing Drew Martin in a football game," she blurted.

The doctor looked at her witheringly. "Oh, come now, Miss Parkinson." His voice became heavy with sarcasm. "Surely you've seen enough of Drew Martin during the past three days. You've been hovering over his bed like some giddy old woman."

She drew her breath in sharply. "That's not true, Doctor," she began defensively. "I've only followed normal clinical procedure, checked to see that they administered the sedation properly—"

The doctor cut her off, his voice icy. "Then perhaps

you'd better go check his sedation now. And while you're there, you can get him ready for the final evaluation. We'll do it tonight."

"Tonight! I thought it was scheduled for tomorrow—"

"Tonight. They're anxious for a report in New York. We'll do it tonight. If all goes well, we'll release him tomorrow."

"Release him!" Despite her professional training, Annie's voice was indignant. "Release him where? And to what? What are you going to do, now that you've messed up that kid's life? Give him a rowboat back to Charleston? Let him hitch-hike back home to Utah to face a manslaughter charge?"

The doctor looked at her uncomprehendingly. "Manslaughter charge?"

"For God's sake, Doctor, you don't think that he can just go home and start attending classes again, do you? He's killed a man!" She stopped abruptly, correcting herself. "No, that's not right. We caused him to kill a man, and now we're about to sacrifice Drew Martin, too—all in the name of medical science."

At first his reaction had been one of amazement that his assistant would question him. But as she challenged his professional judgment, anger had spread over his face.

Now, hearing her question the scientific validity of the experiment, he too lost his professional composure.

"You have no right to challenge this experiment," he told her, striding across the room to stand towering over her. "You have no right to question what we have done, or what will happen tomorrow or the day after that. You are a trained clinical psychologist, Miss Parkinson, and you're involved in an experiment that could prove to be a major breakthrough in understanding the brain-mind relationship."

He continued to stare at her in anger. When he spoke

again, his voice was calmer but still cold, and he spit out the sentences in disdain.

"You were hired to assist on the Utah Experiment because of your excellent record and your high professional standing. I assumed your conduct would be equally professional. But you're acting like an hysterical woman. For your information, Andrew Martin will be released in the care of others who will take him back to Utah and leave him near the home of friends. He will remember nothing of his experience. His condition will be so similar to amnesia that even a specialist will not be able to detect any trace of the drugs that have been administered." He paused a moment. His anger had subsided, but his voice was still frigid. "And ample funds will be provided to assure that he will not be convicted of anything. Now, does that satisfy your maternal instincts?"

She was silent, her eyes averted, staring at the floor.

"Very well. If you have control of yourself, take Martin to the Procedures Room and prepare him. I'll be ready in ten minutes."

"Yes, Doctor." She prepared to leave the room, but the doctor spoke again.

"Oh, yes, Miss Parkinson. Tell Macomb to have the video equipment ready for taping." His anger at the woman was forgotten. His mind went back to the telegram from Hunter, and when he spoke again it was with distaste. "I've been asked to record the procedure for a part of the permanent record."

A short while later he entered the large control room that overlooked the brilliantly lighted Procedures Room. He walked directly to the control console and saw it was already dotted with red and green lights as the electronic gear was activated by Macomb. Through the double-glassed window he could see Annie bending over an inert form on an examining table. As she moved away for a moment, he could observe Drew Martin.

The skin on the youthful face was pallid, the lips set together in a tight, straight line. His eyes were closed except for an occasional fitful fluttering. His blond hair fell back in disarray against the white hospital pillow. Two restraining straps circled his muscular, athletic torso.

Annie again moved to his side, applying a miniscule electrical attachment to a small, shaved portion of his scalp.

The doctor watched her movements, watched her shave a second patch of hair away and complete a second connection. When he was certain that the scene was procedurally correct, he spoke over the intercom.

"Inject the alphapentathol, Miss Parkinson."

Annie removed a hypodermic from the table beside her and plunged it into the young man's arm, then stood back to observe his reaction.

It was almost immediate. As the drug coursed into his body, his eyes opened and stayed open. In place of the listless expression, his face and eyes took on euphoric life. His body moved and began to strain against the straps that held it flat, but when he encountered resistance he instantly relaxed, a smile coming over his face, his eyes taking on a look of pleasant resignation.

The doctor spoke into a microphone on the console. "Can you hear me, Drew?"

At the sound of his name, the young man's head moved slightly. His eyes maintained the look of pleasant resignation as he answered softly, "Yes." His tone was almost dreamlike.

"We are performing an experiment, Drew, to determine the depths of your memory. I will ask you a number of questions, and you will answer them to the best of your ability. The nurse has attached an electrode and a diode to your scalp, and we will occasionally apply an electric stimulus to the right side of your head. Don't be frightened. You will feel no pain. Do you understand me, Drew?"

Martin's head nodded.

"Answer me, Drew. Do you understand me?"

"Yes. I understand."

"What is your name?"

"Andrew Martin."

"What is your full name?"

"John Andrew Martin."

"Where do you live?"

"In Logan, Utah."

"Where are you enrolled in college?"

"At BYU."

"What is your religious faith?"

"Mormon."

"What do you call people who are not members of the Mormon Church?"

"Gentiles."

"How do you feel about Gentiles?"

"I hate them." Despite the harshness of the words, the reply was offered in the same dreamlike voice, the face remaining in the same placid repose.

The doctor continued. "Have you always hated Gentiles, Drew?"

"No. Some of my best friends were Gentiles. Before—" He stopped.

"Some of your best friends were Gentiles, Drew?" the doctor prompted.

"Yes."

"When did you begin to dislike your Gentile friends?"

"Just before I joined the Marauders."

"What are the Marauders?"

"Good Mormons."

"What do they do?"

"They hate the Gentiles."

"Why do they hate the Gentiles, Drew?"
"I don't know. We just hate them."
"Did anyone tell you to hate the Gentiles, Drew?"
"No. No one told me to hate them."
The doctor repeated the question. "Did anyone tell you to hate the Gentiles?"
The eyes became troubled. "No-o-o. No, I don't think so. I can't remember."
"Do you remember what happened on the campus last Saturday night?"
"There was a rock concert."
"Who was the singer?"
"Barry Starr."
"And what happened after the concert, Drew?"
A pause. "The Marauders had a meeting."
"Did you attend?"
"Yes."
"And what did you do?"
"We had a fight."
"Where?"
"In the dormitory. With the Gentiles."
"What happened during the fight, Drew?"
"I don't remember. It all happened so fast."
"What happened during the fight, Drew?"
"I don't remember. The Gentiles were mad. They were ready to fight us. One of them called me a dirty name and came at me. He grabbed my mask. I was ready to hit him, but then I had a gun in my hand. I don't know where I got it."
"And what did you do, Drew?"
"I don't remember."
"What did you do, Drew?"
As he heard the question again, the young man became restless on the table. His head moved from side to side, and for a moment he strained against the restraining straps. His only answer was a moaning sound.

"You must tell me, Drew. Try to remember. What did you do?"

There was agitation in Drew Martin's voice when he finally replied. "I don't know. I don't remember. There was an explosion. I saw blood on his shirt. Someone told me to run. I ran outside. And then somebody grabbed me and stuck a rag over my nose. It smelled funny. I don't remember anything else."

The doctor nodded and sat back, considering. Everything was going as he had expected. Martin had normal recall of the conscious events of the past week. Now, for the difficult part, the subconscious recall. He glanced at his wristwatch, making note of the time: 6:42 P.M.

He had no doubt about his ability to withdraw experiential responses from the hundreds of tiny neurones in Martin's brain. But now he would be seeking out *one particular neurone*—the one tiny brain cell where a subliminal message of revenge had been stored.

If he succeeded with this, then he would be ready for the final experiment. It was the reason he had put up with Hunter and the demands of the Miramar Corporation through the years. His crowning professional achievement: to reach the subconscious and manipulate the behavior of the entire American public, every man and woman and child who came into contact with the mass media.

A frown came across his face as another thought pushed its way into his churning brain. There were other reasons why he had put up with Hunter, of course, reasons he usually chose to ignore. And there was another reason why he was so intent on making Project Jupiter a reality. At last he would have the opportunity to exact revenge for an old wrong. And as that thought formed itself in his mind, a smile of anticipation appeared on his face.

He realized suddenly that Annie was standing by the

patient staring at him, awaiting his instructions. He pulled his thoughts back from the past and approached his evaluation procedure with a renewed determination. There was every chance that it would not prove successful. But, on the other hand—. His hand reached out to the console, flipped a switch. A harsh, metallic sound filled the room. Percussion, electronic strings, a synthesizer. And voices. And then, in the midst of it all, the shrill, insinuating tones of a man's voice.

The doctor spoke. "Do you recognize that sound, Drew?"

"Yeah. It's a record."

"Who is it, Drew?"

"Barry Starr. It's the big record at school. All the DJ's are playing it. It's 'Puppet in Love.' My roommate plays it all the time." He was silent a moment, then he forced himself to direct a question to the doctor. "Why is it playing now?"

"To help you remember the Massacre, Drew. To help you remember why you hate Gentiles."

"Oh."

"Drew, I'm going to help you search your deepest memories and to tell me what you remember. Whatever it is—a sound, a voice, a face, anything—try to describe it to me. When I say the word *recall*, tell me whatever comes to your mind. Do you understand?"

"Yes."

The doctor applied the first electroshock and saw the head of the patient jerk involuntarily. Simultaneously his voice called out, "Recall!"

"I hear something."

"*Recall!*"

"I hear something. A woman's voice. She's saying something to me. But I can't hear what she's saying . . ."

"*Recall!*"

"I heard it again. But I can't understand."

"*Recall!*"

"Now I can hear it. It's my mother's voice. She's calling me."

"What is she saying to you?"

"She's telling me to come away from the river. She's telling me not to fall in the river because I can't swim."

The doctor realized that he had unlocked Drew Martin's memory bank and drawn forth an experiential response from the patient, an experience from his childhood that had remained stored in his memory throughout the intervening years.

He tried again. "*Recall, Drew.*"

"I hear voices again."

"The same voices?"

"No. They're different. There's a lot of them. They're yelling at me. Telling me I did something wrong. Oh-h-h." He moaned. "Oh, everyone is yelling . . ."

"*Recall!*"

"They're still yelling. Make them stop. Now they're screaming. I don't know what to do. What have I done?"

"Where are the voices, Drew? Where are you?"

"I'm in the dormitory at school. I don't know what to do . . ."

"*Recall, Drew.*"

"I don't know what to do . . ."

"*Recall, Drew.*"

"I don't know what to do . . ."

Annie Parkinson straightened from her position beside Drew Martin and looked with excitement through the window at the doctor, but he shook his head. He had merely discovered the neurone where the memory of the riot was stored. That was to have been expected. It was undoubtedly foremost on the mind of the young man. But that wasn't what he sought. He wanted to find the memory *before* the riot, to learn what *motivated* the riot.

His voice called out again, "*Recall.*"

"*Recall.*"

The doctor's voice had lost its edge, his shoulders slumped over the console in fatigue. In the Procedures Room, Annie had pulled a stool to the side of the examining table and now sat there, drained and tired.

The clock on the wall behind her showed that it was after ten.

Drew Martin responded again, his voice unchanged from the dreamlike tone of remembrance that had, for more than three hours, recalled incident after incident from his subconscious.

The doctor sat back in his chair.

"Let's take a break, Annie. Perhaps you'd get us both a cup of coffee?" Gratefully she started to disconnect the electrode from Martin's scalp. "That's all right." The doctor stopped her. "Just leave it hooked up until you return."

He sighed as she left the room. Nothing conclusive. Although they had learned a great deal about the past of Drew Martin, he had been unable to elicit any experiential response relative to the experiment.

Pushing himself back from the console, he stood and stretched. One hand went to the shirt pocket beneath the clinical jacket and withdrew a long slender cigar. The match sputtered in his hand and as he drew the fire into the tobacco he was engulfed in a cloud of smoke.

He walked back to his chair and began a cursory check of the electronic gear, making certain of its function before they continued.

Suddenly he realized that something was not right, something was not as it had been. His eyes shot to the examining table. Finding nothing amiss, he was about to dismiss the sensation when he localized it. It was the sound of the Barry Starr record.

He listened more closely and then he could detect the

difference. Another sound, another voice was mixed with the soundtrack that was playing into the room. He sat forward and adjusted the volume upward on the microphone that hung over Martin's quiet form, and then he realized what it was.

Drew Martin was humming with the record. He was following the music exactly with his own voice, softly and unobtrusively, but nevertheless following it.

The doctor's hand leaped forward and he sent a major electrical shock into the young man's brain, calling out in a voice alive with excitement, "*Recall, Drew! Recall!*"

"I hear music. I hear music somewhere."

"What kind of music?"

"I don't know. It's funny. Lots of high voices singing. I don't like it."

"What does it sound like?"

"It's creepy. The voices are so whiny." He fell silent a moment, and another surge of electricity shot into his brain.

The doctor's body hunched over the console, his senses racing. The patient was hearing the voices—the *other* voices—the sub-audible message that had been embedded in the Starr recording.

"What are the voices saying, Drew?" The surgeon was tense, his voice demanding.

"I can't tell."

"*Recall again, Drew.*"

"They're so hard to understand. Like a ghost's voice."

"*Recall again, Drew.*"

"They're saying . . . they're saying . . . yes, they're saying Brother Joseph . . . and Haun's Mill. And something else."

"*Recall, Drew!*" There was no response, and the doctor spoke again as Annie entered the control room with a cup of steaming coffee.

"*Recall, Drew.* What else do you hear? *Recall, Drew.*"

"Joseph Smith . . . and Haun's Mill . . . and there's something else. Now I can hear it. They're saying, 'Gentiles.' That's what they're saying. They're talking about what the Gentiles did to Brother Smith at Haun's Mill."

"What else, Drew? What else are they saying?"

"I can't hear . . . wait! They're saying another word. But what is it . . ."

"Listen, Drew, and tell me."

He was silent for a moment before he spoke, a look of intense concentration on his face. And then his face broke into a new awareness. "Now I can hear it. Now I remember why I hate the Gentiles."

"*Recall and repeat*, Drew!"

"It's Revenge. They're saying, 'Revenge.' " His voice rose to a high pitch, despite the drug. "Revenge against the Gentiles. Make them pay for what they did. Revenge!"

The doctor slumped in his chair, the energy drained from his body.

Success. Complete, total success. Thank God, he whispered to himself. Thank God.

Chapter 3

The cable car stopped in its near vertical ascent of Nob Hill and a woman stepped to the street, encircled by a horde of other bodies.

All those around her were handsome and sophisticated, stylishly dressed and intent on their own affairs. But as they broke and scattered in every direction, she stood apart as the most handsome and stylish of them all.

She stood for a moment looking up the hill at the imposing structure of the Fairmont and across at the slightly tarnished facade of the Mark Hopkins. Then she turned and walked briskly back down the hill to a renovated nineteenth-century structure, its painted face complementing similar structures about it.

The woman paused at the front doorway, briefly fumbling in her handbag for her key. As she did so, she caught sight of the telegram that had been delivered to her office. Ignoring it, she found the key and let herself into the small entryhall and, a few moments later, into her tiny apartment on the top floor.

Tossing a slim attaché case on a chair, she glanced at her watch and out of habit switched on the television set. She moved into the bedroom, vaguely conscious of the newsman's voice as she pulled the lightweight turtleneck sweater over her head.

She was occupied with her own thoughts, with Hunter's wire. It was miraculous, she thought, that she had been able to pull it all together in such a short period of time. Especially on the Friday after Thanksgiving, when most of the city was still in a holiday mood.

It was even more miraculous that she had been able to reach the man she had called, to arrange an appointment with him at cocktail time. She had assumed that an attorney of his magnitude would be inaccessible, would spend the holiday weekend vacationing, relaxing. People like that must have families, must have some structure in their lives, she reasoned.

But she had reached him rather quickly, all things considered. And he had agreed to meet her before he left San Francisco for the weekend. And now she didn't want to be late. She wanted to make the arrangements tonight. She wanted to be able to send a positive reply to Hunter before the evening was over.

She emerged from the shower and pulled the plastic cap from her head, allowing her long dark hair to fall loosely about her damp shoulders. She slipped into a heavy terrycloth robe, feeling its folds absorb the drops of water that still clung to her body, and moved to the closet to select a dress.

Her hand was reaching out to take a garment from the rack when she heard a word from the other room that pushed all thoughts of clothing from her mind.

"Utah." The announcer was talking about the Utah incident.

She ran across the bedroom to the living area and the newscast and sank into a chair opposite the television. On the screen she saw a map of Utah, followed by photographs of the boy—the same that the nation had seen so many times in the past few days—and heard the announcer discussing the fate of Andrew Martin.

". . . *About midafternoon today Martin wandered aim-*

lessly to the front door of a farmhouse near his hometown of Logan, Utah. He was, and is still, the apparent victim of amnesia, claiming no memory of his activities or whereabouts since last Saturday when he was involved in the shooting death of a fellow student at Brigham Young University.

"*Officials of the Salt Lake City Police Department report that he is in good physical condition except for minor lacerations on the right side of his head. The small cuts and abrasions could be the result, they speculate, of an injury to his head, which could have brought about the amnesia.*

"*Martin has been officially charged with manslaughter in the death of William James Robinson almost a week ago. His parents and officials of the Church of Jesus Christ of Latter-day Saints have been allowed to visit him at the Salt Lake City jail, where he will be held until formalities allow his release.*

"*In another occurrence of the Thanksgiving weekend—*"

The woman rose and flipped off the television. She walked across the room to the window, pushing aside the curtain to stare down at the activity on the street below her. She had known of the complete success of the Utah Experiment from Hunter's telegram, but the coverage on the evening news served to reinforce its importance.

The news commentator couldn't report the *real* news, she thought, the medical breakthrough that Paul had accomplished on the island. She shook her head. It was too bad that she couldn't have been there to witness the final evaluation, to share in Paul's triumph. Earlier she had been a vital part of Paul's research program, until the project demanded a different role of her. And now he was alone on St. Sebastian's with no one to toast his successes. There would be no public acclaim for him, not even recognition by the medical profession, not yet. The project demanded total secrecy. The Miramar Corporation demanded it. Maxwell Hunter demanded it.

Hunter. The thought of him filled her with a vague feeling of discomfort, even though she knew he was on the other side of the continent from her.

She turned and walked to the place she had thrown her attaché case earlier. From it she took a sheaf of papers. She scanned the names at the top of each page and withdrew one.

Collins & Craig. The most successful advertising agency in Atlanta today, perhaps even in the South. Not unlike scores of other successful agencies in Los Angeles and Dallas and Chicago, in every part of the United States. She looked at the other names on the reports in her hand as she had done on countless occasions while she had studied each of them. They all offered the necessary requirements, all satisfied the needs the team would have in the months ahead.

But her eyes went back to the report on the Atlanta agency, and her mind returned to Paul. He had been determined from the outset that Collins & Craig would be the agency. And so had Gorman. Even Hunter concurred in their thinking.

Only she had questioned it, only she had demanded that other agencies be evaluated. And her will had prevailed. Now, she must make her own recommendation.

A frown crossed her face. Paul was obsessed with the selection of the agency, was obsessed with Collins & Craig. She knew that his reasons were personal. And deep rooted. And deep-rooted personal reasons could be dangerous, could obscure good judgment. She would have to watch Paul more closely, she realized; she could not allow him to jeopardize the success of the project.

But, she thought with a shrug, whatever his problem I can handle it. And this is the least I can do for him. If

I can't be there to congratulate him, I can support him in this way.

She withdrew the report, placed it on top of the others. Tonight she would notify Hunter of her selection, would mail a report tomorrow. Collins & Craig was as good a choice as any.

Suddenly she was aware of the time, and she moved quickly back to her bedroom to get dressed.

A short while later she emerged from the building and walked back up the hill to the traffic light. Across the street she could see the hotel, and her watch told her she was on time.

She reached the covered portico of the Stanford-Court and walked under its magnificent stained-glass dome into the elegant lobby. She selected a table as far removed as possible from the bustling cocktail area that spread throughout the lobby and ordered a drink. She prepared to await the arrival of the legendary criminal lawyer.

She was on her second martini when he finally appeared. He was a shaggy lion of a man, his grizzled gray hair cascading over his collar. He stood in the center of the room looking from table to table in his search for her. He saw her almost at once. She was sure of that for she gave him a slight wave of her hand in identification. But he seemed to relish his position of physical prominence, to enjoy whispers that were exchanged at other tables as sophisticated San Franciscans told their out-of-town guests of the presence of the luminary from the world of criminal law.

And then he walked directly to her, pausing before her chair and allowing his eyes to unashamedly study every part of her body. With a courtly bow, he spoke.

"I had no idea that the voice I spoke with this afternoon belonged to such a beautiful woman," he said, sitting down. "I'm delighted that I could see you."

She smiled, the dazzling, provocative smile that had served her so well throughout her life. "I know how terribly busy you are—"

"Busy? My dear, I'd toss away every boring brief and trial transcript in my office if I could see the brilliance of that smile. You are truly a gorgeous woman." His manner was quaint, and obviously practiced.

She smiled again. "I asked you to meet me this afternoon because I want to retain you to represent an acquaintance of mine who is being held on manslaughter charges."

The smile faded from the man's face and his eyes became sharp and wary. "I'm terribly busy at this time—" he started, but she cut him off.

"Let me finish. I believe this particular case might be of interest to you. The young man's name is Andrew Martin."

He thought for a moment, then shot her a look of comprehension. "You mean Drew Martin, the college boy who's been involved in all of this Mormon rioting out in Utah?"

"That's correct. The people that I represent are most anxious that he have the best possible legal counsel." She reached for her handbag, opened it, and extracted a white envelope, sliding it across the table toward him. "At the same time," she continued, "they're anxious to have no public association with the matter. They would prefer you to take the case on a 'public service' basis."

"My dear young lady," he began, "I'm far beyond the point of serving as a public defender, no matter how deserving the case might be."

She was silent, but her gaze moved from his face to the envelope lying before him, and then back to his eyes again.

He reached out and took the envelope, opening it discreetly and thumbing through the currency it held.

"These are thousand-dollar bills," he said tonelessly.
"That's correct. And there are one hundred of them there. I don't know what your customary retainer is—"
He stopped her. "This will be sufficient at the outset," he said. "Tell me about Andrew Martin."

Chapter 4

Steve Gorman steered the compact car into a veritable river of traffic that clogged the Interstate and braked his speed to match that of the holiday motorists in front of him. A chain of red taillights glowed with sporadic bursts of brighter reds as an accident somewhere ahead slowed the line of cars to a trickle. With his progress reduced to this snaillike starting and stopping, he felt his temper begin to rise.

His hand reached out, flipping the knob on the radio. He was assaulted by the voice of a news announcer, and he was about to change the dial to a music station when he caught the words the man was speaking.

"*Andrew Martin, the college student being held in Salt Lake City on manslaughter charges, returned to his home in Logan, Utah, yesterday, apparently the victim of amnesia for the past week. His whereabouts had been unknown since the previous Saturday, when he was involved in the 'Mormon Massacre' that resulted in the death of a fellow student at Brigham Young.*

"*In a Saturday morning press conference, one of America's most noted criminal lawyers announced that he would represent the youthful defendant on a public service basis.*

"*The attorney is flying today from San Francisco to*

Salt Lake City, where he will—"

Gorman shut off the radio. His face was impassive, but his spirits were bright. He nodded slightly as he realized how well the project was going. Now that Drew Martin was out of their hair, now that the Brain Man had proved his point to Hunter—now that all of that was out of the way, he could get down to business.

And the business he would attend to tonight was the most important business of all, he told himself.

Traffic was moving again, and he picked up his speed. As the red marker on the speedometer inched itself higher, he felt that tremor of excitement growing within his body. Tonight he was on familiar terrain. He was not dealing with psychologists or communications czars, nor the phony protocol of the corporate boardroom. He would be dealing with a politician, and his reentry into this world of down-and-dirty, no holds-barred politics filled him with excitement.

He was in downtown Cleveland now and he began to look for the address of the building. He slowed the car to a creep as he scanned storefront after storefront in the retail shopping area.

And then he saw it. The HAPWORTH FOR CONGRESS headquarters, spotlights illuminating the campaign sign, frayed bunting snapping in the brisk autumn wind. He smiled to himself, amused that the razzle-dazzle was still being perpetuated, even though the election had occurred three weeks earlier.

Gorman pulled the car into a parking slot across the street and studied the campaign headquarters.

He found himself gazing into the eyes of Anthony "Hap" Hapworth—bright, intelligent eyes that stared back at him from the three-foot photographs mounted on the plateglass windows of the building. As he looked at Hapworth's photos, he realized that he had never had a face-to-face meeting with the young Congressman, although he knew about Hap Hapworth—all about him. What kind of toothpaste he used, how he liked his steaks. His favorite brand of bourbon. Where he took his women, and which women.

After months of research, after dozens of meetings with private investigators, after digging and snooping and probing into every facet of the man's life, he knew more about Hapworth than Hapworth himself.

But tonight would be the first confrontation between them, and Steve Gorman reveled in the prospect.

Taking the bulging briefcase from the seat beside him, Gorman crossed the nearly deserted street and stood in the shadows for a moment observing the scene within the office. The walls were covered with the usual campaign paraphernalia: photographs and posters and bumper strips; bedraggled boxes and cartons stacked randomly; long tables still covered with pamphlets and brochures proclaiming the candidate's superiority.

But Gorman's eyes did not rest long on the clutter of the office. He focused his attention on the redhead who sat idly at the receptionist's desk, disinterestedly thumbing a magazine. She wore a white silk blouse, unbuttoned casually to reveal a magnificent cleavage. Her breasts strained against the sheer fabric, and Gorman allowed himself a few moments to strip away the white silk to visualize their perfection. He couldn't see her legs beneath the desk, but he knew they would be long and shapely, her hips generous. His eyes moved to her face. Tousled auburn hair. Seductive eyes. A sensuous mouth, set in a petulant frown. She raised a white coffee mug and sipped lingeringly.

Gorman felt a stirring in his groin as he studied her. Jesus, he was horny. A familiar pulsating desire began spreading over his body, but he dismissed the thought from his mind with a grunt of regret and started across the sidewalk to the door. This was not the time for it, he told himself. Perhaps later, back at the hotel. Perhaps even with the redhead. Sometime.

She noticed his movement on the sidewalk and brought herself to attention as she saw the figure approaching the entrance. Gorman saw her slide the coffee mug out of sight, hurriedly close the magazine, and busy herself with random papers on the desk.

He pushed open the door and walked directly to her desk. He caught a faint smell of bourbon in the air and he understood the coffee mug.

She looked up in feigned surprise. "Yes?" she questioned him.

"I'm Steve Gorman," he told her. "I have an appointment with Congressman Hapworth."

"Oh, yes." She beamed at him, and again he felt the urgings. "The Congressman is on the telephone at the moment. I'll tell him you're here." She arose and started across the room, and Gorman saw that his assessment of the rest of her figure had been correct. Her legs were perfect, her hips ample, and they undulated beneath the lightweight wool skirt that she wore.

She turned as she was about to leave the room. "Could I get you a cup of coffee?"

He stared at her in silence for a moment and then allowed a mocking smile to come over his face. "I'd rather have a cup of bourbon. Like you're having, Diana."

She looked at him in surprise and started to protest. And then his use of her first name sank into her mind, and she studied Gorman. "How did you know my name?" she asked.

"I know a lot about the Congressman and his staff," he said enigmatically. "I know that your name is Diana Malloy and that you're a very beautiful woman." The mocking smile was back on his face. "And I also know that you're the private property of Congressman Hapworth."

She drew in her breath in shock, and the petulant look was replaced with an expression of concern. She opened her mouth to phrase a denial but another voice called out through the empty offices.

"Diana!" It was Hapworth calling from another part of the partitioned headquarters office. "Diana, has Gorman arrived yet?"

She turned and left the room, walking hurriedly down the corridor toward the sound of the voice. But before she could reach him, before she could tell him of Gorman's insinuating comments, the Congressman appeared and strode past her toward the reception area and Steve Gorman.

"Mr. Gorman!" He walked directly up to Gorman, seized his hand, and pumped it with political expertise. "Welcome to Cleveland." He had his arm around Gorman's shoulder now, adroitly moving him toward the door to the corridor, steering him down the hallway to his office. He talked as they went. "I'm delighted that you're here. I was a little surprised that you wanted to meet on a Saturday night, but actually, it's just as well. Diana and I can use the time to catch up on a little of the paperwork. The campaign just ended a few weeks ago, you know, and I've got to get back to Washington soon. So I'm glad we could make connections tonight." The running commentary had carried them down the hallway and into a small office equipped with a desk that was overflowing with stacks of papers and other campaign memorabilia.

Now they sat facing each other. The Congressman took a cup of coffee from his desk and sipped at it. "Would you like some coffee?" he inquired, and Gorman shook his head, silently wondering where Hapworth had hidden *his* glass of whiskey.

Gorman studied the figure sitting opposite him impassively. He loved the political arena, loved campaigning, loved the rewards that he could get from politics.

But he hated politicians, and unfortunately they were an essential ingredient.

This specimen, he told himself as his eyes stared wordlessly into Hapworth's, was better than most. At least, the raw material was present—raw material that could be molded into a crowd-pleasing challenger: not too fat, not too thin; not too tall, not too short; not too dark, not too fair. Just right. And still young and fresh enough to have a chance to make it, young and fresh enough to be molded and manipulated into what we want.

But molding and manipulation would be no good without control. That was the vital element. The last time Gorman had molded a candidate into the people's choice, he had lacked control. And without it, he had been tossed out on his ass. He wouldn't make that mistake again. And neither would Hunter. They'd both learned their lesson the hard way, even though it had been with different politicians. Get the upper hand, keep the upper hand.

Gorman proceeded accordingly. "In what year did your family change its name?" he asked abruptly.

The look on Hapworth's face was one of astonishment. He attempted to conceal it by taking another sip of coffee, and then he affected an almost disdainful look as he replied. "Change our name? What are you talking about?"

Gorman spoke again, pulling a file folder from the briefcase that sat at his feet. "The year was 1913. Perhaps even you weren't aware of the exact year, but I'm sure you know that your family name is Heparelli, that your grandfather was an immigrant from Corsica, and that your bloodline is Italian."

Hapworth stared at him in disbelief, and then a look of anger spread over his face. "What goddamn business is it of yours?" he replied.

Good, Gorman thought. He's a fighter. He's got a

backbone. That's more than some of the pricks I've worked with.

Gorman smiled at him. "I don't blame you for getting mad. You've gone to great lengths to conceal the Heparelli name from the voters—just like you've concealed the fact that one of your biggest backers is Gus Franciosa. Not here in Cleveland, where the word might get around. In New York. And the FBI has a dossier on Franciosa that thick. It would make interesting reading for your constituents, wouldn't it?"

Gorman reached down to take another folder from his briefcase. "But I've got my own little dossier—on you. On some of your dealings with Franciosa. All secret, of course."

Hapworth opened his mouth to reply, but Gorman waved him back into silence, tossing the folder onto the cluttered desk for his inspection. As the Congressman tentatively pulled open the folder to leaf through its contents, Gorman proceeded.

"Actually, that's only *one* of the little secrets that you've kept from the voters. There's the matter of your mistress."

Hapworth looked up in shock. "What the hell are you talking about?"

"Not what—who." Gorman jerked his head in the direction of the reception room. "Diana Malloy. That little affair has been going on for several years. That's not public knowledge, is it? Not even to your wife and children. We'll have to find a place for her, put her on ice, get her out of your life." Gorman smiled. The thought pleased him.

Hapworth started to speak, but Gorman silenced him. "Oh, don't worry. We'll keep her available, so you can knock off a piece every now and then. But a mistress doesn't fit in with your conservative image."

Gorman looked up and, satisfied with the shock that

was spreading over the other man's face, plunged on.

"Don't bother to deny it, Congressman. Everything is right here—" he patted his briefcase comfortingly "—plus a lot more. A lot of other juicy items that the press would like to sink their teeth into.

"Item." His voice was like a machine gun as he began his recitation. "The Ohio land deal. That money has been whitewashed so many times it took an entire staff of CPA's to trace it. Income to Hapworth, two hundred eighty-six thousand dollars.

"Item: the new federal dam in Wyoming. The water conservancy district there. Most people don't know that Congressman Spalding cut you in on the deal to get your vote. Income to Hapworth, three hundred forty-two thousand dollars.

"Item: hanky-panky with the State Treasury. Using Ohio's surplus funds to make a bundle. When we found out about your banking shenanigans, we knew you had a brilliant political future. You influenced the State Treasurer to deposit state funds in banks in which you indirectly hold stock. And those banks gave you interestfree loans to *re*invest on sure deals. And I'll have to hand it to you, you're a good businessman. A damned good businessman. Your income from that effort netted you one million eight hundred seventy-three thousand dollars as of yesterday. Not bad for a little Corsican boy who sleeps with his secretary and steals the taxpayer's money."

Hapworth's face was sober now, and he pushed the chair back from the desk, pouring the coffee into the trash basket behind him. He fumbled at a lower desk drawer and a bottle of bourbon appeared. He removed the cap and, with a shaking hand, filled the coffee cup with the dark liquid.

Gorman smiled and stood, reaching out for an extra coffee cup that stood on the edge of the desk. "I believe

I'll have a little drink of that myself, 'Hap.' " His use of the nickname was derisive, and as the other man poured the whiskey into his cup his smile changed into a sneer. He gulped the bourbon in one swallow and reached out to refill his cup.

"Would you like to hear more?" Gorman started again. "I've got lots more, Hap. As a matter of fact, I've saved the best for last. Like to hear it?" Gorman was feeling the whiskey. Quicker than he'd have liked. The realization bothered him for a moment, but he took another sip and it felt warm and good.

"Item: blackmail and death." His voice was low now, low and menacing. Hapworth looked at him for a moment, then dropped his head into his hands, waiting to hear the rest.

"Blackmail and *death,* Congressman. When we saw what a hold you had over the State Treasurer, we looked a little bit further. We found that one of his staff members was a homosexual. And then, just like you, we put two and two together. Or one and one. The State Treasurer and that poor young law student who worked for him. And then you blackmailed them both. And threatened them. *And you drove that young man to suicide.*"

Hapworth was silent, but his head jerked convulsively in his hands.

"But, Hap, you didn't carry that one far enough. What you didn't know is that the kid wrote his parents before he blew his brains out. He confessed the whole thing. And, Hap, *he named names.* Your name!" Gorman's voice rang out in triumph. "And I have the letter."

Silence filled the room. Finally, his face white and drawn, Hapworth raised his head and looked at Gorman. "Who the hell are you?" he asked.

Gorman laughed maliciously. "You know my name. I'm Steve Gor—"

Hapworth cut him off, his voice higher, more agitated. "I know your name, but who the hell *are* you? Who do you work for? My opponent?" He tried to reason it out, but he only became more confused. "But if you worked for him you'd have brought all of this out before the campaign . . ."

Gorman took another sip of whiskey and felt the warmth spread through his mind. He only smiled at Hapworth.

"What do you want?" A note of hysteria was in Hapworth's voice. "What do I have to do to keep you quiet? To keep you from ruining me?"

Gorman exhaled softly and relaxed. Hapworth had capitulated. Gorman had achieved control.

He leaned forward and faced the Congressman. "Ruin you? On the contrary, Hap. The people I'm associated with aren't going to ruin you. They're giving you the chance of a lifetime." He played his trump card. "In just two years, we're going to make you President of the United States."

Chapter 5

In Manhattan the late evening twilight had brought an end to the Thanksgiving weekend. Tomorrow the city would spring into life again, claiming its rightful position as the hub of commerce and industry, of finance and communications and retailing.

A helicopter hovered noisily over the rooftop of the gleaming monolithic structure that dominated scores of its sister structures in breadth and height and, most especially, in the uniqueness of its design.

More than fifty stories below, twilight was abruptly fading into dark on Park Avenue and the elegant twinkle of lights was in sharp contrast to the gaudy brilliance of the streets to the east and west.

The aircraft settled gently on the brilliantly lighted landing pad, and the harsh *whack-whack-whack* of its blades gradually subsided.

A solitary figure emerged from the helicopter and, standing back, waved the pilot away. Then, turning toward the small structure on the rooftop, Maxwell Hunter summoned his private elevator.

He stepped into the cubicle and observed his choice of call buttons: Rooftop . . . Penthouse . . . 52nd Floor. He pushed the second button and soon stepped forth onto polished parquet floors. He was surrounded by elegance. Teakwood, carved and crafted into symmetrical panels, covered the walls and ceilings, even concealed the now silent elevator. A reception desk stood to his right guarding the teakwood-clad corridor that led to the executive offices of The Miramar Corporation.

Hunter touched one piece of the paneling. With the motion an entire section opened, allowing him access to the rooms beyond.

He was in his private apartment, his momentary refuge from the outside world, and here the mood changed from elegant antiquity to the chic contemporary. Light sprang at his touch from huge round globes suspended on slender chrome tubes. The furnishings were steel and glass and sculpted leather, chosen with care by one of the city's finest decorators. Throwing his briefcase and raincoat on an oversized bed, he moved silently through bedroom and sitting room, past a small galley, to another door. As he strode through it, he was transported back to the world of traditional elegance.

He was in his office. The pinnacle office of The Miramar Corporation, headquarters and nerve center for a vast communications empire that ranged from motion pictures to paper pulp mills, from the recording industry to metropolitan newspapers and television stations.

He strode to the functional desk, strangely out of place amidst all of the antique furnishings. As he expected, he found a leather folder of correspondence that his secretary had prepared for him. Taking it, he went back to his apartment and sprawled on a chair in the sitting room.

Shuffling through the routine corrcspondence, he withdrew only that which was of immediate concern to him, that which might have bearing on the project he considered of absolute importance. Not only to him, not just to Miramar. To America itself.

He found a letter from the island. But after scanning it, he realized it was a follow-up to the telegram he had received Thursday night after the successful evaluation of the Utah Experiment, a greater, in-depth report. He laid it aside until later.

A telegram from San Francisco caught his eye, dated Friday at 7:12 P.M. The message was not news to him. He had heard it announced by newsmen from coast to coast. The criminal lawyer on the Coast had taken the bait. It was expected. He had placed the ante high enough to catch his interest. A passage of the telegram caught his eye, however. "Will forward analysis of prospective advertising agencies under separate cover. Concur in choice of Collins & Craig."

Hunter wasn't surprised. He'd accepted the fact long ago that the Atlanta agency would be the operational base for the project, accepted it not so much because Paul had demanded it as because he, personally, didn't care. One advertising agency would do as well as another. But, with Paul's insistence, he had set about the task at hand and had already started a background check on the two principals. In the year ahead, Gorman would complete the confidential dossier, would set them up for acquisition. Hunter smiled to himself. By this time next year, Collins and Craig could be on the road toward becoming millionaires, so long as they played ball with the Project staff. The smile faded. And if they chose not to play ball, he'd own them anyway.

Bringing his attention back to the correspondence folder, Hunter looked for the letter containing her detailed analysis, but he could not find it. He shrugged. It, too, could wait until later.

What he was most interested in was some form of communication from Gorman, and at last he found a Western Union envelope that had been obscured by a larger piece.

He ripped the telegram open, a smile spreading across his face as he read it: HAPWORTH ACCEPTS MY PROPOSITION. WE ARE READY TO PROCEED. WILL RETURN TO NEW YORK MONDAY.

Hunter laid the folder aside and stood, a strange feeling of elation about him. He felt it in his head, throughout his body. And he felt the need to do something about it. Something ceremonial. The words of the steward on his airplane came back to him, and he walked to the tiny galley and swung open the door of the refrigerator. He found a bottle of champagne, and he took it out, studying the label by habit.

It was a needless exercise, he realized. Christine would not allow anything to be placed there that did not meet his rigid specifications. But even if it had been the poorest example of a domestic vineyard, he would not have cared. His need was greater than his connoisseur's taste.

He stripped the paper covering from the neck of the bottle and separated the small strands of wire. Expertly applying gentle pressure to the cork, he was finally rewarded with a resounding explosion.

He filled one of the graceful glasses from the shelf and raised it in a symbolic gesture of salute.

"Project Jupiter is launched," he said aloud.

Part II

Chapter 1

Rick Craig eyed the tall, bronzed blonde who stood on the corner waiting for him to bring the small convertible to a halt. She stepped from the curb, staring back at him insolently as she crossed the intersection, and finally disappeared among the slender palm trees that lined the boulevard.

There's no doubt about it, he told himself as he waited for the light to change. Absolutely no doubt about it. Southern California's still the land of the Golden People.

The sun felt warm and satisfying on his shoulders and he stretched back, trying to soak as much warmth into his body as possible. Clasping his hands behind his neck, he turned his face upward. I might not want to live here, but it's a great place to visit, he thought wryly. And if a man has to work on New Year's Eve, I'd a helluva lot rather be in Los Angeles than shivering in Atlanta.

An irritated toot of a horn reminded him the light had changed and he nosed the Porsche on down the boulevard. Moments later he turned off the main thoroughfare toward the studio. Steering into the confines of the chain-link fence, he waved casually to the guard and proceeded to the enormous soundstage at the end of the street.

Rick pulled over to the curb by an isolated doorway. The red light was not glowing. Good. The final take hadn't started yet.

He pulled the latch and swung open the tiny door, untangling his long legs from where they had been coiled around the intricacies of the steering column and the brake pedal. He swung them out the door, then turned back to take his attache case, pausing a moment to glance at himself in the mirror, to brush his hand through his dark windblown hair.

Grabbing his jacket, he hopped from the small car and approached the heavy metal-clad door. The studio chalkboard greeted him with the same mute message it had borne every day since Christmas. "Soundstage 4 . . . Agency: Collins & Craig/Atlanta . . . Client: FRESH!"

Ignoring the "No Admittance" sign, he pulled the door open and stepped into the dimly lighted recesses of a massive room. His timing, he realized, had been extraordinary.

"OK, everybody. Ten-minute call." Loudspeakers projected the director's voice throughout the set. "Let's see if we can make this one a final take."

Rick threaded his way through the organized chaos of the production studio toward the stairs that led to the viewing room. But as he approached the steps, he saw Laura Talbott blocking his way.

She stood there, tall, statuesque, her figure so ripe that it almost burst the seams of the tight gauze blouse and fashionable black pants she wore. A colorful scarf pulled her long black hair away from her face. My God, he thought to himself, what an extraordinary woman.

A smile played across her crimson lips as she addressed him. "While the cat's been away, the mice have been hard at it." Her green eyes twinkled with good humor. "I guess you heard Ron Spence on the PA. We're ready to go for the final take."

Unconsciously Rick slipped his arm around her waist. "And is your 'star' behaving himself?" A note of distaste was obvious in his voice.

Laura grimaced slightly. "Starr is a pain in the ass. But he's behaving himself. At least, he was a few minutes ago. He's still bitching about the 'redeeming musical value' of the FRESH! music. Still insists on calling it a jingle—"

Rick cut in. "And he's still reminding you that 'Puppet in Love' made the top of the charts for twenty-one weeks. Right?"

Laura nodded.

"Well, I've had about all of Barry Starr that I can take," Rick continued, the sound of irritation rising in his voice. "Maybe it's time I reminded him that 'Puppet in Love' *was* at the top—but *over a year ago.* It's old stuff. As a matter of fact, he's old stuff—"

"Hey Rick, it's all right. I can handle him!" Laura pulled away from him, the smile still on her face but a serious look in her eyes. "And we've got a contract with him, remember? Plus three production spots already in the can. We're not going to toss all that away just because he's difficult to work with."

The amplified voice of the director broke into their conversation. "Ready on the set. Let's go!"

Laura stepped farther away, then leaned back toward Rick. "And besides—I don't believe you care so much about his attitude as you do about the way he flirts with me." Playfully she placed her index finger against the tip of his nose, then kissed him lightly on the lips. "Gotta go," she murmured, and disappeared into the sea of bodies suddenly moving about them.

Rick watched her depart, his brows creased in thought. Then, shrugging the thought away, he climbed the stairs and took his customary post behind the huge soundproof glass windows.

The overhead set lights had already been punched up, transforming the grayness of the sprawling set into the sparkling intimacy of a discotheque. A huge mirrored wall reflected the brilliance and shimmer of the spots, doubled their intensity, multiplied their number.

Another spot appeared, bathing a small podium in a wide circle of light, and the glass ball that hung from the ceiling began to slowly revolve. Its mirrored prisms sought out and reflected still other tiny pinpoints of illumination until everything was frenetically alive with strobelike flashes of light.

A property man was aligning the tables and chairs. Dancers appeared from darkened recesses, snuffing out their cigarettes and smoothing their glittering costumes. Musicians and singers strolled to places of relative isolation, away from the prying angles of the cameras, and the electronic sounds of instruments began to punctuate the air with dissonant chords and whining riffs.

Rick Craig felt a mounting excitement as he waited. These frenzied preparations would do credit to an epic Hollywood musical. He silently shook his head in a mixture of disbelief and awe. No matter how many times he took part in producing a major television commercial, he was always a little amazed at the monumental effort and staggering logistics that were required to stage it.

And it hadn't started here on the soundstage, of course. It had begun months earlier and was culminating today. He checked himself. Not today. It would culminate only when viewers all over America saw the commercial and, hopefully, went to the store to buy a six-pack of FRESH!

"Hi, Rick."

He hadn't heard the door open, and he swung around now to see who had joined him. Brett Stanley ambled across the room, an easy smile on his tanned face, a golf cap perched on his head.

"Hi, Brett. What brings the president of the hottest studio on the coast out here with the working class?" He grinned, extending his hand. "I would have thought you'd be out on the links."

"I have been. Played eighteen this morning." He grasped Rick's hand. "But I thought I'd better check things out before I knock off for the holiday. I want to be sure that Ron Spence is treating you properly."

"Ron's doing a good job. A fine job." Rick was serious now. Below the activity was increasing and he didn't want to miss the take. He continued to talk, but he kept his eyes on the set. "You're damned lucky to have Ron. As a matter of fact, *we're* damned lucky to have him on the FRESH! series."

"You're right on both counts," Stanley replied. "When I took over the old VTR Studio last spring, I set out to get the best. And Ron Spence is the best. He can do things to music and motion picture film that you can't even imagine. He started as a composer-arranger, you know—for some of the biggest recording stars. Then he found there was top money in commercial jingles. I just took him one step further into big-time production." He paused. "And you *are* lucky to get him. He was scheduled for a location shoot this week. But Laura talked him into the FRESH! assignment."

"Laura could talk a man into anything," Rick murmured softly.

Stanley didn't hear him and proceeded. "Speaking of luck, you're doing pretty well yourself. To have Laura Talbott, I mean. Ron says she's the best he's ever worked with. I don't know where you discovered her, but hang on to her—whatever it takes."

Rich was silent. When Stanley had mentioned her name, his eyes automatically searched the set for her. Now he saw Laura's dark head bobbing in animated conversation with Ron Spence, her clipboard balanced on a knee, the inevitable stopwatch clasped in one hand.

Yes, he admitted to himself, he was fortunate to have Laura. She had been a godsend. His mind went back over the months she had been a part of Collins & Craig. Her professionalism, her creative ability, her warmth—all had come to the surface almost instantly after he hired her. But her "discovery" had been pure coincidence.

She had answered a "Help Wanted" advertisement in *Advertising Age*—an ad Collins & Craig had placed to try to recruit new staff members to help serve the FRESH! account. Laura and dozens of others had submitted their résumés, and Laura was one of the lucky ones—one of a score of new employees who had moved to Atlanta.

Rick's thoughts turned back to the year just ending, to the day that they had received the call from the marketing director of FRESH! They were going to change agencies, he had told them, and he had requested a presentation. But it was more than that. FRESH! had been established as a popular regional soft-drink in the South for years. But now they were going national—East and West and North. Collins & Craig had been given a chance to show its stuff, and Collins & Craig won the account over other agencies more than twice its age, more than twice its size.

Laura had been a natural on FRESH! She had discovered Spence and had worked with him to modernize the old jingle into an electrifying up-beat musical sound. With Rick, and scores of other people at the agency, she had introduced the new sound throughout the southeastern part of America. The FRESH! image clicked with the public. Sales soared and cash registers rang and FRESH!—and Collins & Craig—took on a national significance.

This afternoon they would complete the series of

spots that would take FRESH! into test markets all over the country in the winter and spring. In New Hampshire and Florida and Illinois initially, and if the sales results were satisfactory, then on to other tests in Texas and California and Ohio.

And then in the summer another advertising campaign. But this one would be national. Network television—lots of it. Newspapers from coast to coast. Outdoor posters and radio. Transit cards for New York subways and Los Angeles buses and taxicabs in Houston. The whole works. The big time. Jay Collins was delighted. Laura was excited. The entire agency was agog. And through it all Rick had tried to maintain some semblance of sanity.

Now he heard Brett Stanley clear his throat in embarrassment and remembered with a start that the other man was still in the room with him. He turned and saw Stanley at the door.

"I've got to run now," Stanley was saying to him. "I'll watch the shooting session from down on the floor."

"Happy New Year, Brett. Sorry I got lost in my thoughts."

"Happy New Year." He was halfway out the door before he stopped and turned back to Rick. "Oh, by the way, do you and Laura have any plans for the evening? We'd love to have you join—"

Rick waved him away. "We already have plans. Thanks anyway. And thanks for coming by."

Stanley was gone, and Rick turned his gaze back to the set. And inevitably to Laura. She still sat talking to Spence, and now Stanley had joined them.

As Rick continued to watch her, his thoughts turned to their personal relationship. She had entered his agency life in the spring, and his personal life just a short while later. He had taken her to bed one night quite accidentally, and the affair had started. Since that time neither of them had shown any inclination to let the arrangement end.

Now, against his better judgment, against his wishes, the relationship was reaching a fever pitch. He sensed that she was pressing him to make things more permanent, and he knew that sooner or later he would have to come to grips with the situation. Sooner or later? he asked himself. And his mind gave him the answer: later.

Ron Spence's voice cut through the silence in the viewing room and disrupted his thoughts. "Tony, are your dancers ready?" On the stage, he saw the diminutive choreographer look toward Spence and raise one hand with thumb and finger joined together in the OK sign.

Spence proceeded methodically, checking cameramen and musicians, soundmen and technicians. Laura, now silent, sat beside him awaiting his final announcement.

"OK, we're ready for the final take. Barry, will you take your place?"

From the background came a solitary figure, walking slowly and languidly through the flickering particles of light. He stepped onto the podium and was bathed in a brilliant spotlight. Extending one hand to accept a microphone from a waiting soundman, he stood there silently.

Finally he thrust his head back, his face looking toward the ceiling, his eyes closed in mental preparation. Both hands fell to his sides and he stood in repose, awaiting the countdown from the director.

Barry Starr. Within the past year, America's newest rock sensation. Leader of the disco craze. Talented musician, battlescarred performer.

Barry Starr. At the top of the charts since his big hit single "Puppet in Love" took off on college campuses over a year ago. And now under Ron Spence's urgings, the new musical spokesman who would assist FRESH!

in making its musical debut in the marketplaces of America.

He was dressed in silver. Tight pants that were cut to fit the contours of his body, jacket that accentuated his broad shoulders and tapered to a narrow waist. A black frilled shirt stood carelessly open almost to the waist, and silver chains and bangles hung around his neck, a single medallion gleaming in the lights as it lay against his dark chest.

They had worked with Starr through the week, and the disco scene before them was the last of the four-spot series they had produced. A Forties Big Band sound, with Starr crooning into the microphone, his bushy hair slicked back. A jean-clad Barry Starr, thumping and humping an electric guitar in the look, the sound of Elvis. Barry Starr again, backed up by the bubbling champagne sound of Welk.

Four spots, designed for four age groups. Four spots that would be played throughout America as the appeal of FRESH! was methodically tested before its national bow.

"OK. This is the final take. Let's get ready for the countdown." Spence's voice boomed over the set, and Rick could see him set the timing clock before him. He started the verbal countdown.

"Thirty seconds . . . twenty-five . . ."

The preparatory music hit the soundstage like an explosion, the musicians throwing themselves into the well-rehearsed phrases.

"Twenty . . . fifteen . . ."

The dancers reacted. Their jaded faces assumed the fixed smiles of enthusiasm, their bodies grabbed the beat. They were transformed into a well-choreographed, undulating entity, each magnified, each body reflected in the mirror behind them.

"Ten . . . nine . . ."

The singers opened with the lead-in vocal and Starr responded to them instantly, his body jerking, his feet moving, his lips silently mouthing the words.

"Eight . . . seven . . . six . . . five . . ."

The buzz of the telephone sounded like a rifle shot in the silent room. It broke through Rick's intense concentration, causing him to jump.

He ignored it, but again it rang, its insistent sound as startling as a slap in the face.

Rick grabbed it from its cradle, subconsciously afraid that the noise might somehow penetrate the soundproof room and disturb the production.

He put it to his ear. "Mr. Craig?" the operator's voice inquired. "I have an urgent call for you from Atlanta."

Rick mumbled something into the receiver, trying to keep his attention on the production that was already underway on the set.

"Mr. Craig?" The operator was insistent.

"I can't take any calls," Rick snapped.

On the set, the dancers were surrounding Barry Starr, his highpitched voice amplified above the wailing sounds of the back-up singers.

"But Mr. Craig . . ."

He cut her out of his concentration by placing the phone in his lap with her protestations of urgency funneled into his thighs.

Damn, he thought as the company hit the finale. Damn, I've missed it. All of this effort for the final take, and I've missed it.

He saw the dancers hold their final positions, saw the fixed smiles remain in place. He was aware that Barry Starr still had one hand extended into the air, frozen in the theatrical world of make-believe. Then as the director's voice called, "Cut!" the tableau before him sagged out of shape. The bodies literally wilted, the hands dropped heavily to sides. The fixed smiles melted away to reveal again the tired look of boredom.

Quickly he looked at Laura by Brett Stanley's chair, and saw her start toward the viewing room. Her expression said that it had been a good take.

She pushed through the door with excitement still alive on her face. "What did you think of it, Rick?"

"I think we got it," he lied, unable to tell her that he had missed the entire short-lived production.

"I think we did, too." She smiled. "But we can play it back on the videotape monitor to see if there are any obvious flaws—to see if Starr missed his high note or any of the dancers fell over their feet." She paused, then added unnecessarily, "Do you want to take a look at it?"

Rick nodded as he started to get to his feet. The final approval was his. Only he would bear the final responsibility to the client, and only he could make the final pronouncement.

As he stood, the ill-fated telephone fell from his lap to the floor.

"I'll be right in," he told Laura. "This damned phone . . . operator, are you still there?"

"Mr. Craig," an irritated voice responded, despite the fact that less than a minute's time had elapsed, "I'm still here and I'm trying to tell you that you have an urgent call from Atlanta holding for you. It's Mr. John J. Collins, and he says that it *is* urgent. He *must* speak with you."

His reply was unusually sharp. "Tell him that I'm in the final take on the FRESH! spot and that I can't talk to him right now. I'll return the call as quickly as possible."

He hung up the phone and moved to the videotape control room, a mild concern forming in his mind. He had talked with the office earlier, had talked with Jay personally. All had been well. And even though life was always very real and terribly earnest for Jay, it was seldom urgent.

The expressions in the control room told him that the group assembled there felt that it had achieved a keeper. He watched as the monitor played back the videotaped version of the filmed spot, and he agreed with Laura's judgment. It *was* a good one—maybe the best of the series.

He turned to the faces awaiting his reaction and broke into a grin. "It's the best yet! Let's wrap it up and all go have a Happy New Year!"

His eyes caught Laura's, discreetly motioning toward the door, and she answered his glance. He moved out of the room back to the client room to retrieve his jacket and case.

From that vantage point he saw Laura on the set gathering her belongings, again talking with Ron Spence. Barry Starr sauntered up to the group and joined the conversation, casually putting his arm around Laura's waist. As Rick watched, the singer pulled the girl closer to him, molding her pliable body to his own, and then he pulled her to him and kissed her firmly on the mouth.

Rick felt a flush of anger spread over him, and grabbing his coat he stalked toward the door and the stairway to the set. But he pulled himself up short and stopped. Wait a minute, Craig, he told himself. What the hell are you getting so upset about? Because she's letting some greasy rock singer pant around her? Because she's playing the game by *your* rules? After all, isn't that what you want? No attachments, no lasting liaisons? Just an arm's-length relationship?

He walked ahead now, slower and in greater control. Just an arm's-length relationship, he thought wryly. Except in bed.

He picked his way toward the group standing near the director's chair.

". . . and I'll be back out to oversee the final edit," Laura was saying to Spence. "Oh, Rick," she added as he joined the conversation, "Ron says they'll have all the final film ready in a week or so, and I'm coming out to oversee. And while I'm here, Barry has invited me to a party he's having at his beach house. Doesn't that sound like fun?" Her smile was genuine, and she looked at Rick to see if he shared in her pleasure.

"That'll be nice," Rick said, smiling ingenuously. He shook hands with Stanley and then with Barry Starr.

God, he thought to himself, why doesn't that greaser button up his shirt?

The bungalow cottage at the Beverly Wilshire offered a perfect arrangement. A large sitting room in the center separated two individual suites. The living room of each had been converted to make a working office for Rick and for Laura, the center room being reserved for planning conferences. Though interconnected, their bedrooms were discreetly apart.

Now Rick stood in his room stripping off his turtleneck and slacks. Laura had already emerged from her suite and was lying on a poolside chaise. Rick had seen the full-rounded figure, had eyed her bikini appreciatively as she walked past his window while he was making dinner reservations for the celebration he had promised her.

He looked about idly for his swim trunks and stopped in midsearch as another idea came to him. He went to the telephone and dialed room service to order a bottle of iced champagne. As he gave the waiter his instructions, he caught sight of his lean, muscular frame reflected in the mirror.

Not bad for a thirty-eight-year-old man who never gets any exercise anymore, he thought. A little fuller through the middle than in the days when he was the hotshot of the Auburn basketball courts, but still—all things considered—he'd kept pretty trim.

His eyes moved up to his face, outlined in straight black hair that fell back from his forehead and over his ears in a stylish cut. It's amazing what a high-powered stylist and a twenty-dollar bill can do for a farm kid from Georgia, he thought wryly. The face was mature, no longer boyish, not particularly handsome by Rick's standards. But "interesting," he was told, and "appealing" and, more frequently than he liked to hear, "sensitive."

He saw the swim trunks lying on the floor across the room, but as he turned to get them his eyes fell on the circle of gold that danged from the chain around his neck. He reached behind his neck, his fingers fumbling with the tiny clasp to release it.

"Rick, have you seen my sunglasses? I've looked everywhere—"

He turned, the interruption pushing the chain out of his mind, and saw Laura Talbott standing in the open doorway. He watched her, watched her eyes studying his naked body.

She turned to leave, but his voice stopped her. "Laura," he commanded softly, and she stopped and turned back to him. He extended one hand toward her, inviting her to come to him. "We can go to the pool later, Laura."

Her face remained immobile, but her breasts gave him the answer he was seeking, moving slowly then rising and falling as her breath came in shorter, more rapid bursts.

She took a step toward him, pulling at the ties of the bikini, and then with a shrug she shook the flimsy material to the floor and stood before him.

Silently he studied her, savoring the moment. Her breasts were rounded and firm, their symmetry broken only where the golden tan of her skin gave way to a narrow strip of whiteness. With reluctance he let his eyes move away, move down her body, past the golden skin of her stomach to the convexity of her hips and finally to the dark triangular promise that she offered him.

He moved toward her slowly, deliberately. And when he stood in front of her, he extended both hands to bring her face to his. He felt the warmth and moistness of her lips and immersed his mind in it, his lips and tongue searching and exploring. Gently at first, tenderly. And then with a mounting passion. He pulled her toward him, his mouth beginning to move roughly against hers.

Her hands came to his body, found him, and began to sensuously rub and squeeze him into throbbing rigidity. He pulled her closer, pushing himself hard against her. His hands gripped her, pulling her against him, feeling her respond with urgent thrusts.

They stood there, rubbing and pushing against each other, lost in the initial moment of passion. After a moment he broke away and pulled her to the bed. With a single movement he stripped back the covers and pushed her down against the coolness of the crisp sheets. And then his body covered hers.

He ground himself against her and felt her thrusting movement answer his own, felt her legs lock around his until they were pulled still closer together in a writhing oneness.

He wanted to feel her, and his hands found her breasts, taking the nipples and squeezing them into hard points. He felt her hand seeking him, encircling his organ, pulling and pushing it with frenzied motions.

And then she pushed him away, pushed him to his back, and quickly moved over him, straddling his legs. Her hands darted to her head, seeking the pins that carelessly held her dark hair in a knot. He struggled to sit up, struggled to take her breasts in his hands, but the dark hair cascaded around her shoulders and then covered his stomach as her lips found him.

With a groan he sank back against the bed, feeling his groin begin to blaze. Suddenly he knew that he could stand no more, and he lunged up and against her, pushing her backward, engulfing her body under his own.

He knelt over her, letting his erection move across her stomach in ever increasing concentric circles, and he heard her moan in readiness and then he was in her. Slowly at first until her own movements began to accent his short thrusts, and then with one long, hard movement, he penetrated her completely and he felt her lock herself to him and answer his undulating movements.

They moved as one, faster and more forceful until a frantic dizziness began to overcome his mind. A ringing sound filled his ears, a ringing sound that he distantly identified as a telephone, but he gave his mind to the sensations that overcame him and he finally surrendered himself to the prolonged spasms of ecstasy. He felt her body answer him, heard the moaning sound of satisfaction escape her lips, and he was satisfied.

Afterward they said nothing, lying in silence in the darkening room, her head cradled in his arm. He could see the narrow strips of white against her tanned body in the late afternoon coolness of the room, could see his own dark contours reflected in the quick red glow as he flicked his cigarette against the ashtray on his stomach.

And then he fell asleep.

Chapter 2

In Atlanta John Jacob Collins sat very erect behind his desk. His fingers tapped a wooden tattoo with a yellow pencil on the polished wood surface before him, from sharpened point to eraser and back to sharpened point again.

He stared at the digital clock as another numeral dropped into place. 7:19. Another minute had passed. The beat of the pencil increased its tempo.

Twenty minutes after seven on New Year's Eve, Collins thought, and still no return call from Rick. What the hell is he *doing* out there?

Another numeral replaced the other, and then another . . .

The drumming became a little stronger, the eyes a little harder as his anger and frustration mounted.

Maybe he didn't get the message, he thought. No, he countered, I *know* he got the message. I heard the son of a bitch on the phone refusing to talk to me.

Maybe I should place another call to the hotel. He's probably back there by now.

He felt his lips set in an obstinate line. No, goddamnit, Rick's a big boy. And the least he can do is return his goddamned telephone calls. He's a businessman, even if he is the creative director of the hottest agency in Atlanta.

The hottest agency in Atlanta. In the South. The sound of the words echoed through his mind. They weren't his words, although he didn't disagree with them. They were the words that he had heard earlier in the afternoon. Words of praise from New York, from a man who was offering Collins & Craig the world on a silver platter.

And Rick Craig was an essential part of the deal.

His attention drifted from the diabolical clock on his desk to the telephone call he'd received after lunch, and exasperation slowly began to be replaced with excitement.

Joseph Roth. The name had a vague familiarity about it when Dorothy announced the telephone call over the intercom. But it was only when he had Roth on the phone that he remembered.

"Mr. Collins?" He could still hear the cultivated, well-modulated voice. "I'm Joe Roth, executive vice president of The Phoenix Press."

The Phoenix Press. One of the legendary publishing houses of America, the progenitor of thousands of books each year, the parent of Chartwell Books, the paperback octopus whose brightly jacketed tentacles reached into every bookshop, every drugstore, every discount house in America.

Jay Collins associated the name with the company. Joseph Roth was the wonderboy of the publishing world. A name he'd heard about while he was in BBDO's New York office, a reputation that had continued to grow since he came to Atlanta eight years ago.

"Yes, Mr. Roth," he had said, picking up the tenor of the conversation. Calling on his memory, he followed up. "I believe we met at one of those big NBC parties a number of years ago." A ploy, to determine the temperature of the business water.

"Oh really? Possibly so. I don't recall having met you,

but we've been watching the superb work that you and that fellow Craig are doing down there in the Sun Belt. You're the hottest thing in the South. It seems to us that you have a better feeling for the consumer than some of your brothers here on Madison Avenue."

The comment stunned Collins. Whatever he had been prepared for on the last day of the year, it hadn't been such an open statement of praise. Blood rushed to his face and words of reply were lost on his tongue.

But Roth again took the lead. "We've been particularly impressed with your work for FRESH!"

Collins found his tongue. "I'm surprised that you've seen any of that campaign. It's only been a regional campaign in the South. Rick Craig is in Los Angeles right now working on the new television series for the national test campaign. If it all goes well, you should be seeing a lot about FRESH! next summer."

"Oh yes, we've seen the regional spots. We travel quite a lot, you know. As a matter of fact, your television spots are about all that I've found amusing in some of my overnight visits to Raleigh."

Collins remembered another fact misplaced in his mind. The Phoenix Press owned a huge pulp and newsprint mill in the Carolinas. Publishing. Paperback books. Paper mills. The phone call was becoming more interesting by the moment, and Collins seized the brief pause to ask a direct question.

"I'm sure you didn't call me to talk about FRESH! What's on your mind, Mr. Roth?"

In an equally direct manner, Roth unfolded a series of facts in such rapid succession that Collins was hard pressed to make note of them on the legal pad in front of him.

Book sales were good—better than ever. Last year's volume had reached a new high. Revenues of more than two hundred million dollars. But they weren't good enough. The Press had developed a new concept: teach the American public to read again. Help them rediscover the pleasures of the printed page, wean them away from the television screen. It was a massive undertaking, and one that would be backed with a massive advertising budget.

"We anticipate spending as much as ten million dollars in advertising," Roth said pointedly, and Collins gulped.

"That's a lot of money," Collins replied lamely.

"You're damned right it's a lot of money," Roth shot back. "It's an unheard-of amount. The industry high was the one million dollars that Random House spent on their dictionary. But we'll spend twice that amount on each of four different books. And we want to be sure that we have the right agency spending it for us."

Collins was silent. His mind was racing ahead, but he was afraid to speak, afraid of destroying the momentum of Roth's conversation.

"We want television, radio, newspaper. The whole thing. But especially television. Directed to the average man, the average household. We all learned a lesson from *Roots* a few years back." He paused for breath.

"How does Collins & Craig fit into all of this, Mr. Roth?"

"We're going to change agencies. Our current agency isn't big enough. They're not savvy to television. We've talked to a couple of big New York shops, and there are those who feel that we should take a look at agencies in Chicago or San Francisco. But frankly, Mr. Collins—" his voice took on a confidential tone "—we're fascinated with what Collins & Craig has been doing. Vince Astin —he's our president—is willing to give you first crack at it. So am I. Are you interested?"

Collins felt as though he had been submerged without air, and his first thought was that he must surface or drown in a tide of amazement. Despite the constriction in his throat he managed to answer. "Of course," he said, managing a crisp, professional tone.

"Good. We're not committed to Collins & Craig, you understand, but we've checked you out pretty carefully and we'd like to talk to you and Craig day after tomorrow. We'll send the company jet for you."

Collins heart sank. "That really won't be necessary," he began. "And Wednesday is terribly tight timing. My partner is in Los Angeles, and he'll have to get back. And for a presentation of this magnitude we'd need a little more time. How about the end of the week, or next Monday?"

"That wouldn't work out at all," Roth answered bluntly. "Not at all. Vince Astin is leaving on Thursday for a conference in London and a six-week literary circuit on the Continent. We'd like to make the decision before he leaves."

Collins could sense trouble. Rick. Rick Craig would resist any sort of connection with the literary world. And he was planning a vacation in Palm Springs with Laura.

He started hedging. "Certainly, Mr. Roth. I'll be in New York on Wednesday. I'm not certain that Rick Craig can finish up on the coast and be with me—"

"That's part of the deal, Collins." Roth was abrupt. "That's the main reason we're interested in you. Because of Craig's knowledge of literature, because Craig was a best-selling author several years ago. Frankly, if Craig can't be with you, don't bother to come yourself."

The blunt words angered Collins, brought forth a professional jealousy that he hadn't known existed. But he answered judiciously.

"Certainly," he repeated, and then he was silent. The sting to his ego still crowded his thoughts.

"Well?" Roth demanded, but still Collins was silent.

Roth spoke again. "Mr. Collins, perhaps we're inconveniencing you too greatly. If you aren't interested, I'm sure that one of the New York agencies can be more flexible . . ." He let his voice trail off.

Collins did the only thing he could do. "We'll be there on Wednesday, Mr. Roth. Both of us. Where shall we meet your plane?"

Now, four hours later, Jay Collins still sat at his desk, his analytical mood of the afternoon momentarily displacing his frustration with Rick Craig. And then he heard Roth's words again. "If Craig can't be with you, don't bother to come yourself."

The memory snapped him from his reverie with a jerk. The clock indicated 8:04, and his anger returned. He reached for the phone and with short, jabbing motions, dialed the 213 area code and the number of the Beverly Wilshire.

I'll find that son of a bitch if it takes me all night, he told himself.

Chapter 3

Rick Craig lay in the same position as the jangling sound of the telephone cut through to his consciousness. He felt a prickling sensation in his left shoulder where Laura's head still lay, felt her hand on his chest, the warmth of her legs as they pressed against him.

And then the telephone rang again, demanding, insistent, and he struggled to free himself. Pulling away from her, he reached for the noisy instrument and mumbled a greeting into the mouthpiece.

"You son of a bitch, where in the hell have you been?" A torrent of angry words exploded into Rick's ear, and he shook his head, trying to clear his mind. "Do you realize that I've been trying to get you on the goddamned telephone for the last four hours?" The words continued, unabated, and with sudden comprehension, Rick realized that it was Jay Collins and remembered with regret that he had forgotten to return the call earlier in the day.

"I'm sorry, Jay—" he began, but Collins continued as though he had not heard the apology.

"I left word at the studio that it was urgent, I left word at the hotel, I've left word all over town. It's a hell of a note when your own partner can't get in touch with you when something really important comes up."

Rick flipped on the bedside light in the darkened room and pulled himself to the side of the bed. He listened to the tumble of harsh words, trying to determine what exactly the urgency was.

"Jay—" he began, but he couldn't stop the flow of invective. Sighing, he resigned himself to wait it out and looked about for his cigarettes. Laura still lay beside him, her head now propped on one hand, and he motioned her to the crumpled package on the dresser across the room.

"Jay," he started again, and then repeated himself. "Jay!" His voice finally commanded Collins into silence, and he continued. "What the hell is wrong?"

The tirade had been spent, the frustration vented, and Rick heard Collins' voice relax into a more normal tone. He took a lighted cigarette from Laura and pulled a pillow against the headboard, settling back as his associate began to relate the telephone call from New York.

Suddenly Rick sat upright on the bed. "Wait a minute, Jay. Did you say The Phoenix Press? *The* Phoenix Press? With a ten-million-dollar advertising budget? That's absurd. There's never been a publisher in the world who spent *that* much—"

"That's where you're wrong, pal," he heard Collins reply. "It's the first time in history, but Roth told me so himself. And they want Collins & Craig to help them spend it. What do you think of *that?*"

Rick was silent a moment, considering. "I don't think much of it, Jay. Regardless of what Roth told you, I can't believe that they're serious about it." He paused as another thought isolated itself from the hundreds that were racing through his mind. "And if they *are* serious about it, Jay, I can't believe that they'd want an unknown Atlanta agency to handle the account."

"It's because of the work we've done for FRESH!—" Collins began.

"Bullshit." Rick's voice was soft, but it cut through to the other man's consciousness and silenced him. "Bullshit," Rick repeated. "They'd never go off Madison Avenue. And they'd damned sure never come to Atlanta. I know the publishing world, Jay. I worked with them for years. That's not the way they operate. There's something wrong about this deal."

"God*damn,* Rick!" The reply was immediate. "They offer us a ten-million-dollar account and all you can say is, 'There's something wrong.' "

"Something *is* wrong, Jay."

"Something will damned sure *be* wrong if you don't get your ass in gear and catch that Delta flight in the morning." Collins paused for a moment, then his voice took on a note of apology. "I'm sorry that this ruins your plans for a little getaway to Palm Springs, but it can't be helped. There's no way you can miss this one. You'll have to come back to Atlanta tonight or tomorrow."

His comment jolted Rick's mind back from his considerations of The Phoenix Press, back from memories of the publishing world that had long since been locked in a closet of his mind.

"Jay, I can't finish up here and get back in time to go to New York. You'll have to take this one by yourself."

"Of course you can be back in time. There's a flight tonight, another early tomorrow. The morning flight arrives in Atlanta in time for you to meet the plane they're sending from New York. It'll be tight, but you can make it."

"But I still have work to do here."

"I thought you finished this afternoon?"

"We did. We finished filming, but there's still a lot to be done before I can clean up things and come home—"

"Damnit, Rick!" Collins exploded again. "The agency has the chance of a lifetime and you're telling me you've got to clean up things in LA. Don't you understand what I'm saying, man? We've got a chance for a biggie. Almost a fifty-percent growth overnight, maybe a New York office—"

"We can't handle it, Jay. Not on the heels of FRESH!—"

"The hell we can't handle it. We handle anything we go after."

"Come on, Jay. This would mean new people. Lots of new people. Even more than we've already hired. And money. We're already up to our necks in bank loans just to handle the cash flow for FRESH! We can't handle it."

"You're too goddamned conservative, Craig. *This is a ten-million-dollar account.* And they want us. Collins & Craig." His voice took on an edge. "And they want you. In New York. Not because you're one of the best creative directors in the business. Because you know the publishing business."

"Not anymore. That was a long time ago."

"Maybe so, but you're part of the deal." Irritation was becoming obvious in his voice. "Without you, it won't fly. They insist that you be present. Demand it. To be more precise, if Craig doesn't come, they don't want to see Collins."

Rick heard the pronouncement and recognized the irritation in Collins' voice, but he was silent.

Collins pushed the attack a step further. "As for finishing up things out there, can't Laura handle it?"

"Of course Laura can handle it. But . . ."

"But what?"

Rick paused. He was searching for excuses, looking for plausible reasons to mask the feeling of apprehension that had begun to spread over him when Collins had first mentioned The Press.

He finally spoke. "It's just not right, Jay. It's not right for us."

Collins' voice was insinuating. "It's not right for *us*, Rick? Or it's not right for *you?*"

"What do you mean?"

"You know what I mean. You told me once that you'd never get involved in writing again. That you'd put that part of your life away. Are you sure this is not just a personal thing with you?"

I'm not sure of anything, Rick thought, feeling the apprehension in his mind and body like a numbing ache. But he answered positively. "That has nothing to do with it."

"Are you sure?"

"I'm sure. It's just that I don't feel good about this—"

"Rick, I'm not asking you to feel good about it. I'm not asking you to write another novel. All I'm doing is asking you to help me on this presentation. They want to meet you. Hell, maybe that's all you'll have to do. After we get the account, you can put someone else on it. Maybe Laura. But I need *you* on Wednesday. What do you say, pal?"

Rick didn't answer. Laura had risen and slipped into Rick's robe, and now she sat opposite him, her eyes intent on him, awaiting his next reply.

"Well?" Collins pushed him for an answer.

The silence lengthened and finally Rick broke it with a loud sigh. The inevitability of the situation was soaking through, but still he couldn't answer.

Collins' words shot through the telephone. "OK. To hell with you, Craig. It's not your decision anyway. I own as much of this agency as you do, and Smitty owns part of it, too, and he's with me. And you sit out there trying to play God—"

"Calm down, Jay. I'm not doing anything—"

"Oh, yes. You *are* doing something. You're screwing me. And you're screwing the agency out of our big chance." The words picked up in their intensity, his anger mounting. "I can't believe that you'd do this to the agency. But most of all, I can't believe that you'd treat *me* this way. You *owe* me something after I pulled you out of the goddamned gutter and made you what you are today."

"You didn't make me anything, Jay." Rick's anger flared, and he spit the insulting words back into the receiver. "I made myself what I am today. Not you, not anyone else."

Collins came back to him, his voice at once contrite. "I'm sorry, Rick. I lost my temper. I didn't mean—"

"Of course you meant it, or you wouldn't have said it." Rick's voice was icy as he continued. "Maybe you're right. Maybe I do owe you something. For old times' sake. So I'll come. For *Auld Lang Syne.* But let's get one thing straight.

"You may have given me my first job in advertising, but it took two of us to build the agency to where we are today. It only takes one to tear it down. And I don't intend to let that goddamned professional ego of yours take us down the tube. Do you understand what I'm saying?"

There was silence at the other end of the line, and Rick concluded the conversation. "I'll help you with the presentation, Jay, but I won't go along with anything that's not in the best interests of the agency. And I'm not interested in flying on their fancy corporate jet. I'll fly directly to New York and meet you at the hotel." He started to put the receiver down, but an afterthought seized him. "And Jay—"

"Yes?"

"Happy New Year!"

He replaced the receiver, taking care not to let his hand shake, not to reveal the anger and resentment that had flooded over him. He sat there staring in silence at the instrument.

"What happened, Rick?"

For the moment he had forgotten about Laura, and now he looked sharply at her. "Nothing," he replied.

"But something must have happened. You and Jay were fighting. I've never heard you fight before. And what about The Phoenix Press?"

"It's nothing," he repeated, but she continued to look at him, awaiting a further response. "They've asked us to make a presentation, that's all. And it's an account that I don't want to be involved with. It's too big. I don't think we could handle the growth, all the new people. And I don't understand why one of the biggest publishers in New York would want an Atlanta agency—" He stopped, his eyes narrowing as he returned her stare. "Hell, Laura, you heard the entire conversation. You heard what I told Jay. Why are you questioning me now?"

"Because I want to talk about it. If you don't want to be involved with the account, I'll respect your judgment. But don't keep *me* from being involved with the account." He started to speak, but she went on. "Sure, it's big—but we were able to handle the FRESH! account, and we could handle this one too. And I'll agree that it's unusual that they don't want a New York agency. But it's just possible that they like our work. There's nothing wrong about that. Really, Rick, this might be my big chance. I've been your assistant long enough. And I could handle The Phoenix Press, couldn't I? I could serve as creative director. Maybe not as well as you at first, but I'd get better. But you're telling me that you don't want to be involved. Why, Rick?"

"I don't think the agency should be involved, Laura." He underlined the finality of his thought by arising and walking to the bureau. He grabbed a pair of shorts and pulled them on, turning to walk into the sitting room beyond. But Laura was not ready to end the conversation.

"I want that account, Rick. It's important that Collins & Craig have it. It's important that I get to work on it."

He turned and stared at her, amazed at the hunger in her voice. "I've told you that I don't want to talk about it, Laura," he said sharply.

"There are a lot of things you don't want to talk about, aren't there?" She was staring at him, her face beginning to screw up in anger. "Like my future with the agency. Or my future with *you.*"

He felt his own anger rising. "For God's sake, Laura, this isn't the time. I'm not in the mood to—"

"That's the way it always is, isn't it, Rick? When *you're* in the mood. A little while ago you were in the mood for sex, and you satisfied yourself. But now that I'm in the mood to talk about my future, you don't want to talk about it." Her eyes flashed at him from across the room. "Well we're *going* to talk about it. About my future in the agency. And while we're at it, we might as well talk about my place in *your* life, too."

She walked toward him, her voice becoming more penetrating. "I'm tired of being dangled on a chain, Rick." Laura was facing him now, and she stared into his eyes defiantly. "And I'm tired of having you dangle *that* goddamned chain in my face."

Rick realized suddenly that he had forgotten to remove the chain earlier when she had first entered the room, and his hand moved compulsively to the pendant.

"Oh, don't try to cover it up. I noticed it earlier. I couldn't help but notice it, with it hitting my chest every time you kissed me." Her hand moved out, brushing his hand away, taking the gold circle to study it. "What is it, Rick? I've never noticed it before. As many times as I've seen you naked, I've never seen you wear it."

He shook his head and pulled away. "It's none of your affair," he murmured.

"It's time that we made it my affair." Again, she

grabbed the gold pendant, inspecting it. "It's some sort of medallion, isn't it? And there's something engraved on the back. What does it say? 'K.P. to R.C. Til death do us part.' What *is* it, Rick? Was it a wedding gift? Is it something that you wear all the time? Except when you're in bed with me?"

A rocket burst of red flashed over his mind as he heard her words, heard her voice becoming more strident, more demanding. "Cool it, Laura. I don't want to talk about—"

"Of course you don't want to talk about it. Or about her. You've never wanted to talk about her. But God, Rick, that was almost ten years ago. *Ten years*. Surely you've had time to forget her, to forget those days. I've tried to help you, Rick, God only knows that I've tried. But you've shut me out, just like you shut everyone out. What was her name? Kathy? You've never told me anything about her, but other people have. And I'm sorry, Rick, I'm sorry that you lost your wife. But what about *me,* Rick? What about Laura: I'm here, and I'm alive."

He felt himself trembling with anger, furious at this invasion of his private world. The red splotches of violence spread throughout his mind. He wanted to strike out at her, to silence her, but he controlled himself and turned away.

Again Laura reached out to take the chain, holding firmly to the medallion. "This gives me *one* answer, Rick. This tells me where I stand in your personal life. Now what about my professional life? Is this going to ruin my career, too? Is this the *real* reason you don't want anything to do with The Phoenix Press? Maybe it isn't the cash flow or the sudden growth. Maybe it's old memories. Maybe it's *her.*"

He had her wrist in his hand, applying pressure, but she resisted him. "Take your hands off that, Laura."

"I'll take my hands off it!" With one quick, angry

gesture she pulled her wrist from his grip and yanked at the chain. He could feel it cut into his neck, could feel the delicate gold mesh give way. She stood away from him, and held it there for a moment.

He advanced on her. "Give it to me, Laura." His face was black with anger, his voice a low whisper.

"So this is the medallion that you used to wear. No, that you *still* wear," she said, backing away from him. "Why don't you sleep with *it,* instead of me? Because I'm better? I'm better than a piece of gold. Or a memory—"

"Let me have it, Laura."

"To hell with you. To hell with you, Rick Craig." Her eyes defied him as she took another step backward. "I'm up to here with playing it by *your* rules. I say to hell with a writer who can't write anything but ad copy. To hell with the husband who can't lay his dead wife to rest. To hell with the Wonder Boy of Atlanta. The Wonder Boy Writer."

He took another step toward her. *"Laura, give it to me."*

"I'll give to you, all right." She pulled her arm behind her head, and with a furious motion her hand shot forward. The chain flew across the room. "To hell with the medallion and to hell with the Boy Writer."

Rick grabbed her arm and jerked her toward him with such strength that she lost her balance. "Don't you ever say that to me again." She resisted him, but his grip grew firmer and he began to shake her. *"Don't you ever say that to me again!"*

She drew her hand back and brought it forward with all her force against his face. He released her, but in the same moment he pulled his arm across his chest and let it fly forward with such force that it knocked her backward. She stumbled and fell across the bed but recovered herself and started to get up, her hands reaching for him, clawing, scratching.

Rick reached out to grab her hands to fend off her reckless blows. With the movement he fell across her, pinning one of her hands over her head and stilling her body with his own.

He lay there on top of her, breathing heavily. "Don't ever call me that again," he said in a hoarse, choking whisper.

She tried to answer, but her words blurred into small frenzied noises. She struggled against him and with her free hand found his back, and he could feel the burning sensation as her fingernails gouged and clawed against his naked flesh.

Rick struggled to catch her hand, finally pinning it with the other over her head.

"You son of a bitch." Her face was only inches away from him, and she spit the words at him with vehemence. "Why don't you take that goddamned gold medallion to bed?"

She struggled against him, overpowered by the weight of his body. The robe she wore had pulled away, and her naked breasts rubbed against his chest, her legs and thighs thrusting against his body. For the first time he realized that he was hard and that he wanted her.

Her lips opened again to speak, but his mouth was on them, smothering the words back into her throat. For a moment she continued to fight him, but then her movements subsided and he felt her lips respond and her body become limp in his arms.

Later, the evening air on the terrace outside their room chilled him, but he sat lost in thought, smoking one cigarette after another. From across the pool he heard the sound of music from the hotel's ballroom. At first he paid it little attention; but finally the melody sank through his concentration.

Should auld acquaintance be forgot and never brought to mind . . .

It was midnight, and the band was playing "Auld Lang Syne." He listened to it, the words forming in his mind as a rush of bittersweet memories flooded over him.

Oh, Kathy, he said to himself. For God's sake, release me.

Chapter 4

Steve Gorman emerged from the elevator and found himself surrounded by dark wood paneling.

Shit, he told himself. This is all I need this afternoon. A meeting in this goddamned mausoleum.

Gorman paused a moment before the massive gilded frame and studied himself in the mirror. God, I look as bad as I feel, he thought. His memories of the New Year's Eve celebration were blurred, but the taste of bourbon was still heavy in his mouth. He had gulped aspirin since his alarm clock had jangled him awake, had taken a shot of whiskey neat to still his stomach. But his head still throbbed. His nerves felt like raw meat.

With an effort he pulled his shoulders back and tried a smile. It seemed to work and he smiled again. Good. Hunter wouldn't approve his drinking so much, wouldn't understand his blackout. And he damned sure wouldn't tolerate dull reactions. Not any time. But especially not today.

He glanced at the reception desk to his right and was vaguely surprised to find it empty. Surprised and a little resentful. If Hunter was going to call a goddamned meeting on New Year's Day—and during the Rose Bowl game, at that—the least he could do was make the whole staff show up for work.

Then he heard the clacking noise of a typewriter and he moved toward the sound, feeling a little better. At least *someone* else was going to share in his misery. Someone besides Hunter and Roth. But as he rounded the corner and came into view of the typist, he felt the depression return. It was Christine Childs.

He approached the desk and spoke. "Good afternoon, Miss Childs."

She looked up for a moment and then, without a sign of recognition, returned her attention to the half-filled page before her.

Christine Childs was old and efficient and loyal. And mean. She had guarded the executive chambers with a relentless passion for years. Her position was legend and her icy stare had been enough to make even the strongest quake a little.

"Is Mr. Hunter in?" Gorman again interrupted her typing and now she directed the stare at him.

"Of course he's here. But the meeting isn't until two-thirty. You're early. So is he," she said, nodding her head to the small receiving room behind Gorman's back. "You'll both have to wait until he's ready."

Gorman turned to see Joe Roth sitting uncomfortably on the edge of an impeccably upholstered wingback chair, thumbing idly through the pages of *Fortune*. As he approached, the other man acknowledged his presence with a nod.

Gorman sat opposite him and busied himself with a search for a cigarette. He studied Roth, and a feeling of dislike spread over him.

Another goddamn phony from the Business School, Gorman thought. But, he added grudgingly, he's a smart phony. Smart enough to turn The Phoenix Press into a goddamned money machine. Smart enough to corner the market on best-sellers last year. And smart enough to get along with Mac Hunter.

"Got a light, Joe?" Gorman's request were the first words either man had uttered, and now Roth closed the pages of the magazine and fumbled in his coat pocket. His hand finally emerged with a slender gold lighter. As he extended his arm, Gorman saw a gold bracelet carelessly dangling from Roth's wrist, saw the well-manicured fingers flick a tiny burst of flame from the lighter.

But he noticed something else. Something that helped ease the pounding in his head.

Joe Roth's hand was shaking.

Bluntly Gorman called it to his attention. "A little nervous, Joe?" He nodded to the other man's hand and was rewarded with a look of realization as Roth withdrew the lighter and held it firmly between both hands.

Roth shrugged and started to reach for the magazine again. But Gorman pursued the matter. His voice was deliberately low, filled with a gravelly sound, out of the earshot of Christine and her clacking typewriter.

"I don't blame you, Joe. For being nervous. You're not used to coming up here to Camelot all alone, are you? Without all of the other Knights of the Round Table here to protect you? There's safety in numbers, isn't there, Joe? When you've got all of your sidekicks from the Board with you, you can count on them to take some of the heat. But when you're all alone, you start squirming."

Roth had, in fact, been moving about in the chair. But at Gorman's words, he pulled himself erect. His eyes narrowed as he studied the man opposite him, then he again chose to disregard Gorman's comments.

"Hands shaking, squirming in your chair," Gorman taunted. "Better keep a tight one, Joe. God only knows what you might do when you get into the Royal Chambers."

"Don't be absurd—"

Gorman's laugh was a single sound, a guttural, mirthless bark that came from deep inside his chest. "I'm not being absurd, Joe. And you know it. Because Hunter's given you a priority assignment, and he doesn't want it fucked up. He wants to *own* that advertising agency, Joe. Possess it. And them. Just like he owns The Phoenix Press, Joe. Just like he owns you. And if everything goes OK, he'll be all smiles." Again he punctuated the air with the guttural one-note laugh. "Correction. He's never all smiles. But everything will be all right. But if you haven't pulled your end of the deal off, our Good and Benevolent King—" he barked again at the irony of the words "—will turn into something else. *A mean, dirty son of a bitch.*"

Gorman could see the obvious distaste that Roth felt for him mirrored on his face. But despite himself the other man gulped audibly, and Gorman was satisfied. He had gotten under that phony Harvard reserve, had made the bastard sweat a little.

"I've done everything I was supposed to do, everything Mr. Hunter told me to do," Roth began. "By every rule of business acquisition we should be able to own controlling interest in Collins & Craig—"

"Yes, Miss Childs?" Gorman ignored him, looking instead at Christine Childs, who had left her typewriter to stand before them. He used his boardroom voice, his Mac Hunter voice, polished and smooth, the sound of the gutter temporarily pushed aside.

She stood there for a moment, her eyes shooting, birdlike, from one to the other, trying to piece together what they had been talking about. After a moment, she said, "Mr. Hunter will see you now." Needlessly she extended one arm to direct them toward the massive wooden door.

"Thank you, Miss Childs," Gorman said, standing. You old bitch, he added under his breath. Turning to Roth, he added aloud, "Coming, Joe?"

Together they approached the door to Hunter's office. A highly polished bronze plate was its only adornment, and Gorman's eyes scanned the words engraved on the metal.

R. MAXWELL HUNTER III
Chairman of the Board
The Miramar Corporation

He pushed through the door, causing Roth to bring up the rear, and inside the threshold he stopped.

Maxwell Hunter sat at the massive desk, his back turned toward the door, his figure silhouetted against the Manhattan skyline. He was silent and made no effort to acknowledge their presence.

Gorman heard the door close behind him, felt Roth come abreast of him and stop. Both men stood silently, neither prepared to break the silence of the room.

Finally Hunter swung the chair around and faced them. Black eyes darted out from under heavy brows and his mouth was closed in a thin, straight line.

"Good afternoon, gentlemen." The voice was deep, almost harsh. He delivered the greeting crisply without any attempt at amenity and followed it with another statement. "I'm ready for your report."

"Everything is proceeding according to plan," Roth began in an enthusiastic voice, as he took one of the two chairs opposite the desk. "All of the players have been rehearsed and the curtain will rise tonight—"

"Goddamnit, Roth," Hunter's voice was sharp and hard, cutting through the words like a machine gun, the black eyes boring into Roth to accentuate Hunter's irritation. "I know you consider that you've done a masterful job in 'orchestrating this little drama,' as you continually refer to it. But I asked you for a report, not a theater review."

Gorman's staccato laugh punctuated Hunter's comment, and the older man turned to glare at him. But he met a smooth, bland expression and he focused his attention back on Roth.

"Please give me the report." The anger was gone, replaced by the earlier businesslike tone. "In business terms, not the jargon of the publishing industry. Or whatever it is. Are you ready?"

"Yes sir," Roth answered. He leaned forward, reaching for his briefcase. Gorman sought out his eyes, but Roth avoided looking at him. He removed a pad from the case, and Gorman could see his hands begin to shake. But when he spoke, it was in a precise, almost academic voice.

"Our goal has been to acquire Collins & Craig, an Atlanta-based advertising agency, either totally or through majority ownership.

"From the outset research had indicated that an outright tender would be rejected—not by Collins, but probably by Craig and possibly by the minority owner, Logan Smith.

"The strategy has been this: offer The Phoenix press—"

"I *know* what the strategy is, Roth." Hunter interrupted, the underlying current of irritation again evident. "I developed the goddamned strategy, and I don't want to hear it again. Just give me a current status report."

"Yes, sir." Roth paused, clearing his throat. He consulted his legal pad and began. "They'll be on their way to New York within the hour. On the Miramar jet. Collins and Logan Smith—"

Hunter looked up sharply, his mouth open to speak, and Roth quickly answered the question in his eyes.

"—along with Rick Craig, who is flying commercially from Los Angeles."

Hunter grunted his acceptance.

"I called Collins yesterday," Roth continued. "He reacted as we anticipated. He asked for more time, asked to come alone. Without Craig. But he finally gave in to my demands. I called again this morning—got him out of bed—and he again agreed to my demand that he bring Smith and all their current financial data. That way he won't have time to doctor up the figures."

Hunter nodded. "Is the consultant here already?"

"Yes, sir. Aaron Carlsen arrived this morning."

"Does he know what to say?"

"Exactly. After we've built them up, dangled the carrot in front of their nose, Carlsen will tear them down.

"He'll tell them that they are understaffed to take on an account of this magnitude. They need more people. *Many* more people. High-priced people.

"He'll suggest that they open a service office in Manhattan. That, too, takes money.

"He will call their attention to the need for working capital for start-up production.

"And finally, Carlsen will call their attention to their extreme undercapitalization, to the note payable to Security Founders in Atlanta. They need more money. Badly. And because they are undercapitalized, Carlsen will not recommend that The Press retain Collins & Craig as its agency.

"In short, come up with more cash—a lot more cash—or forget it."

Absorbed in Roth's monologue, Hunter had swung himself away from the men and was again staring out the window.

"What about the Atlanta banks?" he asked.

"We've shut them off already. Security Founders is interested in getting some of the action from Miramar, and they'll play ball with us. They'll refuse any further loans. In fact, they'll even demand immediate payment on the existing note, if we wish. They'll cooperate. And so will all of the other Atlanta banks."

Roth fell silent for a moment. Finally he spoke again. "And that leaves them little choice. If they want to handle The Press, if they want other business from Miramar, they'll have to sell the controlling interest of their agency in exchange for cash *plus* a substantial loan for working capital. Sell the stock to a silent partner. Sell the stock to Maxwell Hunter."

At the sound of his name, Hunter turned back to face them. He stared at Roth for a moment in silence. When he spoke, his voice was softer, more thoughtful than it had been earlier.

"Just one more question. Will it work?"

"What do you mean?"

"Will it work? Will they accept the offer, when it's made? Can we gain control of Collins & Craig?"

Unconsciously Roth began to squirm in the chair. "My assignment was to set up the mechanics of an acquisition. And I've made all of the arrangements that you wanted. Even to the extent of sacrificing The Phoenix Press to an Atlanta agency, or spending *far more* for advertising than we should—"

"I didn't ask you about the arrangements or the expenditure." Hunter's voice was sharp. "I asked you if it will work. Will it?"

At first Roth was silent, his eyes averted, looking down at the floor. Then with a shrug he met Hunter's eyes.

"I don't know."

"Will they accept the offer?" Hunter persisted.

"I honestly don't know. That's not my area of responsibility," Roth began, directing his gaze at Gorman. "From the beginning we agreed that I'd handle arrangements and that Gorman would handle personalities. Maybe you'd better ask him if it will work."

Gorman felt a dryness in his mouth, felt the headache

returning. Now it's my turn, he thought to himself. He waited for Hunter to turn his penetrating gaze away from Roth, waited for the black eyes to bore into him.

But Hunter kept his eyes fixed on Roth. "I'll get around to Gorman in a minute. But right now, I'm interested in your opinion. *Will it work?*"

Roth took a deep breath and exhaled it noisily. Again he shrugged his shoulders. "I don't know, Mr. Hunter. Most agencies would jump at the chance to have Mac Hunter as a silent partner, to have the stability of The Miramar Corporation behind them. But this isn't your regular Madison Avenue advertising agency."

"Go on, Joe." It was the first time Hunter had used Roth's first name, and with it Roth relaxed a bit. "I'm interested in your opinion, Joe. Do you think we can bring it off?"

"Yes. Yes, I think you can pull it off. But it's going to be difficult. I don't know what type of persuasion Gorman's going to use, but this man Craig isn't going to be an easy nut to crack.

"If it were just Jay Collins you were dealing with, it would be a relatively simple thing. You can read the man like an open book. He's a competitor. He plays the game to win, usually at someone else's expense. He wants to be Number One. Professionally and personally. Being a winner is far more important to him than money. He's already come a long way. He's kicked and scratched his way up the business ladder, and he's screwed his way up the social ladder. He would regard this as a giant step forward. It would make him the biggest in the South or the Midwest. In time, bigger than any West Coast independent if you gave him all of the Miramar business. But his professional ego makes him want Madison Avenue, too. And he'll be able to make a triumphal entry back into New York. The way we have it arranged, the only thing that will be missing is a tickertape parade down Madison Avenue." He paused reflectively.

"No, Collins isn't the problem. It's Craig." Roth reached down into his case and took out a folder marked "Confidential." He removed a sheet and tossed the folder onto the desk before him. "You know the facts. You've read his confidential dossier as often as I have. And, as I said a moment ago, Rick Craig won't be an easy nut to crack."

Roth began to read from the sheet of paper in his hand. "Born and raised near a small town in Georgia. Father killed in action in World War II. Educated at Auburn. All-American Basketball honorable mention. Graduated with honors. Married the summer after graduation. Enrolled in graduate study at Columbia. Later took up residence in Aspen, Colorado. Published first novel in 1966, published *The Brilliant Dream* in 1968. On the best-seller list for twenty-three weeks, the recipient of the National Book Award.

"Received enormous publicity, went on the lecture circuit. Began drinking heavily. Success went to his head. Rifts appeared in the marriage. Kathleen Craig was killed ten years ago by a hit and run driver in New York City. Craig went into a deep depression. Moved back to Colorado but suffered writer's block. Eventually joined the hippie subculture, got into drugs in a big way. Almost lost his life when fire destroyed a house where he had been hired as caretaker. Went on the skids for a couple of years, then met Jay Collins, who was in Aspen supervising a film for BBDO. Craig served as a script consultant and later, when his mother developed a terminal illness, he asked Collins for a job in Atlanta as copywriter. They formed Collins & Craig six years ago, and they have enjoyed an enormous success. But he's still a very troubled man and very attached to the agency.

"In all this time since his wife was killed, he's never left himself open again. He's a loner. Won't let anyone get close to him." Roth looked at Gorman. "As a matter of fact, I'd be most interested in just how you intend to approach him."

Gorman smiled offhandedly and ignored the opening. But silently he agreed with Roth. Craig was a tough one. And now the time was getting short. He was aware of the dryness in his mouth again, conscious of the pounding within his skull. At any moment he would feel Hunter's penetrating stare, would hear Hunter's insistent demand that he reveal his strategy.

Roth's voice droned on, but Gorman ignored it. He reached forward to take the "Confidential" folder from the desk, and leafed through the contents, hoping that his manner appeared to be casual. His eyes darted from page to page, searching frantically one last time for the key to Rick Craig.

Suddenly he found it. And he realized that the key had been there all along, in the form of the Stock Option between Craig and Logan Smith, the agency's controller. But somehow, he hadn't seen it. Until now.

His eyes scanned the photostatic copy again. And it was there, clear and concise.

On January 1, Rick Craig would sell an additional fifty shares of agency stock to Logan Smith. Fifty shares. An insignificant amount. So insignificant that he had overlooked it earlier. But even fifty shares could destroy the balance of ownership that had existed between Collins and Craig.

Gorman flipped back through the documents, reviewing the ownership of agency stock, his mind computing totals quickly and with a growing excitement. And he was right. On January 1, Logan Smith would own a total of 5 percent of the stock. Collins would own 48 percent. And by selling the additional fifty shares, Craig would own only 47 percent.

On January 1, Logan Smith became the most important figure in the agency. And Logan Smith was vulnerable. Steve Gorman knew precisely how to control him.

Gorman's sharp, barking laugh shot through the room, interrupting the incessant flow of words from Joe Roth. Hunter swung around to him, his eyes cutting into him, demanding an explanation for the interruption.

"All of this discussion about Rick Craig is interesting, of course," he began, "but it's totally irrelevant."

Irrelevant. It was a phony word, a Joe Roth word, and he was pleased to see the look of consternation it produced on Roth's face. He proceeded, and he chose the same word to emphasize his point. "It's irrelevant because *Rick Craig is irrelevant.* For that matter, so is Jay Collins."

Gorman leaned down to take Roth's legal pad, ripping away the sheets Roth had read from, and letting them fall haphazardly to the floor. He took a pencil from his pocket and, standing, he addressed the others.

"It's really a matter of simple addition, Joe," he said, scribbling names and numbers on the pad for both men to see. When he finished, he tossed the pad on the desk for Hunter to inspect.

"You haven't asked me for *my* opinion yet, Mac," Gorman said, "but I'm going to give it to you. *Yes,* it will work. *Yes,* they'll accept the offer. *Yes,* we can gain control of Collins & Craig."

Gorman had the high cards, and Logan Smith was his ace in the hole. Confidence spread through his body, soothing his nerves, stilling the throbbing in his head. "The answer is yes, because *I'm going to make it work.* Tonight."

Chapter 5

"Wanna take a hansom ride through Central Park, mister?"

The old man stopped him, blocking Rick Craig's way. An old horse, already tired by midafternoon, stood mutely in the street, the jaunty artificial flowers affixed to his harness contrasting sharply with the tattered blanket that protected it from the January wind.

"Take a hansom ride, mister?" the man repeated, and Rick shook his head and walked on. The two of them, horse and driver, seemed vaguely out of place to him, a lingering concession to an earlier time, a memory from the past.

He stood on the corner observing the deserted intersection where Fifty-eighth and Fifty-ninth converged on Fifth Avenue, awkwardly conforming themselves to the massive, towering bulk of the Plaza.

A memory from the past. He reflected on his earlier thought. This whole trip was like a memory from the past, and he heard the words again. Words and phrases that had echoed, ghostlike, through his memory since his arrival at the hotel.

"We'll stay at the Plaza, won't we, Rick? After all, if Scott and Zelda could swim in the fountain, we can at least spend our honeymoon there . . ."

Rick smiled, remembering Kathy's enthusiasm in planning their wedding trip, remembering the honeymoon itself. He stepped from the curb, pulling the collar of his trench coat up against the sharp wind, and approached the fountain in front of the hotel.

They had been married that summer after graduation. The perfectly matched couple, their friends said. Kathy and Rick. The beautiful and gracious young Southern woman and the handsome basketball star. She, a talented painter; he, a budding young writer. They'd spent every penny of his hard-earned savings here at the Plaza before they moved to the other side of town, where he started on his master's work at Columbia. Those had been happy times, frustrating but happy. Before they moved to Colorado. Before *The Brilliant Dream*.

It was funny, he reflected, gazing up at the grayed stone and Gothic parapets of the venerable old building. The Plaza had been a part of their life, a part of the happy times. And now after all these years he was back at the Plaza. Remembering.

"I'll expect you to take good care of my daughter . . ."

Another voice. Kathy's father. He had first met Kathy's parents here at the Plaza. Rick remembered his nervousness, his apprehension as Kathy firmly gripped his hand and led him through the crowded tables of the Palm Court. A violin had been playing somewhere in the background. And they had welcomed him into their group and shortly after into their family.

Rick frowned as he thought of the wall of recrimination that had grown between them after her death.

But in the beginning, their respect for one another had been enormous. Her father was a physician who, despite his Yankee upbringing, had distinguished himself as a noted surgeon and sponsor of the arts in Savannah. He was sophisticated and urbane, witty and intellectual, and he had clearly idolized Kathy. He had studied in

New York, interned in Montreal, selected Savannah for his residency. But New York had been his city, and Kathy's incurably romantic notions about Manhattan were part and parcel of her father's own.

And Kathy's mother. As deeply ingrained with Southern heritage as with her Irish ancestry. She had countered her husband's romantic notions with humor and the wisdom of her centuries-old heritage, and when her laugh rang out, as it was likely to do, Rick could instantly hear Kathy's own laugh.

Rick's thoughts lingered on them a moment. I wonder where they are? I wonder what they're doing now?

He stood and walked back toward the entrance of the hotel. Past the hansom cab and the doorman, up the steps of the main entrance, and he heard another voice, not in his memory but alive and excited and calling out to him.

"Rick!"

He turned and looked down to the street. Jay Collins was stepping from a long dark limousine, the driver standing beside the open door.

Rick raised one hand in greeting and watched as Collins emerged and supervised the unloading of luggage.

He fits the role, Rick thought to himself. His eyes moved over his associate from his bald scalp with its fringe of reddish blond hair past his craggy, pitted face, to the chalk-stripe gray suit and the fashionable camelhair polo coat. Despite his physical limitations, he was every inch the prosperous executive. And now, Rick realized, he even had the props to go with it. A uniformed chauffeur in a corporate limousine for a dramatic entrance at one of New York's luxury hotels. It's too bad he can't see himself, Rick thought. He'd like the image.

The thought lingered in Rick's mind. Jay *would* like the image. Perhaps too much. The promise of The Phoenix Press and the world of Madison Avenue might be too much for Collins to assimilate. Too much for the agency to withstand. He remembered Collins' impulsive words from the evening before, felt his own anger flash over him again.

But Collins was bounding up the steps, a broad smile spread over his face. "Rick! I'm glad you're here. Look who I've brought with me."

Rick looked back to the limousine and saw another familiar figure retrieving a briefcase from the pile of luggage on the curb.

"What's Smitty doing with you? I didn't know he was coming up for the presentation—"

"I didn't either, until this morning. But I got a call *at home—*" he emphasized the point with a knowing look "—before I was out of bed this morning. Roth again. He asked me to bring all of our current financial data with me. Said they had reviewed our creative stuff but that they were concerned with our financial stability. Wanted to see proof that we're solvent."

Logan Smith had joined the other men now, and he extended his hand to Rick. "Hi, Rick. Didn't expect to see me, did you?"

"No," Rick took his hand, "and I still don't know what you're doing here."

Collins resumed his explanation. "When Roth called, he asked me to bring the financial reports. And he insisted that I bring along our controller to interpret them. Because they've retained Aaron Carlsen to examine our financials and give us the stamp of approval."

Collins had herded the group through the revolving door and stood awaiting the arrival of the doorman with the luggage cart.

"*Aaron Carlsen,*" he repeated for emphasis. "Do you know who Aaron Carlsen is, Rick? He's a financial consultant to agencies and advertisers. As a matter of fact, he's *the* financial consultant."

Collins whirled around, his eyes taking in the setting before him. "The Plaza is all right," he noted. "Especially since they fixed it up. Personally, I would have preferred the Pierre—" He broke off in midthought as the doorman appeared. "This way, boy. We're checking in."

He turned and started around the Court, leading Smitty and the doorman in a processional to the reception desk. Glancing over his shoulder, he saw Rick standing in the same spot and returned to him.

"Aaron Carlsen is big business, Rick. They wouldn't have hired him if they didn't mean business. And I'm ready for the big time." He took an envelope from his pocket and thrust it into Rick's hand. "Our first meeting is tonight at six," he said, nodding toward the envelope and leaving to join the others.

Rick could feel the quality of the heavy paper as he pulled a sheet of notepaper from the envelope. At the top was the engraved crest of The Phoenix Press, the unique, interlocking *P*'s that had come to be synonymous with America's oldest publishing house. Beneath the insignia was the name of Joseph Roth, and his identification: Executive Vice President.

"Welcome to New York, Mr. Collins," the heavy handwriting said. "I had hoped to be on hand personally to meet you, but another commitment prevents it. Mr. Steve Gorman will join you in the Oak Bar at 6:00 P.M. Please give him the financial documentation, which we discussed earlier today by telephone, so that Mr. Carlsen may have the evening to analyze it.

"I look forward to meeting you, Mr. Craig, and Mr. Smith tomorrow at 10:00 A.M. and to your presentation."

Rick looked up to see Collins again approaching him, followed by Smitty and a bellman.

"Come on," Collins called out to him, jingling the

heavy key in his hand, and Rick joined the entourage as they approached an elevator. "We'll have a chance to freshen up before we meet this Gorman fellow. He's obviously one of Roth's flunkies who doesn't object to working on a holiday."

The three of them stood in the doorway of the oak-paneled bar, a surge of bodies crowding before them, silhouetting themselves against the turn-of-the-century murals that lined the room. The city—or, at least, the Plaza—had come to life again after the long New Year's afternoon.

Collins edged his way past the jam of people and caught the attention of the *maitre d'*, moving his lips close to the man's head to make himself heard over the hubbub. The harried man automatically frowned, shaking his head and turning his attention back to the other people clamoring to be seated. But he stopped and turned back to Collins, his face covered with sudden comprehension. Smiling, he ignored the other guests in the doorway and took Collins by the elbow, leading him toward the rear of the room.

There, a solitary figure sat at a table, forming an island of emptiness in the throng that surged around him. When he saw them moving in his direction, he stood to greet the trio of visitors, his hand stretching out in welcome.

Steve Gorman. The man Roth had mentioned in his note.

As they joined him at his table, Rick eyed the New Yorker speculatively, deciding he fit the mold: vested suit, small-patterned tie, button-down shirt; a slightly supercilious manner; the detached, almost bored look that put an invisible barrier between him and the tide of humanity that flowed around him.

Steve Gorman looked like all of the other men in the room. Almost.

But something caused Rick to study the younger man more closely. Early thirties he guessed. A big man, tall and fit, his jacket unable to conceal broad shoulders and powerful arms. And although the lines around his eyes seemed etched too deeply for his relative youth, his skin was tanned and ruddy, a healthy contrast to the pallid faces at the tables around them.

But it was his eyes that commanded Rick's attention. Gorman's eyes were sharp and clear, darting from one face to another, lingering on one for a moment, then passing on to unabashedly study the next and to catalogue and mentally file away his findings.

His eyes were on Jay Collins now, studying him, carefully gauging his reactions to Gorman's words. He was painting the glories of the corporate life, the magnificence of Manhattan. And as the other man responded with enthusiasm, Gorman embellished the subject. Had their trip on the company jet been comfortable? Had the steward taken care of their needs? He had just returned from a trip on the same plane, he noted. To the Bahamas. That explained his suntan, he said. And it explained his run-down condition: a client had been with him, and they had taken a couple of girls and . . .

His voice trailed off, but his eyes were intent on Jay and he winked. And suddenly, Rick observed, Jay Collins began to relax and to warm to the conversation with Gorman.

A silence fell over the table as the waiter brought another round of drinks, and Rick diverted his attention to the mural behind the bar. Finally he was aware that the silence persisted, and he looked back to find Gorman's penetrating gaze silently fixed upon him. Slowly a sardonic smile came over Gorman's face and he spoke.

"So you're Rick Craig," he said. "The famous Author-turned-Ad Man. It's not every day we have the opportunity to wrap up both talents in one person."

Gorman's eyes had not left him, and Rick felt himself

flushing under the scrutiny like a strange breed of animal being exhibited at a zoo.

He returned Gorman's stare. "Yes, I'm Rick Craig," he answered evenly, and Gorman continued to stare at him. Finally Rick spoke again. He tried to make his voice pleasant, but he had the instinctive feeling that he was addressing an adversary and his tone reflected it. "And who are *you*, Mr. Gorman? Are you Mr. Roth's assistant?"

Gorman's laugh was like a rifleshot crackling through the room, and a look of genuine amusement came over his face. "Roth's assistant?" The staccato bark rang out again. "No. I'm associated with The Miramar Corporation—"

Collins voice interrupted. "The Miramar Corporation? The communications conglomerate? But what does that have to do with The Phoenix Press?"

Gorman laughed again. "We own them," he said bluntly. "We own a lot of companies. Miramar Pictures Corporation, of course. That's our oldest and best known. They've been one of America's top motion picture producers almost since the days of talkies. And we own Miramar Cinema International. They're the distributors for Miramar Pictures, domestically and abroad.

"And we're into publishing in a fairly big way, too. The Press, we've already mentioned. And Chartwell Books, the paperback house.

"And major daily newspapers in Miami and Los Angeles. And a weekly on Long Island.

"And the magazine group. We publish five different trade magazines. And we'll soon be announcing the acquisition of a very important fashion trade paper.

"Our Forestry Products Division in North Carolina furnishes newsprint and pulp for the publishing operation.

"And we're into television, too. Three stations: in Texas, California, and Missouri. And a cable television operation.

"And—" Gorman paused for breath, then shrugged his shoulders. "Oh, there are a few more. Television production companies, a couple of recording studios, printing houses, engravers. A lot of smaller, related businesses. Miramar has had a major acquisition program for the past five, six years. And it's worked like clockwork. We find a company that fits our pattern. We pay top dollar—book value *plus.* We've made millionaires out of more than a few of them. Then we provide working capital or expansion capital. We provide marketing know-how. And we *all* make money. In our kind of a deal, nobody loses."

Collins had listened with rapt attention, and now he silently shook his head in agreement with Gorman. "You're right. Nobody loses. Everybody's a winner."

"Everybody is a winner?" Rick was speaking not so much to Gorman as to Jay Collins, but he only asked a part of the question that was in his mind. What about those people who don't want to be swallowed up by a giant conglomerate? What about those people who don't like the corporate way of doing things?

Gorman looked at him again, his brows pulled together in thought. But when he spoke, he directed his remarks toward Collins, ignoring Rick.

"Everybody is a winner. I'm a living example. I just made the transition from private entrepreneur to corporate boardroom a couple of years ago. And it made me a wealthy man." He paused a moment and the smile came back to his face. "As a matter of fact, I'm a former ad man myself. I owned my own public relations agency. Primarily political advertising, campaign consultation."

Collins snapped his fingers in realization. "Wait a minute, Steve Gorman. Steven A. Gorman Associates.

SAGA." Gorman nodded. "You're the man who elected the President. Why, hell yes, you're the man who took the President out of backwoods politics and sent him to the White House. Your name used to be spread across every issue of *Ad Age.*" He paused a moment, reflecting. "I knew that you'd gotten out of the business, but I thought you were on the White House staff—"

Gorman stopped him. "I was." His face was expressionless, but his voice had an edge to it.

Collins started to speak again, to follow the line of questioning he had started. But he thought better of it and closed his mouth without comment. Gorman finally broke the silence.

"I found the private sector to be more to my liking." His voice was more natural now, and a smile was on his face. "And a hell of a lot more lucrative," he said, winking at Collins again.

"But, all of that has nothing to do with the matters at hand." Gorman abruptly turned the conversation to business. "Did you bring the financial information with you? The data that Joe Roth asked you to bring?"

Smitty jumped into activity and after fumbling in his briefcase for a moment pulled forth a voluminous file. Placing it on the table before them, he opened the folder and took up the first report.

Gorman waved his remarks aside, replacing the report in the folder and closing it.

"I'm sure that Aaron Carlsen can understand it. You'll have a chance to meet with him tomorrow morning. I hope the information is as good as we think it is," he said pointedly. "If it can stand up under Carlsen's scrutiny, and Miramar's, it could be very important to you."

Collins sat forward in his chair. "What do you mean, Steve?"

Gorman put the folder into his own case and snapped

the lock closed. And then he dropped the bombshell.

"The Miramar companies spend millions and millions of dollars in advertising every year. The Press is just a drop in the bucket. There's no reason why they shouldn't be spending it through Collins & Craig."

He prepared to leave, but he looked abruptly back at Collins. "Do you have dinner plans this evening?"

"No-o-o, nothing definite. We'll probably just eat here in the hotel—"

"I'm tied up with Aaron Carlsen for a while. But later in the evening, I'm going to drop in at a little party at a friend's apartment." He took a business card from his pocket and scribbled an address on it. "Maybe you'd like to join me. One of the producers from Miramar Pictures is here to interview a couple of Broadway actresses who are trying to make it big in Hollywood. You never know—it might get interesting later in the evening." He smiled, his inference unmistakable. "If I can count on you, I'll have them bring along a friend—"

He had directed the invitation to Collins alone and now, belatedly, he made a halfhearted attempt to include the other two men. "Both of you are welcome, too, of course. If you're interested, I'll see how many extra women I can dig up—"

Smitty shook his head. "No, thanks. I've got an old college buddy here and I'm going to try to see . . ."

Gorman nodded and moved his eyes to Rick. They stared at each other for a moment, and Rick silently shook his head.

"Whatever you wish," Gorman said, and focused back on Jay Collins, reaching across the table to hand him the business card. "But I *can* count on you?"

"Certainly," Collins answered, a flattered smile on his face. "I'd love to—"

"Good," Gorman said. and then he left.

They watched him pick his way through the thinning

crowd and finally disappear through the door. "God *damn!*" Collins exploded, a look of amazement on his face. "God*damn,* Rick, did you hear what he said? 'Millions and millions of dollars in advertising.' And there's no reason why they shouldn't be spending it through us. God*damn!*"

Rick turned Gorman's words over in his mind and the insanity of it all overwhelmed him. Yesterday in Los Angeles he had sensed something wrong about the phone call from The Phoenix Press. Today his concern was magnified tenfold by the glib enticement offered by Steve Gorman.

But the look and sound of excitement in Jay Collins told him that this was not the time to discuss his misgivings. It would only result in a further argument, deeper scars in their relationship. He finally answered calmly. "It sounds fantastic. But don't get your hopes up yet, Jay. First, we've got to get by the consultant."

Smitty broke into the conversation. "And that worries me. He's going to see how short on cash we really are. And I'll bet he's not going to like it."

"Short of cash, hell. We're the hottest thing going. They know it and we know it. We're on the verge of the biggest breakthrough in the history of the agency, and you're worried about what some broken-down old consultant is going to say." Rick was amazed at how shallow Collins' earlier depth of respect had become. Collins continued. "I'm a hell of a lot more interested in what Steve Gorman has to say."

Collins summoned a passing waiter. "Waiter! Bring me a double Scotch on the rocks." He looked at the card he held in his hand. "And Gorman asked me to join him later tonight. Another chance to get to know him, to tell him about the agency. By tomorrow morning, I'll have that son of a bitch eating out of my hand."

He sat back in his chair, expansively sipping at the

drink, his eyes roving the room. "Man, this is where it's happening. New York. The Big Apple. Hell, right here in this room. The cocktail hour at *the* Plaza. Not the Peachtree Plaza."

Collins' eyes continued to scan the room, but suddenly they riveted themselves on the doorway of the bar. He bent his head forward, one hand at his brow in a gesture of concentration. He looked back toward the door. "Rick, I know that woman. I remember her from when I worked here before, but I can't remember her name."

Rick looked up and saw a beautiful young woman and a distinguished older man move in their direction, and he quickly averted his eyes as they were seated at an adjoining table.

Collins continued to stare, almost mesmerized in his attempt to recall the woman's name, and finally Rick drew his attention back to his own table. "Jay, you're becoming obvious. Her escort is beginning to look you over, too."

"I'm sorry," Collins replied in a low voice. "But I know her—at least I did. I never forget a good-looking woman. As a matter of fact, I tried to date her. That's right! She was in the personnel department of J. Walter Thompson. If only I could remember her name—"

"What difference does it make?" Rick was tiring of Jay's preoccupation. "You already have plans for the evening. And she obviously has plans, too."

"If only I could remember her name," Collins repeated. And then, providentially, the *maitre d'* walked through the room, paging softly "Miss Suzanne Carmichael . . . Miss Carmichael, please." Jay snapped his fingers in recollection. "That's it, Suzanne Carmichael," and he watched as the man at the next table stood and summoned the waiter.

He handed her a message, and she ripped it open and

scanned it briefly, grimacing as she handed it to the man with her. He read it, and they conversed briefly, then he stood. "I'll take care of it for you," they heard him say. "I'll probably have to see him personally. Tonight. Can you get home alone?"

Jay seized the opportunity. He was on his feet before her escort could move away, insisting that she join them, doggedly trying to refresh her memory and convince her that she had known him.

Her voice was brittle and sophisticated as she responded to his introduction. "Collins?" She shook her head. "I'm sorry. It's been so many years . . ." She turned to Rick to acknowledge the introduction. She studied him for a moment, and her brows pulled together in thought. "Wait a minute. Jay Collins. And Rick Craig. Collins & Craig. *The* Collins & Craig. From Atlanta. What a remarkable coincidence that I'd run into you like this. A few days ago, I'd never heard your name. But now my telephone's ringing off the wall. You've got the whole industry stirred up because of The Phoenix Press."

"The whole industry?" he asked incredulously. "Stirred up? Just because we're making a pitch to The Phoenix Press? I'm surprised that The Press would attract that much interest on Madison Avenue."

"It's not just The Press. It's the magnitude of their new marketing concept. I don't know how word got out, but it's all over town that this will be the first major marketing development in the publishing world in fifty years. Maybe forever." The tired sophistication in her voice was replaced with an animated sound of interest. "From where I stand, it looks as if you're going to be needing a whole new staff for The Press. Maybe a New York office, too—"

"Just where *do* you stand, Miss Carmichael? Why do you know so much about all of this?" It was the first time that Rick had spoken and his voice was curt, almost rude. Purposefully so. He still felt resentment at his encounter with Gorman, and Suzanne Carmichael's brittle chatter was doing nothing to dispel his feelings.

"I'm sorry." Her voice was genuine, and she fumbled in her bag for a business card. She pushed it across the table. "Let mc offer the professional services of Carmichael and Findlay. We specialize in executive placement in advertising and marketing. That's why I know about Collins & Craig, about the plans of The Press. Just a small rumor is enough to make every disgruntled account executive and creative director in New York start pounding on my door. And they *are* pounding on my door because the rumors are flying—not just about The Press, but about Miramar, too."

She concentrated her attention on Collins. Her voice was matter-of-fact. "And rumor has it that you're the new fair-haired boys of Mac Hunter of Miramar—"

"Mac Hunter?" Collins said. "We don't even know Mac Hunter—"

"You will, darling. You will. And maybe he'll buy you out and make millionaires out of both of you."

Millionaires. There was the reference again, the same thing Gorman had told them. And even though Suzanne Carmichael was a very beautiful woman, Rick felt the same vague sense of distaste come over him as he had experienced with Gorman.

He shifted his weight back in the chair, preparing to push himself away from the table, to excuse himself from the group. But astonishingly Jay Collins was already moving to his feet in an effort to extricate himself.

"I'm terribly sorry, Suzanne," he murmured, voicing his need to freshen up before joining a friend at a party. Then he was gone, followed shortly by Smitty with the same excuse he had mumbled to Gorman about an old college friend. And, contrary to his wishes, Rick Craig found himself alone at the table with Suzanne Carmichael.

She took another sip from her glass and settled back to look at him. "So you're Rick Craig," she said.

Later he would realize that the words were spoken without malice, with genuine interest and curiosity. But now he heard Steve Gorman, not Suzanne Carmichael. And his anger at Gorman and The Phoenix Press and Jay Collins, his frustration with the entire untenable situation welled up in him and focused on this stranger who had suddenly become his companion.

"And you're a Lady Headhunter," he lashed back. "Are you out for another scalp to hang on your belt, along with all the others? I'd think Collins & Craig would be too small to interest you."

She stared at him in surprise, an uncomprehending look on her face. Then she pushed her drink away and started gathering her things together. "It's obvious that I've overstayed my welcome," she told him. "I'm terribly sorry that something I said offended you, Mr. Craig, but before I leave, let me clear up a couple of points." Her voice was icy, impersonal.

"I don't like the word *headhunter.* I find that it has almost the same connotations as the word *prostitute.*"

Rick already regretted his outburst and he opened his mouth to speak, but she went on without a pause. "You're under no obligation whatsoever, Mr. Craig, to use professional services in your search for qualified creative people. But if you *do* become the agency for The Phoenix Press, and if you *should* choose to use us, or anyone else for that matter, you should understand from the outset that we're not headhunters. We're professionals. And we specialize in the area of advertising. There are a vast number of agencies and companies looking for top-notch people, there are a lot of top-notch people looking for better jobs. All we try to do is form a bridge so that they can get together."

Again Rick started to speak but she ignored him, pushing her chair back and standing. "Good night, Mr. Craig."

She walked through the remnants of the cocktail crowd and left the bar. For a moment, Rick sat in a state of shock. Then he reacted. Pulling a couple of bills from the roll in his pocket, he threw them on the table and hurried after her.

He caught up with her at the curb as she was trying to hail a taxi and fumbled awkwardly with words of apology. When a taxi pulled up in front of them, she pulled open the door and slid onto the seat. He pushed his way in beside her.

Jay Collins sat on the edge of the back seat of the taxi, offering the driver unsolicited assistance in finding the address. They were in the upper eighties, in one of the most fashionable parts of elegant Park Avenue, and the surroundings heightened his sense of anticipation.

For a fleeting moment he felt a flash of remorse at his abrupt departure from the group at the bar. Not so much at deserting Rick for the evening as at leaving a good-looking woman. A good-looking woman always offered a certain promise.

But this promised more. Steve Gorman promised more. And Jay Collins could almost smell the action that he knew would come.

"There it is," he exclaimed, and the taxi driver grunted his awareness of the address as he pulled to the curb. Collins shoved a wad of wrinkled bills in the driver's hand and without waiting for change stepped under the canopy that stretched to the street. He still held Gorman's card in his hand and he anxiously doublechecked the handwritten address against the ornate lettering on the bronze plate by the front door. Satisfied, he rang and was greeted peremptorily by a uniformed doorman, one eyebrow raised questioningly.

"Mr. Gentry's apartment. Number Six-C," Collins told him, and the man stood aside, directing him down a marble-tiled hallway past rows of other discreet bronze plaques to an elevator.

Minutes later he stood before Apartment 6-C and rang the bell. After a moment the door opened slightly and Collins looked up, anticipating Gorman's welcoming features. Instead he was confronted with a dark, swarthy face that eyed him suspiciously. The man made no move to open the door farther, and Collins looked at the card to be certain he was at the correct address. Satisfied, he looked back at the man.

"Steve Gorman suggested that I drop by—"

The instant opening of the door made further words unnecessary. The short dark man revealed himself fully now. He wore a white linen suit and a dark shirt, set off with a white tie—an incongruous look, Collins thought, for this January night. But the suspicious look had melted into a smile. "Mr. Collins? Come in. Mr. Gorman is expecting you."

He turned and led Collins down a hallway with mirrored walls and potted plants into a large, softly lighted room. In white, Collins noted. All in white. White walls. White carpeting. White overstuffed sectionals facing into a white antique mantel where a fire crackled in the fireplace. White lacquered furniture with only a trace of glass and chrome. Even the tasteful graphics on the walls were predominantly white, a splotch of color here and there relieving the monotone of the room.

He could see a man sprawled on the couch, his back to Collins. A striking blonde stood at the fireplace sipping from a champagne glass. Her platinum hair was piled on her head nonchalantly, her high cheekbones accented with red, a carmine pout painted on her lips. Her dress, too, was white, its shimmering cloth clinging sensuously to her breasts and hips and long, lithe legs. She eyed Collins for a moment without interest and then directed her gaze and her words to the man before her.

"Jay!"

At the sound of his name Collins turned and saw Steve Gorman striding toward him. The other man looked self-assured, comfortable in his surroundings. He pumped Collins' hand, seizing his arm to propel him toward the small alcove where he had been sitting. He slid back on a barstool at the diminutive bar, motioning Collins to another.

"Cynthia, this is Mr. Collins. Fix him a drink and make him welcome. He drinks . . ."

"Chivas Regal," Cynthia murmured, tossing her red hair back over a shoulder as she leaned forward to take an empty glass. Collins studied her, his attention drawn away from Gorman and the others by her movements, by the breasts that strained against the halter top of her gown as she bent over the bar. She handed him the glass.

"How did you know I drank Scotch?" he asked.

She was moving around the bar now, seating herself next to him. "You *look* like a man who drinks Scotch. And I'd only serve you Chivas." She took the glass from his hand and sipped at it, and when she handed it back to him her fingers played lightly over his hand. "Mr. Gorman tells me that you're very big in advertising. That you'll soon own one of the biggest agencies in New York. That you're going to handle all of the Miramar business. I hope you'll consider me for some television work . . ."

Collins laughed deprecatingly, looking around to seek Gorman's reaction. He was surprised to find the seat next to him empty. He turned his attention back to Cynthia as he felt her hand on his thigh, moving slowly, sensuously, caressing the skin beneath the cloth of his trousers.

Collins slipped his arm around her waist and pulled

her closer to him, placing his glass to her lips for another sip. He felt her hand continue its upward movement.

At the front door Gorman paused long enough to peel a couple of hundred-dollar bills from the roll in his pocket. "Thanks, Vince. Give this to the girl. That should be enough for a couple of hours of her time." He thought a moment, then added another hundred to the outstretched palm. "Make it three hours. And tell her to make it a night that the country boy will never forget."

"You won't be wanting a room tonight, Mr. Gorman? One of the other girls will be free in a little while—"

"Not tonight, Vince. I've got work to do." Pulling a coat over his broad shoulders, Gorman walked down the mirrored hallway and left Apartment 6-C.

Logan Smith let himself into his room, whistling softly under his breath. He felt a twinge of remorse at the white lie he'd told Rick Craig, a cock and bull story about wanting to have dinner with an old college roommate and his wife. But remembering the woman he'd left Rick with, he couldn't feel too bad.

He peeled out of his business suit, tossing it carelessly on the bed. He paused long enough to take a bottle of Jack Daniel's from his suitcase and pour himself a preparatory drink for his own night on the town.

As he pulled on the faded denims and contoured body shirt, he felt more comfortable. He took another drink of the raw whiskey and surveyed himself in the mirror. With the change of clothing came a change of personality. From the fiscally intent young mind sprang a free spirit.

The Village, he thought. That's probably the best place to start. I wonder if that groupie bar is still open? If not, he told himself, there'll be another. There's always a group that's willing to play if you look hard enough.

Then, throwing a leather jacket over his shoulders, he left the room. He was ready to swing without the watchful eyes of Atlanta, or of Susan, or—most of all—of Collins & Craig. Thank God, he thought, they were both occupied tonight.

Outside another young man braced his back against a lamppost and placed one foot against it for support. Randy Elliot had taken up a vantage point at this particular corner of Central Park South because he could see both entrances to the hotel, could be alert to his mark if he should appear.

Jeez, he thought, he'd had some unusual assignments since he first met these people. Some AC, some DC. But none of them too unpleasant. Several of them actually rather nice. And the pay! It was always good and it helped tide him over when he didn't have a chorus job in a musical.

And the pay for this job was the best yet. Two hundred bucks for one night's work. He smiled to himself. Work? Hell, this was play. And it was all set up. Three girls primed and waiting at a bar. Another guy ready to join the group on signal. The key to the apartment in his pocket.

Two hundred bucks for a piece of cake, he repeated to himself as he pulled a pack of cigarettes from the tight jeans and put a match to one. Plus another fifty to do a bit as a waiter at "21" tomorrow, if it all came off as they expected.

At that moment his watchful eyes told him he was on. He abandoned the lamppost and moved quickly to the corner, crossing the street against the traffic. As he reached the corner of the Plaza, he scrutinized the young man standing there, mentally comparing him with the photograph he had studied. It was the same guy. The denim-clad figure walked toward him, then past him to a waiting taxi.

Randy moved leisurely toward the second taxi in line and opened the rear door. He pulled a bill from his pocket and held it before the driver's eyes. "I want you to follow that cab in front of us, and I don't want you to lose him."

The ageless black entertainer finished a familiar refrain and, with the final chord, he sat motionless in the spotlight while restrained applause filled the supperclub.

Rick Craig joined the others about him, but his motions were perfunctory. His attention was not on the performer, but on the woman who sat opposite him.

Her response was neither perfunctory nor restrained. Suzanne Carmichael's hands clapped together enthusiastically in tribute to the legendary entertainer, her eyes filled with excitement, a look of rapt attention on her face. She shot him a glance, a smile, and he answered her. And then her attention was back with the singer.

Rick studied her. He had done so throughout their evening together, in quick, stolen glances when her attention was directed elsewhere. But now, his face obscured by shadows and her attention on the small stage, he was free to stare at her without embarrassment.

She was beautiful. Perhaps the most classically beautiful woman that Rick Craig had ever known. Her hair was long, so dark it gave off a blue-black radiance, and it waved softly about her face. The face itself was finely sculpted, the features patrician, the complexion clear and lustrous. And her glittering dark eyes could, according to her mood, snap with anger or sparkle with excitement.

The soft fabric of her dinner dress emphasized her breasts and the slender symmetry of her willowy body.

Around her neck, a simple gold chain, and on one hand, a diamond dinner ring.

Rick saw other words begin to shape themselves on the man's lips, heard a new sound fill the room. But his attention, his thoughts, remained on the woman opposite him. What kind of woman *is* Suzanne Carmichael? he asked himself.

At the Oak Bar she had been fashionable and sophisticated. And abrasive. But later, after the initial awkwardness of the situation, he had found her intelligent and literate and gentle. And beautiful.

He pondered the change in her personality, and then it became clear to him. At the Oak Bar, she had worn a mask. A mask of sophistication. A protective covering, her wall against the outside world.

The idea took hold. Suzanne had worn a mask, just like the mask that Rick had worn for so many years, his shield of protection against further pain.

But Suzanne had cast off the veneer, had let him see her as she truly was.

Why can't I? he asked himself. Why can't I? The thought was numbing, debilitating, a question he could not answer. Dear God, he said to himself, *why can't I?*

He tried to address himself to the question, to answer it, but a heavy chord from the piano demanded his attention and he looked at the stage. The singer's voice was raised in the crescendo of the finale.

And before he could face the tormenting question in his mind, the song was ended and, finally, the performer out of sight. And once again, as he had done for so many years, he could lock the question away and ignore it, hide it beneath his own mask.

He rose and took Suzanne by the arm and together they were swept out of the café, engulfed in an ocean of people all trying to leave at once. Under the fringed hotel canopy they stopped, forming a small island in the flow of humanity.

Rick looked at her, not ready for the evening to end. "I'd like another cup of coffee," he said with a grin.

"Do you like espresso?" she asked impulsively.

"I love it," he answered, and she took his hand.

"Then come on," she instructed him. "I know the best espresso bar in New York. And it's close enough to walk."

The night was clear and still. And unusually warm for January, he commented as he pulled her closer to him. They walked on in silence for a moment before he spoke again.

"You're different," he announced abruptly.

"Different?" she responded. "Different from what?"

"Different from the kind of person I thought you were when we met in the Oak Bar."

"And what kind of person did you think I was?"

"A New York bitch."

She looked up at him in surprise and pondered the matter for a moment. "I suppose I was," she admitted. "But that was before I got to know you." Her look became accusing. "And you've got to admit that you asked for it. You were pretty much of a bastard yourself."

They walked on in silence until finally he looked down at her and spoke.

"Oh, by the way. Happy New Year."

She laughed. "Happy New Year to you, too, Rick. And the best of everything."

"The best of everything," he murmured, almost to himself, his thoughts returning with a jolt to the circumstances of his presence in New York. "I wonder what this year will bring?"

"The Phoenix Press?" she asked directly. "Somehow after spending an evening with you, I'm not sure you really want The Press."

"I'm not sure that I do, either." He shook his head and took a deep breath of air, trying to clear the conflicting thoughts that were beginning to gather there again. "It seems almost impossible that The Phoenix Press only entered my life yesterday. And in just twenty-four hours, it's ballooned into The Press, and The Miramar Corporation, and a New York office, and somebody named Mac Hunter and God-only-knows what else." He paused a moment and his voice took on a bitter note. "Oh, yes. And Steve Gorman."

He felt her body tense and he looked down at her. "Do you know Steve Gorman, Suzanne?"

She was silent for several steps before answering. "Yes," she finally said. "I know Steve Gorman." She pulled away from him. "And I know Mac Hunter, too. So will you, by this time tomorrow. He's chairman of The Miramar Corporation. He owns The Phoenix Press. He's Gorman's boss."

Rick was silent for a moment. "Tell me what you know about them."

"I really can't do that, darling." The brittleness, the protective cover again. "I know more than I'd like to."

They walked on in silence and finally she spoke again, this time in the voice Rick had come to know. "That sounded bitchy, didn't it? But I really mean it, you see. The Miramar Corporation is a good customer of mine. And it wouldn't be wise for me to go around talking about Maxwell Hunter, would it? Not even to you, Rick. Maybe most of all not to you." Again she was silent. "I wouldn't want you to get hurt, Rick. There's no reason for it." She repeated herself. *"There's no reason for it."*

"Wait a minute," Rick protested. "This Mac Hunter character couldn't hurt me—"

"Don't argue, Rick. Just listen to me. And remember one thing: whatever Hunter wants, Hunter gets."

Rick felt a tremor come over her body and he slipped his arm around her waist again. "What about Gorman?" he ventured.

"Since Gorman became Hunter's administrative assistant it's not wise to talk about him, either. Or to cross him. But the whole city used to talk about him. I guess I can tell you what they say, what's been printed about him.

"Steve Gorman had a public relations agency in Chicago. Not public relations—political relations, really. He handled several winning candidates and began to make a name for himself nationally. Came to the attention of the national committee. And then he took up with the President, before he even became a candidate. And Gorman literally elected the man President.

"He did it only for one reason: he knew what the voter wanted and how to make the candidate look good." Suzanne looked at him a moment, then continued. "Steve Gorman is a political gutfighter. And remember this: whatever the situation demands, Gorman can understand it and see that it happens.

"Mac Hunter did *not* back the President," she said. "He's too conservative for that. But when Gorman was kicked out of the White House, Hunter picked him up."

Rick interrupted. "Gorman was thrown out of the White House? Why?"

"No one ever knew, exactly. Except Gorman and the President, I guess. Rumor had it that he got involved in a dishonest deal, involving *big* dollars, and the President wouldn't stand for it.

"At any rate, Gorman showed up in New York shortly after that as Hunter's assistant."

She stopped and turned toward the entrance of a brownstone front and began to pull Rick up its steps. "But enough about Steve Gorman. Here's the espresso bar I told you about."

As they entered the front door and walked toward a small elevator, Rick looked about him. "Funny, this doesn't look like a café. And I don't see any espresso bar . . ."

"You will," she answered pulling him into the elevator. A moment later, on an upper floor, she inserted a key in a lock. Stepping inside, she offered him her hand, announcing with a flourish, "Welcome to the finest espresso bar in Manhattan—the Café Carmichael."

She led him into the apartment and then whirled around and faced him, amusement still present on her face. He moved to her, putting his hands on her waist and drawing her to him. For a moment she looked seriously into his eyes. Then the amused look returned and she pushed away and walked into the living room.

She looked about the room. "You'll have to admit that the decor is excellent. But the service is lousy. I'd better get busy. Tomorrow's a working day, and you've got to be on your toes."

She went to an open bar and attacked a brass-and-chrome machine with skill. Rick sat on a stool opposite her for a moment, then stood and walked about the apartment. He walked into a second room, a small library, and stood before the bookcases studying the titles, trying to piece together the personality from the books she read. His hand suddenly reached out and took one from the shelf and flipped it open. Then, with a look of surprise on his face, he walked back to the bar and laid it on the counter in front of her.

He pointed to an inscription on the flyleaf, "Best regards, Rick Craig." He looked at her, his brows knit together in thought. "I don't remember signing this. I don't remember meeting you before."

"You wouldn't." She laughed. "You signed it during an autograph session at a little shop on Third Avenue.

All those years ago. Your wife was with you, and the two of you were beautiful and charming and gracious. She was—"

Suzanne stopped, not knowing how to proceed, and changed the subject. "I read your book, of course. A couple of times. I thought it was a beautiful story." Her eyes remained fastened on the espresso machine as she continued. "A beautiful story, written by a very talented man."

Rick looked at her intently, afraid that he would find the sophisticated smile he had seen earlier. But she was intent on her work. He cautiously awaited her next comment, the first of the probing questions he had come to expect. But he was rewarded only with her silence, her own privacy respecting his right to privacy.

In response his lips formed the silent words, "Thank you."

Coming around the bar now, she placed a cup of steaming Italian coffee in his hands, and continued her conversation. "I read your earlier novel, too. It wasn't as good," she added honestly. "I was always sorry that there wasn't a third book."

"So was I," he responded, and then became silent, mulling over his coffee cup. He spoke again. "You're not the usual type of person that a man meets in New York," he began hesitantly. "As a matter of fact, you're not a very usual type of woman. You don't ask the usual kind of questions." He paused and then answered the inquiring look in her eyes. "You know, questions like 'Why don't you write anymore?' or 'When's the next big one coming out?' or 'What ever happened to your wife?' I never seem to have an answer for that type of question."

She shrugged off the question in his eyes. "When a man is ready, he'll discuss those things."

Rick took the coffee cup from her hands, setting it on

the bar. He took her face in his hands, bending down to kiss her softly, exploringly. Rick stood before her, pulling her up, encircling her waist with his arm. "You're a beautiful woman," he murmured, and then wordlessly he broke away and took one of her hands, gently pulling her toward another part of the house.

For a moment she seemed ready to follow him, but then she pulled back and stopped, her hand brushing across his face as she kissed him quickly, tenderly.

"No, Rick," she said, shaking her head slowly, almost dreamily. He again pulled her toward him, and again she resisted. "No," she repeated with more determination.

"Why, Suzanne?"

"Why? For a lot of reasons. I'm sure that women are easy for you, Rick. You're a very handsome man and you're terribly exciting. Maybe too handsome. And maybe I find you too exciting. Maybe you're the first man I've known in a long time who was genuinely sensitive, a genuine pleasure to be with.

"Or, maybe it's because I don't get business that way. By sleeping with my clients." She had moved away now, had found his trench coat. She held it out to him and her voice regained its professional qualities. "And maybe it's because it's late and it's time for you to go back to your hotel."

She pulled him gently toward the front door and reluctantly he responded. They stood wordlessly at the doorway for a moment, and then he pulled her toward him and kissed her again.

"Thanks," he said. "Thanks for showing me the Café Carmichael. And thanks for sharing a little piece of yourself with me. Maybe, sometime . . ."

"Sometime?" she prompted him.

"Maybe, sometime, I can do the same with you." And without a backward look, he turned and walked to the elevator. A few moments later he was on the streets of Manhattan, engulfed by the darkness of the night.

High above the street, the executive offices of The Miramar Corporation were engulfed by the same darkness. Every light in the chairman's suite was extinguished except for a single brilliant beam that cut through the blackness and carried flickering colored images from a motion picture projector to a viewing screen across the room.

A silvery vapor of smoke drifted upward, transformed by the light of the projector into a wispy, ghostlike trail. It diffused itself throughout the room and, finally, into the consciousness of Mac Hunter. The smell irritated him, and he looked at the figure sitting opposite him. A faint red glow lighted the other man's face for a moment before another cloud of smoke dispelled itself into the room, its acrid stench again assaulting Hunter's nostrils.

Hunter suddenly leaned forward, his head silhouetted momentarily on the screen as he groped for an ashtray and sent it sliding across the coffee table toward his companion.

"Goddamnit, Paul, get rid of that cigar."

At that moment the film ended and the screen went white. The overhead lights suddenly glared forth and Hunter sat there, his eyes squinted together against the new brilliance flooding the room.

The office was in total disarray. Stacks of file folders were piled haphazardly on the floor, random sheets of charted graph paper were scattered over the coffee table, overflowing onto the Oriental rug beneath, spilling over a stack of heavy volumes of computerized data. Obscuring a portion of the marble fireplace was a standing easel, holding the reproduction of a newspaper advertisement proclaiming the name "HAPWORTH!"

Hunter was aware of Steve Gorman busying himself

at the projector, running the film back through, unthreading it, replacing it in the canister beside the machine. But his attention was fixed on the older man sitting across the low table from him, indifferently stubbing out a long slender cigar. Hunter's dark brows pulled together and he held the man in his eyes, studying him, and he felt another wave of irritation sweep over him. He didn't understand it. It wasn't the cigar, he realized. Hunter had long since become accustomed to the cigars.

Perhaps it was the older man's attitude, his smug aloofness. His superior disregard for Hunter's wishes. Or perhaps, he reflected, I've worked with him for too many years. Perhaps the time had come to end his association with Paul Prescott.

He considered the idea, then discarded it. Not because he doubted its validity—it was probably a completely accurate analysis of the situation. But because it was impractical, counterproductive. Because he still needed Paul Prescott. At least for a few more months.

Prescott pushed the ashtray away and sat back in the chair, folding his arms across his chest and silently returning Hunter's stare. Finally he removed the heavy horn-rimmed glasses and, holding them professorially before him, continued his earlier discourse.

"The campaign film has been in use in New Hampshire for about four weeks, now. Before that, it was—"

"The campaign film?" Hunter cut him off, his voice sharp, caustic. The irritation he had felt before was spreading through his body into his mind, translating itself into hostility. "Was *that* the campaign film that you've talked about so incessantly? That cost thousands upon thousands of collars to produce? That demanded the talents of Hollywood's finest? Was that the result of years of psychological research and a king's-ransom-worth of technical equipment?"

He was rewarded with a look of flushed indignation on the other man's face and he continued. "Really, Paul. You disappoint me." Sarcasm dripped from his voice as he launched into a longstanding cat-and-mouse game, trying to break through the immaculate reserve of his associate.

Hunter's usual tactics—the tactics that worked so well with most of his underlings—didn't work with Paul Prescott, because Prescott did not consider himself an underling. He never had, not since the beginning of their relationship. And, in a way, Hunter respected him for that. Perhaps that was one reason why the relationship had lasted this long.

But nevertheless Hunter enjoyed playing the game and the brief look of anxiety he had produced on Prescott's face spurred him on. "Really, Paul," he repeated. "Is that the subliminal epic that's supposed to put Hapworth in the White House? I had expected better of you."

"Oh, come now, Mac," Prescott responded. His face was bland again, his voice calm. "Come now. Despite the fact that you own a billion-dollar media empire, you've never understood communications. And you've *certainly* never understood the ideas behind subliminal communication. You said these same things about Barry Starr's recording of 'Puppet in Love." But it worked. Brilliantly. And this will work, too." The silver-haired man paused. "Will work? It *is* working. We've just received the latest surveys and we know it's working.

"But before we go ahead, let's get one thing straight. You asked me here tonight to give you a status report, not to play games. I'll show you the samples of the work we're doing. I'll show you the subliminal inserts in the film you're so critical of. But I won't play cat-and-mouse. It's much too late and I'm much too tired." The doctor rose and walked to the projector.

Hunter watched him, considering. It was a victory of sorts, perhaps all that he would achieve. Mentally he shrugged it away. Tonight he would let the mouse get away. Unless another opportunity presented itself.

He directed himself back to the film, the caustic tone still in his voice. "Tell me why that piece of trash is so 'brilliant.' "

"Because I *made* it brilliant," Prescott snapped back. "Because my assistants on the island planned it brilliantly and the technicians in Los Angeles executed it brilliantly." The doctor was rethreading the film into the projector. "I'll grant you that the film seems quite innocuous. Much like any other political campaign film. But you didn't *see* it, really. And neither do the housewives and working girls in New Hampshire. They don't *see* our message—or hear it or consciously comprehend it. *But they feel it subconsciously.*"

He ran the projector forward to a precise frame and, signaling Gorman to extinguish the lights, he ran the scene, reversed the projector, then ran it again. He repeated the process in slow motion.

"You didn't see anything, did you? Even in slow motion. But let's see it again, and this time note the slight blip—it's barely discernible—between the time Hapworth shakes the hand of the young woman in the shopping center and the scene outside the factory."

Again the film was shown. "I see the blip," Hunter said. "Is that where it starts?"

"Right. This is our first intrusion on their subconscious. And from here until the end of the film we literally bombard them with the special message—in this case, a message for the eighteen- to thirty-five-year-old female. But we have five different appeals for five different demographic groups. Appeals that play on their emotions to convince them that Hapworth is the best man for them. Not just for America. The best man for *them.*"

"Let me see the insert."

"In a moment. Before you see it, let me tell you about it. Before the women in New Hampshire saw this film they said the same things you did. They found Hapworth 'weak' and 'ineffective.' What were some of the other spontaneous comments from the benchmark study, Steve?"

Gorman, sitting near the flickering screen, grabbed a bulky computer printout and flipped through its pages until his finger jabbed at one of the charts. "*Weak and inneffective,* like you said. And *unknown . . . too conservative . . . part of the nut fringe . . . nice looking but a cold fish . . . he can't win . . . looks like he's dishonest . . . he leaves me cold . . . sterile.*"

"Not exactly a winner's image," Prescott said. "As a matter of fact, a loser's image. And no chance for a victory. Not even for a third or fourth place in the primary." As he talked, Prescott had taken a second projector, bulky and awkward looking, from a case on the floor and began setting it up in tandem with the first machine. He fell silent for a moment as he worked, then stepped back to check the synchronization of the two projectors. Satisfied, he nodded toward them as he explained.

"This is a tachistoscope. It dates back to the initial experiments with mechanically induced subliminal perception in the late fifties, the early sixties. Remember the popcorn experiment? During a six-week test in a movie theater, more than forty-five thousand movie patrons perceived subliminal suggestions flashed on the screen: 'Hungry? Eat Popcorn.' They sold half again as much popcorn as usual. And the machine they used was a tachistoscope. It's simply a film projector with a high-speed shutter that flashes subliminal messages every five seconds at one three-thousandth of a second. It's outmoded and outdated. But I'm using it tonight because *this is the only way I can show you the subliminal inserts.* Because with the more sophisticated Light Intensity

Technique that we've now perfected, *the messages are totally invisible.*" He reached forward and patted the projector containing the subliminal film to emphasize the point. "There is no way that the subliminal messages in this film, or in our television commercials, can be detected, not even under ultraviolet scrutiny, once it has been conformed onto the regular film and left the laboratory. And with LIT, we have greater flexibility: we can provide intermittent subliminal inserts, as we've done with the campaign film, *or a continuous, separate message that plays in tandem with the regular message,* as we're doing with the television commercials. Think of it, gentlemen. A totally contained, completely separate message, produced at a level of light intensity below the level the conscious eye can perceive, and then superimposed over the regular message. Literally two in one. But they never knew they've seen *this* one. They just react to it.

"*And no one can detect it*—not the television station, not the sponsor, not the advertising agency that created the regular message. It means that you could—"

"Goddamnit, Prescott!" Hunter's voice cut sharply into the monologue. "I've heard all of this before. I know you've mastered the art of psychological bullshit. Now I want to see how you've done on pornography. Are you going to show me those goddamned inserts or not?"

Prescott's features screwed up into a scowl. "Of course," he said coldly. "Steve, would you get the lights?"

The screen again filled with the image of Anthony Hapworth, the film cued to the moment of the first insert. Slowly, frame by frame, the scene unfolded. Hapworth moved with jerky, Chaplinesque motions, then slowed even more, the film resembling an old-fashioned nickelodeon.

Finally he stopped. There on the screen where the

smiling politician had been only a moment before was a naked man. And slightly to his rear was a naked woman.

The film progressed. Five seconds of Hapworth, then quick, insistent flashes of the handsome young face. Flashing words: HAPWORTH . . . VIRILE. Hapworth again. And then the insistent flashes of the muscular body in the first stages of sexual arousal. HAPWORTH . . . MASCULINE. From Hapworth to the man. And then to the woman. And to the man and woman together. Hard-core closeups of their passionate embrace, of their heaving bodies. Back to Hapworth's simpering smile. And constantly interspersed between each scene the words HAPWORTH . . . VIRILE . . . HAPWORTH . . . MASCULINE.

The film resumed its normal speed and Prescott picked up on his commentary. "There are many, many additional inserts, of course, but it will take too long to study the detail of each of them. I'll just point out where they occur. Here's one. And another. And here . . . and another here." His narrative was filled with long pauses as the film played itself out. "And beginning here, there's one every five seconds until the end."

At last the film ran out and the doctor switched off the projector, moving toward the electrical switch. In the brilliance that followed he whirled back around to face Mac Hunter, a mixture of triumph and bitterness in his voice.

"Subliminal epic? Call it that if you want, Mac. But call it successful, too. Because it's working!" Prescott stalked to the chair where Gorman sat, grabbing the computer printout from his hands and letting his eyes run down the page. "Listen to what *those same women* said after they had seen the film. *Strong candidate . . . best for the country . . . masculine . . . vigorous . . . I find him exciting . . . didn't realize he was so tough . . . a real man.*

"The film is working—just the way this newspaper ad

is going to work." Prescott was becoming more agitated as he took a newspaper proof from the easel and held it in front of Hunter's face. "Take a look. This advertisement is designed to give a double dose of subconscious stimuli. Strong subliminal association, a strong invisible message.

"Take a look at the photograph. Hapworth out in front in a crowd scene, people pushing to get next to him. He's talking to a woman. Not a man, a woman. He's in shirt sleeves. But his torso is airbrushed, to make his shoulders broader, his biceps seem bigger, his waist smaller. And he's wearing a tie. But notice how it's blowing in the wind? It's sticking out from his body. A phallic symbol that was planned as carefully as his body position and his hand gesture—and that's another classic phallic symbol. See how his forefinger is extended, how his other fingers are cupped under?"

Hunter started to open his mouth, but Prescott's words continued to spew forth. "No, don't tell me that the viewer won't recognize all these symbols. I realize that not one person in a thousand could even understand what I've just described to you. *But they'll sense it.* And they'll feel the significance in the headline: AMERICA *COMES* TO A LEADER . . . AMERICA *COMES* TO HAPWORTH.

"And if all of that doesn't attract their attention, our silent message will." With a flourish, Prescott flipped over a piece of clear acetate, covering the ad in its entirety. On it were printed and scrawled tiny words, words that appeared all over the face of the ad, forming a mosaic of pattern and design. SEX . . . VIRILE . . . SEX.

"The words are called embeds and they're invisible to conscious perception—you probably couldn't see them without the acetate key. But they can be perceived instantly at the subconscious level. These embeds can be designed into the layout or airbrushed onto it. Or added to the original photograph, as they were here: regular photograph at one one-hundred-and-fiftieth of a second, double exposure for the embed at one one-thousandth of a second. Or painted on an engraving plate and lightly etched in acid."

Prescott turned to place the newspaper proof back on the easel. His anger had diminished now, but a look of bitterness was still about him.

"The man on the street might call these examples subliminal advertising, but I prefer to think of the campaign film and this newspaper advertisement as experimental devices. Experimental devices that have successfully reached the subconscious mind and molded and manipulated it into a predetermined course of action."

He looked at Hunter and the bitterness was apparent in his voice. "Or you, Mac, might prefer to call it psychological bullshit. But the medical profession will call it the most magnificent breakthrough since Wilbur Penfield proved that there *is* a subconscious. Even the most doubting of my colleagues would term it a success—already. Now. After the Utah Experiment. After the surveys from New Hampshire. But after the primaries! After the New Hampshire results are actually a matter of public record, after Florida and Illinois and California and all the rest, they'll call it an unqualified success and a major step—"

"Bullshit." Gorman's voice crackled through the room.

Prescott whirled away from Hunter and toward the younger man. "What do you mean? How dare you—"

"Bullshit, Doctor. This project isn't going to be a success until Anthony Hapworth is sitting in the White House. And when it is a success, when Hapworth is elected, even then your *distinguished colleagues—*" the disdain was obvious in his voice "—aren't going to know a goddamned thing about it. Because you're never going to tell them. Your job's not to go down in medical history, Dr. Prescott. I thought Mr. Hunter made that perfectly clear last summer when we had to recall all of the copies of *Mind Control* that you sneaked out and had printed and handed out to your distinguished colleagues." He paused a moment to catch his breath, then continued. "No, your job's not to go down in medical history. Your job is merely to design the subliminal advertising that'll get Hapworth elected."

Prescott was silent for a moment, his eyes locked with Gorman's, a look of extreme distaste on his face. When he replied his voice was tightly controlled.

"Yes, that *is* my job isn't it? *Merely* to design the subliminal advertising. To create the subliminal materials and make them work. To manipulate the mind of the world, without letting the world know that its mind is being manipulated."

Gorman started to speak, but Prescott waved him into silence.

"That makes me the designer, the fabricator. The producer of the product. Almost like a manufacturer, if you will." He repeated the phrase, warming to the comparison. "That's right. A manufacturer. I manufacture it and you sell it, Steve. You develop the sales strategies and write the marketing plans and study the demographics. And then you use the mechandise I create to *buy and sell results.* You're just a merchant, aren't you? A merchant, buying and selling." He whirled around to confront Hunter. "And so are you, Mac. Just a merchant. Except the commodity that you're buying and selling isn't wheat or gold or steel. It's the human mind."

The old man paused dramatically, looking from Hunter to Gorman. Then, pulling himself erect, he turned his back on both of them and walked away. "That concludes my report, gentlemen."

Hunter glared after him, opening his mouth to speak, to call him back for the last word. But then he closed it again.

Prescott had walked to the small bar at the back of the office. His face was flushed, his hands trembling as he threw ice cubes into a glass and covered them with vodka. He took a sip, then a gulp. Then without warning he lifted the glass to his lips and drained it.

Hunter watched him fill the glass again and take another drink. A smile of satisfaction spread over his face. There's more than one way to win the game, he told himself.

He turned back to Gorman. "Give me your report," he commanded.

"The film has had an enormous impact." Gorman was winding up. "It's been responsible for a gain of eighteen percentage points for Hapworth in just the past two weeks."

A smirk involuntarily played across his face as he saw Mac Hunter's surprised reaction to his announcement. Shit yes, Hunter, he thought. We're winning. So get off my back. I saw you go after Roth today until the poor bastard almost threw up. And now you've driven that pathetic old man back to the bottle. But you're not going to get me, you son of a bitch, because I'm going to stay one step ahead of you.

"All of this has been accomplished without spending a penny for paid advertising," Gorman went on, using his boardroom voice, the protective coloring he had learned to adopt when he was thrashing his way through the Miramar corporate jungle. "But we've reached the point where we *will* use media advertising. And putting it all together for us, in neat little subliminal packages, will be our new advertising agency—Collins & Craig, of Atlanta. And they won't even know what they're doing."

"Collins & Craig?" Gorman looked around to see Paul Prescott standing beside him, a fresh drink in his hand. "Did I hear you say Collins & Craig? What's the status of the acquisition plan? Do we own them? Is it going to work? Where are they tonight? In Atlanta? Here, in New York?"

"The situation is going to work. I have it under control," Gorman answered tersely, trying to turn his attention back to Hunter.

"Where are they? Here in New York?" the doctor persisted.

"Yes, they're here in New York," Gorman snapped. He looked back at Hunter. "I've got them exactly where I want them. Jay Collins is tucked away in a high-class whorehouse. Logan Smith's been intercepted and they've taken him to the apartment."

"What about Rick Craig?" Prescott's voice was higher, more insistent.

"Rick Craig's not important," Gorman retorted. "He's a troublemaker anyway. I'd like to get rid of him, to make things so unpleasant that he'll sell out and get out of the agency. If we don't, he'll continually mess things up—"

"Rick Craig stays! He stays at the agency." Prescott's voice was higher, more agitated. He turned to Hunter. "Craig stays, Mac. That was part of the original deal. Craig stays. Don't let Gorman get rid of him. Not now or anytime in the future. Because if Rick Craig leaves, so do I. That's the deal we made—"

"Goddamn!" Gorman exploded. "What the hell is going on? You wanted to acquire an advertising agency. Not a New York agency. It had to be an Atlanta agency. So I could have gotten a dozen Atlanta agencies, but it had to be a *special* one. So I set out to buy an agency that doesn't even know it wants to sell. And I'm about to pull it off. But, damnit, this is too much. When we *know* that Craig's going to cause trouble, you still insist that we keep the son of a bitch as a part of the deal." He looked at Hunter. "What the hell is—"

"Shut up." Hunter's voice was deep, demanding, and he silenced Gorman's outburst with a shake of his head. Then he turned to Prescott and his manner changed. "It's all right, Paul. A deal is a deal," he said soothingly. "Rick Craig stays."

The lights were flashing in Rick Craig's mind as he tossed fitfully in his sleep, splashing his brain with splotches of color. His dream world was lighted up like a pinball machine and Rick was the steel ball, buffered and propelled from one thing to another.

White lights of the television studio and dancers and soft drink bottles. The purple light of Barry Starr. With a harsh metallic sound, he bounced into the blue light of Laura Talbott, staring at him, questioning him. The amber of The Phoenix Press. And then green, green for go, green for Jay. The ball rolled down the board, and now lights were all around him. The soft lights of Suzanne's apartment, the bright lights of Fifth Avenue, the discreet lights of the Plaza. And suddenly the red light of Miramar, of Miramar and Mac Hunter, revolving and blinking and shrieking away at his exhausted brain.

He sat up in bed, his body covered with perspiration. How long had he slept? He had stayed at Suzanne's until well after midnight. He turned on the lamp, grabbed for his watch. He hadn't slept long. Not long enough.

With a groan he rolled out of bed and walked to the bathroom for a glass of water, trying to separate the dream from the reality that faced him. Sleep was out of the question, he realized. At least for now.

A walk. Maybe a walk would do it. Long walks, late-evening walks—since the first days in New York they had served a therapeutic purpose. Maybe again tonight.

He pulled on his shorts and reached for the clothes he

had worn earlier. Grabbing his trench coat, he let himself out of the door.

It was late, very late. But even at this hour the Plaza was still awake. His steps carried him past the Palm Court and he paused a moment. A violin was playing.

But he turned away from the Palm Court and the throbbing violin and walked from the hotel with determination, as if purposeful activity would help dispel the thoughts that were beginning to flood his mind. Thoughts of New York. Bittersweet memories of his days there with Kathy.

Rick's steps propelled him across Fifth Avenue and along Fifty-ninth. Up Park Avenue, down side streets. Up and down, back and forth. Criss-crossing, backtracking. Walking. Remembering. Trying to forget.

They had been magnificently, passionately in love. And New York had been good for them that first summer. The violin in the Palm Court, carriage rides in Central Park. Ferry rides. The Empire State Building and the Statue of Liberty. Hours in the Metropolitan. And then graduate studies at Columbia that fall. Married students housing. Strolling through the falling leaves. Watching the ice skaters at Rockefeller Center. Late hours bent over a typewriter, trying to frame and mold his thoughts into a novel. And Kathy's dogged belief in his talent, so great that she was willing to leave the city and move with him to the mountains of Colorado. Those had been the good days, the happy days.

One foot mechanically placed itself in front of the other and Rick Craig continued to walk the deserted streets. Snatches of the melody played through his mind, fighting with the memories of the good times and the bad. A fragment of the lyric went through his mind and he fought to recall it. And then to answer it. Was I the only one? Was I only thinking of myself, never of Kathy?

Rick shuddered a little as other thoughts passed across his mind. Another time in New York. The successful days. The triumphant return from Aspen. He had made it big. His first novel had been published. And then *The Brilliant Dream* was on the *Times* list, acclaimed by most of the critics in town. Rick was a star. A bestselling novelist. An author. Author. AUTHOR! And Kathy. Kathy had seen it coming, had tried to ward it off. Had fought to keep him on balance, to keep their marriage on course.

But then came the National Book Award and any sense of humility deserted him. An overnight sensation. A critically acclaimed author, handsome and charming and virile. Good copy for the jaded journalists and tired talk-show hosts. A mixture of the South and the rugged Rockies. Possessor of a beautiful, charming young wife, herself an accomplished painter and photographer—but no! Rick could hear his mind reacting, his ego establishing itself. Enough about Kathy and her photography. I'm the star. This is my show.

They had made it through the awards function, but Rick couldn't put it behind him. And when New York tired of him, turned its back on him, he turned to other cities. San Francisco and St. Louis and Philadelphia. Atlanta and New Orleans and Boston. Places where they were still eager to lionize him, to heap lavish attention on him.

Kathy's good sense had no longer been able to penetrate his thinking. He began to harbor grudges, to resent her advice, to suspect her of professional jealousy. He no longer invited her to accompany him to all of the places where the literary intelligentsia were still eager to probe his mind, where the smart young socialites were eager to explore his face and body.

From city to city, from bedroom to bedroom. More alcohol and sex. Another feeding of the ego. Throughout the summer and fall and into winter. And then winter turned to spring and a new winner of the NBA was named and Rick Craig's world began to crumble.

Now, on this night, Rick was walking up Madison, his steps subconsciously directing him to where it all ended. And he remembered the final spring. The bad days. The tragic days.

It was customary for the previous year's winner to be on hand in New York when the new NBA presentations were made. But Kathy hadn't liked New York that spring, hadn't liked Rick too well, either. And she refused to accompany him. He insisted, demanded. And finally they had come. To the Plaza. And to a round of luncheons and cocktail parties from one end of town to the other. Parties that gave Rick opportunity after opportunity to further deaden his brain, already numb from alcohol. He had floated through the week in a haze of drunken glory, glory that was slipping away as he lost his place in the literary limelight. It had reached a peak the night of the presentation banquet at the Hotel Carlyle, the night he would turn over his coveted award and become a has-been.

Now Rick's steps took him to the corner of Seventy-sixth and Madison, to the Carlyle, and he stood there staring at the surroundings that had engraved themselves, in bits and pieces, onto his memory. He saw the doors of the hotel, saw them open, saw people from a late show spill into the street. He watched them gather there under the canopy anxiously looking for taxicabs. And he remembered.

That night had been a drunken nightmare, one of those fade-out, fade-in evenings where certain scenes stood out like brilliantly lighted vignettes, only to black out of sight and memory.

Rick remembered one of those vignettes—not clearly, not all of it. But he remembered. Kathy was standing under the same canopy, looking furiously down Madison for a cab. He had come through the doors, drunk and belligerent, looking for her.

"Where the hell do you think you're going?"

"I'm going home," she snapped back, her eyes burning with anger.

"You mean back to the hotel?" he slurred, stepping up to her and grabbing her arm.

"No, I mean *home.*"

"You're not going anywhere without me. Come on back and we'll have one more drink and then I'll take you back to the hotel."

She had jerked her arm away, flaring at his physical restraint, and turned her back on him.

"Come back," he remembered shouting, following her, and his movement had forced her even farther down the darkened, deserted side street. He had run to catch up, caught her by the shoulder, spun her around. And she had resisted his grasp, knocking the highball glass out of his hand and shattering it on the sidewalk.

And Rick remembered his reaction, his words. And the words she had spoken in return.

He had taken her by both shoulders, his drunken anger reaching a peak, and shook her small body with all his force. "You're not walking out on Rick Craig. You've hated me ever since I won the award last year. You've been jealous of me because *you* didn't make it big as an artist. But by God, I'm not going to let you walk out on *me.*"

She had tried to pull away, but his grip was too tight. Finally her body had gone limp. "Hate you? Jealous of you? I don't even know what you're talking about." Her voice had been calm, almost analytical. "Remember when I used to call you Rick Craig, Boy Writer? I knew you then and I loved you. But, dear God, Rick, I don't know you anymore. Who are you? What have you become? Someday you'll wake up and see the truth—that you're still just plain Rick Craig, Boy Writer. But hate you? Be jealous of you? Good Lord, no, I don't hate you. *I pity you.*"

And then he had faded out, the blackness of the side street encompassing his body and his memory.

And then—a few moments later? minutes? an hour?—another scene, other words came back to him. ". . . home . . . I want to go home . . ." The words haunted him still, along with the memory of the car. Out of the dark it had come, a small car with headlights not yet turned on, with enormous speed that could only have been generated by another drunken mind, with speed so great that it struck her body and tossed it across the darkened street.

"Kathy!" he had called out, running toward her crumpled body. "Kathy, Kathy!" he screamed.

Now he stood between parked cars in the darkness of Seventy-sixth Street, breathing heavily, his mind filled with a torrent of red flashes from the ambulance that had come to remove her body. And when another darkened car sped down the street on this January night, he involuntarily replayed the scene.

"Kathy!" he called out. "Kathy!"

The cab driver, mistaking the words for the summons of a taxi, screeched to a halt, switched on his lights, and stood waiting for the fare to approach. When nothing happened, he backed up until the tall man standing between the parked cars came into view. He rolled down the window and said, "You want a taxi or not, mister?"

The guy was a strange one, for sure. But he seemed harmless enough. He just stood there in the headlights' glare, looking confused. Then he mumbled something about a taxi, but the way he said it, it sounded more like somebody's name.

"Come on, mister, I ain't got all night. Do you want a cab or don't you?"

The man opened the door and stepped into the back seat. "Take me back to the Plaza," he said in a strained voice.

Chapter 6

The huge oak door opened silently and the young woman appeared again, this time bearing a silver tray with a polished carafe and two coffee cups centered on saucers of fine English china. She placed them at one end of a long conference table.

"If there's anything more that I can do for you while you're waiting . . ."

Her question trailed off as Jay Collins smiled and said with a deprecating gesture of his hand, "Nothing at all. We'll wait until they're ready for the presentation."

The girl motioned to the rear of the room. "The projectionist will be in the equipment room, and if you'll just push the button—" Not contented with her instructions, she walked past him to the other end of the table "—this button, here, you see—then the projectionist will handle the rest."

Collins smiled his thanks, and she left him alone with Rick Craig in the recesses of the conference room at The Phoenix Press. Smitty had already left them, to closet himself with Aaron Carlsen, and now all they could do was wait.

He poured the black coffee into a cup after flipping the saucer over to study the hallmark. The quality of the china was in keeping with everything else in the room.

Heavy English doors encircled by oak paneling. An oversized marble fireplace, and over it the portrait of a man. The founder, Collins surmised, although he had not bothered to study the bronze plate beneath it. Brass wall sconces. Crystal vases with fresh flowers.

Collins took a sip of coffee and glanced at his watch. Still ten minutes before the presentation was scheduled to begin. Ten gut-wrenching, finger-drumming minutes to kill. Ten minutes of worry about the words he had chosen to say, ten minutes to speculate about the success of his efforts.

These were the moments that Collins dreaded the most. Those final moments when, prepped and rehearsed, all he could do was wait.

He walked to the window that covered one wall and looked beyond the courtyard below to Madison Avenue. It hadn't changed much. Hadn't changed at all, so far as he could tell, from the days when he had started out here. A new high-rise here and there, but Con Ed still had the streets blocked, the people still rushed along oblivious to one another, the traffic noises still reached their periodic crescendo of sound.

Things hadn't changed, he reflected, but a lot of water had gone under the bridge since those days.

He'd always known that New York was the place for him. He'd recognized it early, in college, and had decided that the advertising business was as good as any other. And slowly he had begun to develop a master plan. He applied himself to his marketing studies, to learning the techniques of communications. And he applied himself to people, too, honing his power of persuasion, learning how to manipulate and juggle his fellow students and professors into the roles he wished them to play.

The talent had served him well in the army. He entered as an officer, and early in his brief career he loosed his power of persuasion on a senior career officer in the Pentagon. A few weeks later he got his orders for Europe—Paris, to be exact—and there he applied himself to learning the ways of the Continent.

When he returned, he came to New York, determined to take Madison Avenue by storm. He studied the scene with care, researched the top advertising agencies relentlessly. And his efforts had paid off. His charm and persuasiveness—coupled with a brief affair with an unattractive assistant personnel director—landed him a job with the agency of his choice.

His rise had been rapid, and in those early days in the agency he polished the traits of personal magnetism that had already begun to serve him so well.

He had never been a handsome man, hardly even attractive. Nevertheless he found that women were attracted to him, and he manipulated one after another into his bed. He married, of course, and for awhile—only briefly—he dropped his other romantic liaisons. Helen was a beautiful young woman, the daughter of an important client, and although he didn't love her, she answered perfectly one more of his requisites for success. They eventually moved to Connecticut, joined the country club, and started a family.

He kicked and clawed and climbed his way up the ladder, but his meteoric rise wasn't due to his charms and chicanery alone. Collins was good. He realized it, and the management committee at the agency realized it, too. He believed in the free enterprise system, and he understood the traditional function of marketing. He comprehended the picture totally and he knew and respected the role that advertising played in making the cash registers ring in the marketplaces of the world.

When a premature heart attack sidelined the manager of their Atlanta office, he knew that this was another step that must be taken. He presented his credentials to the executive committee, and despite his age stepped over at least a dozen other men and moved his young family to the city that was already becoming the cultural and business hub of the South.

His rise to prominence on Peachtree Street did not come as quickly as on Madison Avenue. In Atlanta things took more time. But the same lessons served him well, including afternoon affairs with a number of prominent young women.

Slowly but surely the groundwork was laid, the credentials were gathered to allow Jay Collins' realization of the next step in the master plan, the formation of his own advertising agency. Only two essential ingredients were missing: the control of at least one major account—an account of such significance that it could prompt several lesser advertisers to follow suit—and a creative teammate whose brilliance with the written word or moving picture could match his own expertise in the marketing field.

In the summer of 1972 the answers to both requirements appeared. Jay Collins seduced Sarah Jamison, the wife of the president of a burgeoning plastics empire, and the daughter of its chairman and founder. And shortly thereafter Jay Collins took a chance on a down-and-out young writer he had met on a filming location in Aspen and hired Rick Craig for a minor creative position in the Atlanta office.

At the time, he remembered now, he had placed far greater importance on the first event than on the second. But eight years later Sarah Jamison had moved on to other conquests and he to a myriad of other women. His liaison with Rick Craig, however, had produced sensational results. And beginning today, Collins thought, he would begin his conquest of the street that lay before his eyes. And his return to Manhattan would be with style.

He looked down at his watch again and saw that the

appointed hour had arrived. As he turned to speak to Rick, the secretary appeared again. "Mr. Roth is on his way."

Collins sprang toward the door and stood there watching five men walk slowly toward him. A tall blond man, graying at the temples. That would be Joe Roth. An older, distinguished-looking man. That would be Vince Astin, the president. Collins dismissed the next two as flunkies. Vice presidents, he had been told, marketing men for The Press and for Chartwell Books. He focused his attention on the man at the rear. Steve Gorman.

As they reached the threshold, Collins stepped forward, his hand outstretched, and for a moment the room became a sea of confusion and hand shaking and introductions. And then the amenities were out of the way, and Jay Collins stood at the head of the conference table.

"Gentlemen, we're delighted to be with you in the offices of The Phoenix Press today and to discuss with you the capabilities of Collins & Craig . . ."

More than two hours later Collins was still talking. The interim period had been filled with logical, persuasive salesmanship, with quiet and provocative discussions of the creative process, using motion pictures and sample reels of television commercials, providing a glowing appraisal of the capabilities of the agency.

Now the group was reassembled at the "21" Club around a large table in a private dining room. Roth was elaborating on the innovative marketing plan he intended to launch, and Collins countered with machine gun blasts of questions. The dialogue was one of precision: question asked, question answered; question asked, question answered.

A waiter handed Roth a message, and he excused

himself, giving Collins the opportunity to silently listen and observe. The final curtain on the performance had not fallen, but the intermission offered him welcome respite.

Collins glanced around the table. Smitty and Aaron Carlsen were engaged in their financial discussions, and Rick was engrossed with the marketing man for Chartwell.

Only Steve Gorman sat in silence—a silence he had maintained since the presentation began. Collins tried to catch Gorman's eye, to establish the rapport he had felt the evening before. But Gorman seemed intent on Logan Smith. He stared at the young controller, watching his animated reaction to Carlsen's questions.

At that moment a new and different waiter approached the table with a leatherbound humidor of cigars, passing from man to man for his selection. As he reached Smitty and presented the box to him, he leaned forward and said something directly into the young man's ear.

Collins would not have wasted further time watching the exchange had it not been for his associate's startled reaction. In the process of raising a coffee cup to his lips, Smitty shot his head around and met the eyes of the waiter. The instant of confrontation was so unexpected that the cup, poised in midair, was motionless for a moment as Smitty's face registered recognition and then total and complete shock. Then, as the shock from his brain spread throughout his body, the cup clattered to the table, overturning on the white linen and spilling into his lap.

Collins' eyes flashed back to the waiter, and he saw the man smile and wink almost imperceptibly at Smitty. And then he turned and left the room.

Another waiter—one that Collins recognized from earlier—came through the door and set about cleaning the place setting and providing napkins to repair the damage to Smitty's pants. But still Smitty sat in stunned silence, his face drained of color, staring mutely at the door.

Finally heeding the waiter's assurances, he focused his attention on the people about him and managed an embarrassed smile, excusing himself to repair the damages to his clothing and composure in the privacy of the men's room.

Collins watched him leave. Maybe the kid is sick, he told himself, and he pushed his chair back to see if he could help. But before he could get to his feet, he saw Joe Roth returning to the table.

"Gentlemen," he said to the group, a broad smile on his face, "I just bumped into Mac Hunter as he was leaving." He paused a moment to lend sufficient emphasis to his words. "He's going to join us for a moment. To meet our guests from Atlanta."

Roth turned his head toward the door and, as if on cue, R. Maxwell Hunter III entered the room and officially entered the lives of Jay Collins and Rick Craig.

"He's quite a guy, isn't he?" Jay Collins murmured.

It was the first time since their takeoff that the silence had been broken in the elegant, pressurized cabin of the Gulfstream. He sat at the rear of the aircraft with Rick Craig and when his comment brought no response from his companion, Collins lapsed back into his own thoughts and interpretations of the day's events.

Mac Hunter had not simply entered the room, Collins remembered. Instead, he had engulfed it, possessed it. Not with his personal magnetism, his personality. It was something different. Almost like finding oneself surrounded by heavy fog. Hunter was all encompassing, all pervasive.

Perhaps it was the eyes, Collins mused. Black and penetrating, they sat below heavy dark brows that were naturally arched into inverted *V*'s, producing an almost demonic look. His mouth was set in a dark field, a perennial five o'clock shadow. Coupled with the dark bushy brows it produced a remarkable contrast to the white, almost pallid skin. Luxuriant black hair without a trace of gray added further to the black-and-white contrast of the man.

He was a big man, almost as tall as Rick. A big man with big hands. Dark and massive, covered with hair. Hands that engulfed your own hands as he gripped them.

"He's quite a guy, isn't he?" Collins repeated, louder this time, to get Rick's attention.

Rick looked at him for a moment before answering, studying him. "Yeah, quite a guy," he finally replied. "Quite a frightening guy, if you ask me."

"Frightening?" Collins shook his head in disagreement. "Strong, for sure. Tough as nails. And used to having his own way. But not frightening." He paused, then completed the thought, "At least he doesn't frighten me."

"I'll bet that Joe Roth would pay a pretty penny to be able to make that statement."

"Roth? Did he seem to be frightened of the big man?"

"Scared out of his wits."

"Maybe so. That's his problem. Steve Gorman damned sure didn't seem to be afraid of him." Collins dismissed the matter. "All I know is that Mac Hunter held out the world to us today—on a silver platter. And I'm not frightened of *that* prospect."

"Held out the world? Sure, Jay, he promised us more of the advertising if we performed for The Press—"

"Hold on." Collins stopped him. "He was much more specific. He talked about the total industrial program for the pulp mills and—"

"Let me finish. If he did hold out 'the world,' Aaron Carlsen jerked it back. We can't comply with their requirements."

Collins was silent for a moment, his face immobile. He felt the slight throbbing motion begin in his jaws as he began to clench his teeth together in irritation. "Of course we can comply with their requirements. They're a little stiff, stiffer than I thought they'd be. But we *can* comply with them, and by God we *will.*"

"Good God, Jay." Rick's voice was incredulous. "You're the one who has always preached fiscal common sense. Now you're saying that we ought to go out on a limb just to snag a big new account. We've done all right in the past without someone telling us how to run our business, and we'll keep on doing it."

Collins was silent again, his jaw muscles throbbing. When he finally answered, his voice was soft, matter-of-fact. "You're right, Rick. We've done pretty well in the past." He continued, the voice still soft but a hard edge coming through with each word. "But you're wrong, too. Because we're going to do even better *with* The Miramar Corporation. It would take us six or eight more years to get to this point on our own, and by God, I intend to get there. Now. If you've got cold feet, then just keep on doing your thing and let me handle the deal. But don't kid yourself, Rick. I *can* handle it." He looked to the front of the cabin. "Smitty! Get back here. And bring your notes with you." He turned back to Rick, his eyes defiant.

Logan Smith joined them, necktie pulled loose, shirtsleeves rolled up, and a yellow legal pad in his hand.

"Have you got the key points extracted from the tape yet?" Collins challenged.

"Yeah, I've been through the whole thing again." He fell into one of the swivel chairs opposite Collins. "I've made notes on it. I'm glad we put it on tape. I couldn't keep up with Aaron Carlsen, once he got rolling."

Collins signaled the steward, requesting another drink. "Let's hear it." he demanded.

"All right. It boils down to this. We can have The Phoenix Press and maybe a lot more business from Miramar if we're willing—" he stopped, correcting himself "—if we're *able* to meet three requirements.

"First, open a New York office." Smitty consulted his notes. "Old Aaron speaks like a textbook. Here's what he said. 'The day-to-day relationship would be enhanced with a suite of offices that would lend prestige and provide enough working space for a service and media team.' "

"OK, Smitty," Collins cut in. "We can handle it. Agencies come and go like trains out of Grand Central Station. We can find the space. And I'll manage the New York office."

"What about your accounts in Atlanta?" Rick asked.

"I'll handle both of them," Collins shot back at him. Then his voice softened. "I thought it was nice of Steve Gorman to suggest a reception for some of the other New York agency heads and media bigwigs. That would help get us off on the right foot, let them know that Collins & Craig is coming to town in style." He considered the idea silently for a moment, then turned back to Smitty. "Go ahead."

"Next, expanded personnel. That one won't be as easy as the first. The Carlsen report is academic, but there's no doubt that he knows the business. He said, 'The overnight acquisition of a major account means the overnight acquisition of a sufficient staff to handle the business.' " Smitty looked up from his notes. "Even though The Press is pretty hardnosed in their demands for staff, they've taken a lot of the guesswork out of it for us. The Carlsen report is almost a personnel acquisition manual, and a damned good guideline on the cost of New York talent—"

Collins cut him off. "We don't need the Carlsen report to tell us what to do. New York's full of headhunters." He looked at Rick. "Hell, you had dinner with one of them last night."

"Sure, Jay," Rick answered. "New York is full of qualified people, and they're the biggest job-hoppers in the world. But how are we going to pay for them?"

"That's what worries me," Smitty added. "They don't come cheap." He looked seriously at Collins. "Jay, what they demand is impossible. They want us to increase our payroll costs by fifty percent, maybe more. And we don't have the money in the bank to pay that kind of money now. And the income won't start coming in from The Press for three or four months. Maybe longer. Put that together with all of the other costs—the New York office, start-up costs, additional travel, entertainment, everything—I don't see how we can handle the deal."

Collins rattled the ice cubes in his highball glass impatiently and motioned to the steward. "We can handle it," he retorted, sitting up and reaching out. "Let me see the goddamned list."

His eyes scanned the page. It read like the personnel roster of a good-sized advertising agency. Account supervisor . . . two account executives . . . director of creative services group . . . graphic specialist . . . broadcast specialists . . . The list went through the ranks: media buyers, artists, copy writers, media assistants, executive secretaries, production supervisors, accounting clerks, typists . . . the list was endless, and the figure at the bottom of the page was staggering: almost six hundred thousand for salaries alone.

Smitty was right, he told himself, keeping his eyes glued to the yellow paper in his hand. It would *not* be cheap. And the lagtime before The Press started producing income would be almost impossible to deal with. He felt a wrenching in his stomach but his face remained impassive.

Smitty was talking again. ". . . Carlsen is operating

under the same fiscal theory that we've always operated under. Once the money starts flowing, there wouldn't be a problem. He figures that we ought to be able to retain thirteen percent of the billing as gross income. I figure we can do better than that. But even at thirteen percent, we'd realize one million three hundred thousand dollars in the first full year. You can buy a lot of artists and account executives with that kind of dough. And if you use industry averages of payroll to gross income, you could *afford* to spend a helluva lot more on payroll than the figures on that sheet show. And there'd still be plenty of money left over to pay for a New York office and all of those other things I mentioned. Plus a nice bonus for the owners." Smitty smiled at the thought, but his face clouded over again. "But it's the lagtime that could kill us. And that brings us to the third requirement.

"This is the real blockbuster. The undercapitalization of Collins & Craig."

Smitty leaned back and eyed the two men before him. He drew in a long breath and expelled it.

"Gentlemen, I'm afraid they have us by the balls. We are, in fact, undercapitalized and we have been ever since Collins & Craig went into business. And they've put their finger on our weakest spot. Our financial condition is weak. We've kept our retained earnings at a minimum—we've spent the money to get good people and keep them. We've gone to in-house computers, on-staff research people. We've been leaders in the industry. Hell, we haven't even taken the money out ourselves. We've kept it in the agency. And we're too young to have accumulated much in the way of net worth and working capital. And that's what we need. That's what they demand that we obtain. And—" he summed up his remarks "—for that very reason, that may be the reason that we're not able to handle The Phoenix Press. We can't swing the money."

Collins had been staring out the darkened window of

the aircraft, but this negative note drew his attention back into the cabin and his eyes focused on Smitty.

"What did you say?" he asked.

"I said that we may not be able to meet their demands. That we may have to throw in the towel."

"God*damn!*" His growing irritation finally exploded in anger. "Now you're singing the same sad song that he is," he said, jerking his head toward Rick. He saw Smitty seek out Rick's eyes, recognized the mutual concern that was mirrored in both men's expressions, and he became even more angry. "Don't give me anymore of that 'throw in the towel' stuff. We *can* make it and we *will* make it. Goddamnit, *I'll* make it myself if I have to."

Smitty retorted softly with his calm, analytical accountant's reasoning. "Jay, facts are facts and figures are figures—"

"Goddamnit, don't give me that old one about figures don't lie!"

"Figures *don't* lie, Jay. And the figures are there in black and white. We don't have the money to qualify for the account."

"We may not have the cash now, but we damned sure will have it."

Rick entered the conversation, realizing the growing intensity of Collins' feelings, seeing the conflict arising among the three of them. "We're talking about over five hundred thousand dollars, Jay. A half million. It would take us years to accumulate that kind of money."

"Years, hell. It only takes a few minutes to sign our name at Security Founders. We'll borrow the money."

"We've already got a loan with Security Founders, Jay. And the bank's not going to increase it by a half million dollars. Let's be realistic—"

"I am being realistic," Collins snapped. "Todd Chastain's a friend of mine. He'll do whatever I ask him."

Smitty broke in. "Chastain's been put out to pasture. He can't approve that big a loan anyway. And they have a new man in the bank. From New York. To clean up a lot of Chastain's sloppy loans. And I understand he's a mean bastard."

"I'm a mean bastard, too. And I can handle it."

"*You're not going to handle anything unless all three of us agree to it.*" It was Rick Craig's voice, and Collins snapped his head around to face his partner. He was surprised at the look on Rick's face, at the determination in his tone. "I told you the other night, Jay," Rick continued. "And I'll tell you again. I don't intend to let you flush the agency down the drain because of your professional ego."

Collins stared at Rick in silence, his jaws grinding together in an effort to control his temper. Finally he stood and started to move toward the front part of the cabin. Before he left, he addressed himself to Rick.

"I'm ready for life in the executive suite," he said in a tight, controlled voice. "I've waited a long time for it to happen, and I don't intend to let it slip away. I'm ready to be a part of Mac Hunter's world, and I'm going to make it happen."

He repeated himself, his voice an icy monotone. "*I'm going to make it happen.*"

Chapter 7

"You stupid son of a bitch." Despite his anger, Jay Collins found a certain satisfaction in venting his frustrations on the hapless account executive seated before him. "Your ineptitude—*your sheer ineptitude*—has very nearly cost us the Security Founders account."

The man opened his mouth to protest the charge being leveled at him, but Collins went on. "I was at the bank this morning to talk about additional expansion capital, but all I heard about was what a lousy job the agency is doing for the bank."

"Jay, I don't know what you're talking about—"

"Then you'd damn well better *find out* what I'm talking about. You're the account executive, aren't you? It's got to be pretty bad when it comes to the attention of the executive committee—not the marketing committee, the *executive* committee. And I was told by that smartass bastard from New York—"

"Jay, I tried to warn you about him, but you wouldn't listen."

"I was told by Mr. Samuel Barnes that the creative product was slipping, wasn't keeping up with the competition. Deposits are down. The last campaign for savings wasn't productive."

"Jay, honest to God, I wasn't aware of any of that."

"You weren't aware." The voice was heavy with sarcasm. "That's the trouble, Jenkins. You haven't been aware of the results you've produced. You haven't been on top of your account."

Jay fell silent for a moment. Those goddamned, lousy bastards, he thought. How *could* they turn me down on that loan? It's a gilt-edged guarantee. The Phoenix Press. Miramar. And they know it as well as I do. He heard Barnes' words again. "We decline to make the commitment at the present time." Decline to make the commitment? Bullshit. That's a banker's way of saying he doesn't trust you.

Jenkins hadn't spoken, hadn't dared to voice any further protests. Now he moved, diverting Collins' thought back to matters at hand.

"Ok, Jenkins. That's all for now. Get your ass out of here and get it on the ball. Find out what's wrong. I'll expect a full written report on my desk in the morning."

The man rose without further comment, grateful to be dismissed, and hurried to the door.

Collins watched his departure without any visible emotion. He was aware that he had vented his anger and frustration on an individual who was probably blameless, yet he didn't care. It helped relieve the mounting tension he felt, the feeling of impending despair that he was beginning to sense. The realization that perhaps, after all, he wasn't going to make it happen.

The past two days had been hell. On Thursday morning, back in the office after the New York presentation, he had been forced to face the facts and descend the Mount Olympus on which he had placed himself the evening before. After the anger and the rash promises he had made to Craig and Smith on the Gulfstream, he knew he had to perform and he set about preparing a methodical game plan. He had called Todd Chastain at Security Founders first thing, and since it was too wet and cold to play golf, had arranged lunch at the club. Todd always reacted better to an informal situation, and he wanted the best possible reaction.

Then he had telephoned a friend who sat on the board of the First, making a tentative thrust about a loan. A fall-back position in case Security Founders wouldn't lend him the entire half million. But he had received bad news. The First was taking a very conservative attitude toward all lending. Especially to large loans. And first priority would go to their own customers, of course. Not to an advertising agency that represented their biggest competitor.

He had toyed with the idea of calling other Atlanta banks, but he resisted the indignity of such a move. And then another thought had seized him, and he relaxed with it. If Security Founders *should* refuse, he had an alternate plan that would work. Without any embarrassment to him or to the agency.

He had left to meet Chastain with confidence, but when they met in the men's grill, he had found Todd to be curiously noncommittal. Finally he loosened up over martinis, and Jay realized that Smitty was right. Todd had lost a considerable amount of power at the bank. A matter of bad loans, Todd explained. In fact, the Board had imported a hatchet man from New York to help clean up their financial act. Samuel T. Barnes—"Slashin' Sam," Todd had called him—had been given immediate and positive control of all lending functions.

That had been yesterday. By midmorning today, "Slashin' Sam" had lived up to his name. Not only had the cold-eyed bastard turned him down, but he had threatened to call their existing loan, to demand immediate payment. And then he'd had the nerve to lecture Collins on the exigencies of the advertising agency business. Finally he had delivered his *coup de grâce* and completely turned the tables on him.

"Mr. Collins," Barnes had told him, "I'm hardly the one to tell you this. You'll hear about it from our marketing committee. But I understand there is widespread dissatisfaction within the executive committee about the agency's performance on our account."

Just like that, Collins thought. But it was a brilliant move, he had to admit. Forcing him to change his offense to a defense without giving him sufficient warning to even follow the play, much less to review the game plan.

The buzz of his intercom interrupted his reverie, and he picked up the phone. He listened a moment then spoke. "No, I don't want to talk to him. Tell him I'm in a meeting." He started to replace the instrument, then spoke again. "And Dorothy, after you get rid of him, I have a number of important phone calls to make. I don't want to be disturbed for the rest of the afternoon. If there's anything of importance let me have it now."

After she had departed, he sat looking at the messages she had placed on his desk.

A call from a client. Not important. Yet.

A call from the manager of the Atlanta office of *Advertising Age*. Wanting confirmation of acquisition of The Phoenix Press account. Premature. That could wait.

And a sealed envelope with his name on the front, written in Rick's scrawled penmanship. He had avoided Rick and Smitty all day because he wasn't ready to talk to them. But his curiosity overcame him, and he ripped open the envelope to find a brief message on Rick's memo stationery.

"Before any commitment to additional agency loans is made, it is imperative that Smitty and I see you. We cannot risk everything we have built to satisfy The Phoenix Press. We'll be available all afternoon. Let us know when you can talk."

With a grunt of disgust, Collins threw Rick's note on

his desk and reached for the phone again. "Dorothy, I want to talk to Leo Knowles of the American Bank of Commerce in Birmingham. And after I talk to him, I want to talk to the president or CEO of *every bank we handle.* All of them. And tell them it's urgent."

So be it, he thought. If one big bank won't handle the loan, we'll give a bunch of smaller ones a piece of the action. And to hell with Security Founders *and* Rick Craig.

At Dorothy's signal, he took the phone and greeted his client ebulliently. "Leo? How's the weather over there in Birmingham?"

". . . then I can expect your letter of commitment no later than Wednesday?" Collins said, snubbing a cigarette out and dropping it in the growing pile in the ashtray. He smiled and ended the conversation. "Thanks, John, for your assistance. And the next time I'm in New Orleans, I want to take you to dinner at that new place in the Quarter. I still remember the evening we spent there."

He hung up and blanced at the clock. Quitting time. And, with satisfaction, he reviewed the results of his afternoon's work. He pencilled the New Orleans commitment onto the growing total and circled the figure at the bottom of the line: $375,000. Not bad for one afternoon's work. And he still had calls working to Shreveport and Jackson.

By God, I've done it. And I've done it all alone. Without any help from the others. He walked to the bar and poured himself a drink.

This calls for a little celebration, he thought, and he sat back at his desk, allowing himself to relax for the first time since he began his telephone marathon.

Suddenly he wanted to be with someone, to share his moment of triumph. Helen crossed his mind, but he ruled her out. He crossed Rick and Smitty off the list. They were the last ones he wanted to talk to. And this wasn't the kind of thing you'd want to share with one of your bed partners.

He thought a moment longer, beginning to realize how insular his personal life had become. Where were all the friends of the years gone by?

With a sigh he drained the glass. Might as well go on home. Maybe stop off at the club again, have a drink with whoever's there. He stood, ripping the top sheet from the legal pad, smiling again at the magic total at the bottom of the page. Cramming it into his briefcase, he scooped up the phone messages and threw them in. He strode across the room and grabbed the door handle to fling open his office door.

In stunned silence he stared at the two figures sitting there.

"As I told you in my note," Rick said pointedly, "Smitty and I want to talk to you—today." He walked to Jay, taking him quietly by the arm and leading him back into his office. "To start off with, Jay," Rick said, "You only own forty-eight percent of Collins & Craig. And that's not enough to do what you're trying to do."

Helen Collins heard the car brake to a stop in the circular driveway, heard the front door of their stately Georgian home slam shut. She laid aside her book in anticipation as she heard Jay coming up the stairs. Earlier in the afternoon, he had refused to talk to her on the phone. Dorothy had told her he was trying to wrap up The Phoenix Press, and Helen hoped he had been successful. It was so important to him. And if he got it, maybe he'd get over the bad mood he always seemed to be in lately.

When he appeared in the doorway of their bedroom, she knew her anticipation had been poorly measured.

He barely spoke as he walked past her into his dressing room.

"I kept dinner warm for us," she began, but he cut her off abruptly.

"I don't want any dinner, Helen. I've got work to do."

"What's wrong, Jay? I thought you were about to wrap up The Phoenix Press?"

"Well, Rick Craig has just unwrapped it," he called out from the dressing room. "It'll probably take mc all night to think it out." He reappeared dressed in pajamas and robe. "I'm going to work in the study," he snapped. "Don't wait up for me."

Helen got to her feet and followed him down the stairs. "Jay," she called after him, "I haven't eaten either. I waited for you so we could have dinner together." At the landing she paused and put up her hand to help her keep her balance. She'd had a few highballs to help relieve the depression and it took her a moment to regain her balance.

"Jay!" she called out again, but her only answer was the slamming of the study door.

She walked on down the stairs, toward the living room. She felt the despondency come over her again, the godawful loneliness. Perhaps another drink will help, she thought. Or maybe a couple of drinks. Who in the hell cares, anyway? Certainly not Jay Collins.

Collins sat in the study of his home lost in thought, oblivious to the fire that crackled in the fireplace before him. The anger of his meeting with his partners had gradually subsided during his long drive home. But in its place was a deep resentment. Slowly he was beginning to admit to himself that he was running into a blank wall. The deal was falling apart. Because of Rick and Smitty, the opportunity of a lifetime was about to disappear.

He flipped open his attaché case to get a legal pad and

pencil. As he rummaged for the pad, his eyes were drawn to the cassette from the New York meeting. Thoughtfully he picked it up and toyed with it as he thought back to the events of the presentation. Finally he walked to his desk and inserted the cassette in a tape recorder and sat back to listen word for word to the transcription of Wednesday's meeting.

At midnight he sat upright and stared at the recorder. He reached out, stopped its forward motion, and rewound it to listen to a segment of the conversation again. He heard it a third time, heard the voice of Aaron Carlsen speaking.

". . . the undercapitalization of the agency is not a crime nor a sin. It is a result of rapid growth, a weakness that shows a far greater strength. But it must be corrected by negotiating a loan with a financial institution. The only other alternative to gain working capital is through the sale of agency stock to another party. The silent partner method."

And he heard Steve Gorman's voice break onto the tape. "I'm surprised that Hunter hasn't already propositioned you for part ownership of your agency. He usually doesn't do business with anyone unless he's got a piece of the action."

Collins played the message once again, listening to the crucial words. ". . . *the sale of agency stock to another party . . . surprised that Hunter hasn't already propositioned you for part ownership of your agency.*"

Collins' hand slowly reached out to silence the machine, and sat back in deep thought. Finally he nodded silently to himself and reached for the telephone.

"Operator," he said, "I want to place a person-to-person call to New York City. To Mr. Steve Gorman."

A clap of thunder broke through Rick Craig's sleep and roused him. He gradually became aware of the early morning rainstorm and then of the persistent ringing of his doorbell. Propping himself on an elbow, he grabbed his wristwatch. Not yet six o'clock. Who in the hell would be at his door?

He rolled out of bed, grabbed a robe, and stumbled out of the bedroom. Switching on the light, he threw open the door. There before him, crisp and meticulous in a navy suit, was Jay Collins. His face was stern and he stared at Rick for a moment before pushing past him into the apartment.

Rick turned to follow him, rubbing a hand over his unshaven face. "I hadn't expected an early morning conference, Jay."

"I hadn't expected a late afternoon conference yesterday, but I got one." Collins' brows were pulled together in a frown, his mood serious. He walked to the draped window, and with a quick motion pulled the curtains apart to reveal a broad expanse of glass. He silently pondered the raindrops falling against the window for a moment and then turned to face Rick.

"Last night I offered to sell all of the outstanding shares of agency stock to a silent partner."

The eyes of the two men locked together until Rick spoke. "I see," he said quietly. "And who did you make this offer to?"

"To Mac Hunter. In exchange for The Phoenix Press. For a couple of other Miramar accounts. For a total of fifteen million dollars in billings."

"And what does Mr. Hunter want in exchange?"

"I don't know, yet. To share in the profits, I assume. That's what he usually wants. And there'll be a lot of profits to share. But I haven't talked to Hunter yet. Only to Steve Gorman. You can ask him yourself. We're meeting him on Monday night."

Rick ignored the statement and focused back on Collins' opening declaration. "Wait just a minute. Let me get this straight. You offered Mac Hunter all of the unissued shares of the corporation? And now you're telling me that all he wants to do is share in the profits? The profits of what, Jay? Of an *advertising agency?*" His voice was incredulous. "Use your head, Jay. Compare the profits of Collins & Craig with the profits from Miramar Pictures. With his television stations and newspapers. And you're still telling me that Hunter will be interested because of a small share of small profits? Come on, Jay. If Mac Hunter is interested in Collins & Craig, it's damned sure not for profits. He's got something else on his mind."

"You're too suspicious, Rick. You've been a writer too long. After all, we're just talking about a business deal. About selling Mac Hunter some stock—"

"Are you sure, Jay? Are you sure we're not talking about selling Mac Hunter our souls?"

Collins opened his mouth to reply, and then a curious look came over his face and he locked Rick's eyes in a long, hard look. "Maybe so, Rick. Maybe so. And if that's the way it is, so be it."

Rick looked at the face before him, recognized the hungry look in the eyes of this man who had been so close to him. The same hungry look that had been in his own eyes once, the same determination to plunge headlong into destruction. He shook his head and started to speak, but Collins had picked up the subject again.

"Hunter is sending a plane for you and me and Smitty on Monday afternoon. We're going to his private island off the Carolina coast—St. Sebastian's."

"What makes you think that Smitty will be interested? Or that I'll even go with you?"

"Gorman is going to invite Smitty, and I'll make certain that he's on the plane. But I want you on it, too. I *expect* you to be on it."

"And if I'm not?"

"If you're not, then there won't be anything to talk about, because by this time Tuesday morning there won't be any Collins & Craig. I'll move to dissolve the corporation. Or else I'll take all the accounts with me and walk out. It'll be Collins & Associates. A division of The Miramar Corporation."

Rick heard the threat and accepted it. Jay could probably do it, could disband the corporation and take enough of the accounts to open his own agency. He weighed the matter a moment before he spoke.

"I'll be on the plane, Jay." His voice was hard, bitter. "But not because of your threat. I'll be on the plane to do everything possible to keep the agency from being split apart. I'll do anything in my power to keep that from happening. Anything except sell my soul."

Across town Logan Smith sat at his kitchen table, trying to decipher the morning's news from the soggy newspaper spread before him.

He took a sip of strong coffee and when the telephone rang answered it after the first ring. No sense in awakening Susan and the kids this early, he thought. He wasn't prepared for the voice that greeted him.

"Mr. Smith? This is Randy Elliott in New York. Remember me? We spent some time together last Thursday evening. And then I saw you at lunch the next day. Remember?"

Smitty's hand began to tremble slightly, and his voice was unsure as he answered the question. "Yes, I think I remember—"

The other voice cut him off, an insinuating laugh mixed with the words. "Of course you remember, Smitty. And if you don't, I have some photographs that'll refresh your mind."

The words came like a thunderbolt. Smitty's hand was shaking badly now, his mind racing incoherently past the words he was hearing.

Elliott continued. "Well, anyway, I'm working for The Miramar Corporation now. For Mr. Steve Gorman. He wanted me to give you a message. Mr. Gorman is sending a plane to Atlanta next week to pick up you and Mr. Collins and Mr. Craig. To go to an island somewhere. To talk about buying some stock from you. Something like that. Anyway, Mr. Gorman wanted me to encourage you to be there. He wanted me to say that *it would be to your advantage* to be on that plane. Do you understand the message?"

Smitty was silent, his throat too dry to answer. Finally as the silence became prolonged, he was able to choke out one word.

"Yes," he answered.

"Good," the other voice replied. "Oh, by the way, Smitty. Mr. Gorman will bring those photographs with him. He said he'd give them to you on the island."

And then the line was dead, and Logan Smith stood in the neat kitchen of his new home in Atlanta. Slowly he walked back to the kitchen table, his mind numbed, a dazed stare on his face.

Chapter 8

Rick Craig pulled the trench coat closer about him as though the khaki fabric could shield him not only from the cold mist and ocean spray but from the rocking, dipping movement of the boat as well.

The gray skies that covered Atlanta that Monday had spread across Georgia. He and Smitty and Jay Collins had flown through rough and choppy weather to Brunswick in one of the smaller Miramar planes and transferred to a waiting boat that was already pitching from the movement of the waves in the channel.

Finally, when they had cleared the channel and reached the relatively short stretch of open ocean, Rick had retreated from the cabin and from Jay Collins. His relations with Collins had been strained, almost to the breaking point. Today, as they approached a confrontation with Mac Hunter, he had even less patience with Collins than usual. And so he left Jay alone with Smitty, regaling the younger man with his dreams for the future.

Climbing to the bridge, he had instantly felt the chill. But he felt the freshness of the air, the mist in his face, and he luxuriated in its cleansing qualities. He moved a few steps forward to the helm, taking hold of the polished chrome bar to steady himself.

"Ever been out to the island before?" Rick looked to

his left and saw a gnarled hand extended for a handshake. He looked up past a voluminous yellow slicker to find a weather-beaten old face.

"No, I haven't," he answered, taking the old man's hand. It felt tough, leathery, and it was immediately disengaged from Rick's clasp and replaced on the wheel of the boat.

"My name's Jonathan Chadwick," the pilot told him. "But most folks around here just call me John." The amenities completed, John turned his attention back to the swelling sea before him, closing his mouth in silence.

Rick respected his stillness, welcomed the opportunity for the wind to fill his lungs, to help wipe away the cobwebs that had fastened themselves to his brain.

Finally he spoke, directing a question to John. "Do you work for Mr. Hunter?"

The old man nodded. It was obvious that he didn't intend to say anything more, and Rick looked back at the gray sea in front of them. He was almost startled when he heard the voice again.

"Shouldn't rightly say that I work for Mr. Hunter, though he's the man who pays my wages." He fell silent again, and Rick watched him, silently prodding him along to finish the thought. "Actually, I work for the island. Have for fifty, sixty years. Too long to remember. Ever since I was a boy. Work for the island, and whoever happens to be its owner. Used to live out here, 'til the missus got crippled up with arthritis and couldn't get around too good anymore. Mr. Hunter was good about it. He kept me on the payroll. Found us a little place in town. It was just as well. That was about the time they started fixing everything up. 'Restorin' it,' they called it. The house got all fancied up. The old quarters, too. Turned them into a fancy guest house for all of Mr. Hunter's friends. Hauled all that fancy equipment into the old stables, even added on to it. Once they got finished with it all, it was too fancy for the likes of me and Anna. And too much goin' on. Too many folks comin' and goin' all the time. We're better off in town."

"Do people still live out here?" Rick asked. "When Mr. Hunter's not here?"

"Oh, lots of people," John answered him quickly. "Live right here on the island." He looked at Rick, nodding his head in emphasis. "Why, it takes a lot of people to operate—"

Suddenly the old man broke off, a strange look coming over his face. His eyes searched Rick's and a look of concern appeared in his eyes.

"I been talking too much," he said, and he turned his face back to the open sea, his mouth clamping shut.

"Who lives here, John?" Rick asked, not pressing for an answer so much as making conversation.

The old man shook his head, and Rick repeated his question. "Oh," John finally said, "the cook, the caretaker, people like that." His eyes still focused ahead, and Rick felt him drawing away into an uneasy silence.

"There's the island." John broke the stillness with his pronouncement.

Rick followed the stubby finger beyond the starboard side of the craft and he could see for the first time the panorama of Mac Hunter's island.

Before him was a wide expanse of gray beach, stretching from the left to the right around the entire perimeter of the small body of land. On the right a tip of land extended out into the sea, and the churning winter waves dissipated themselves on the colorless sand of the beach. Behind the sand a gentle rise of barren ground was punctuated only with small clumps of gray vegetation and the spikes of reeds that rose to be silhouetted against the sky.

The barrenness of the land was broken dramatically by a forest that extended to the left as far as he could see, forming a dark backdrop for the fringe of beach that protected it from the ocean.

Seeking a narrow inlet where the waters were calmer, the boat slowed and approached a rustic boat dock. A stocky man on the dock called to John and threw a landing rope aboard. Another stood ready to help the visitors step to the dock. Shortly Craig and Collins and Smith were loaded in a strange-looking contraption hitched to two horses. An antique railway carriage, Rick heard the driver say. They used them in Savannah to haul passengers from the depot to the hotel about the time of the Civil War, and Mr. Hunter greeted all his guests that way.

They were moving now, slowly, leisurely along the road leading from the dock into the forest that surrounded them. The gray of the afternoon became even darker as the rain-filled skies were obscured behind the overhanging boughs of the huge oak trees and towering sea pines. Spanish moss hung from their limbs and vegetation grew up on both sides of the tunnel-like road that cut its way through the undergrowth of the centuries.

The stillness was overpowering, silencing even the running commentary of Jay Collins.

Finally they emerged into the open air again to climb to higher ground, traversing a road that skirted the edge of the forest and overlooked miles of gray beach.

Collins was talking again, but he stopped abruptly as his attention was diverted to the beach below. Coming into sight was a figure on horseback, approaching them at a fast gallop, gradually coming even with them.

The rider was crouched over the horse, his right hand beating the flanks of the animal to urge even more speed. He was bareheaded, the wind pulling the blond hair back over his head, and he looked straight ahead and whipped the horse into even greater speeds.

It was Steve Gorman.

His appearance drained further comment from Collins and they rode on in silence. Finally, rounding a curve in the roadway, they drew up in front of a long white building, the guest lodge.

The rustic exterior could not prepare a visitor for the elegance of the interior. Thick carpeting was underfoot. Natural paneling covered the walls, converging on a single rock wall where an enormous fireplace blazed with a fire that helped dispel the afternoon's gloom.

Collins quickly found the bar, and was soon busy fixing drinks. He had resumed his nonstop monologue, and Rick felt his control wearing thin. Dear God, he thought to himself as he walked to the fireplace, will he never stop? Will he never realize that this isn't a normal business situation where he can charm himself into getting his way?

Collins thrust a glass of Chablis into his hand, and Rick looked at it without interest. He turned to stare into the flames, hardly aware that Collins had addressed himself to the framed photographs and hunting trophies that hung at random over the stone wall. He let his mind divorce itself from Collins' words, let his thoughts return again to the past week.

One week. Seven lousy days. Just a week ago he had sat in a hotel room in California and listened as The Phoenix Press had entered his life. And now, a week later, their tightly knit partnership had disintegrated into civil warfare. The irony of his thought struck him, and he involuntarily smiled. A Civil War. A War Between the States. How appropriate that it was being fought in the citadels of the South.

". . . this plaque says that these deer were killed right here on the island." Collins' words intruded on his thoughts and Rick turned to look at him, to see him carefully scrutinizing the brass plates under the mounted forms.

I can't believe it, Rick thought. I can't believe that he could be so calloused to what he's doing . . .

"I've heard that the fishing is good, too," Collins said. "Sea trout, mullet, spot-tailed bass like that big one over there over the fireplace—"

"Christ Almighty!" Rick's exclamation, punctuated with the sound of his glass being slammed against the manteltop, broke through Collins' discourse. Both of the other men stared at him in surprise.

"Good God, Jay, we're not down here to hear about the goddamned spot-tailed bass."

"I was only talking about the hunting on the island, the fishing—"

"Jay, you haven't even begun to hear about the hunting on the island. Or *being* hunted."

Collins' eyes narrowed. "Being hunted? What in hell is that supposed to mean?"

Logan Smith watched the two men before him. He heard their words of anger, saw their eyes locked on one another, and a feeling of depression spread through his body.

He stood and left the room. As he proceeded down the corridor to his room he could hear the accusations being tossed back and forth, the voices becoming more heated in argument.

He closed the door behind him and sank down on the bed. He scanned the contents of the guest room. His clothing had been carefully hung in the closet, his toilet articles neatly laid out in the bathroom. His eyes fell on a desk in the corner, and he saw a large envelope propped on its surface. He moved to it and saw that his name was written across the front in a bold scrawl.

He ripped it open and pulled forth a piece of notepaper attached with a clip to a photograph. Slipping the notepaper away, he stared in disbelief at the photograph. Again he felt a tremble go through his body.

It can't be, his mind told him. It's not possible. That didn't happen.

The tremble was replaced with a shudder, and he put the print back in the envelope as if that simple gesture would remove it from his life. But the fear was still with him, and he stood and placed the envelope under the pillows of the bed, staring at it for a long moment as though he expected it to appear again before him.

And then he remembered the note that had been attached. He found it on the floor where it had fallen and tried to focus on its words. He read them again and again. Then he sank to a chair beside the bed, letting the notepaper flutter back to the floor to rest under the end of the bed.

Smitty reached into his shirt pocket and withdrew a cigarette, putting a match to its end. Taking a long drag, he blew smoke across the room, and as the air left his body he lay his head back against the chair and stared in silence at the ceiling.

Gorman reined the horse back as he emerged from the forest and approached the long, low-slung stone building. The symmetry of its shake-shingled roof was broken by a confusion of antennae and aerials and other electronic accouterments, and his thoughts uneasily reverted to the trio from Atlanta that he had seen on the highroad a short while earlier.

I hope they didn't see all of this, he told himself. I hope they're not aware of Paul's laboratory and the clinic. But just as quickly he dismissed the concern from his mind. What the hell difference did it make? In just a few hours they'd be a part of the family anyway.

He jumped from the horse, throwing the reins over the low-hanging branch of a tree. A couple of strides took him to the recessed doorway and he pushed his way inside to encounter Annie Parkinson standing in the foyer.

"He's waiting for you in the film room," she said without being asked. "He's been here for more than an hour."

Gorman ignored her reproof and walked down the hall, slapping the leather crop against the heavy cord of the riding pants. He strode through the swinging doors and came upon Brett Stanley, sitting lackadaisically at a desk.

"Good afternoon," Gorman greeted him.

"Good evening is more like it," Stanley replied.

"What the hell is that supposed to mean?" Gorman bristled.

"It means that you're over an hour late and that Paul Prescott is nowhere to be found. It means that I've come all the way out here from the West Coast so you can approve four television spots. It means that I've got to fly back tonight. The least you can do is help me stay on my timetable."

"Cut the crap, Stanley. I didn't ask you to come out here. Mac Hunter *told* you to bring the spots out for approval. So don't bitch to me." Gorman turned toward a glass-enclosed control room, then stopped and faced Stanley again.

"Did you bring the girl?"

Stanley stared at him for a moment in distaste. Then he nodded. "Yeah, I brought her. She's up at the Manor House. But this is the last time, Gorman."

"The last time for what?"

"The last time I pimp for you. From here on out you can get your own women."

"You'll do it whenever I ask you to do it," Gorman growled. "And don't you forget it."

"No, I *won't* do it. Not anymore. And if I have to go to Hunter, I will." At the sound of Hunter's name, Gorman blinked and swallowed, and Stanley proceeded. "And besides, I'm running out of girls. I don't know what you do to them, but one time with Steve Gorman and that's enough. More than enough. In fact, I can't even get them to talk about it."

Gorman considered for a moment and decided to let the matter rest. He shrugged. "Different strokes for different folks," he muttered, turning back toward the control room. "Are you ready to show the spots?"

Stanley moved toward the room. "I'm ready. But where's Paul? Isn't he going to approve them too?"

"Dr. Prescott is taking a sabbatical for the weekend. Which is the nice way to say that he didn't have the guts to stay on the island while his old friend Rick Craig is here."

Stanley stopped short. "Rick Craig is here? On St. Sebastian's? Jesus, Gorman, why didn't you tell me? I know Craig. And if he sees me—"

"I told you to cut the crap, Stanley. After tonight it won't make any difference. We're acquiring Collins & Craig. Officially. Out in the open. Tonight."

Stanley whistled through his teeth. "Thank God. All this cloak and dagger stuff is about to give me an ulcer."

"It's not over yet. Not until I tell you that it's safe. For the time being, at least, you'll have to stay in the closet. We're going to acquire Collins & Craig, but that doesn't mean Rick Craig is going to be playing on the team. Something tells me that he's going to be making trouble for all of us."

Stanley flicked off the overhead lights and walked to the projector. "You don't like Craig, do you, Gorman?"

"No," Gorman replied tonelessly. "I don't like Craig. As a matter of fact, I think I dislike him. Very much."

He fell into silence as the screen was filled with a sparkling disco scene, and America's hottest rock star began to sing about FRESH!

The three of them made the drive to the Manor House in considerable style. The same driver had returned for them, but this time he wore a smart black uniform and drove a Mercedes sedan.

At the front door of the house Rick allowed his companions to precede him. He paused a moment, staring at the heavy oak doors.

I wonder what they'll hit me with *this* time? he thought grimly. Then he pulled himself erect and joined the others.

They stood in a dimly lighted baronial entryhall, waiting with a servant to be ushered to another part of the house. Shortly they entered a brilliantly lighted room of mammoth proportions. For a moment Rick's eyes scanned the antique furnishing, the handsome *objets d'art*, finally coming to rest on a figure at the other end of the room. Standing with his legs spread apart and his body outlined by a roaring fire, stood Steve Gorman.

He still wore riding pants and boots, but he had added a jacket and a scarf tucked casually into his open-necked shirt. He held a riding crop and for a moment he said nothing, slapping the leather against his open palm.

Then his face broke into a smile and he approached them. "Welcome to St. Sebastian's," he said, walking to Collins and taking his hand, ignoring the others. He turned back around and the hand holding the riding crop swept expansively over the rest of the room in a single motion. "What do you think of it?" he asked, turning back to Collins. "What do you think of the Miramar Manor House? This is one of the little perks that comes with Mac Hunter," he said to Collins. "Like Apartment 6-C. Like a lot of other good things."

Gorman gestured Collins to the other end of the room, then turned to face Logan Smith and Rick Craig. "Good evening, Smitty." His voice was strange, Rick thought. A little sarcastic, but more than that. Insinuating. "And Mr. Craig." The tone was gone now, replaced with a wintry sound of formality. "I'm surprised to find you here. Despite what Jay said, I didn't think you'd come. But I'm delighted . . ."

He moved away from them, fixing drinks, serving them. He played the role of a gracious host, entertaining them with stories of the restoration of the island, his voice polished and sophisticated. But his eyes were hard and intent, and they seemed to be trained on Smitty rather than the others. He went back to refill his drink. Too quickly, Rick thought. And a short time later, he went back again.

Then he addressed them. "Gentlemen, I believe dinner is being served. If you'll just come with me—"

"Dinner?" It was Jay Collins who interrupted him. "We can't eat yet, not 'til Mr. Hunter joins us—"

"Oh, didn't I tell you?" Gorman tossed off the question as if it had no importance. "Mac can't be with us tonight. He had another pressing meeting in Manhattan."

"But . . ."

"But?" Gorman prompted Collins.

"But, I thought . . ." Collins stopped, unsure of his words. "Well, I mean, I thought that we were here to discuss a rather important business matter—"

"We are." Gorman's tone was sharp. "We certainly are. A damned important business matter." Some of the sophistication of his earlier conversation was missing, and his eyes switched from one to the other of them. "But we don't need Mac Hunter to discuss it. I'm prepared to discuss it. And I'm prepared to make you an offer. Tonight." He whirled and walked back to the bar, sloshing bourbon over the ice cubes in his glass.

"But first let's have dinner." He had switched tones again. "I'm sure you'll like what Jacques has prepared. He's Hunter's private chef, you know. Brought him here from Grenouille in New York . . ."

* * *

The dinner had ended and Gorman pushed himself away from the table, his chair sliding across the polished parquet of the floor.

"Well," he said, rising abruptly and leading them from the room. "Now that that's out of the way, we can get down to business."

They moved back into the large room again, and the three men from Atlanta took chairs around the fireplace.

Gorman's eyes went back to the bar. "But first," he said, "let me get us a little after-dinner drink." He moved in that direction but suddenly he stopped, his eyes focusing on a figure who had entered the room beyond them.

"Lisa," he called out. "I'm glad you've joined us. Come here, Lisa. Gentlemen, allow me to present Lisa Hope."

A tall, striking blonde walked past them and took Gorman's outstretched hand, looking into his eyes for a moment before she kissed him lightly on the cheek. She was dressed in white satin overalls, the suspender straps crossed over her bare back and fastened by large rhinestone buttons to a bib that strained against her chest. Her long hair was pulled back into a bun and stabbed through with rhinestone-tipped pins.

Gorman took her hand and held it high, letting his eyes scan her body from head to toe. "She's a delightful creature, isn't she, gentlemen? What some people might call a good-looking broad. And you ought to see her when she's taken off her little overalls and pulled those goddamned pins from her hair."

The smile left the young woman's face and she turned to Gorman with a frown.

"Now, now, Lisa. Don't get mad just because I'm discussing your gorgeous body." Holding her hand again, he began to swing it slowly back and forth, and as her body picked up the rhythm, the smile returned to her face. He twirled her back and forth as though he were exhibiting a choice possession, and the girl executed a graceful pirouette, the smile fixed on her face.

Dropping her hand, he stepped back and as though addressing a child, said to her, "Lisa, you may act as hostess tonight." His voice became harder. "Get us a drink. You know what I'm having. Ask the others what they want."

She turned to them, smiling, but he was speaking again. "Lisa's entire point of existence on this little trip is to please me, isn't it, Lisa? She has no thoughts, she has no feelings, she has no ambitions other than to appear in a new movie that Miramar is producing. And to get that part, she'll do anything I say. Won't you, Lisa?"

A frightened look came over her face as she stood staring at Gorman. She turned her head nervously to look at the others, but Gorman pulled her eyes back to him with his staccato laugh.

"But, remember that we're in the South. Not in New York. And now that we're down here, you must do it in the true tradition of the mistress of a Southern manor house. Like Scarlett O'Hara, Lisa. You must curtsy first."

She looked at him in bewilderment, and finally deciding that he was not serious moved toward Rick, whose eyes were widened in an incredulous gaze at the scene he was witnessing.

"Lisa," the voice snapped out, and she stopped and turned back to him. "I said to curtsy."

For the first time she spoke. Her voice was small, frightened. "Curtsy? But Steve, I—"

"*Curtsy, Lisa.* You're an actress, aren't you? Let's see you act."

Displaying a weak smile, Lisa began to form the awkward movement of a curtsy, her motions stifled by the tight satin pants. As she brought one high-heeled foot behind the other, she began to lose her balance. Struggling to right herself, she collapsed, an ungainly tangle of satin-clad legs sprawled on the carpet.

Gorman's short laugh shot out and repeated itself. He walked over to stand over her, his legs spread apart in the same pose he had affected when the men entered the room. "Get up, Lisa," he said, laughing even harder.

Rick was on his feet. He walked toward the helpless girl and with a disdainful look at Gorman offered her his hand.

With his action Gorman stopped laughing. He extended his own hand toward the girl. She looked in confusion from one man to the other.

"Take your choice, Lisa," Gorman snarled. "But before you do it, be sure you know what you're giving up."

The girl was silent a moment. Then without hesitation she took Gorman's hand and began to get to her feet. A smile was back on her face as she stood, a smile that broadened into a stagy, theatrical look. She allowed Gorman to encircle her waist with his arm.

"That's a good girl, Lisa. Now go on back upstairs and wait for me. I'll be along soon."

She pulled away willingly, anxious to leave the scene of her embarrassment.

Rick was still standing beside Gorman in front of the fireplace. He heard the short laugh break the silence and slowly he turned his head to find Gorman looking directly at him. The two men stood there staring at each other. Anger smouldered inside Rick, but he felt another emotion as well. This is it, he told himself. The confrontation. The moment of truth. The two of us, side by side.

He turned to face Jay Collins and Logan Smith. "There's no point in playing this little charade any further. Both of you know where I stand." He heard the words of Gorman in his mind, and he repeated them.

"Take your choice. But before you do it, be sure you know what you're giving up."

Why? Rick questioned himself as he kicked up a toeful of the decaying bark that covered the dark ground beside the guest lodge.

He climbed the steps to the porch that circled the building and slumped into one of the rustic wooden chairs outside his room. Why are these people determined to take control of Collins & Craig?

But another question displaced that one in his mind. A question far more pertinent.

And if they do, where does that leave me?

He lit a cigarette and sat there in the darkness. The rain had stopped, but big angry clouds still churned across the sky. Occasionally they would part, revealing a starry sky above them, and the light of the moon would briefly illuminate the landscape around the lodge.

In the darkness Rick could discern the muted lights on the landing of the steps to the beach. He could hear the incessant, dull roar of the ocean and the muffled splash as the waves rushed up on the beach. A sound that usually brought peacefulness to his mind.

But not tonight. With a sigh he flipped the cigarette into the darkness and raised his tall body from the chair. His hand found the knob to the door of his room, and he quietly let himself in.

His room was dark, but a slender sliver of light shone beneath the bathroom door that connected with Smitty's. He was surprised that the meeting was over, but glad. Glad to finally learn thc score.

He walked to the door and into the bathroom and was startled to find Smitty's adjoining door wide open, the lights in the room blazing. "Smitty?" he called tentatively, and receiving no response, ducked his head into the room calling Smitty's name again. The room was empty.

He shrugged. Maybe it was just as well. Maybe Smitty was holding his ground. Maybe he hadn't sold out yet.

Rick started to leave the room and his eye caught sight of something under the end of the bed; he stooped to pick it up. It was an involuntary action, done without curiosity, but as he started to put the small piece of paper back on the end of the bed, his eyes caught sight of a single name at the bottom of the page.

Steve Gorman.

Without compunction, he scanned the rest of the handwritten message.

Thoughtfully he placed the notepaper on the bed and returned to his own room, mulling the words in his mind, trying to interpret their significance.

"Tonight you stand to gain a great deal. Or to lose everything. Before you make your final decision, you should hear my offer. Meet me at 11:00 at the foot of the steps to the beach."

There had been a postscript on the note. Something about photographs, about a man named Randy Elliott.

He looked at his watch. It was already after 11:30. Rick pulled off his tie and jacket and grabbed a dark windbreaker from the open suitcase on the bed. Extinguishing the overhead light, he quietly let himself out of the room.

Outside he walked noiselessly toward the dim light that marked the stairway to the beach, and on through the thinning vegetation toward the sound of the surf. He stumbled over a piece of driftwood, and as the sand beneath his feet became more level, he knew he was nearing the water.

A break in the clouds filled the scene with moonlight, and Rick searched the broad expanse of beach for the sight of another figure. There was no one.

The clouds covered the moon again, and he stood there in darkness, turning his head in both directions, his eyes trying to penetrate the black of night. And then in the distance he saw a tiny dot of red, the faint glow of a cigarette. He started walking slowly in that direction, and as he saw the red glow again, he picked up his gait to a silent trot.

He jogged along, his eyes still searching, and he was rewarded with a flicker of light. A match applied to the end of a second cigarette. He was much closer now, and he slowed his pace so that the flat thuds of his feet on the sand would not be noticed.

He kept moving toward them, and finally he could discern voices. He slowed his pace even more, straining to hear the words the men were saying.

At that moment the clouds parted again for an instant, revealing the forms of two men and the grayed outline of a wooden structure beyond them. He stopped and pulled close to the ground, catching his breath. He heard footsteps, sounding hollow on a wooden platform. Then the sound of a door being opened. And finally he saw light coming through the windows of what appeared to be a boathouse.

Rick crept forward quietly. His own feet touched the wooden plank leading over the waters of the inlet that the boathouse straddled, and he continued.

He was at a window now, standing beside it, inching his head from the darkness into the bright shaft of light until he could see inside. Smitty stood with his back to Rick at the edge of the dock. Gorman was sitting at a table, his chair tilted back in a posture of nonchalance. He was speaking, but Rick could only hear a faint murmur, see his lips moving.

Smitty whirled around, anger on his face, and said something. Smitty continued talking, his hands lending agitation to his words. Rick saw Gorman reach into his coat and pull forth a large envelope and throw it on the table. The angry sound of Smitty's voice reached him and he saw the young man whirl around and stalk toward the door.

Rick flattened himself against the wall as the door swung open and Smitty walked out the door onto the platform. Gorman's voice called after him.

"Before you get so goddamned righteous, kid, you'd better take a look at what's in this envelope."

Smitty stopped in midstride just a few feet away from Rick, then slowly walked back into the room and closed the door behind him.

Again Rick moved his face back to the window. Smitty's back was to him again, but it was obvious that he had taken the envelope and was staring at its contents. Suddenly his shoulders sagged, the life gone out of them. He sank into a chair opposite Gorman, putting both elbows on the table, cupping his down-turned face.

Gorman stood, preparing to leave, and before Rick dodged back into the night, he saw the man pull another envelope from his pocket and hand it to Smitty. The door opened and Gorman came out of the boathouse, walking back in the direction of the guest lodge.

Rick waited until he was out of sight, out of hearing distance, and then he walked silently to the open door. Smitty still sat in the same position. Rick stepped inside the threshold.

"Hello, Smitty." His voice sounded unusually loud, bouncing off the walls of the empty room.

The other man jerked in shock, his shoulders stiffening, his head raising and twisting around. It took a moment for the shock of recognition to sink into his mind. Before he could speak, Rick advanced into the room.

"What's in the envelopes, Smitty?"

The words brought a further look of shock to Logan Smith's face, but they cut through the stupor of his mind and he reacted quickly, turning and scooping the contents back into the envelope.

Rick stepped up to him, grabbed his shoulder. "What's in the envelopes, Smitty?" But the other man shook himself free and stood, pushing the chair over to the floor in his haste, and thrust the envelopes inside his coat, holding them tightly, the look of fright on his face.

Silently the two men faced each other, and finally Smitty was able to speak. His voice was toneless. "What are you doing here?"

"I've been here all long," Rick answered. "I saw Gorman give you the envelopes. And now I want to know what's in them. I want to know what he's using to get to *you.*"

"It's none of your business, Rick."

"What in the hell do you mean, 'none of my business'?" He reached out and grabbed Smitty by the arm. "I want to know what's going on, Smitty."

Smitty remained immobilzed for a moment, then he pulled out of Rick's grasp.

"I hope to hell you never find out what's going on," he answered.

"Are you throwing your lot in with Gorman, Smitty? With Miramar? With the kind of life you saw up there earlier, with that pitiful Lisa? Have they found a way to buy you, too, Smitty?"

With a choked sound of emotion, Smitty answered. "I guess you're right, Rick. I guess they've found a way." He turned and almost ran from the boathouse, and Rick stood there alone.

Chapter 9

"It was over before it started," Rick Craig said moodily, staring at the Coors bottle sitting before him on the polished mahogany surface of the bar counter. "They had all the high cards, and I didn't even know the name of the game until it was too late."

He lifted the bottle from the bar in a mock toast toward the man sitting next to him and added, with a wary smile, "You'll have to admit, Dan, that the stakes were awfully high. When the dealer is willing to ante up that much, he's got to want something damned badly."

Dan Osborne nodded impassively, his eyes intent on Rick and the bottle he held in his hand, oblivious to the frenzied activity and the brilliant plumage of the *après-ski* crowd that jostled against them.

Aspen was at the height of the February ski season and though the old bar at the Red Onion was normally the refuge of the regulars against the tourists, tonight the flatlanders had invaded it in force.

A particularly noisy outburst took Osborne's attention for a moment and he glared over his shoulder. Then he returned his attention to Rick, leaning nearer to him so he could hear the quiet voice of the other man.

"And Maxwell Hunter wanted Collins & Craig," Rick continued. "God only knows why, but he wanted

Collins & Craig. Not just an advertising agency. There must have been a couple of dozen New York agencies who would have jumped at the chance.

"But he zeroed in on us. And he knew his target. He threw out The Phoenix Press as the bait—he must have thought that The Press would hook me. When that didn't work, he threw in millions of dollars worth of other Miramar business, and pure, simple *greed* hooked Jay."

He paused, taking a long draw from the beer bottle in his hand. When he spoke again, his voice was lower, with a bitter edge to it. "And he stooped to God-only-knows-what to bring poor Smitty into the deal." He paused again contemplatively and then went on in the same tone. "There's something very, very wrong about this whole deal, something evil. I can feel it. There has to be a *reason*. There has to be a reason why Maxwell Hunter wanted Collins & Craig."

For the first time the other man spoke.

"What do you intend to do about it?" he asked.

Rick swiveled his body toward the bar and cupped the bottle in both hands, slumping over the counter and staring at its surface.

"I don't know, Dan." He shook his head silently. "I don't know what I'm going to do about it. All I know is that I tried it for four or five weeks after we got back from the island, and it didn't work. It wasn't the same. I guess it won't ever be the same again. I don't know what I'd expected, but there was a barrier between all of us—Jay and me, Smitty and me."

"What did the girl think of all this?"

"Laura?" Rick shrugged his shoulders. "She's torn between the two sides. She's sympathetic toward me, but she's excited about the professional prospects. Laura's having a hard time separating her professional life from her personal life. She claims she loves me, wants to marry me. But this is a big opportunity for her, and she's excited about it."

"She wants to marry you?" Osborne raised his eyebrows as he asked the question, and Rick answered him with a silent nod. "And what about you? Do you want to marry her?"

Rick expelled a loud sigh and looked at the man next to him. He shook his head. "No. Not yet, Dan. Maybe someday. But, you know, I keep measuring every woman against—" He broke off and studied the label on the beer bottle. Finally he directed his troubled eyes back to Dan Osborne. "And I haven't found her yet. I met a woman in New York when we were up there to make the presentation. She was different. Something about her that I couldn't quite put my finger on. Maybe . . ." His voice trailed off, and he looked away from his friend, back to the bottle on the mahogany bar.

They sat in silence for a moment, and finally Rick spoke again. "I don't know what I'm going to do about it, Dan. I guess that's why I'm here. I needed someone to talk to, someone who could help me get my act back together. You did that once before when you saved my life in the fire, so here I am again."

Osborne shrugged off the remark with a laugh. "OK, Rick," he said, "but I won't hang out my Shrink Sign until the morning. Right now, it looks to me like you need to have a little fun."

Their conversation was broken as a youthful blonde in a light blue turtleneck sweather interposed herself between them, eyeing both men appraisingly and then demanding the bartender's attention.

As she leaned over the bar, her breasts fell against her sweater and it was almost as though nothing separated them from the scrutiny of the two men. They moved freely as she moved, well rounded and upturned with the firmness of youth. As she straightened back up, having accomplished her mission with a fresh bottle of beer, she smiled, first at one and then the other, and pushed her shoulders back, revealing the perfectly formed nipples that stood out against the fabric.

Both men had fallen silent, watching the brief tableau appreciatively. As she moved away, Dan reached for her arm and pulled her back toward him. He kissed her lightly on the cheek and then moved his lips toward her ear, speaking quietly with her for a moment.

She drew away and eyed him, a slight smile on her face. Shrugging her shoulders nonchalantly, she again left the bar.

Rick laughed and looked at Dan. With a broad grin still on his face, he said, "I see that Aspen hasn't changed a lot."

"Oh, the city's changed," Osborne answered, "but the people haven't. They come and go every time the season changes, but they're still the same people—just with different faces." He stood, pulling a couple of bills from his pocket and throwing them on the bar. "I haven't seen this one around before, but she's just another ski bunny."

Waving to the bartender, he took Rick's arm and started toward the door. "Let's get out of here. There's a new Mexican restaurant around the corner—downstairs, where Sunny's used to be. Let's get a pitcher of Sangria and some enchiladas."

As he reached the door and pushed his way through, he said over his shoulder, "And besides, the barmaid's an old friend of yours."

Before he followed Osborne into the cold mountain air, Rick stopped and took another glance at the denim-clad throngs that jammed the small barroom. His eyes wandered to the historic bar itself, to the carved figures of a small boy and girl who sat jauntily atop the ornate backbar, presiding mutely over the proceedings as they had since the turn of the century.

It certainly hasn't changed, he thought. Not since the days when he lived in Aspen, not even since the days of the silver boom. The same yellowed photographs of Victorian prizefighters lined the walls, the same chipped tiles covered the floor.

And the same people lined the bar. The same people, just with different faces.

He stepped into the cold night air and walked with Osborne across the snow-covered mall. Rick pulled the leather jacket tighter against his body, matching his normal stride to the shorter steps of Dan Osborne's stocky, muscular frame.

For a long while they said nothing, but finally Osborne broke the silence.

"I'm glad you called." He looked at Rick briefly. "It's been a long time. A lot of water has gone under the bridge." They walked in silence again for a moment, and then he added, "Ginny will be glad to see you, too."

Ginny. Another name, another memory from a time in his life that he had tried to erase. His first instinct was to stop, to turn around, to suggest another restaurant. Then, realizing the inevitability of the situation, he accepted it.

"I'm glad I called you, too, Dan," he finally answered. "And I'm glad you were home, and not still in the Himalayas taking pictures of mountains." Ignoring the reference to Ginny, he went on. "A lot of water *has* gone under the bridge, Dan, since you were peddling pictures of wildflowers to the tourists and pulling drunken writers out of burning houses." He looked at Osborne, but the other man kept his eyes on the cobblestones beneath his feet. "It's been pretty easy to keep up with your work, you know. As a matter of fact, it's hard to pick up any book on photography without seeing the name of Daniel Osborne prominently displayed. You've come a long way, baby, as they say in my business."

Osborne ignored the compliment and turned abruptly, steering Rick into a passageway off the street and toward a stairwell that led to a snow-covered patio below. Together they clumped down the metal steps and pushed into a tiny cocktail lounge, claiming two seats at the bar.

"Bartender!" Dan Osborne called out, tossing another bill on the brightly colored tiles of the bar top. "I want a pitcher of Sangria and a kiss from the prettiest barmaid in Pitkin County!"

The woman behind the bar remained intent on the open drawer of the cash register, her back turned toward the new customers. But over her shoulder came a retort, uttered in a soft, husky voice that carried through the noise that filled the room.

"I've told you before, Osborne, we don't serve firewater to halfbreeds," she said in mock sternness. Placing the change on the plastic tray and handing it to the waitress, she turned to face them, her eyes searching among the faces that lined the bar for the familiar look of Dan Osborne.

Without noticing the face of the man who stood beside Osborne, she smiled and continued in the same bantering tone. "And besides, when did you switch over from the hard stuff to Sangria? I thought you were a Margarita drinker?"

Unexpectedly, without plan, Rick broke into the conversation.

"I'm the one who's switched off the hard stuff, Ginny," he said quietly. "Give Dan a Margarita. I'll stick to wine."

Ginny moved her gaze to this new voice that had entered the conversation, the smile still spread across her lips. As the presence of Rick Craig before her gradually soaked into her consciousness, the smile faded from her face. She stood almost immobilized, oblivious to the sound or activities around her, staring at his face, her dark eyes looking so intently at his eyes that he could almost feel them piercing into his mind.

Finally, her face still impassive, her lips formed words and in the husky voice that Rick remembered so well she said, "Hello, Rick."

Then, aware of the awkwardness of her reaction, she recovered her composure and moved toward him, leaning across the bar and extending her hand.

"It's good to see you again, Rick. It's been a long time." Turning to Osborne, she picked up the bantering tone she had used earlier. "Although I can't say much for your choice of companions." She extended her hand to him. "Welcome home, Dan'l. It's always good to have you back."

She busied herself making drinks, all the while making idle conversation. "Where was it this time, India? When did you get back?" Not waiting for an answer, she placed the glasses in front of them and continued. "Will it be two for dinner? I'll give your names to Carl. He'll be able to seat you in just a moment. . ."

And she was gone. Rick's eyes followed her from behind the bar, across the room, and he waited in anticipation for her return to the bar. But she only smiled vaguely in their direction and directed her attention to other customers.

For moments Rick was lost in thought, and Osborne respected his silence. Finally Rick pulled himself back to the present and turned to his companion. "I'm surprised to see Ginny working in a bar," he said thoughtfully.

Dan laughed as he stood, responding to a signal from the *maître d'*.

"She's not working in a bar, Rick. She *owns* the bar. The restaurant, too. Our Ginny has become quite a successful businesswoman."

The young man in the red ski sweater was intent, a frown spread across his bearded face, as he removed the final plate from the table, placed it precariously atop the others, and backed away from the secluded corner of the dining room.

"He looks more like a ski instructor than a waiter. So does the *maitre d'*," Rick Craig speculated, watching the figure disappear through the swinging doors into the recesses of the kitchen.

"He is," Dan Osborne answered brusquely, reaching out for the carafe of Sangria wine and filling their glasses to the brim. "They all are. You remember how it is, Rick. A lot of these people will do *anything* at night in order to be on the slopes during the daytime."

As he raised the dark red wine to his lips, his eyes drifted across the room and fixed themselves there in concentration. Following his gaze, Rick saw the blonde in the blue turtleneck sweater seated with another young woman at a table across the room. When Dan looked back at him, Rick smiled, nodding his understanding.

Osborne continued the conversation he had dominated since they had ordered dinner.

"I shouldn't be critical. I'm always just as anxious as the rest of 'em for the season to open. Always hate to see it close, too." He jammed a cigarette into his lips and pulled a weather-beaten Zippo lighter from his pocket, still speaking as he puffed the flame into the tobacco.

"Everyone's praying for a good snow tonight," he explained. "We need it. And one's predicted." He pulled the cigarette from his mouth and flicked an imaginary ash from its bright red tip into the ashtray.

"Then it'll be hell 'til the middle of April. You've never *seen* so damned many people, Rick. Lots more than when you lived here. At Christmas, it was so jammed in Aspen and Snowmass that you couldn't stir 'em all with a stick. Like I said, I always look forward to getting back on the skis, but you couldn't *pay* me to spend the Christmas season here. Or spring break, either."

As Dan Osborne paused a moment to take a long drag from the cigarette, Rick studied the figure sitting opposite him. Hair bleached blond by the sun that beat upon the beaches and mountaintops of the world. A face permanently tanned and weathered by a love for the outdoors, deeply etched with the creases and lines of a genuine lust for life and laughter. A blondish mustache that bristled and sagged over his upper lip, almost obscuring it from view. Still a renegade, Rick thought. A maverick who had made it to the top in the world of international photography because his talent was, fortunately, greater than his lack of diplomacy.

Osborne reached two muscular arms over his head and behind him in a luxurious stretch. His clothing was so predictable that it might have been the same that he wore ten years before: faded jeans and turtleneck, topped off with a Levi jacket worn and threadbare from a lifetime of washings.

Settling his arms back on the table and downing the last of his wine, he continued. "As a matter of fact, they're going to pay me *not* to spend my springtime in the Rockies." Noting the question on Rick's face, he went on. "I'm going to be one of the featured speakers at the Southern California Design Institute."

He snubbed his cigarette out and looked up at Rick, grinning. "You never thought they'd ever get me behind a college lectern, did you? Well, neither did I. But I'm doing more of that sort of thing these days. As a matter of fact, on *both* sides of the aisle—as guest speaker and as student, too. I've taken part in the International Design Conference—here, at the Aspen Institute—for the past three summers. Hell of an experience. Matter of fact, Rick, you should come out next summer. If it's half as good as the one last summer—"

Osborne abruptly stopped himself in midsentence with a snap of his fingers as a different thought came to his mind. He continued, jabbing his finger toward Rick to emphasize his next statement.

"By God, I almost forgot. I met your father-in-law here last summer. He was a speaker at the Conference."

The shock was evident on Rick's face. "Paul Prescott? You saw Paul Prescott last summer?"

"Yeah, at the Design Conference—"

Rick interrupted his answer with another question. "What the hell was Paul doing at a design conference? He's a neurosurgeon—"

"Not any longer," Osborne shot back. "He's into research. Has been for a number of years, apparently. He talked to us on the subject of subconscious perception—you know, what gets through to the subconscious part of the brain that the conscious part doesn't even comprehend. Damned interesting stuff. He's even written a book on it. Lots of Freudian overtones, that kind of thing."

His comments were lost on Rick, who had gone into a world of private thoughts. Taking his wineglass between thumb and forefinger, he turned it slowly back and forth, watching the glint of the candle reflect from the empty glass.

"Paul Prescott," he mused. "Paul Prescott here in Aspen." Abruptly he looked back at Osborne. "What a remarkable coincidence. And you met him?"

Osborne nodded his answer and Rick again stared moodily at the glass before him. Suddenly Osborne brought the front legs of his chair to the floor with a crack, from the precarious balance he had been making. "In case you're wondering, I didn't tell him that I knew you. Or that I knew Kathy. I didn't see any point in opening up old wounds."

He broke off his commentary as the waiter approached and placed the bill before them on a small plastic tray. Rick's hand moved toward the tray, but Osborne had already peeled more bills off and thrown them down. He jumped abruptly to his feet.

"What we need, ol' buddy, is a nightcap. Let's go across the street to the Paragon."

They walked through the nearly deserted restaurant into the lounge where Carl, the *maitre d'*, now tended bar for the few remaining patrons. Osborne's arm shot out to expose his wristwatch. Noting the time, his voice boomed out across the silent room.

"Goddamn, Carl, it's not even eleven o'clock yet. Where the hell *is* everyone?"

A smile spread across Carl's face and he jerked a thumb toward the front door. "Hell, man, they're all outside. Probably dancing in the streets. While you've been sitting back there talking, it's been snowing. A heavy snow. The slopes are going to be good tomorrow."

Osborne buttoned his frayed jacket and rubbed his hands together in simulated glee. "Let's get on over to the Paragon," he said to Rick. "By now, the prayer meeting will be in full progress. We ought to get there before they sacrifice somebody to the Snow Gods."

As he moved toward the door, Rick's eyes searched the rooms for a sight of Ginny. He approached the bar and spoke quietly with the young man named Carl.

"Is Ginny still around?" he asked.

"No, sir," the man answered. "She took off early tonight. Left just a little while after you and Dan came in."

Rick turned toward the waiting figure by the front door. Despite his earlier reluctance at the thought of meeting Ginny again, he felt a tinge of irritation at her obvious lack of interest in his return. With a slight nod of his head, he dismissed the thought from his mind and spoke to Osborne.

"Lead me to the Paragon," he said. "I've got a prayer or two, myself. Hell, Dan," he slapped his companion on the shoulder, "if this white stuff keeps falling, we might even get old Rick on the slopes!"

"I haven't seen so many people since I . . ."

The girl's words were lost amidst the throbbing sounds of the room. Indicating that he had not heard her, Rick moved his head nearer her lips as she repeated the comment.

"I said, I haven't seen so many people since I spent New Year's Eve on Bourbon Street."

Rick smiled and was about to answer when a hand reached through the people lining the bar and pulled her away to the dance floor. His eyes followed the couple as they pushed their way to the tiny wooden square where other bodies moved to the undulating rhythm of the disco music.

He caught sight of Dan's stocky frame approaching, followed by the inevitable blonde in the blue turtleneck. Osborne pushed his way to Rick's side, reaching into his pocket to produce a single key.

"Here's a key to the house," he said. "You can have the upstairs bedroom. The downstairs bedroom will be off limits tonight." He winked, and, turning back to the girl, enveloped her small waist with his arm and led her toward the front door.

Rick watched them leave, then let his eyes scan the room contemplatively as he sipped from the beer bottle in his hand. A feeling spread over him with Dan's departure, a feeling he finally isolated and defined, surprised, as loneliness. Loneliness, amidst scores of people, the same loneliness *they* felt and sought to relieve.

Without the familiar link of Dan Osborne from Aspen Past to Aspen Present, without a personal tie to the panorama of people that spread before him, he realized he was just another of the faces. Just another ski bum who was willing to do anything at night . . .

The thought filled him with discontent and he stood up abruptly, tilting the bottle and downing its contents in one gulp.

On the street, the cold air was fresh and clean and welcome in his lungs, the silence of the deserted mall a pleasant respite from the din of the discotheque. For a moment he stood quietly, gulping in great gasps of fresh air and feeling his mind become more clear with each breath.

Then he started walking. Slowly at first, enjoying the solitude of the moment and scrutinizing the changes that had occurred on the street he had once known so well. Past darkened storefronts and silent restaurants he walked, realizing that, like the people, the institutions of the city remained unchanged. Only their public faces were different.

He turned onto a darkened side street and his pace quickened. The chill of the winter air began to creep through his clothing, and he realized that he would welcome the warmth of Dan Osborne's home, despite Dan's preoccupation of the evening.

He was oblivious to the car that had crept along behind him, guided only by its parking lights. But as he stepped into the street, he saw it and paused to let it pass. He was surprised when it drew slowly abreast of him and stopped.

He could see the window being lowered, could detect the glow of a cigarette from the dark interior. And then he heard Ginny York's husky voice.

"I'll buy you a nightcap, Rick." The words flowed through the snow-filled air and swept over him, bringing a flood of warmth and desire and memory to Rick Craig.

He bent down to look into the car, and saw her features outlined softly in the pale lights from the dashboard. And then she spoke again. "For the good times, Rick."

He pulled open the door of the small car and slid into the seat beside her.

The sound of her bedroom door aroused him from his sleep, and he was vaguely conscious of a figure approaching the bed and standing beside him. A soft, cool hand touched his bare shoulder, gently shaking him, and Ginny's unmistakable chuckle brought him to full consciousness.

"I've brought you orange juice," she said, and her laugh filled the room. "Isn't it remarkable that after all these years I remembered about the orange juice?"

In the half light that seeped into the room, Rick could see her standing beside him. He raised himself on one elbow, extending his other arm to take the glass she held outstretched.

She spoke again. "You've slept away half the morning, love, and I haven't much time before I have to go to the restaurant." She stepped away from the bed and turned. "I'll bring some coffee for both of us."

When she returned, she set the tray on the table beside the bed and went to the windows, adjusting the drapes so that the soft light of morning diffused itself throughout the room.

Rick pulled himself up in the bed, taking her pillow from the other side and propping himself against it. When she returned to pour coffee for him, he reached out for her, moving over to make room for her to sit beside him.

She raised her own coffee cup toward her lips, pausing

momentarily and extending it slightly toward him.

"For the good times, Rick," she said.

"For the good times, Ginny," he echoed, and then continued. "And there *were* some good times. Some bad ones, too. You helped put me back together. Dan pulled me out of the fire, but you pulled me out of the gutter. I'll always remember that, Ginny."

She leaned forward and kissed him softly on the lips, and as she pulled away her hand remained on his chest, moving lightly, lovingly over his body.

Rick pulled her to him, his hand sliding into the opening of her robe and caressing her breasts. As their lips parted, he moved his knees up in the bed making a backrest for her to lean against, and wordlessly they stared at each other. Their hands played across each other's bodies, exploring, probing, caressing.

At first their actions were detached, almost dreamlike. But as they became more aroused, their movements were more deliberate. Rick cupped one breast in his hand. His thumb and forefinger gently massaged it, gradually becoming more forceful, seeking to arouse in her the passion he was beginning to feel in his own body.

As Ginny responded, he sat up in bed, taking her in his arms and pulling her to him. He kicked away the bedclothes and stretched his naked body to pull her closer to him. His fingers sought the belt of her robe, unfastening it, pulling it away from her shoulders and off her body.

For a moment he drew away from her, exploring her nakedness with his eyes. And then he bent over her, pulling the passion from her lips into his and engulfing her body with his own.

Afterward, he sprawled spread-eagled across the bed, one arm thrown over his eyes, dozing in his contentment. He was vaguely conscious of Ginny's presence in the room, of the sounds of her dressing and preparing herself for her workday.

He roused himself as she sat on the bed next to him again. For a moment they looked at each other, remembering the times that had gone before.

He spoke. "What would you say if I asked you to come back to Atlanta with me?"

She laughed. "I'd say you missed your chance. Seven or eight years ago I'd have done almost anything to be with you, Rick. To stay with you. But it was too soon, too soon after Kathy. You weren't ready for it. Last night and this morning, they *were* for the good times. But I don't want to see you again while you're in Aspen." She kissed him lightly and quickly. "I can't let Rick Craig back into my life. It's too painful getting him out of it again."

He took her hand, nodding his understanding, and then she stood and walked away. "Lock the door when you leave," she called out, and he heard her footsteps in another part of the house, heard a door close. Then he was alone.

Rick eyed the pale yellow house as he approached it, its muted color turned brighter by the brilliant mountain sunshine. Obviously it had been built as a monument to Victorian splendor, and it dominated its neighbors in both size and the ferocity of its rococo turnings.

Dan had done a good job in restoring it to its former elegance, he thought as he mounted the steps to the porch, kicking the snow from his shoes before he approached the elaborate front door.

Turning to enter the house, he saw for the first time a white piece of paper, hastily Scotch-taped to one of the panes of cut glass that were set into the wood. His name was scrawled across it in Dan Osborne's flamboyant handwriting. He removed the note and tried the handle, then fumbled in his pocket for the key Osborne had given him.

Inside, he saw his suitcase still sitting in the middle of the room where they had left it on his arrival the night before. Rick sank into a chair, his eyes focused on one of the dangling luggage tags that hung from the bag. ATL. Atlanta. FRESH! Collins & Craig. Mac Hunter. It all rushed back over him with a wave of depression. His problems were still with him.

Pulling his thoughts back to the present, he opened the paper he still held in his hand. The first sentence brought a smile to his face.

"When I told you to steer clear of my bedroom last night, I didn't mean you had to vacate the premises," Osborne wrote. "I hope you enjoyed yourself as much as I did! Sorry I missed you this morning, but the ski slopes wait for no man. I scrounged a parka and ski pants from a buddy. They're on your bed. Hope they fit. You can rent the rest. The keys to the Jeep are on your bed, too. Meet me at the warming house for lunch."

Skiing, Rick thought. How many years had it been since he had skied? He remembered the rush of speed, the feeling of freedom he'd always experienced, and with the memory a smile came to his face. Why not? he said to himself. Maybe the mountain air will clear some of these cobwebs from my mind.

With anticipation came enthusiasm, and he jumped to his feet and moved across the room toward the stairs, stooping to pick up his suitcase as he passed it. His eye again noted the pesky luggage tag that had reminded him earlier of the world waiting for him outside Aspen. He grasped it in his hand and with a sharp motion tore it from the handle. Then, setting the bag on the first step, he methodically balled the heavy paper into a wad and, assuming the classic free-throw position, he tossed the tiny ball across the room. It landed neatly in the center of the fireplace. Score a point for Craig, he thought, as he bounded up the stairs.

* * *

The late afternoon sun still tipped the peaks that surrounded the little resort community, but the darkening gloom of winter obscured the two men as they stomped through the snow between Jeep and house. Their footsteps were heavy on the wooden steps, their voices light and carefree on the crisp evening air.

Through the back door they went, into the drying room to deposit skis and boots, to peel out of sodden gloves and caps, and finally to emerge in the kitchen of Dan Osborne's home.

With a touch of his hand Osborne flooded the room with light, revealing a stark modernity that contrasted almost harshly with the Victorian facade of the old house.

"Fix us a drink while I start a fire," Osborne instructed, gesturing toward the open door that led into the den. "I'll have a very dry martini—use the Bombay gin. The olives are in the little refrigerator under the bar." He turned to make his exit toward an invisible stack of firewood, and called back over his shoulder. "There's a jug of burgundy, too, and plenty of cold beer."

Walking toward the bar, Rick Craig paused in midstep to survey the room that lay before him and the striking panorama it offered of Ajax Mountain. An entire wall was made of glass, plain and unadorned with curtains or draperies. Through it, the sun still struck the tip of Ajax while the lesser peaks around it had already succumbed to the approaching evening. Tiny dots of light had begun to twinkle on the mountainside. A long row of evergreens had been strategically planted just beyond the redwood deck that ran the full length of the window, screening out the undesirable and framing the bottom side of the panoramic view.

The room itself was almost as striking. Two bubbles of plastic overhead formed skylights symmetrically split by the straight lines of a black flue that ascended from the freestanding fireplace in the middle of the room.

The room was furnished tastefully—almost elegantly, yet in a way that complemented the lifestyle of its flamboyant bachelor inhabitant. And all around the room on every wall were photographs by Osborne—Photographs by Osborne, they almost called out. Large and small, brilliantly colored or starkly contrasting in tones of black and white, a collection that could grace the panels of the finest art museums.

In the middle of the photographs a cartoon drawing stood out and Rick went over to inspect it. He found the drawing of an old miner dangling precipitously over a canyon. He was suspended from a long rope, his mining gear, his saddle, his mule, all his worldly possessions dangling below him. He gripped a single, gnarled tree that protruded from the edge of the canyon. On his face was a look of desperation. And below the drawing, a simple caption: "Hang in there, ol' buddy."

Rick's silent inspection was interrupted by Osborne himself, who entered the room staggering under a huge load of wood.

"Let me help you," he said, springing toward the photographer to relieve him of a part of the load.

"Help me, hell," the photographer replied, walking past Rick toward the fireplace in the center of the room. "The only help I need is the martini I asked you to fix. If I'm going to give you room and board, you're going to have to work for it." He busied himself with the fire, occasionally muttering an oath to a log or a crumbled piece of newspaper.

When Rick turned toward him again with the prescribed martini in his hand, Osborne was stretched luxuriously against the large sectional sofa that encircled half of the fireplace. Accepting the drink with one hand, his other swept expansively around the room.

"What do you think of the digs? Not bad for a hack photographer, huh?" And without waiting for comment from Rick, proceeded. "This room and the kitchen are add-ons—to the original house, I mean. We've got a good choice of some of the best architects in the business here in Aspen, so I hired one of them and told him to do it up right. What the hell—" he interrupted himself to take a sip of the drink "—I've got plenty of money now and nobody except myself to spend it on."

He paused reflectively. "And besides, I like the house. When I get home, I don't want to leave it. I'm very comfortable here. As a matter of fact, I think we'll throw a couple of steaks on the grill and stay here tonight." He burrowed himself into the deep cushions and closed his eyes.

Then suddenly, as a new thought struck him, he jumped from the couch and walked across the room. Rick watched him rummage through the drawers of a desk and saw him emerge with a magazinelike publication. As he walked back to the couch, he tossed the booklet at Rick.

"In case you'll give consideration to coming to the Design Conference at the Institute next summer, here's last year's program. Stick it in your briefcase and take it home with you. It'll serve as a reminder. Hell, you can even have free room and board," he said with a grin, gesturing with one thumb toward the upstairs bedroom.

Osborne plopped himself back onto the couch in the same position he had held a moment before, and again closed his eyes, listening in silence to the occasional click of the ice cubes in the small glass he held in his hand.

They sat in silence that was punctuated only by the fire's staccato popping, Osborne dozing in his contentment, Rick idly thumbing through the Conference catalog. A page caught his eye, and for a long moment he stared at the photograph of the man he had once known so well, the man who had never forgiven him for the loss of his daughter. The irony of the circumstance—his encountering Paul Prescott here in this room through the friend he had sought out during another time of personal trial—the irony of the circumstance was too much for him.

With a mumbled comment he threw the magazine aside and stood, walking to the window and staring in silence at the darkening scene before him. Osborne opened his eyes and sat up, "I must have been dozing," he said. "Did you just say something?"

At first, Rick did not answer. Then he turned from the window and faced Osborne. Gesturing to the open catalog on the couch, he laughed sardonically. "It just occurred to me what a shock it would have been if I had attended the Institute *last* summer. A shock for both of us."

Osborne rose and headed back to the bar to replenish his drink. "It might have been a shock, but you would have learned something from the old boy. He's a damned smart cookie."

Speaking over his shoulder from the bar, he continued. "I think I told you he's written a book. I'll give it to you before you leave. It's all theory, of course, but it's a damned interesting subject."

Turning from the bar, he moved toward the kitchen. "I'm going to put those steaks on the grill while I can still see straight," he said, indicating the martini glass in his hand. "Be back in a minute. Help yourself to another beer."

When he returned, Rick was sitting at the desk speaking into the telephone. Raising his eyebrows in question, Osborne looked at Rick as he replaced the instrument.

"I'm going home at the end of the week, Dan," Rick said. "I've just made reservations." Walking to the fireplace, he put one foot on the rough surface of the massive, circular hearth and stared into the flames.

"I guess I realized out there on that mountain today just how important the agency is to me. It's been my whole life. It helped me get my self-respect back, gave me something to be proud of." He looked up at Osborne and stared directly into his eyes. "I'm not going to run from it, I'm not going to pull out and start my own agency. By God, I'm going back to Atlanta to find out the reason why.

"That's it, Dan—there has to be a reason why. A reason why MacHunter wants my agency, why he's gone to all this trouble to get it. There has to be a reason, and I intend to find it."

Osborne stared at him a moment, a smile on his face. Finally he winked broadly at Rick. "Hang in there, ol' buddy," he said.

Chapter 10

The small child pulled at her mother's hand, darting first to the left and then to the right as they preceded Rick Craig down the narrow passenger tunnel.

Rick tried to bypass the child on one side and then the other, but wherever he moved, the child seemed uncannily to be there. He marveled at the girl's energy. They had been delayed in Denver by a heavy snowstorm, hadn't been able to board until the early hours of the morning. Now, after hours in the air, they were finally on the ground in Atlanta, and the child's exuberance was unmatched by any other passenger on the flight.

Rick slowed his steps and fell in behind them, finally emerging in a brightly decorated passenger lounge. Pushing his way toward the luggage claim area, Rick wondered at the number of people crowding the Atlanta terminal so early in the morning. He glanced at his watch. Almost six o'clock. Time for a shower and a change of clothes before going to the office.

And then he realized. He had left his Porsche parked in the basement of the office building. Worse still, he had left the keys with his secretary—keys to his car, his apartment, even the keys to the office. With a sigh, he hitched his shoulder bag up tighter and proceeded to the nearest exit, intent only on finding a taxi and retrieving his keyring.

He didn't awaken until the taxi braked to a stop in front of the downtown high-rise office building. Hopping out, he paid the fare and added a tip, then loaded himself with the luggage and went inside. He searched the lobby for the security guard, and finally saw him rounding the corner by an elevator bank.

"Hi, Charlie," he called out. "How about letting me into the office so I can get my car keys and get out of here before the eight o'clock rush?"

"Sure, Mr. Craig. Just a minute—let me sign you in." The older man pencilled Rick's arrival into a ledger and turned to join him at the elevator. "Been out of town, huh?" he said, following Rick into the elevator and supplying a running monologue of small talk as the elevator whisked upward.

Rick listened with only half of his consciousness. His eyes were fastened on the lighted numerals above the door, and as he saw his floor approaching, he took his luggage and prepared to leave the car. As the doors whooshed open, he stared ahead of him in surprise.

There where the huge panels of glass should have welcomed him, where the gilded logo should hang, now hung a large, discolored painter's tarpaulin. And on an easel in front of it a sign.

"Collins & Craig is expanding . . ." the message told him ". . . to the 31st Floor. Please pardon the temporary inconvenience! Please turn to the left, where our receptionist will assist you."

Charlie was still speaking. "As a matter of fact, Mr. Craig, you won't even need a key. Since everything's so torn up, there's no way to lock up at night. But with the guard downstairs, you really don't need to worry about it . . ." They had come to a barricade, and a scarred steel desk and secretarial chair sat forlornly in the hall.

"Just inside there, Mr. Craig," Charlie told him, and with a smile departed. Another paint cloth covered the wall, and he pulled it aside to see a gaping hole where a wall had once been. He stepped through, his hand searching in the darkness for a light switch. He found himself in the media department. Or what had been the media department. Where the individual offices had been partitioned to provide private cubicles for the time and space buyers, there was now a vast openness. And another easel. With another message.

"You are now standing in the new Collins & Craig reception room. The girl at the desk will be happy to guide you to your destination."

Rick sank into one of the folding metal chairs that lined the bare walls of the room and pulled a cigarette out of his pocket. Lighting it and inhaling deeply, he reflected on the changes that had occurred during his absence.

They move rather quickly, he told himself. And a feeling of bitterness began to settle over him.

His thoughts were interrupted by a man's head, stuck through the dropcloth covering the new entrance. The full figure appeared, clad in blue overalls and a denim workshirt, struggling to move a sawhorse into the room.

He looked with surprise at Rick. "You're here pretty early, aren't you, buddy? You sure you got the right—"

"It's OK, buddy. I'm the owner," Rick answered, tossing his half-finished cigarette to the floor. "Or I *was* the owner," he added, grinding the cigarette out in disgust.

The carpenter continued to eye him suspiciously for a moment. Then, accepting his explanation, he went about his work. "If you're the owner, maybe you can tell me why this remodel is such a goddamned crash project? Overtime every day 'til we get it done. That's what they told me. Overtime every day 'til we get it done."

Rick picked up his bag and attaché case and started down a long, darkened hallway. "I don't know, buddy.

That's a question I can't answer." As he walked down the corridor, he completed the thought. "There are a lot of questions I can't answer."

Rick pushed open the door to his office and in the half light scanned the familiar surroundings to be sure that everything was still in place. Turning to flick the light switch, his eyes stopped on the wall behind him. The painting was missing. Someone had taken Kathy's painting from his office.

He saw two large boxes sitting behind his desk, boxes loaded with file folders and office supplies, with framed certificates and desktop pieces. *His* certificates. *His* desk supplies. And leaning against the boxes stood Kathy's painting.

Those dirty bastards, he thought, not yet focusing on who might be responsible for this invasion of his domain. His eyes fell to the desktop. A different pen and pencil set, different appointment pad with someone else's handwriting.

Someone else, Rick thought. But I wonder who? I wonder who the hell has moved into *my* office?

He pulled open the desk drawer, looking for a clue. Paper clips and pencils and other anonymous paraphernalia cluttered its interior. But in the second drawer, he found his answer. He saw a slim hardback book bound in a brilliant magenta. He pushed it aside to get at the leatherbound notepad that lay beneath it. A name was stamped on its cover in gold, and Rick stared at it in a mounting fury.

Steve Gorman had moved into Rick Craig's office.

Diana Malloy stepped around a sawhorse and edged past a couple of carpenters, taking care to keep the white wool skirt and sweater free from the litter of the reception area. She nodded a "Good Morning" to the girl at the reception desk, making a mental note to start associating names with the many new faces she encountered every day.

Moving down the hall to her office, she busied herself with the chore of getting ready to go to work. She heard a sound from the next office. He's here early today, she thought, but she had no reason to go into his office until she was summoned.

The new arrangement was not pleasant for Diana. She had been quite content with her role as private secretary and confidante to Anthony Hapworth, quite content to share his office by day and his bed on those nights he could sneak away from his wife.

But now she was sharing neither. Hap was traipsing all over the country, calling her from New Hampshire and California and Ohio, giving her hurried instructions and dictating memos into her tape recorder. He was convinced that he was going to be the next President. *President!* But so were they. God! With all the money they were pouring into the primaries, they had to be serious about it.

Serious? A grimace crossed her face. They were serious about it, all right. So damned serious she never saw Hap. So serious they had forced her off the campaign staff. And forced her down here with all these Georgia crackers to be a secretary to Steve Gorman.

So far, it hadn't been an easy job. From the first, he'd tried to play the old game with her. And when she'd kept away from him, he'd become more persistent. Calling her apartment at night, his remarks so suggestive they were almost obscene. God, she thought, if he wants to screw me, why doesn't he just come right out and ask? Then at least I'd have something concrete to report to Hap. So he could go to Mr. Hunter with it. She sighed. She'd have to speak with Gorman today. Tell him to cool it. And if that didn't work, she'd have to tell Hap.

She pushed a red button on the tape recorder and

heard Hap's voice, dictating a memorandum. Pulling a sheet of paper from her desk, she put it in the typewriter, ready to concentrate on the task at hand. It was some moments before she felt the presence of someone else in the room and she glanced up to the door to Gorman's office. She was startled to see a tall, dark-haired man leaning against the door jamb, a scowl on his face.

"And just who in the hell are *you?*" Rick Craig asked.

Shortly after nine o'clock, Steve Gorman traced his way down the now familiar hallway of the agency.

Thank God he hadn't had to go to the airport this morning. The meeting the evening before had been long enough, and afterward he'd stopped off to have a few drinks to relax. The taste in his mouth now reminded him that he'd relaxed a little too much.

His thoughts turned to the meeting the evening before. It had been a long one—but an important one, he reminded himself. Things were finally falling into place, people were fitting into the roles he'd assigned them.

His hand reached out and jiggled the knob on his office door. That goddamned carpenter still hadn't gotten the lock installed!

He pushed open the door and stopped in shock.

Rick Craig was sitting behind the desk, his feet propped on the edge, his hands clasped to cradle his head against the high back of the chair.

His eyes locked on Gorman's and he said in a flat monotone, "Our office hours begin at eight-thirty, Gorman."

Gorman was taken aback and he stood there a moment before entering and closing the door behind him. "I didn't expect you back today."

"Obviously," he heard the other man say. "If you'd had another day, you'd probably have sold all of my goddamned furniture, too."

"I can explain about the new office arrangement—" Gorman began.

"Maybe you'd better. Explain the new office arrangement—and a lot of other things, too."

Gorman went on, a frown forming on his face. "Jay Collins wanted to clear it with you, but he didn't know where to reach you. *No one* knew where to reach you. We thought maybe you'd taken a powder, maybe you'd pulled out on the deal. So we assumed that when you came back you'd rather be with your creative people—"

"Don't assume anything, Gorman."

"We'll discuss it further when Collins gets back from New York. In the meantime, you can sit—"

"We don't have to wait for Jay to get back to discuss anything, Gorman. This is my office, and it will *stay* my office. You can take your crap—" he gestured to the box beside the desk containing a jumbled mess of folders and legal pads, topped off with the leather notepad cover and the slender magenta volume "—and get it out of here." Rick Craig pulled his feet from the desk and stood, raising himself to his full height. "And while you're at it, take that red-headed broad next door with you."

Gorman only glanced at the box, returning his eyes quickly to Rick's.

"Actually, Gorman, I'm not nearly as interested in *where* you're officing as in *why*. I wasn't aware that *you* were part of the deal. Suppose you start off by explaining what Mac Hunter's hatchet man is doing in Atlanta."

Gorman's eyes narrowed at Rick's choice of words, and he fought to keep his anger in check. When he spoke, his tone was cold and methodical.

"I'm here because Mac Hunter *wants* me here. And I'll stay for the same reason." He paused, letting the words express his position, his eyes boring into Rick, the hostility that had been present on the island no longer veiled. "I'm here to protect the interests of The Miramar Corporation. To help you get started. To help you hire enough people to be able to handle it."

Gorman paused briefly, his eyes narrowing in contempt. "Hell, Craig, you've got to hire a minimum of thirty-five *new* employees, and you haven't even lifted a finger yet." He smirked at the other man, and continued pointedly. "On top of that, you've got to hire even more people just to replace all of the dead weight that we've gotten rid of in the last ten days."

The point eluded Rick, so intent was his attention on the man who stood before him. He walked toward Gorman and they stood there, face to face, separated only by the invisible wall of hatred between them.

"You'd like to get rid of *me,* too, wouldn't you, Gorman?" Rick challenged.

"Shit, yes." The epithet mirrored the depth of Gorman's feeling. "Shit, yes, Craig, I'd like to get rid of you. I'd like to pick you up and throw you out of that window—" he jerked his head toward the glass beyond the desk "—but Mac Hunter won't let me. He insists that you stay on board." He paused, swallowing hard. When he spoke again, his voice was softer, more measured, but his body held its rigid stance before Rick.

"And some day, I will. Some day, I'll get rid of Rick Craig." Again he paused, and they stood there facing each other. Then Gorman's tensed body relaxed and he turned away.

"But, in the meantime, I intend to keep my eyes on this business. In particular, I'm looking out for The Phoenix Press and FRESH! and—"

"FRESH!" Rick called out the name in surprise. "What the hell do you have to do with FRESH!?"

Gorman's pleasure was obvious. "Oh, didn't you

know?" he replied casually, one eyebrow raising as a smile came over his face. "Mac Hunter's been a silent partner in the bottling company for a year or two. But last week he bought the controlling interest."

Rick stared at him in stunned silence, but Gorman, satisfied with his parting shot, turned and walked toward the desk. He reached down and effortlessly hoisted the heavy box to one shoulder and walked to the door.

At the threshold he turned to face Rick. "Let's get one thing straight, Craig. I represent the man who owns a significant part of this advertising agency. A greater part than *you* do. And whatever he says—*and whatever I say*—will go." Opening the door, he moved into the hall.

"You may have won this little skirmish, Craig, but the war is just beginning."

Rick walked into the room that housed the secretarial pool, his ears besieged by the clattering of the machines and the voices of the women who manned them. His eyes sought the familiar gray head.

He spotted her in the midst of the younger women, and he moved through the island of desks toward his long-time secretary. The clatter of the typewriters subsided, machine by machine, as the other women became aware of his presence, and they looked at him with expectant faces as he approached Martha Tyler.

He stood before her a moment before she glanced up, and when she did, a broad smile of relief came over her face.

"Oh, Mr. Craig," she began, but he cut her off.

"Martha, I've come to take you back to your own office," he said, loud enough for every woman in the room to hear. Extending his arm with a flair, he led her from the room, and he was aware of the applause and unmuted cheers that accompanied their exit.

"They're pushing me too hard, Martha. I'm pretty

easy-going, but they're pushing too hard. I guess they thought I'd roll over and play dead. But I won't budge another step, and the sooner they know it, the better."

He sat protectively on the edge of her desk as she rearranged her possessions. She had listened in silence, but now she looked up, her face troubled.

"I'm awfully glad you're back, Mr. Craig," she said. "I didn't understand what was happening when they moved me downstairs. I haven't understood anything that's been happening. I've been afraid. I was just happy to still have a job. So many of the others . . ." Her voice wandered off, her eyes seeking an answer from him.

"*What* others, Martha? What are you talking about?"

"You haven't heard?" There was a look of surprise on her face, a look replaced by slow comprehension. She continued gently in the manner of someone breaking bad news.

"All of the people who have been terminated in the last week, Mr. Craig. And there have been a lot of them. Maybe ten or twelve. Maybe more. By the end of the week, we sort of lost count. When they told me to move to the secretarial pool, I was just grateful that I wasn't fired." Tears began to come to her eyes. "Oh, Mr. Craig, I'm *so* glad that you're back. *Everyone* is glad that you're back. Maybe you can tell us what's going to happen—"

Rick broke into her conversation with a question. "What reason have they been given, Martha? Why have they been fired?"

"I don't know—all sorts of reasons. They told Becky Wolf in Accounting that it was to streamline the department, and they told a couple of copywriters that they were being replaced with New York people—and there are already some New York people here. And 'lack of productivity'—that's a word they're using. And 'cutting down on the overhead.' They told—"

Another voice hurtled into the conversation, a big, booming voice.

"They told Joe Greenberg that he wasn't worth a crap as an artist!"

Rick whirled around to identify the intruder and saw a big, grizzled bear of a man standing in the open doorway.

"Joe!" he called out, still not comprehending the words the other man had spoken. He walked toward him, his hand extended, a smile on his face. "How's it coming, Joe?"

Joe Greenberg stood there in silence, arms folded over a barrel chest, not making a movement to accept Rick's outstretched hand.

"What's wrong, Joe?" Rick asked, dropping his arm again to his side.

"What's wrong? Not a goddamned thing, Rick. Except that I'm out on the street looking for a job." His face set in a look of bitterness. "*Looking for a job.* After six years of sweating it out to make Collins & Craig the best shop in the South. Then, zap! Just like that. You're out on your ass, Joe. Go find something else. Get another job to help make the payments on that fancy new house you just bought. You're not good enough for Collins & Craig any longer. You don't understand the new chain of command." He paused and looked squarely into Rick's eyes.

"I just came by to pick up my severance pay this morning," he continued. "And I thought I'd come by to see if you had the guts to tell me to my face."

Rick moved toward his own office. "Come in here, Joe. I need to talk to you."

Rick eyed the lumbering hulk of a man who now sat across his desk. He remembered the day that Joe Greenberg had first presented himself to Rick, seeking a job as an artist. Then Rick had thought he looked more like a lumberjack than an artist. A strong powerful body, broad shoulders that were uncomfortable in the confines of the jacket he wore. And hands that were more like huge hams, hands that were big enough to grip an axe or a jackhammer.

But when those hands gripped a sketching pencil, when the massive shoulders hunched over a drawing board, he had proved his talent time and time again during the years he had been with the agency. From one award-winning campaign to another, he had distinguished himself in Atlanta and the South, and had climbed to the top of the heap as Senior Art Director of the agency.

And now this same figure sat before him, still looking more like a lumberjack than an artist, the hands again clasped in his lap, the tousled black hair now salted with gray, telling him an incredible story.

It had started with a newspaper ad for FRESH!, Greenberg had told him. Laura Talbott had instructed him to use the New York engraver for the series of engravings that would appear in newspapers in New Hampshire, where the new test market campaign would appear. What's wrong with Lew Barnes with Allied, Greenberg had asked. Laura had shrugged her shoulders. Since we're using the new engraver for The Phoenix Press, we've been instructed to use them for FRESH!, also, he had been told.

And he had sent the artwork to them. But when the proof came back, it was faulty. No good. Something was funny about it, Greenberg had stated. It was cloudy, muddy. Not clear. It almost looked as if something had been superimposed over the original artwork.

And so, doing the job he had been trained to do, he had rejected the proof and demanded another. A second proof had been delivered, but not to Greenberg's attention. Instead, he had found it on Laura's desk, marked to her attention. And he had taken it and studied it. Again, an inferior job. And this time he had taken matters into his own hands, and had called Fine Arts in New York and told them off.

And then he had given the artwork to Lew Barnes in Atlanta. The result? A good, sharp, clear proof, worthy of the agency's efforts. And he had approved the job and allowed the engravings to be sent to the newspapers in time to meet the deadline. The ad had appeared as scheduled.

And then the trouble began.

First, instructions from Laura Talbott that she would make all final approvals on the FRESH! account. Greenberg had told her she wasn't qualified to approve print materials, since her specialty was broadcast.

Second, instructions from Jay Collins that in the future Laura would serve as the Creative Director on both The Press and FRESH! Rick was stunned, but he concealed his feelings from Greenberg. FRESH! had been placed under the direction of Laura, had been taken away from him.

And finally, Steve Gorman had ordered Greenberg to send *all* engravings to New York, and Greenberg had gone on to tell Gorman that he was not qualified to make such a decision.

The result had been his immediate termination.

Now he sat looking at Rick, his eyes awaiting an explanation.

"Rick," he said, "I was only trying to do my job, only trying to do what I knew you'd have expected."

"I know, Joe," Rick answered with a sigh. "I know." Then he stood. "I didn't know anything about it. I don't know what's been going on around here. But I'll find out. And I can guarantee you that."

He reached across the desk and took the other man's hand, and after Greenberg had left his office, he sat staring from his window at the Atlanta skyline.

Finally he whirled in his chair and picked up the telephone on his desk, his finger angrily jabbing out a number on the intercom.

"Smitty?" he asked, when he heard the other voice

answer. Brushing over the words his associate offered, he made a concise demand. "I want a list of every person who has been terminated in the last two weeks. And I want the reason for the termination. And I want it *now,*" he said, slamming the receiver against the cradle.

Then his hand reached out again, punching out Jay Collins' number.

After a number of rings, he heard Dorothy's voice come on the line.

"Let me talk with Jay, Dorothy," he said, and listened to her reply. "No, I hadn't heard about the new Manhattan offices, and I'm not interested in hearing about them. When do you expect him?" He paused again, then with a sigh answered her. "All right, Dorothy. Tell him I want to see him—first thing this afternoon."

This time he dialed Laura's number. Another voice answered, and he learned that Laura would be out of the office for the day, filming on location. She couldn't be reached. "If she calls in," he instructed the voice, "tell her I want to see her before the day is out."

His hand was still on the phone when his door burst open and the carpenter he had spoken with earlier stood before him.

"This Mr. Gorman's office?" he asked bluntly.

"No, by God, this is Rick Craig's office. And it's going to stay that way."

The meaning was lost on the laborer, who scrutinized a work order he held in his hand. "Yeah, that's right," he countered, "that's what the nameplate on the door says. But I have this work order that says I'm to remove the nameplate and put a new one on." He held up a nameplate for inspection, and Rick read it from across the room in stunned silence. "Steven A. Gorman, Executive Vice President."

Executive Vice Presicent. *Executive Vice President.* Steve Gorman? Good God, Rick thought, this is complete insanity. He continued to stare at the words in disbelief, and finally he heard the carpenter speaking again.

"I'm also supposed to install deadbolt locks on this door and the one next to it," the man said, nodding his head toward Martha's office.

Rick sat mutely, still contemplating the matter, and finally the other man turned to the nameplate with a screwdriver.

"Hold it, buddy." Rick's mind was functioning again. "Forget about the nameplate. But go ahead with the locks. That might be a good idea after all."

He rose to cross the room, continuing his instructions as he approached the carpenter. "As a matter of fact, I'll take *that* one . . ." He reached out to take Gorman's name from the man's hand, but the carpenter resisted.

"Hold on, buddy," he said. "Who says you've got the authority—"

"He's got the authority!"

Rick looked quickly toward the open door to see Logan Smith standing there.

The carpenter eyed him, then relinquished his hold on the nameplate. "Whatever you say, Mr. Smith," he said with a shrug, then shuffled down the hall, mumbling to himself under his breath.

Smitty stood there, his eyes reading the words on the plate in Rick's hands, and a sardonic smile came over his face.

"Score a point for the home team," he murmured and, taking the nameplate from Rick's hands, he walked across the room and dropped it in the wastebasket under Rick's desk. When he returned, he was solemn, the smile gone from his face.

"Here are the figures and names you wanted," he said, extending a sheet with typed information on it.

"Smitty, what the hell has been going on here while I've been gone?" Rick asked.

"You can see for yourself. We've been cleaning house."

"Who has been cleaning house?" Rick shot back.

"We've been cleaning house. Mr. Collins, the chairman, and Mr. Smith, the treasurer, *and Mr. Gorman,* the new Executive Vice President. Don't forget Mr. Gorman. At the orders of Mr. Hunter, the new owner.

"It makes a lot of sense, doesn't it?" he asked ironically. "We need to hire thirty-five or forty *new* people, so we start out by firing our old employees." A look of bitterness came over him, and he turned to leave.

"Smitty!" Rick called him back. "What's it all about?"

Logan Smith shook his head.

"Smitty, what are they doing to Collins & Craig? What are they doing to *you?"*

The younger man stared at him without words, without expression.

Rick started again. "Smitty, I don't know what went on between you and Gorman that night on the island, I don't know what they have over you—"

Another figure appeared in the hallway, and when Smitty saw it was Steve Gorman, he jerked his arm away from Rick's grasp as if by conditioned reflex.

He looked Rick in the eye and a strange look came over his face. His eyes fluttered toward Gorman, but he looked back at Rick and said, without a trace of emotion. *"What* night on the island? I don't know what you're talking about, Rick. Now just leave me alone."

He was gone, followed down the hallway by Gorman, and Rick stood alone in the doorway to his office, the events of the morning fighting with each other in his mind. Finally, he shook his head as if to clear it and walked back into his office, searching for his jacket. Maybe he could sort it out over lunch, he told himself.

"Mr. Craig?" Martha stopped him. "You wanted to

know when Mr. Collins arrived. He's in his office now, but he says he can't see you for an hour or so. Sometime after lunch. Dorothy suggested one-thirty—"

"An hour or so?" Rick was astonished. "Since when do I have to have an appointment to see my own partner?" he shot back at her, anger and resentment welling up in him.

"I don't know, Mr. Craig . . ." Martha answered helplessly.

"Never mind, Martha." He reversed his steps and headed for Jay Collins' office. As he stalked down the hall, his mood became blacker with each step and when he burst into the outer office, he glared at Collins' secretary.

"Is Jay in there?" he asked, jerking his head toward the door.

"Yes, but he's on the phone. He said he'd see you at—"

"He'll see me now, whether he's ready or not."

Rick threw open the door and stood there. Collins was lounging back in his chair, one foot casually propped on the edge of the desk, his voice ebullient and full.

"Get off the phone," Rick commanded, slamming the door and walking to the desk. "I want to talk to you."

Collins eyed him a moment, then looked back to the receiver and continued his conversation.

Rick walked behind the desk and physically pulled the instrument from the other man's hand, slamming it back into the cradle.

"I said get off the phone. I want to talk to you, and I want to talk to you now. Since when do I have to wait an hour to see you? Since you became Mr. Big of Madison Avenue? Since you went on Mac Hunter's payroll?"

Collins had recovered from the shock of Rick's violent entry, but his ego still stung from Rick's action. He leaped to his feet, pushing the desk chair behind him and sending it rolling against the wall. His eyes were hard.

"And since when do you barge in here and grab the phone out of my hand?" He placed a hand against Rick's chest and began to push him from behind the desk. "And since when do you try to bully *me?* You may be bigger than I am, Craig, but I'm not taking that kind of crap from you or anybody else." He gave a final shove and stood his ground, glowering at Rick, his breath coming in short, quick bursts.

The two men stood facing each other, staring into each other's eyes. Finally Rick sank into a chair and shook his head in frustration.

"I'm not trying to bully anyone, Jay. All I'm trying to do is find out what's happening. I'm up to *here—*" his finger drew an imaginary line on a level with his throat "—with this intrigue. Goddamn, Jay, what the hell is going on?"

Despite his outburst, Rick's tone approached a conversational level, but Collins remained rigid, his lips clamped together. When he answered it was in a terse, uncommunicative tone.

"What's going on? Business as usual, Rick. Business as usual, except that we've been carrying on without *your* services. We've launched the test campaign for FRESH! in New Hampshire, and we're getting ready for Florida and Illinois. And we did it without your help. Laura handled the emergencies—" his eyes narrowed and he added pointedly "*—in your absence.* The next time you decide to take a secret sabbatical, maybe you'll let *someone* know. We just *might* need to reach you."

"From what I've seen this morning, it doesn't appear that you need me for much of anything. You've done a lot of things without my assistance. Or my knowledge."

Collins shrugged. "Life goes on—even without Rick

Craig. What things are you speaking of?"

"The office expansion—acquiring an entire floor of added office space. Acquiring offices in New York. Naming Steve Gorman as Executive Vice President. Moving me out of my office. Firing Joe Greenberg. Firing a dozen others for no apparent reason. Sending Martha to the secretarial pool." He paused a moment, and the bitterness was obvious in his voice. "And creating another Creative Group—putting Laura Talbott in charge of it, removing FRESH! from my control."

As Rick ticked each item off his imaginary list, he felt his anger returning. "Yes, Jay, you *have* been busy. What's the explanation?"

"The explanation?" Jay returned his question in the same dry voice. "The explanation is simple, Rick. We're growing. I realize that you don't like growth, that you fought me every step of the way, but we're growing in spite of you. And when you grow, you have to take action. You can't go running away to lick your wounds."

The personal vindictiveness failed to pierce Rick, but Collins smiled nonetheless, and continued.

"But you didn't ask for a lecture, did you? You asked for an explanation. Let's start at the beginning," and with precision, he began an emotionless recitation.

"The office expansion? Simple, Rick. We acquired a major new account, remember? And when that happens, you have to hire new people. But you've got to have some place for them to sit, right? A floor in this building was available. You weren't available for consultation, the other stockholders were. We voted to lease another floor of office space.

"The acquisition of New York offices? That was a requirement with The Phoenix Press, remember? I heard about suitable space in a satisfactory location. You weren't available for consultation, the other stockholders were. We voted to lease New York space and hired an architect to begin the remodeling.

"Steve Gorman? Our new majority stockholder wanted a representative on hand to oversee the transition. It was deemed advisable to give him a title, so his authority wouldn't be questioned by the staff. Again, you weren't available. We voted him Executive Vice President.

"Your offices. Yes, I can see how that might bother you. That was my decision. I felt you'd rather be near the creative staff rather than the executive staff. If that ruffled your feathers, I'm sorry. But I understand you took matters into your own hands and kicked Gorman out of your office. That was a mistake. But it was *your* mistake, not mine.

"And your secretary. No harm intended, no harm done. We put her in the secretarial pool until you returned to choose an office. As I understand, you've already restored her to her 'rightful' place.

"And then we come to the mass firings, as you call them. God, Rick, you make it sound like the Final Solution, or something equally evil. We cut out the duplications in jobs. We cleared out a lot of the dead weight. We got rid of a lot of unproductive talent."

For the first time, Rick broke into the conversation. "*Unproductive talent?* Goddamn, Jay, some of those people were the finest in Atlanta—"

"The finest in Atlanta won't cut it any longer, not when we're playing in the big time," Collins answered coldly. "And besides, what does it matter to you? All of them were in Laura's new Creative Group—we didn't touch *any* of the people who would work in your Group."

"Did Laura make the choices of who was to be terminated?"

Collins hesitated. "No, as a matter of fact, I did. With Steve Gorman."

"Who made the decision about Joe Greenberg?"

For the first time Jay lost some of his control. He dropped his eyes to the desk, rubbed one palm over his smooth scalp. But just as quickly he continued.

"Joe Greenberg made the unfortunate mistake of telling Steve Gorman to take the job and cram it. He told him he didn't know his ass about artwork or advertising. He suggested that he take his New York ideas and go jump in the Hudson River. And that's a mistake that you only make *once.* Gorman fired him on the spot."

"I want him back," Rick retorted. "On *my* Creative Group."

"Not a chance," Jay said.

"I want him back," Rick repeated.

"Rick, there's *no way* that Steve Gorman will let Joe Greenberg set foot back in these offices, except to pick up his termination pay."

"What the hell does Steve Gorman have to say about my art staff? Joe Greenberg is the best goddamned art director in the South, and *I want him back.*"

Jay looked at him for a moment, an unbelieving expression appearing on his face. He shook his head slowly from side to side and then exhaled a short sigh, leaning across the table and speaking softly to Rick.

"What does Steve Gorman have to say about it? Everything. *Everything,*" he repeated for emphasis. "I know you've had a rough time, Rick," he said, and for the first time a look approaching compassion was present on his face. "But it hasn't been a bed of roses here, either. It's a new ballgame, Rick, with new rules and a new umpire."

Rick started to speak, but Jay held up his hand to cut him off. "I know, I know. You're about to say that I asked for it. And I did. And I still want it. And I'm going to have it. But that doesn't mean that I always think that the end justifies the means.

"And I didn't think Joe Greenberg should be fired. For that matter, I didn't think several of our employees should be fired. But especially Joe. And, Rick, I fought for Joe and his job. I fought for reinstatement, for a second chance. I told Gorman he was the best in the South. But I lost the battle."

Seeing the look of determination in Rick's eyes, Jay shook his head again. "You'll lose the battle, too, Rick, if you decide to fight it."

Rick nodded silently, remembering Gorman's parting thrust earlier: "You may have won this little skirmish . . ."

The two men looked at each other for a moment, a ray of understanding established between them. "As a matter of fact," Collins continued, "Gorman is still madder than hell at Joe. Some idiotic claim that Joe took a FRESH! proof home with him—one of the faulty proofs. I asked Joe about it and he admitted it. He took one of the bad ones, one of the good ones. Said he wanted one of each so he could prove that he did the right thing about the engraving. But Gorman is in a fury. He wants the proof back. He's threatening legal action. Or worse."

Collins shook his head in exasperation. "You asked what's going on around here, Rick? *That's* what's going on—"

His words were cut short by the sound of his intercom, and he picked up the telephone and spoke with his secretary. He listened to her message, and then sat upright in his chair, reaching for a legal pad and pencil. "Tell Mr. Hunter that I'll be with him in just a moment," he said.

Looking at Rick, he said, "It's Mac Hunter. I'd appreciate it if you wouldn't grab the phone out of my hand on *this* call."

Rick looked at him in silence, then rose to leave the

office. As he approached the door, he heard Jay's voice call to him.

"Rick," he began, but he looked away, focusing his obvious discomfort on the telephone. "There's something you ought to know, something that has a bearing on both of us. Mac Hunter has made an offer to buy all of *my* stock in the corporation—in addition to the unissued stock he's already purchased. It's a good offer: an excellent management contract, an enormous salary, a lot of other fringes. He's even offered me a seat on the Board of Directors of The Miramar Corporation."

Jay looked away from the telephone and met Rick's eyes. "When I answer this phone call, I'm going to accept his offer."

Rick looked at him mutely for a moment, then turned again to leave. As he pulled the door closed behind him, he heard Jay's voice jovially speaking into the receiver.

"Mac? I just got back to the office a little while ago. Yes, everything is on schedule for FRESH! . . ."

He stared at the sentences on the half-completed sheet of paper in the typewriter before him and mulled the words over in his mind. *"Please consider this my formal letter of resignation from Collins & Craig . . . the shares of stock in the corporation owned by me, Richard J. Craig, may be sold at book value . . . I will continue to manage my Creative Group until such time . . ."*

Rick Craig stared at the words, mentally completing the letter in his mind. Momentous words, befitting a momentous decision. But impersonal words when they were reduced to black type on the white paper. His hands went back to the keys of the typewriter, but although his mind willed them to write, they refused to function.

He stared at the sheet a moment longer, and then in frustration he ripped it from the carriage and wadded it into a wrinkled ball, dropping it to join other wrinkled white balls of paper in the basket beneath his desk.

He sank back into his chair and stared at the ceiling, and again he remembered the grizzled old miner hanging tenaciously to a gnarled limb at the edge of a canyon. With a sigh he pushed himself away from the typewriter and stood. "Hang in there, ol' buddy," he murmured to himself.

Rick looked across the room and saw his luggage sitting beside the door. A suitcase, a shoulder bag, an attaché case, all sitting where he had dropped them this morning when he had flicked on the lights.

All I wanted, he thought grimly, was my car keys. A shower and a change of clothes. His hand rubbed the dark stubble on his cheek and he shrugged. Slipping into his jacket, he loaded himself with the luggage and walked out the door. Maybe a shower and a change of clothes isn't such a bad idea, he told himself.

As he stood waiting for the elevator to arrive, another thought came to his mind and he realized its inevitability.

One more confrontation and then it will be complete, he thought. And I might as well get it over with.

The chill of winter settled with the dusk over the apartment courtyard and Rick Craig shifted his position on the granite bench where he had been waiting. He groped in his pocket for a cigarette, touching a light to it, and pulled his jacket tighter around him.

And then he heard her coming, her heels clacking against the pebbled surface of the walkway. When the figure was almost upon him, he stood and spoke.

"Hello, Laura," he said softly.

Laura Talbott gave a little gasp and whirled to face him, backing away, trying to distinguish his features in the fading light.

"It's me, Laura. Rick."

"Rick!" Her sound was half anger, half relief. "You frightened me. You shouldn't sit out here in the dark and jump out at me—"

"Let me help you with the groceries, Laura," he interjected, taking the brown bag from her arms and turning to walk to the door of her apartment. After a few steps, he turned and saw her standing motionless behind him. "Well," he said lightly, "aren't you going to ask me in for a glass of wine?"

She was at the door now, fumbling in her handbag for the key. "Of course you can come in, Rick." There was a note of irritation in her voice as she opened the door and turned on the light. "It's just that you frightened me. And I didn't expect you . . ."

Rick walked past her to deposit the grocery bag on the counter, perching himself on a stool. Laura walked into the living room, turning on lamps and slipping her coat from her shoulders. A small exclamation escaped her as she looked around the room.

"The apartment is a mess," she said to him. "I forgot that I didn't have time this morning to clean it up. I had a—" She stopped abruptly, a frown on her face. She started again, rephrasing her remark. "I had some people in last night, and they stayed awfully late. I didn't take the time this morning . . ."

Her remark faded off as she walked into the room and began to gather glasses from the tables. Rick followed her with his eyes. She was right, he admitted to himself. The apartment *was* a mess. Glasses and coffee cups, ashtrays filled to the overflowing. Papers and books scattered on the coffee table. And the place even smelled bad, he thought distastefully. A heavy, acrid odor of stale nicotine permeated the room.

Rick threw his coat over the counter and walked in to join her. "Let me help," he told her, taking a couple of ashtrays and walking back to the kitchen. "No wonder the place smells so bad," he said lightly, turning back to her and extending one of the ashtrays for her inspection. "You ought to outlaw cigar smokers from your apartment."

Laura was beside him, taking the ashtrays from his hands. "There's really no need for you to help me clean up," she instructed him, a smile replacing the frown he had noticed earlier. "Why don't you make yourself really useful and go out to my car and get those other grocery sacks—"

When he returned, lugging two heavy bags in his arms, he was amazed at the transformation. The dishes were removed, the ashtrays back in place, cleaned of their debris. Laura was just leaving the living room, an aerosol can in her hand and a pinelike aroma cutting away the staleness.

"Now," she said. "Let me get you a glass of wine. And—" she looked at him squarely "—for God's sake, tell me where you've been! You left without telling anyone, even me, where you were going, and we've all been frantic—"

"I had to get away, Laura. It doesn't really matter where I've been. All that matters is that I'm back, ready to get with it again." He threw himself into an overstuffed chair in the living room with a sigh. "At least, that's what I thought when I went into the office this morning. Now, I'm not sure what I'm going to do."

"What do you mean?" She spoke quickly, her eyes studying him intently.

"I'm not sure that there's anything left to get with."

"Don't be silly, Rick. There's even more than when you went away. We've grown, Rick. And we're growing even bigger. And we need you. I've managed as well as I could while you've been away—"

"So I hear." His voice was dry, his eyes watching her

reaction. "From all I've been able to gather, you've managed rather well."

"So that's what's bothering you," she replied, placing a wineglass in front of him and sitting to face him. "You're upset because we've split into two Creative Groups. Because they've made me head of one of them. But, Rick, it was the only thing to do—"

"Of course it was the only thing to do, Laura. It was something I would have done myself under normal circumstances. There's too much to be done to work under the old structure. And you were ready for it—I've trained you for it. I'm not concerned with the fact that it happened, Laura. I don't like *how* it happened. And I don't like a lot of other things that have been going on. The firings. Kicking people like Joe Greenberg out in the cold, for no good reason—"

"Joe made a bad mistake. He crossed Steve Gorman."

"I made a bad mistake, too, Laura—if crossing Steve Gorman is a bad deal. I kicked the son of a bitch out of my office this morning."

"I know. I heard about it." She allowed a brief smile to cross her face. "I thought that might happen when you returned." She paused a moment, drawing into her own thoughts. The smile faded from her face, her brief moment of amusement lost in her reflections. "Gorman *is* a son of a bitch," she murmured, punctuating the statement with a nod of her head.

But then she drew herself back into the conversation. "But you didn't make a mistake, Rick. There's a big difference between Joe Greenberg and Rick Craig."

"What do you mean, Laura?"

"Joe Greenberg was an employee. A good artist, but an employee. You're an owner. A founding partner. A stockholder. Gorman can't get rid of you that easily."

"Jay Collins was an owner, too. A founding partner.

A stockholder. Until today. He sold out to Mac Hunter. Smitty sold out to Mac Hunter, on the island. *You've* sold out to Mac Hunter, in your own way. Maybe I ought to do the same and get the hell out of here."

"Oh, no, Rick. You can't do that." Her reaction surprised Rick. He had expected a defensiveness about his accusation of her loyalty, but she ignored it, focusing her attention on his threat of leaving the agency. "You mustn't do that, Rick. *You mustn't leave Collins & Craig.*"

"Why not, Laura? Why shouldn't I? It's not the same agency I've always known, never will be again. I might as well join all the rest of you."

Again she ignored the reference to her part in the matter. "No, Rick. You can't leave Collins & Craig." She stood and moved beside him, one hand beseechingly on his knee. "When you were gone, we were afraid you wouldn't come back. And now that you're here, you mustn't leave again. We need you, Rick. I need you."

"Come off it, Laura. Nobody needs me. The new regime doesn't even want me—"

"That's where you're wrong, Rick. They do want you. Even Hunter. Especially Hunter. He's not a bad man, an evil person. He wants you to stay at Collins & Craig. It's important that you stay—"

"How would *you* know how Mac Hunter feels, Laura?"

The question stopped her. Laura looked at him for a moment, then looked away. She started to speak again, but closed her mouth.

Rick repeated the question, fascinated with her reaction. "How would you know *what's* important to Mac Hunter? You don't even know him."

She remained silent, her eyes studying the glass in her hand.

Rick pursued the matter. "You don't even know Mac Hunter, Laura. *Or do you?*"

Still she was silent, and the question began to grow greater in Rick's mind. "Or do you know Mac Hunter, Laura? Has he promised you a seat on his board of directors, too, Laura? Or a place in his bed?"

"Of course not," she snapped out at him. "He hasn't promised me anything—"

"But you *do* know him. That's right, isn't it, Laura?"

"No—" she began.

"Then how can you assure me that he isn't a 'bad man, an evil person'? How would you know *what* he's like, if you don't know him?"

Laura stood and walked away, trying to compose herself, trying to answer his question. Rick stood, too, watching her movements in silence.

Finally she broke the stillness in the room. "I'm only assuming that he's not a bad person—"

"Assumptions can be dangerous, Laura. When you're dealing with Hunter." He walked to the chair where he had thrown his coat. "Perhaps you're right, Laura. I shouldn't leave Collins & Craig. Not at this particular time, anyway."

She looked at him, relief on her face. "Oh, Rick, I'm so glad to hear you say that. We need you—"

"That's not the reason that I'm staying, Laura. Not because the agency needs me. Because I need the agency. *At least until I can find out what's going on.*"

Part III

Chapter 1

"Good!" Rick Craig looked at the layouts displayed before him and scanned the television storyboard. "Even better than good." He grinned at the creative team that sat opposite him. "It's great. Right on target. Just what the client ordered. When can we have comp layouts to show?"

The young man shook his head. "I don't know, Rick," he said doubtfully. "At the earliest, next week. But probably the week after—"

"Two weeks!" It was more of an exclamation than a question. "But Jenkins needs it to show to the client on Monday. We can't take two weeks—"

"Rick, we'll try. But we're covered up. The whole creative department is covered up. Hell, we're working nights and weekends already, but we're so short-handed, what with the 'housecleaning' last month—"

"I know," Rick answered. "What about farming it out to a freelancer?"

"We've got most of the good ones already covered up."

"What about Laura's Creative Group?"

"They're covered up, too. They're doing the new campaign for The Press and they're in worse shape than we are."

Rick pondered the matter for a moment, but his thoughts were interrupted by the other person before him. "Rick, there's one possibility . . ." he began.

"What? We've got to get this ready. We've already put the client off twice. What's the possibility?"

"Joe Greenberg. This kind of thing is Joe's cup of tea. He could knock out the comps and the storyboard in a few hours."

"Great. Give it to Joe."

"You've got to be kidding, Rick. You know Gorman's orders. Not only did he fire Greenberg, he won't let us give him any freelance work until Joe returns that damned FRESH! proof."

Rick mulled the matter over a moment. "Maybe you can't give it to *Joe,* but you can give it to *me.* For the Greenberg-Craig Studio." He watched their surprise with amusement. "Hadn't you heard? Joe and I are in partnership in a freelance studio. He does the artwork, I get him the business." His face became more serious. "I figured it was the least I could do. Give me the job jacket. I'll have the comps for you by Monday."

"No kidding? Great! But does Gorman know?"

"To hell with Gorman—" Rick paused, thinking. "On second thought, maybe he ought to know. And I ought to be the one to tell him." He reached for his telephone.

The writer stopped him before he could dial the intercom. "You can't. Can't tell Gorman, I mean. He's out of town today. Diana said he was in New York for a day or two."

Rick nodded. "OK. Forget Gorman. Give me the job order. I'll be seeing Joe tonight and I'll give him the job. You'll have it by Monday."

After they were gone he sat back in his chair contemplating the matter. He had taken care of Joe Greenberg, had set him up in business. But that hadn't solved the problem. Collins & Craig faced a severe staff shortage, a shortage that had grown worse and worse since the firings of a few weeks ago.

At a time when they needed to staff up to handle The Phoenix Press, all of the new Miramar business, more and more of their existing people were leaving the agency. Quietly, without fanfare. Without ever expressing their real reasons for resigning. But Rick could sense that the word was out on the grapevine: something is wrong at Collins & Craig. An indefinable word, but a warning that spread from office to office. Something is wrong. Better get out while the getting is good.

And then it had spread to other agencies. Something is wrong at Collins & Craig, ever since they got tangled up with Miramar. And when Rick tried to recruit other artists and copywriters and photographers from other Atlanta agencies, he was met with a polite but firm refusal. The hot shop of Atlanta was still hot, but it had lost its glamour. A few months earlier, people would have fought for a chance just to interview. Now they were cautious, careful, waiting for the dust to settle.

He sighed. Laura had already taken steps to correct the problem in her Group: interview in New York. The answer seemed obvious to Laura, to Jay Collins. To Steve Gorman. Probably even to Mac Hunter. But not to Rick. He couldn't bring himself to acquiesce to their demands. Not quite yet, anyway.

A sharp buzz of his intercom interrupted his thoughts and he sat up to take the phone.

"Mr. Craig?" he heard Martha ask. "There's a lady here to see you." She paused, and a smile came into her voice. "She says she wants to take you to lunch."

His eyes scanned his appointment pad, but he found no name awaiting him. "Who is it, Martha?" he asked.

"Her name is Suzanne Carmichael," the secretary replied.

* * *

Rick leaned across the restaurant table, his elbows straddling his coffee cup, his chin resting on his clenched fists. His eyes were focused on the woman across from him.

Her long dark hair was pulled up and knotted in a simple bun at the back of her head, framing her delicate features in an air of professionalism, more pronounced today than on their initial encounter. Her clothing accentuated the look: dark blue blazer and white turtleneck sweater, a single medallion falling against her chest from a long gold chain.

All in all, Rick decided, strictly professional. The Complete Personnel Consultant. Nevertheless, he admitted to himself, he was delighted with the sight of her.

He pulled his thoughts back to the conversation.

"I think you're being awfully short-sighted, Rick," Suzanne was telling him. "I have some excellent prospects lined up for Laura to interview in New York later this week. Some *excellent* prospects." She paused a moment, leaning down for a slender attaché case. "Listen to some of these," she said, withdrawing a handful of application forms.

"I have a Copy Chief. Age thirty-four. Masters in English. Eleven years' experience with a good New York agency that's billing about thirty-five million. He wants a position with greater growth potential." She threw the application on the white linen cloth and continued.

"I have an Illustrator/Designer. Excellent portfolio. No formal education, but twenty-five years' experience in all forms of advertising art. Currently a top hand with an outstanding freelance studio in Manhattan. But his kids are teenagers and one of them has a drug problem. He wants to leave New York for a smaller metropolitan market." She threw the paper on the table with the other.

"I have a young man whose credentials are excellent. He wants to become a Creative Director, but he's stymied in his present situation.

"I have a woman. A broadcast writer with experience in acting as well. Very good in voiceover work.

"I have a—" She stopped. "Darn it, Rick, I have a hell of a lot of good people who could help you out of the bind you're in. The advertising industry in New York is full of people who can't wait to get away, to find a future in a nicer part of the country. But it's like I told you earlier. You're being short-sighted."

Rick considered, realizing the inevitability of his problem. Then he spoke with finality. "I'll come up with Laura for the interviews on Friday."

"But you can't!" Her exclamation was spontaneous, and as he looked sharply at her she tried to temper the severity of her tone. "I mean, Friday's interviews are set up for Laura, for her Creative Group. People we've lined up to work on The Press account, on FRESH! I'm not sure—"

"What makes you think I wouldn't be interested in the people she's interviewing?"

"That's not what I meant. It's Laura. She probably wouldn't want—" She fumbled for words. "I mean, I don't think she—"

"You mean that Laura wouldn't want me to interfere in her Group, to meddle in her accounts? Maybe not, Suzanne. But I'm still the Creative Director of Collins & Craig, and Laura still reports to me, even though she's got Hunter and Gorman eating out of her hand." He took a sip from his coffee cup, then eyed her levelly. "I'll be in New York on Friday. I'll tell Laura about it this afternoon. And if I like what I see, you can set up some interviews for *my* Group next week."

"Get me that goddamned proof!"

Hunter's hand slapped against the wooden surface of his desk, his eyes glaring furiously from beneath the heavy brows.

"I've told you, Mac—"

"You've told me nothing. All you've given me is excuses. Week after week. *And now I want the goddamned proof!*"

"I've done everything that I could—" Steve Gorman started, but Hunter again cut him off.

"You haven't done enough. You haven't got the proof away from that artist."

"I wasn't the one who let him have it in the first place—"

"No, Sid Ephraim did that. He didn't exercise proper control with the engraving. A faulty job. A subliminal message that could be seen with the naked eye. Incriminating evidence. And then he let the proof get away from Fine Arts. Not one proof, *two* proofs. Sid Ephraim was the screw-up, and by God he's paid dearly for it." Hunter's voice was hard and cold now, the anger gone from it. His eyes held Gorman, penetrated into him. "And so will you, Steve, if—"

"I'll get the proof over the weekend." Gorman's voice was controlled, but as he spoke his tongue flicked out to dampen his lips. He remained silent for a moment, one hand clenching and unclenching itself.

"That's not soon enough, Steve."

"I can't be in two places at once," Gorman shot back defensively. "I can't be in Atlanta chasing down the goddamned proof and in New York for the meeting and the interviews."

"You're not going to be in New York. You're not going to participate in the interviews."

Gorman heard the pronouncement with surprise, and for a moment his shock stilled the clenching of his fist. "What do you mean I'm not going to participate in the interviews? That's part of the plan, that's essential—"

"That's been changed. I just got a message from Atlanta a short while ago." Hunter nodded his head toward the phone on his desk. "Rick Craig is coming to New York for the interviews."

"Craig? Coming here?"

Hunter nodded.

"But that's not part of our plan. We can't let him—"

"Why not?" A smile was on Hunter's face as he posed the question. He seemed to savor the idea. "Why not? We're prepared for him." He thumped his hand on a thick manila file on his desk. "Every one of our people has a legitimate background in the agency business. Every résumé in this folder will stand his scrutiny. And every person will be prepared to answer his questions after the meeting Thursday night. All we have to do is guide Craig to the proper choice. As a matter of fact, it will work better this way. Much better. When our people go to work in Atlanta, they'll be Rick Craig's people, too."

"But it's too risky. She may not be able to handle it alone. She needs my help—"

"She can handle it."

Gorman's eyes remained fastened on Hunter and he was silent. When he finally spoke, his voice had an unnatural tone to it.

"Rick Craig. Rick Craig is messing things up again. And I don't like Rick Craig—I never have. He's been the one person who's kept Project Jupiter from moving smoothly from the very beginning. This thing's bigger than Rick Craig. He needs to be *removed* . . ."

His voice trailed off, but his eyes continued to blink. He could feel a vague pain from his balled fist, clenched so tightly that the fingernails bit into the skin of his palm.

"We're going to elect a president," he said to Hunter,

his voice louder than it had been, his eyes focusing on the other man's face. "We're going to elect a president and Rick Craig's not going to stop us. And if he tries to, he's going to have to be *removed.*"

Gorman felt Hunter's eyes on him, studying him, watching his reactions. He was aware that the other man stood suddenly, walked around the desk to stand beside him. He felt Hunter's hand on his shoulder, patting him softly.

"That's right, Steve." Hunter's voice was soft, almost gentle. "Project Jupiter *is* bigger than Rick Craig. And perhaps he does need to be removed—some day. But not now."

Gorman stared up at the other man, trying to assimilate this uncharacteristic attitude. His eyes continued to blink nervously, but gradually the motions of his hand subsided and his body lost some of its tenseness. After a moment his face, too, relaxed, and a semblance of a smile came across it.

"And when the time comes, Steve, you can be the one to do it." Hunter stood there another moment, then walked away to the expanse of glass that looked out over Manhattan. As he spoke, his voice had lost the softness. He was again crisp and businesslike. "But in the meantime, Steve, get back to Atlanta and get that proof out of Greenberg's portfolio."

Hunter stood at the window, looking at the scene below. "And then, Steve, get down to Miami. By this time next week, all of our people will be in place in Atlanta. We'll have the agency under control. And you can move on to the campaign. The Florida primary is next. We'll win that one. And then Illinois. Everything is going according to plan. The FRESH! spots are already running in the Chicago area. The introductory campaign for The Phoenix Press comes next."

Hunter was lost in his thoughts now, his voice dropping to a level that Gorman could barely discern, his face hidden from view. "We're selling soft drinks, and we'll be selling a book. But all the while, we're selling Anthony Hapworth." He chuckled softly and stood there in silence.

He turned and a darker look came over his face. "But we won't be selling anything if we let that FRESH! proof trip us up the way the tapes tripped *them* up. Get back to Atlanta, Steve. Tonight or tomorrow. And get that proof in your hands by Friday."

Steve Gorman walked up Park Avenue. The tension he had experienced in Hunter's office had begun to dissipate itself, and as it drained away it was replaced with a growing exhaustion.

I need to relax, he told himself. I need a drink.

Down a side street he saw a bar and shortly he was sliding onto a stool at the deserted counter. "Give me a double bourbon. Neat." When the drink was set before him, he tossed it off in a single gulp. "Another."

Again he tossed it off. "Give me another," he instructed the bartender. "On the rocks. With a water chaser."

He grasped the new glass comfortingly and sat there, eyes closed, sipping the bourbon. Fragments of his conversation with Hunter played through his mind. *Get back to Atlanta . . . get the proof by Friday.* He opened his eyes to stare at the glass before him. Hunter was right. The proof was the only incriminating evidence in existence. And he'd get it. One way or the other he'd get it back from that bastard Greenberg. *You're not going to participate in the interviews . . . Rick Craig is coming to New York.* Rick Craig. Again. Rick Craig, fucking things up. *Rick Craig needs to be removed.* He heard Hunter's voice, and nodded his head in silent agreement. *You can be the one to do it.*

Gorman smiled and ordered another drink. He was relaxed now. He knew what to do.

Diana Malloy sat at her desk watching the clock.

Almost five o'clock, she told herself. And another day gone.

She started putting her things away, preparing to leave for the evening, pondering the work that Logan Smith had just given her.

Despite the extra work that Smitty generated, she was glad that she and Gorman had been assigned an office next to him—glad because it gave her at least temporary relief from the constant insinuations and sexual innuendoes that Gorman made.

God, she thought to herself with a slight shudder. Every time I walk into Gorman's office, he undresses me with his eyes. And Hap hasn't done anything about it.

She was about to leave when the buzz of the intercom sounded. She brought the receiver to her ear and listened to the receptionist's voice.

Long distance? Who would be calling her long distance at this time of day? And then, with a sinking feeling, she realized that it was probably Gorman calling from New York. Calling with another goddamned memo or letter to dictate, one last thing to do before she left for the day.

Well, she told herself, he can just dictate it on the recorder. And I'll transcribe it in the morning. To hell with him!

She pulled a blank cassette from the drawer, inserting it into the tape recorder that always sat on her desk. She attached the sensing device to the base of the receiver, pushed the "On" button, and was ready to go.

Her finger reached out to push a blinking button on the console, and she brought the receiver to her ear.

"Diana Malloy," she said briskly into the instrument.

"Diana?" a familiar voice answered her.

"Hap! It's you! I was expecting a call from Gorman. But I'm so glad it's you. Where are you calling from?"

"I'm calling from Miami. Can you talk? Are you alone?"

"Yes . . ." she answered uncertainly and, noting the door to Smitty's office, quickly added ". . . no! Wait a minute." She rose and went across the room, softly closing the door to insure her privacy.

"Now," she said when she returned. "I had to close the door to Smitty's office."

"Are you alone now?"

"Yes. What are you calling about?"

"Before I get into that, tell me about Gorman. Is he still giving you trouble?"

"Oh, yes, Hap. It's all I can do to fight him off. You've got to do something about it."

"I'm going to. I'll go to Hunter, if I have to. But in the meantime, stay away from him. He's crazy. He's into real kinky things with sex. You wouldn't believe the things he tried to do with a girl he picked up in a bar in Concord during the New Hampshire primary. *Real* kinky things. With drugs. And ropes. Stay away from him, Diana. Until I can get him off your case."

"I'll stay away from him. Don't worry." She paused. "What are you calling about?"

Suddenly the terse tone that had been in his voice dissolved into jubilation. "Get yourself ready, baby. I'm coming to Atlanta. Tonight."

"For a meeting? Gorman's in New York—"

"Not for a meeting, baby. To see you. To spend the night with you. I really miss you, Diana. I need you."

"I need you, too, Hap. Thank God you're going to be here. Even just for a night. Wait a minute. I'll take the day off tomorrow, and we can sleep in—"

"Take the day off tomorrow, and Friday, too. Because I've found a place down here where we can spend the weekend. I'm going to bring you back to Miami with me. Just for a few days. But be careful. Don't let anyone know that I'm going to be in Atlanta, or that you're coming to Miami. If Hunter found out that we were together, he'd have my ass . . ."

Rick Craig pushed open the heavy glass door of his apartment building, glancing at his watch. Time enough for a shower and shave before his dinner date with Suzanne Carmichael, he told himself. He paused a moment at the wall containing a series of stainless steel mailboxes and looked through the window of his slot.

Turning the key, he pulled the door open and tried to remove the bulky package that had been wedged there. When it finally came out into his hands, his eyes scanned the envelope. A bold scrawl in the upper left corner told him the sender: Dan Osborne, Aspen, Colorado.

In his apartment he threw his trench coat across a chair while he ripped open the envelope and extracted the contents. It was a book of some kind, he realized, bound in a brilliant magenta fabric stamped in gold. No letter, no further message.

He eyed the thin volume in the brilliant binding and the brief words on the cover. *Mind Control,* he read, and flipped open the cover. On the title page the title was repeated and amplified. *"The Role of the Sub-Conscious in Influencing Human Behavior."* And below the title, the name of the author. Dr. Paul W. Prescott, M.D.

Paul's book. Dan had promised to find it and send it, but Rick had totally forgotten the incident. He stared at the volume in his hands. Something about it rang a bell, something more than his conversation with Osborne. Somewhere he had seen the book before. He searched his mind, but when he could not find an answer, he tossed the book aside and dismissed the thought.

Pulling his tie loose and stripping off his jacket, he left the room. But the book reappeared in his memory, nagging at him, forcing him to try to recall another place, another time, when he had seen a similar volume. Again, the elusive thread from the past slipped away from his grasp.

He was in the shower when it came to him. His mind focused on the scene with perfect clarity. It was the morning he had returned from Aspen as he had pulled open the drawers of his desk trying to discover who had moved his belongings. And his mind saw the same slender purple volume sitting on top of a black notebook, a notebook stamped with the name of Steve Gorman.

He stepped from the shower, towelling off quickly and moving toward his bedroom and the book. Again he inspected the title page. "A Research Paper delivered before the American Medical Association and reprinted for private distribution by the author." His eyes dropped to the final words on the page and were riveted there in surprise. "Published by The Phoenix Press . . . New York."

Rick stared at the words and pondered their meaning. He sank into the chair for a moment, turning another page to find himself confronted with a quotation from Hippocrates.

> Men ought to know that from the brain and from the brain only arise our pleasures, joys, laughter and jests as well as our sorrows, pains, griefs and tears . . . It is the same thing that makes us mad or delirious, inspires us with dread and fear, whether by night or by day, brings sleeplessness, inopportune mistakes, aimless anxieties, absentmindedness and acts that are contrary to habit . . .

He turned to the first page of text and began to read.

"During a time of widespread reappraisal of human society, it becomes increasingly clear that the subconscious is the key that can unlock the vast storehouses of the mind and that can, in fact, allow the control of human behavior . . ."

He snapped the book closed. He would be late for his date with Suzanne. And Paul's book would make interesting reading on the flight to New York. *Very* interesting reading, he thought to himself grimly.

Chapter 2

The skyline of Manhattan, gray and wintry looking in its first throes of spring, had given way to the high-rise apartments and hospitals of the river drive. And the river had finally been left behind in favor of the elegance of the upper seventies.

The taxi driver steered his way down the one-way street, a solitary vehicle negotiating the solitude of the shallow canyon between the rows of fashionable brownstone townhouses on either side of the street.

The two women sat in silence in the back seat, one of them studying the surroundings with interest, the othe: hardly aware of a neighborhood that had long since become commonplace.

The cab pulled to the curb and Suzanne Carmichael moved forward on the seat, automatically searching her bag for the money for the driver.

The trip to New York with Laura Talbott had been an awkward one. Laura had not been pleased by Rick Craig's sudden announcement that he was joining them in New York for the interviews, had been irritated when Suzanne had agreed to a dinner date with Rick the previous evening.

But now it was over and she sighed her relief as she took a bill from her coin purse to hand to the driver.

Laura's hand stopped her. "Don't bother, Suzanne. I'll pay the cabby when he drops me at my hotel." She smiled, urging Suzanne out of the cab. "I'll see you tomorrow."

"Yes. Thank you, Laura." Suzanne stepped to the street, drawing her attaché case and luggage behind her. But before she could close the door, Laura called out to her again.

"Suzanne!"

She bent forward and leaned back into the cab, and found Laura with a perplexed expression on her face.

"I'm sorry, Suzanne," Laura began. "Sorry that I've been such a bitch. About Rick, I mean. He's a hard man to get close to, a hard man to catch. There's a wall around him that no one's been able to crash. There was a time when I thought I could, when I was almost ready to throw aside my career, everything I've worked for. But—" She stopped, a distant look in her eyes. "But." She shrugged the sentence away, focusing her attention back on the other woman. "What I wanted to say was, if you're interested in him, I wish you luck."

With a slight wave of her hand she urged the driver on and left Suzanne standing on the curb staring after the taxicab in silence. She stood motionless for a moment, then with a quick shake of her head she faced the building in front of her. The brownstone was accented by a neat wrought-iron fence and a well-manicured box hedge, and beyond the hedge a short flight of steps led down to her offices.

Entering the diminutive reception area, she saw the bright face of Angela peer around the corner of her office.

"Miss Carmichael! Am I glad you're back. All hell has been breaking loose here." She held up a folder bulging with papers. "We've got a fistful of new applications. Everyone in New York seems to want to move to Atlanta."

Suzanne eyed the folder disinterestedly. She walked past her secretary into her own office, motioning the girl to accompany her.

"We won't have time to consider any new ones. We've already done the preliminaries and made the basic decisions." She threw her coat on a loveseat across the room and moved to a broad slab of glass supported by polished chrome sawhorses.

"There's one you'd better look at," Angie persisted. "Christine Childs sent it over this morning. She said Mr. Hunter wants you to include this one with the others he sent you."

Suzanne took the application and scanned it, a look of irritation coming over her face. She whirled around and walked to the telephone, her finger punching out a number with precision. As it was ringing, she gestured Angie out of the room and sank into the chair behind the desk.

"Miss Childs? This is Suzanne Carmichael. Tell Mr. Hunter that I need to talk with him." She paused. "No, Miss Childs, I need to talk to him now."

She waited impatiently, her enameled nails beating a tattoo on the glass desk.

"Mac!" Her voice said the word insistently. "I need to see you, Mac. About the interviews. Can you meet me this afternoon?"

Laura Talbott pushed open the rococo grill of the wrought-iron gate and walked to the door of "21," stepping from the chill into the warmth and color of its plaid carpeting. She brushed past the *maitre d'* and turned toward the bar, stopping only briefly in the doorway to let her eyes scan the room. She saw him sitting at the bar, holding a stemmed glass filled with clear liquid and studying the outline of the olive that rested at its base.

Laura pushed past the others until she stood beside him, waiting for him to turn his head in her direction, waiting for him to welcome her back to New York. After a moment he became aware of her presence and turned to face her, and she rewarded him with a dazzling smile.

"My dear," he said, replacing the glass on the bar and rising to take her hand. "It's been a long time. Too long."

In Atlanta Rick Craig stood at his office window watching the red ball of sun sink out of sight on the outskirts of the city. After the cold and wetness of the winter the city was coming to life again as slowly and inevitably the first signs of spring began to appear.

Too bad, he told himself, that the interviews tomorrow couldn't have been scheduled in Atlanta. New York will be cold and blustery, he predicted. And not too pleasant. Just like Laura's mood since he announced his intention to join them: cold and blustery and not too pleasant.

But Suzanne will be there, he reminded himself. And whatever Laura's mood, Suzanne will be warm and pleasant.

With a shrug he turned back to his desk and the slim volume that had occupied his attention for the past minutes. Rick picked up Prescott's book and thumbed the pages, reading the underlined passages again.

". . . the subconscious is the key that can unlock the vast storehouses of the mind . . . the human mind can be molded, manipulated . . . the motion picture or television medium is especially effective with its double image, double message . . . the print medium should not be overlooked . . . through control of the photoengraving process a hidden message can be embedded."

Shaking his head, he slammed the volume shut and tossed it in his attaché case. Heavy, he admitted—just as Dan Osborne had warned him. And certainly too academic for easy reading. But nevertheless fascinating.

And if Steve Gorman found it of interest, then he would find out why.

Rick looked at the clock on his wall. Almost time for his appointment with Joe Greenberg, to give Joe the job for comp layouts he'd promised his Group for Monday. He grabbed the case and slipped on his coat and, locking the agency doors behind him, headed for the elevator.

The car shot him down to the lobby floor, and he transferred to another elevator that would take him to the underground parking garage.

As the door slid open, Rick stepped forth onto the shadowy concrete surface of the cavernous parking garage. In the scant light he could see the few remaining vehicles standing like silent sentinels as he walked on the oil-stained pavement toward his Porsche parked in solitude in a far corner.

His thoughts were on Paul Prescott's writings, completely immersed in the intricacies of the concept. As a result he did not notice the small Mustang edging its way from its parking stall.

Perhaps it was the sound of the accelerating engine that first drew his attention, a sound of heavy motor revolutions accompanied by tires gaining momentum. A sound that was amiss to his ears in the silence of the empty garage. That car is going too fast, he thought and as he whirled around to connect the sound with a sight of the offending driver, his eyes were blinded by the sudden shaft of light that sprang from the headlights of the small car that was bearing down on him.

The car hurtled forward, never veering in its headlong path, and for an almost fatal moment, Rick Craig stood motionless, transfixed by the notion that the car would alter its course, would finally see him and swerve aside. But finally, as the distance was narrowed to a few feet, Rick Craig realized that its course was set and its aim deadly.

He whirled to his right and fought to gain momentum

to escape the oncoming vehicle. His free arm flailed at the air. One leg shot forward in a giant step, but his foot landed on an oil slick and he collapsed against the pavement. And the car was upon him.

Somehow his other foot found traction and he pushed his body forward, his fingertips digging in the concrete to assist the frantic scramble to safety.

The car rushed past, the driver only a shadowy blur. As it passed Rick's huddled figure, one wheel caught the edge of the attaché case that lay where he had dropped it. The momentum flipped it against the underside of the vehicle and the back wheel threw it free.

With an enormous screeching sound, the car braked and slid into a noisy turn. Accelerating again, it flew onto the exit ramp and was gone.

The trembling in Rick's knees had subsided, his hand was relatively stable as he touched the lighter to a cigarette. He turned the Porsche into a well-manicured street in the pleasant suburb where Joe Greenberg lived.

Though his mind coherently searched for the street address, his thoughts were filled with anger and frustration at the insane driver who had so nearly run him down.

He walked across the grass and stood under the porch light.

He waited, uncomfortable in his mission. His hands brushed at the grime from the parking garage that still stained his jacket and trousers. Again, he rang the bell. And a third time. Finally he turned to leave.

As he stepped off the porch, he heard a sound behind him and turned to see the door opened and a tiny figure outlined against the soft light from within the house.

"Is Joe here?" he said as he returned to find a wizened old woman. She looked at him in silence, her nervousness emphasized by one hand holding firmly to the screen door that separated them.

"Is Joe here?" he inquired again, and this time the old woman shook her head.

"No," she answered, her voice little more than a high-pitched croak.

"I'm Rick Craig," he said. "Can you tell me where I could find him?"

"Joe's not here," she said tremulously. "He's at the hospital. Miriam and the children are with him. I'm Miriam's mother and I'm all alone. Now please go away." She started to close the door, but Rick called to her.

"At the hospital? Is something wrong?"

"Joe's been hurt. He was run over this afternoon by a hit and run driver."

Her words stunned Rick. He opened his mouth to speak, but before he could utter another question, she slammed the door and was gone.

"Miriam!" Rick walked past the attendant at the Intensive Care desk toward the chair where Miriam Greenberg sat. "I just found you. Your mother couldn't tell me where they had taken Joe. How is he? What's his condition? Miriam, what the hell happened?"

Rick knelt before the haggard-looking woman and took one of her hands in his own.

"Miriam, is Joe going to be all right? How badly is he hurt?"

Miriam Greenberg stared at him expressionlessly for a moment before she answered, and when she spoke her voice was as flat as her countenance.

"Joe's going to live," she said, and fell silent again.

"How extensive are his injuries?" Rick pursued his questioning.

"A concussion. A broken hip." With a shrug of her shoulders, she added, "Several broken ribs," as though the ribcage seemed insignificant by comparison. "His face was cut badly," she went on, withdrawing her hand from Rick's and wiping at her eyes. "But he'll live, thank God."

Rick moved to sit beside her, and as he did he saw Adam Greenberg, Joe's oldest son, sitting across the room. "How did it happen?" he asked them.

"It happened late this afternoon. Joe had an interview for some work for the new studio and he was hit crossing the street to get his car, on a downtown street. There weren't any witnesses. We don't even know what kind of a car it was, except what Joe could tell the police. 'A little car,' he kept mumbling. That's all he said, 'A little car.' And he kept asking about his portfolio."

"What about his portfolio?"

"It's missing," she answered. "We've searched for it, but it's gone. It had all of his samples in it—he had it with him for the interview. But it's gone."

Rick stood up, galvanized. A small, compact car. A short while earlier a similar car had aimed at him. A missing portfolio of samples. A portfolio that had contained a copy of the controversial FRESH! proof.

Finally, assured that there was nothing he could do, he turned to leave, and as he walked through the corridors of the hospital Jay Collins' words came back to him. *Gorman is in a fury . . . threatening legal action . . . or worse.* And the faint red light of danger began to glow more vividly at the base of Rick Craig's skull.

On the way back to his apartment building, Rick weighed the absurdity of his suspicion against the overwhelming circumstances of the day. But he could find no satisfactory answer.

Shortly after ten o'clock in the evening, Dr. Paul Prescott walked into the conference room of The Phoenix Press and took a place at the head of the table. At the sight of him, the men who had been clustered together broke apart to take their seats around the long table.

Prescott surveyed the group cursorily. All present except one, he thought to himself. But she was the most important of all. Where in the hell is she? he questioned. His hand went inside his coat and extracted a leather case and shortly the cigar produced billows of smoke as he puffed it into activity. He decided to proceed.

"Good evening," he announced. "The purpose of our meeting tonight is, quite literally, to come out of hiding. To come into the open. I have worked with each of you individually in the past months, but you have known each other only by a series of code names. Tonight we will discard the code names under which we have functioned for so long. Tonight we will become known to each other by sight as well as by sound."

Prescott paused. His fingers thumped the ash of the cigar into a metal bowl, and focused on a casually dressed young man at the far end of the table. "Good evening, Zeus," he said.

He was rewarded with a smile and a wave of the younger man's hand, but the reaction from the others around the table was more pronounced. At the sound of the name, each turned to study the man carefully, a mixture of curiosity and interest on their faces.

"Allow me to introduce Brett Stanley, one of our team members who accomplished his placement several months ago at VTR Studios in Los Angeles. Brett, we're delighted that you could forsake the beaches of Southern California for the blustery skies of Manhattan."

A broader smile broke across the sun-tanned face and he replied. "New York's still my home, Paul. *Despite* the lousy weather."

Prescott's eyes moved around the table and settled on a middle-aged man in a chalk-stripe suit. "And Sid Ephraim, one of the older members of our group.

You've known him as Vulcan."

Ephraim nodded curtly, his face expressionless.

Prescott continued. "Sid is Executive Vice President of Fine Arts Engraving Company here in New York. The workrooms of Fine Arts have been the laboratories where we have perfected our process for embedding a subliminal message in advertisements for the print media—newspapers, magazines, posters, brochures, and the like."

Focusing his remarks on the newer members of the group, Prescott continued his explanation. "And Brett Stanley has introduced in Los Angeles the subliminal technology that he developed here in New York. After we acquired VTR, he equipped an antiquated studio with a solid core of technicians who can implant an almost invisible message in motion picture film."

Stanley started to speak, but Prescott continued. "And through his work with some of the most gifted musical arrangers in the movie industry—Ron Spence, for example—he has mastered the art of the subaudible suggestion. I believe that the experiment in Utah and the Barry Starr record proved *that* point. Right, Brett?"

"Right!" A note of sarcasm was in his voice as he continued. "Barry still thinks he hit the top of the charts because of his talent! The stupid son of a bitch never understood that his fans weren't reacting to his singing. They were reacting to our song. And they never even realized they were hearing it."

Around the table the heads nodded in silent comprehension—except for one man. He held a dull, blank look on his face, his head turning back and forth between Stanley and Prescott. He was dressed in a shabby black suit, and the sallowness of his complexion was in sharp contrast to the healthy good looks of the Californian.

Noting his confusion, Prescott continued with the introductions. "And may I introduce the other members of our team: Joe Martin . . . John Finley . . ." He continued around the table, introducing each, until his eyes came to rest on the pale man. "And Jake Smith, who has become a part of our group only this week. You'll learn more about Mr. Smith's specialty later in the evening." Prescott cleared his throat and looked out over the faces.

"As I have said, tonight we have discarded the code names. With one important exception. In the future only one code name will be used—for reasons of top security. And that name is Minerva—"

At that moment, the door to the conference room swung open and every head turned to look at the new figure who entered the room. A woman stood in the doorway, her hand poised on the knob as she surveyed the scene before her.

She hesitated momentarily, aware that her entrance had distracted their attention, then quickly closed the door and moved to the table.

"Gentlemen," Prescott announced, "her timing is as perfect as ever. Join me in welcoming Minerva—by far the most beautiful member of our team."

The woman placed a case on the table and sat down. She nodded briefly to the faces around the table, running her hand under her long, dark hair to pull it from her shoulders. "Please go ahead, Paul," she said crisply.

"I was about to comment," he proceeded, "on the importance of this meeting. It marks one of the few times when we will be gathered together on a face-to-face basis. In the past each of us has worked independently to perfect our own technique, whether it be in photography or mechanical art or cinematography. In the future we will continue to practice those talents independently.

"But the time has come when this inner group must

know each other by sight and by proper name. For instance, on a shooting or editing assignment, it is vital that Brett Stanley know the rest of us by sight. It is essential that Sid Ephraim know on sight those persons who can be trusted—to avoid another dangerous mistake like the proof for the FRESH! advertisement.

"It was important that we show our faces to each other for another reason." He nodded to the woman sitting to his right. "In the past you've referred to this woman as Minerva, a name that is equally appropriate in describing the goddess of wisdom or of arts. But tomorrow, four of you will meet Minerva to interview for positions with Collins & Craig's Atlanta office. You must recognize that of the three people who will be interviewing you, Minerva is your friend and ally."

Prescott raised one hand in warning. "Show no signs of recognition, of course. But remember Minerva. Remember that she is an ally, no matter how antagonistic her questioning might seem.

"For those reasons she is here to rehearse you tonight for your interview tomorrow. Interviews for the positions of writer . . . photographer . . . production manager . . . and keyline-retouching artist . . . illustrator . . . copywriter." His eyes had passed to each of them as he mentioned their positions.

Suddenly, the woman's voice shot out and her finger pointed to the newcomer.

"You. What's your name? What position are you applying for?"

The man stared at her in silence, gulping as he collected his thoughts.

"Let's go," she repeated in irritation. "What's your name? What position? What are your qualifications?"

The man finally spoke, his eyes darting from the woman to Prescott. "Do you want my real name?" he stammered. "Or my new name?"

"Goddamnit, Smith," she shot out vehemently, "this is a rehearsal for your interview tomorrow. Of course we want your new name! I'll be there to help, but I can't do it all. Now, let's hear your qualifications."

Smith sat in silence for a moment, then searched in an inner pocket frantically until he pulled forth a dog-eared file card filled with tiny, meticulous handwriting.

"My name is Jakob Schmidt," he read in a singsong voice. "I am a craftsman by trade. I am applying for a position as retouching artist or keyline artist. I have had many years experience—"

The monologue was broken by the crack of a feminine hand falling with force against the flat surface of the conference table.

"That won't do the job, Smith. We've spent a lot of time and money in setting up a new identity for you, and you obviously haven't done your homework." She leaned across the table, pointing a finger at him threateningly. "But let me tell you, Mr. Smith, that you *will* do your homework before tomorrow, or you'll be right back where you came from."

Smith's mouth was agape and he started to speak, but her tirade was not finished.

"It would be easier for you to admit that you're a convicted forger, that you've spent a lifetime doing detailed handwork on engraving plates. It would be easier to say that your experience in retouching has been on forged documents and currency. It would be easier because it's the truth. But when did you become interested in the truth? Since when did an ex-con like you get worried about a little white lie?"

Smith had pulled himself up in indignation. "There's no need to tell all of these people about that—"

"There's every need, Smith. They need to understand that you're a common criminal and that we've arranged your release from prison on parole. They need to know that you've signed a contract with us just like they have. And that if you botch up on this job, you go straight back to prison."

Her eyes went around the table. "There's every reason for all of you to know that we're not playing games. We're in this for keeps. And while the rest of you aren't convicted criminals like Smith, we've got enough on each of you to put an end to your careers. And we won't hesitate to do that. We've paid you big money, we'll continue paying you big money. But if you make a mistake—" her eyes were hard and merciless "—we'll get you. And don't *ever* forget it."

She looked back across the table at Smith. "Just sit still and don't open your mouth. Listen to the others. After the meeting, I'll rehearse you privately."

Focusing her attention on the other faces, she chose one and pointed her finger directly at him.

"You," she said. "What's your name? What's the position you're applying for?"

The man sat forward in his chair. Although his hand trembled slightly, he lit a cigarette and smiled ingratiatingly and began. "I'm Joe Martin," he said, "and I'm interested in a position as a photographer. My application shows you where I've worked—mainly on the West Coast—but I have my portfolio here and I'd like to show you some of my work . . ."

At last it was over. With the exception of the benighted Jake Smith, it had gone rather well, Prescott thought to himself. Very well, he conceded. The last man in particular—John Finley—had fielded the questions relating to the job of production manager extremely smoothly.

Prescott stood and smiled. "I realize it's getting late, and you have to be back here early in the morning. But let me give you a few final words. Tomorrow you'll be offered jobs at Collins & Craig. You'll move to Atlanta. You'll be assigned to the FRESH! and The Phoenix Press accounts, the vehicle that will carry our messages to the American public.

"And when you're in place in your new jobs, you'll do the work assigned to you. You'll become friends with your co-workers. You'll develop a loyalty to the agency.

"At the same time, you'll carry out your specialized assignments in the security of the studio you will set up in your home. You may seek the counsel of each other —in private, of course. And you may call me at the Clinic at any time.

"But be careful. Don't allow your materials to fall into other hands." Prescott looked directly at Sid Ephraim, who accepted the censure with a scowl. "We will not tolerate another incident such as the one that occurred at Fine Arts.

"And finally, trust *no one* unless he is properly identified. We will add new employees and craftsmen to our team as our workload increases. We will always attempt to notify everyone of such additions. If for any reason you do not receive notification, one word will assure you of their authenticity. The word *Minerva.*"

Prescott paused and leaned forward, supporting himself with his hands on the table. His face was serious, his brows knit together in concentration. He closed the meeting, speaking slowly, emphasizing each word.

"Gentlemen, tomorrow we enter the final phase of Project Jupiter."

"I'm sorry, sir. Mr. Hunter cannot be reached at this time. This is his answering service. May I take a message?"

For a moment Steve Gorman did not answer the New York operator. Instead he drained the bourbon from the glass on the table beside the bed. When he finally spoke, his voice was thick, the words piling heedlessly upon each other.

"Tell the sonuvabitch that Gorman called. Tell him that everything's under control. Tell him I got the proof." He paused, chuckling aloud as another thought came to his clouded mind. "And tell him that I got Greenberg and Craig, too."

The operator's puzzled voice came back to him, attempting to decipher his cryptic message. With rising irritation he ended the conversation. "Just tell him that Gorman has got the proof. Can you understand that? Gorman has got the proof."

Gorman slammed the receiver back on the phone and eyed it with eyes that were hardly able to focus. He'd exonerated himself with Hunter. He'd recovered the evidence. He had handled somebody else's screw-up. He had done as Hunter wanted. He reflected on his activities since he returned to Atlanta, remembered the look on Rick Craig's face in the parking garage, and his breath came a little quicker with the stimulation.

He lurched off the bed where he had been sprawled and walked across his bedroom toward the bottle of whiskey. He sloshed the liquid into the glass, spilling a part of it on the floor. As he raised the glass to his lips, his eyes fell on the plastic pouch that lay beside the whiskey bottle, a pouch filled with a white, powdery substance that reminded him of the immediate pleasures that lay before him.

Setting the glass aside, he picked up the pouch and turned to the opposite side of the room and the silent figure awaiting him.

The girl was a stranger to him, someone he'd met in a cheap bar. And now she was naked and her hands were tied behind her, secured to a large ring on the wall. Her mouth was taped to prevent any sound escaping her, but her eyes were frantic with fear. The wall to which she was tied was covered with mirrors, and Gorman saw his own naked body reflected, saw himself begin to stiffen in anticipation. Slowly he advanced toward the young woman. His fingers produced a quantity of the white powder and he took it clumsily into his nostrils and into his system. Tossing the pouch aside, he stood there, his legs spread apart, his hands dropped to his hips, as he awaited the sensation he had already begun to feel. The desire heightened, spreading from his groin throughout his entire body.

Slowly he pulled his arm back, and then with a powerful blow he slapped the girl across her face.

Chapter 3

The windshield wiper made a noisy *clack* as it whisked away the raindrops from the windshield of the veteran taxicab. But the sound was lost on the ears of Rick Craig.

He sat in the back seat lost in thought, staring sightlessly at the panorama of early rush hour in midtown Manhattan. On his lap was Paul Prescott's book, held firmly in his hands with an index finger carefully guarding the page he had been reading.

Suddenly he directed his attention back to the book, opening it quickly and reading again the passage that had prompted his concentration.

"Medical science, assisted by commercial research organizations and often funded by huge, multinational corporations, has made enormous progress in learning how the human mind can be molded, manipulated, and even almost totally controlled."

Again, the phrase jolted his comprehension. ". . . *progress in learning how the human mind can be molded, manipulated . . . almost totally controlled.*"

Mind control. The subject of the book. An area of study that Paul Prescott had spent years in researching. And there, in black and white, Prescott was suggesting that the human mind could be totally controlled.

The jolt of brakes brought him back to the present, and the cab driver prepared to deposit him on the curb in front of the venerable courtyard of The Phoenix Press.

Slipping the book into his briefcase, he paid the driver, pulled the briefcase and an overnighter out of the cab with him, and turned to face the building. He stood there for a moment, his mind still echoing the preposterous idea that Prescott advanced in his research paper.

"*. . . the human mind can be molded, manipulated, almost totally controlled.*" The phrase echoed in his mind as he mounted the steps and presented himself to the receptionist in the lobby. Shortly he entered a conference room on an upper floor and found himself alone. The only trace of his associates was Laura Talbott's attaché case on the conference table.

Welcoming the solitude, he walked across the room and sank heavily into one of the chairs circling the table. His thoughts again reverted to the academic jargon of Prescott's book.

". . . seduction symbolism . . . domination of human behavior . . . the unconscious mechanism of the brain . . . oral wish fulfillment fantasies."

He shook his head slowly back and forth. The depth of the neurosurgeon's academic terminology made it difficult for a layman to follow. But then he thought of the other words—words that he, as a professional communicator, *could* understand, if not totally comprehend—and his head stopped its motion.

"Photographic embeds . . . subaudible tones and harmonies of rock music . . . light intensity projections through motion picture film . . . the 'popcorn experiment' of the late fifties . . . subliminal persuasion through advertising."

And through it all, the frightening message of Paul

Prescott recurred in his brain: *the human mind can be molded, manipulated, almost totally controlled.*

"Hello, Rick."

The voice came so unexpectedly that he jumped and jerked his head toward the open door of the conference room. Laura stood on the threshold, and as he rose to greet her she entered the room and approached him with one hand extended in greeting. Her manner was cordial, but the tension in their relationship was apparent.

"I've been visiting with Joe Roth, and one of the vice presidents of marketing. They've gone over the rest of the 'blockbusters' with me—the ones that will follow *A Time for Terror*—and we'll get galley proofs before we leave. *A Time for Terror* is doing great in the first two markets. We'll start the same spots in Illinois right away. Then follow it up with Texas and California to tie in with an author tour. Then in the summer we'll go national." She paused a moment. "That's fortunate, isn't it?"

"What do you mean?"

Laura's voice was brittle and businesslike. "It's fortunate for us that the states they've chosen for the first campaign are the same as the states we've been using for FRESH! It'll save us a lot of media work."

Rick thought about what she'd said. Laura was right. It *was* fortunate. But it was more than that—it was almost uncanny that two major national advertisers would choose the same states for isolated, specialized campaigns. He was about to comment on the unusual coincidence when he saw Suzanne Carmichael walk into the room.

"Good morning." She came directly to Rick, giving him a warm smile and briefly taking his hand. Then she turned to Laura, the smile fading somewhat as she faced the other woman, and spoke. "I've decided to take your advice, Laura. Thanks for the tip."

Rick looked from one woman to the other, trying to decipher her cryptic remark. But the moment was gone, and Suzanne turned to the conference table, anxious to get down to business.

"There's a waiting room down the hall that's filled to capacity with eager advertising people. If we want to stay on schedule, we'd better get started."

As they gathered themselves around the table, Suzanne continued. "I've scheduled the interviews at twenty-minute intervals. You've both studied the résumés and you'll have the chance to see samples of their creative work. We've already weeded out a lot of people on the preliminaries. We'll weed even more out today, and you can talk to any one of them a second time, if you wish. Oh yes—I've added one more to the list. An excellent retoucher." She handed them the new application form. "If you'll get your own files of the résumés out, we can look them over briefly before we begin."

Rick snapped open the lid of the case and absently riffled through the assorted papers, putting the brightly colored volume on the table beside the open case.

He heard a muted gasp, the sound of air drawn in surprise into the lungs of one of the women. He looked up, and found both of them watching him and looking at the book on the table before him. He looked from one of them to the other and then explained.

"It's only a book I've been reading," he said lightly. "It has nothing to do with the interviews."

Laura reached across the table and took the book. "Is it one of The Press' spring selections?"

"Hardly," he answered. "It's a research paper, actually. A private, limited printing." He paused, then added, "I once knew the author rather well."

"*Mind Control,* by Dr. Paul Prescott, M.D. That sounds awfully heavy, Rick."

It *is* awfully heavy, he thought. Heavy and frightening. But he kept the thought to himself. He took the book from Laura and laid it back in his case beneath the stack of application folders. When he looked up, Laura was studying the folders in front of her. But Suzanne's eyes were focused on a tip of the book still visible.

"That's an interesting subject, Rick," she commented. "Where did you get your copy of the book? From the author?"

"No, I got it from—" Rick stopped, shaking his head. Something about this conversation bothered him, something about the entire incident with the book. "Let's get on with the interviews," he said.

Suzanne continued to stare at the book for a moment but finally she took a schedule sheet in hand and began. "We'll start off with the pure craftsmen and leave the creative types until after lunch. The first person we'll see is our new applicant. He's a highly experienced retouching artist who just recently arrived in the United States from Germany. His name is Jakob Schmidt . . ."

The luncheon had been exceptional. It was faultlessly served in the boardroom by a white-jacketed waiter, and Joe Roth had joined them to discuss in some detail the promotional campaign for *A Time for Terror*.

But now their conversation turned to the interviews.

"I think Jakob Schmidt is the obvious choice for the retoucher, don't you, Rick?" Laura questioned.

Rick nodded in agreement, and Suzanne smiled. "I'm glad you feel that way. He was my choice, too, but he conducted himself so badly during the interview—"

"You helped him along nicely, Suzanne." Laura smiled.

"That's all part of my job," she replied, ignoring the hint of sarcasm in Laura's voice. "But what did you think of the production managers?"

"That's not as easy," Laura countered. "There are

two that are pretty evenly matched." She paused and then said tentatively, "Robert Smith . . ."

Suzanne interrupted. "Either Robert Smith or John Finley. Finley probably has the better credentials—"

Rick cut into the women's conversation. "Bob Smith seemed a little more our type, don't you think, Laura?"

"I'm not sure. Finley *was* awfully impressive."

"It's your choice, of course," Suzanne said. "But now, we need to talk to several photographers. They'll be waiting for us upstairs." She paused, glancing at her watch. "We still have a few moments. Laura, would you like to freshen up?"

"Yes," Laura replied, pushing her chair away from the table. "If you'll give me directions . . ."

"I need to make a telephone call to my office," Suzanne said, walking toward the door. "Come along. I'll show you."

Rick watched the two women speak briefly in the hall, and then depart in separate directions. He lit a cigarette, preparing himself to kill five or ten minutes before the afternoon session got underway.

She walked quietly and quickly down the hall, approaching the upper conference room almost stealthily. With a guarded movement she slowly pushed the door open and, seeing the room empty, slipped through the door and closed it.

That's good, she thought. Everything as we left it and the others aren't back yet. Rick's briefcase was still open as it had been throughout the morning. Pulling the file folders aside, she saw the book. Quickly she removed it and placed the folders carefully back in place. Holding the book behind her, she turned and hurried to the door.

Again she opened the door stealthily and peered into the empty hall.

Good, she repeated to herself, leaving the room and

moving down the hall toward the stairway. As she walked, the question that had claimed her attention most of the morning again recurred to her.

How in God's name did Rick Craig get a copy of Paul's book?

She disappeared into a doorway marked EXIT, and her heels clattered against the steps in the isolated security of the stairwell as she retraced her steps to the executive offices.

A short while later, the three of them gathered again in the conference room and took the same chairs they had occupied all morning.

Suzanne opened the meeting with a new résumé form. "The first photographer we'll talk to is an applicant I only heard from yesterday afternoon, but he's such an outstanding person that I asked him to come. His name is Joe Martin . . ."

As Logan Smith returned from lunch, he found the executive corridor of Collins & Craig's Atlanta office to be almost deserted. He had known Rick and Laura would be out of town, that Jay was on a business trip to New Orleans. But as he passed Steve Gorman's darkened office and saw Diana Malloy's vacant desk, he grimaced.

The cats are away, he thought to himself with a shake of his head. And the mice are playing.

Settling himself at his desk, he reviewed the exhaustive outline he had prepared in the morning for the special report that Mac Hunter had demanded.

Damn, Smitty thought to himself. It would have been so much simpler if Diana had not phoned in to announce that she was sick. He could have dictated the report. But in her absence he would have to laboriously write it by hand.

And then a thought struck him. Wasn't Diana always fiddling with the tape recorder on her desk? Didn't Gorman sometimes telephone dictation into the tape recorder? Rising from his chair, Smitty walked to her office and spied the tape recorder on her desk. Detaching the plug, he picked it up and returned to his own office to unravel its mechanical intricacies.

A cassette was already in the chamber. It's probably a clean tape, he thought, but I'd better check it . . .

His finger touched the rewind button and he watched the tape return itself on its spool. When the motion stopped, he pushed another button, expecting to hear the silence of an unused tape.

"Diana Malloy." He heard Diana's voice flood the room, and Smitty fumbled quickly with the recorder, attempting to locate the volume control. Before he could lower the volume, another voice—a man—was added to the first.

"Diana?"

"Hap! It's you! I was expecting a call from Gorman. But I'm so glad it's you. Where are you calling from?"

Smitty had no intention of eavesdropping, but he lingered a moment before he switched off the machine, and he heard the conversation continue.

"I'm calling from Miami. Can you talk? Are you alone?"

"Yes . . . no! Wait a minute . . . now. I had to close the door to Smitty's office."

Logan Smith stared at the recorder in disbelief for a moment, and then pulled his hand back from where it had hovered above the "off" switch. With a firm set of his jaw he leaned back in his chair and listened.

A click of the telephone signalled the end of the conversation between Diana Malloy and Anthony Hapworth, but Smitty sat motionless in the ensuing silence, staring at the small black box in front of him, the full impact of the words that he had heard taking hold. Finally he reached forward to rewind the machine and, after a moment, prepared to listen to the entire tape again. "Diana Malloy," he heard her begin, and he swung his chair around to stare out of the window as he listened to the damning conversation.

When it was over he stopped the machine and sat reflecting on what he had learned, trying to conceive a course of action. His preoccupation with the tape had been so complete that he had not observed a figure appear in the doorway of his office and stand there leaning against the door jamb.

"Smitty, you're a sneaky little bastard."

Steve Gorman's words exploded in the room like a grenade, creating a shock wave in their wake. They were spoken with malevolence, accompanied by the staccato laugh.

He sat in silence for a moment, his back still turned to Gorman's insolent figure. The circumstances of the past few months went through his mind, and suddenly he knew what he must do. Finally he spoke.

"Hello, Steve," he said. "I thought you were still in New York." Smitty turned slowly in his chair, and when he saw Gorman standing there, he forced a slow smile to his face. "That was an interesting conversation, wasn't it?"

"Damned interesting," Gorman said, pulling himself erect and walking into the room. "Interesting enough to take care of Diana Malloy—and Anthony Hapworth, too."

Smitty reached forward, his eyes leaving Gorman long enough to frantically search for the ejection lever. Quickly he pushed it and the tape fell into his hand.

Gorman advanced toward him. "Give me the tape," he said softly.

Smitty stood and slipped the tape into his trouser

pocket. "No, Steve, I think *I'll* keep it." He fought to keep the tremor that was building throughout his body from showing in his voice.

"Give me the tape, Smitty." The voice was louder, more demanding.

"No, Steve." Smitty tried to make his voice firm yet relaxed. He swallowed and proceeded. "What's sauce for the goose is sauce for the gander, Steve. You have your photographs, and now I have my tape. Two can play the game, Steve. And up until now, it's been a little lopsided."

Gorman stopped before Smitty's desk, his face bearing an incredulous look. "What the hell are you talking about?" His voice, like his face, was filled with shock at the younger man's defiance.

Seizing the advantage, Smitty turned and walked casually around the desk, edging himself toward the open door to the hallway. He took the tape from his pocket and casually flipped it in the air, catching it quickly and restoring it to its place of safekeeping. "What's the tape worth to you, Steve?" he asked, moving himself closer to the door. "What's it worth to Mac Hunter?"

"You *are* a sneaky little bastard." There was something akin to admiration in Gorman's eyes. "But you're out of your league." Gorman spit out the words, and with them recovered his position of advantage. He stepped back quickly to block the doorway and stood there, legs outstretched and massive shoulders barring Smitty's escape route. A black look came over his face, and he stretched out his hand. "Give me that tape, Smitty."

Logan Smith understood the situation. He shrugged his shoulders and forced a grin to his face. "Sure, Steve," he said and walked toward the other man, his hand reaching into his pocket to retrieve the tape.

He quickly pulled his hand from his pocket and stuck

it forward toward Gorman's outstretched palm. As Gorman diverted his eyes to take the cassette, Smitty sprang forward, taking the man's hand and throwing a foot forward. In a classic judo movement, Steve Gorman was caught totally unprepared and found himself flying through the air. He collapsed on a chair and against the floor with a force that pushed the air from his lungs and left him motionless.

Smitty's karate training had served him well, and he knew he must end what he had begun. With a single movement, he was straddling Gorman's inert form and reaching down to take hold of the lapels on the other man's coat.

At last leaving Gorman's unconscious body prone on the floor of the office, Logan Smith grabbed for his jacket and ran down the hall. Not to the elevator, but to the stairwell and down several flights of stairs until he emerged on a lower floor and casually approached the elevator.

A short while later, he was in his car and driving up the exit ramp to freedom.

To freedom? His analytical mind told him otherwise. To momentary freedom, at least—a chance to think, to plan a course of action. A chance at last to exonerate himself in Rick Craig's eyes. And in his own, as well.

And so he drove. And thought. And by late afternoon he had devised a course of action.

Rick Craig stalked down the corridor of the hotel. He jabbed a key at the door of his room and slammed it behind him, stripping off his suit coat and throwing it on the bed.

Walking to the chair, he threw himself down and stretched his arm to look at his wristwatch.

Eleven-thirty. The evening was gone, and with it his

plans to spend it with Suzanne. First it had been Laura, unnecessarily prolonging the interviews by demanding that they see, once again, the applicant Joe Martin—the photographer they had eventually hired. And then it had been Joe Roth, appearing from out of nowhere and insisting that the three of them join him for dinner to discuss the marketing plan and creative program that Laura had already set into motion for The Press.

And finally it had been Suzanne herself. When he had taken her home, she had declined his offers of a nightcap. And when he had taken her to the door, she had stated firmly that the Café Carmichael was closed for the evening.

He walked to the window of the hotel room and, with a frustrated jerk of his hand, he drew the heavy drapes apart and stood looking over the lights of the city. The traffic raced along the streets below—tiny, antlike people who moved about, doing their individual thing, lost amidst the hubbub in their own lives, their own problems.

Alone, he thought. We're *all* alone. Alone in a crowd. Here, in a city of millions of people, he stood, like most of them, alone and lonely.

Standing there, his legs spread apart and hands shoved into his pockets, his shoulders jerked involuntarily upward in a gesture of futility. With a forced determination, he moved back into the center of the room. His fingers pulled at the knot of his tie and he began to undress for bed.

He extinguished the lights except for the lamp beside the bed, and threw back the spread and blanket. Piling the pillows on top of each other, he turned to his attaché case and Paul Prescott's book.

His hands felt under the folders still stuffed with applications, but his fingers encountered only the leather lining of the case. Using both hands, he searched again for the slender volume. Finally he brought the case to the bed with him, setting it on his knees and sorting through its contents more thoroughly. And then the realization struck him. The book was gone.

He must have left it at The Press, he thought. But he remembered putting it back in his case, remembered scanning the room when they had finally left. And the conference table had been bare.

He set the case aside and went to the closet to his trench coat, feeling inside its roomy pockets to see if he might have slipped it there. But as his hands groped against the poplin fabric, he knew he would find nothing.

I know I had it, he told himself. Both Laura and Suzanne saw it, commented on it.

Both Laura and Suzanne. Both women knew that he had the Prescott book. And other than Laura and Suzanne, only one other person knew about the book: Dan Osborne.

Both Laura and Suzanne. Then one of them must have taken it from his case. But which one? And why?

He was dressed now and on the street, walking and mulling over a perplexing question: why would anyone remove the book from his briefcase? And he could reach only one answer: someone wanted to prevent his reading the book.

But why? Why would anyone care? Why would someone want to prevent his exposure to Paul Prescott's theories of mind control? What possible bearing could it have on his life?

He came to an intersection, and as he waited for the light to change, another thought came to him, a thought more disturbing in its way than the other. He realized that he could not clearly remember—in fact, had hardly been able to understand—the premises that the book set forth.

He walked on, searching his memory for a key to the question. A phrase returned to his mind, the same phrase that had demanded his attention earlier in the day.

"The human mind can be molded, manipulated, almost totally controlled."

Prescott had stated the fact simply, he remembered. Had supported it with documented research activity. And earlier Rick had absorbed the phrase with intellectual interest. Now, as the words returned to him, the circumstances made them ominous.

The unconscious mind, he remembered, and then corrected himself. The *subconscious* mind. That was the key, the whole premise. The subconscious mind can accept thoughts and ideas that the conscious mind might not accept. Or which the conscious mind might reject if it were aware of them.

He remembered Prescott's discussion of the "popcorn experiment" of the Fifties, remembered vaguely his own awareness of the national notoriety that it caused. Abbreviated messages had been inserted in motion picture film—messages so brief that the conscious eye didn't register them, that the conscious mind didn't comprehend. Subliminal messages. But the subconscious mind *had* received the messages and had responded by telling the viewer that he was hungry, thirsty. And inexplicably hundreds of moviegoers had risen from their seats and gone to the concession stand to buy popcorn and soft drinks.

Prescott had discussed techniques far more sophisticated than those primitive efforts, had dealt with far more insidious ideas, with thoughts of mind-bending proportions.

Motion pictures. And television. Some of it was coming back to him, some of the techniques that Rick's professional training allowed him to understand. Entire sequences or phrases or motivational suggestions could be passed along to the subconscious—messages that were not evident to the conscious mind of the viewer, messages that were virtually invisible through the control of light intensity. But messages that could be read by the subconscious mind. And acted upon.

And hidden messages could be placed on the printed page, Rick remembered now. Messages embedded into the regular photograph or artwork, messages not visible to the naked eye but visible to the subconscious mind.

And the ear. It worked with the ear as well, according to Prescott. Subaudible stimulation, he called it. Sounds that worked with the human ear in the same way as the high-frequency whistle that had long been used to silently summon guard dogs.

He had found it interesting, Rick recalled as he walked. Interesting, but not particularly pertinent. And even now as he played the academic theories back through his mind, he could find no particular pertinence to himself, to Collins & Craig. But if there were not a link, then why had the book been taken?

His mind was still racing when he rounded a corner and saw the spotlighted facade of the Plaza looming before him. He stopped, staring at it in fascination.

The Plaza. Again. It was uncanny how it wove in and out of all of his days in New York, how it had become an inextricable part of his life.

He approached the hotel, walking more slowly now, the questions that had filled his mind lessened somewhat by its presence. Old memories flooded through his brain. He reached the fountain and stopped a moment. On impulse he approached the side entrance and climbed the steps.

Inside the late evening crowd seemed oblivious to the hour. Violin music flooded the Palm Court, waiters hustled back and forth to serve the varied assortment of people who sat there. Guests mingled around the marble columns of the perimeter, pausing to inspect the merchandise displayed in the tiny boutiques. Men in black tie and women in long gowns hurried past him, intent on reclaiming their cars and embarking on the long drive back to the suburbs.

Rick paused a moment at the entrance to the court, deliberating. Finally he approached the *maitre d'*. Perhaps a cup of coffee would help clear his mind.

Before he could be seated, he heard a voice calling out from somewhere. Along with the *maitre d'* and the others milling around him, Rick turned his head toward the lobby, trying to discern the words of the angry guest.

"Get your hands off me!" The voice was closer now, the words more apparent. "This is an outrage. Get your hands off me, I told you."

Every head in the sprawling room was turned, trying to spot the source of the disturbance. The violinist kept bravely about his task, but the low murmur of conversation had stopped. And still the words of indignation kept flowing.

"I'm not ready to go home. And if I were, I'd be perfectly capable of getting there myself. Without your help."

Rick smiled. An imbiber who had strayed into the vineyard a little too far, he guessed, and dismissed it from his mind.

But then the source of the words appeared around the corner of the court, and the smile faded from his face. Walking toward him with a crimson flush covering his face and a uniformed chauffeur holding staunchly to his elbow, was Paul Prescott.

Rick watched in amazement as the two men came closer. He saw the chauffeur guiding Prescott through the crowd, more forcibly now, and saw Prescott react. Suddenly stopping, shaking the other man's grip from his arm, he straightened his tie, ran a hand over his long silver hair, and spoke again, in a loud defiant voice.

"I believe I'll stop here at the Palm Court for a spot of brandy."

The chauffeur grasped his arm again, moving him forward against his will, speaking quietly into his ear. But his words brought another outraged display of indignation.

"Leave me alone. I'm not ready to leave. And I don't give a good goddamn *what* Mr. Hunter says!"

The words electrified Rick as the significance of the scene shot through his mind. Paul Prescott. Here. Tonight. With a chauffeur who had been sent to retrieve him. Mac Hunter's chauffeur.

Rick saw the chauffeur forcibly lead Prescott toward the side entrance, and found himself watching, staring unashamedly after them. And then Rick, too, approached the side entrance and pushed through the revolving door.

They were still standing at the top of the steps and Rick drew to one side in the shadow of one of the massive columns. The chauffeur was angry now, tired of maintaining the reserve he had exhibited inside. He took Prescott by the shoulders and shook him, grabbing his arm again and pulling him down the steps. The older man stumbled and almost fell, but the chauffeur had him in such a ferocious grip that he was literally dragged toward a limousine waiting at the curb. As they approached the rear door Prescott broke away and started to run into the street, but the younger man was after him and had him again. With an exclamation, he yanked the door open and threw the old man into the back seat.

In the brief moment that the interior lights flashed on, Rick saw that the two men were not alone. Another passenger was in the back seat, reaching out a jeweled hand to help pull Prescott into the car.

It was a woman. Rick couldn't see her face—only the back of a sleek, fashionable head with long dark hair pulled back into a knot—and he shook his head in confusion. Was his mind playing tricks on him, or was she vaguely familiar?

The car screeched away, but Rick remained in the shadow of the building, his mind deadened by a numbing question. Paul Prescott. Mac Hunter. A woman. And, tieing all of them to him, the book. Paul Prescott's book.

I wonder who she is? his mind dully asked.

Damn, he thought, viciously grinding out the cigarette in the flimsy hotel ashtray. Damn. I hate being made a fool of.

Rick leaned forward and jerked the top off the carafe, sloshing black coffee into the cup in front of him and taking a quick gulp.

He turned toward the window, his eyes searching the shadowy gray outline of the Manhattan skyline, and reviewed the facts, as skimpy as they were.

And the facts added up to exactly nothing.

He lit another cigarette and realized instantly how foul it tasted. He tossed it into the coffee cup, staring with disgust at the soggy mess before him. Somehow his action broke the intensity of his concentration and his rigid body gave way and he slumped back into the chair.

He felt the tiredness now, the aching, exhausting tiredness. He rubbed his eyes, gritty from a sleepless night, and his head fell back against the chair. The wave of fatigue coursed through his body, erasing the vision of a dark-haired woman in the back of Mac Hunter's limousine.

With great effort he heaved himself out of the chair, pausing only to close the heavy drapes. His fingertips tugged at the buttons of his shirt and he dropped it where it fell. His hands gripped his belt and he stepped out of the trousers that fell to the floor, leaving them in a heap beside the bed.

He moved into the bathroom and turned the shower to "hot" and stepped under its restorative spray.

As the sound of the shower obliterated all other sounds in the room, the telephone cried out angrily, insistently, again and again until finally it became silent.

Rick emerged from the bathroom, his body still glistening with water. The towel fell to the floor, to join his clothes in a tangled mess, and he threw himself across the bed to sleep.

Logan Smith sat on the small boat dock watching dawn gradually illuminate the sky, seeing the familiar shapes of the lake slowly take substance and form. The night sounds slowly gave way to the silence that always preceded another day.

It's time to get moving, he told himself. Gorman has probably already matched up the phone number with the location of the cabin, already knows where I am.

Yet he continued to sit motionless.

I wonder how Gorman got the number up here? he asked himself. I told Susan not to tell anyone I was here. Only Rick. But Gorman's smart. He found a way to get the number. He'll find out where the cabin's located, too. And he'll probably be here before long.

But still he sat transfixed with the tranquil scene before him, occupied with his own thoughts.

I wonder what it means? I wonder what they're up to? I wonder what Anthony Hapworth was really trying to tell Diana . . .

Smitty shook his head, the questions again going unanswered as they had since the afternoon before.

At least the tape is safe, he assured himself. At least Rick will have a chance to hear it. If something happens to me, someone will know.

A worry crossed his mind. *If* Rick gets it. I wish I could have located him. I tried all night, even called just a few minutes ago. He should have been back in his room by now. But I'll just have to trust that he'll get the tape. And my letter.

Somewhere far away a faint sound broke through the stillness around him. Smitty cocked his head toward the roadway, listening. Finally he could discern the sound more clearly, coming closer. The sound of an automobile, driving over the gravel road at a breakneck speed.

He jumped to his feet and grabbed his suit coat from the end of the dock, taking off at a fast trot for his own car. Midway he stopped, then resumed his course at a more leisurely pace.

I'm tired of running, he told himself, tired of hiding. And the tape is safe. What else can Gorman do to me?

As he reached his car, he saw a small white Mustang barrel around the bend in the road and roar into the driveway to the cabin.

A shrill sound shot through Rick's hotel room and through his mind. He lay motionless, and the phone rang again. And again. He pulled it to his mouth and answered it.

"Rick?" It was Jay Collins' voice. "Thank God, I caught you before you left. You've got to come home, Rick. As soon as you can." He paused, and then plunged ahead. "Smitty is missing. His wife thinks he's dead."

Chapter 4

"Susan was awfully anxious to see you," Jay Collins told him as they pulled away from the terminal building and headed through the dusk toward Atlanta. "When she first called me about Smitty, she asked for you in particular. That's when I called you in New York."

Collins continued to speak, briefing him on Logan Smith's disappearance as they drove to Smitty's home.

Smitty had left the office abruptly sometime after lunch on Friday. No one had seen him leave. He had called Susan late in the afternoon to say that he was going to spend the night at their cabin at the lake, that he wanted to think out a problem at the office. He hadn't bothered to change clothes, hadn't packed any overnight gear. That evening, according to Susan, he had called again to say he'd arrived safely. And that was the last contact she had had with him.

After trying to reach him repeatedly, she had driven to the lake the next afternoon. The cabin was deserted, Smitty's car parked beside it, the keys still in the ignition. A rowboat was floating at random on the lake. The police were called, and after their investigation they suspected accidental drowning.

Now as they pulled into the familiar neighborhood where Smitty lived, Collins parked at a curb already crowded with cars. The two men walked across the lawn to the front door and rang. A woman answered the door and led them into a room filled with people.

When Susan Smith saw him, she threw herself into Rick's arms and sobbed quietly against his shoulder. Finally she calmed herself. Looking about her almost furtively, she took his hand and pulled him after her into the privacy of a bedroom.

"Rick," she said, "I had to talk to you alone. Did you ever reach Smitty yesterday afternoon? Do you know where he is?"

Rick looked at her, shaking his head in confusion.

"Did you talk to him, Rick? After you called the house for him?"

"I didn't call the house for Smitty, Susan."

"But you must have. I took the call myself. The operator said it was person-to-person for Smitty. From Rick Craig. And I gave the operator the number at the cabin . . ."

Again Rick shook his head. "I didn't call him, Susan. I don't know what you're talking about."

"But someone did—" She broke off with a gasp. "*Someone* did, Rick. And I gave them the number." A growing realization was on her face. "I gave them the number. I told them where he was. I did it. Even though he told me not to tell *anyone* where he was. 'Don't tell anyone.' That's what he told me. 'Don't tell anyone where I am, except for Rick.' " Susan broke into quiet sobs again. "He was afraid. He was hiding from someone. And I did it to him. I told them where he was."

Rick put his arms around her consolingly. But his voice was firm. "Listen to me, Susan. Get control of yourself. This is important. Who, Susan? Who was he hiding from? Who was he afraid of?"

"I don't know, Rick." She had stopped crying, and her voice was calmer. "I don't know. He said to say he was out of town on business if anyone called for him. Except you. And there were a couple of calls. One of the secretaries at the office. And then a man. I didn't recognize his voice, and he wouldn't leave a name. And then the long distance operator."

Rick nodded, realizing that she knew nothing more. He tried desperately to put the events into some context. "Did he say anything else, Susan?"

"Nothing." She paused, turning to go back to the others. "Except—" She paused again, remembering. "Except one thing. He said, 'I may have sold my stock, but by God I haven't sold my soul.' What is it, Rick? What's going on?"

She looked at him with a question in her eyes, but Rick could only shake his head. He joined her at the door to the hallway.

"We'll find him, Susan," he told her, his voice filled with false optimism.

"Maybe so, Rick. God only knows that I hope so. But I can tell you one thing for certain. Smitty didn't drown accidentally. And when the police drag the lake, they won't find him. Because he didn't go out on that lake."

Rick looked at her inquiringly, and she continued in a firm voice. "Don't you see, Rick? They haven't found any of his clothing. They didn't find his jacket. And Smitty would never have gone out on the lake in his suit coat." She nodded, assured that she was right. "He was at the cabin. But he's not there any longer."

Jay Collins pulled into the lighted driveway of Rick's apartment building and stuck out his hand. "Stay on top of it, will you, Rick? Do whatever you can for Susan. I've got to catch a seven o'clock flight for New York in the morning, and I'll be gone all week."

Rick vaguely nodded his agreement. His thoughts so preoccupied him that he had not noticed Collins' outstretched hand, and he made no effort to get out of the car. He sat there in silence, staring into the darkness that surrounded them. Suddenly he felt Collins' hand slapping him on the shoulder.

"Buck up, pal. It's a tough deal, but you can't let it get you down." Collins' voice was unnecessarily hearty, his manner too solicitous, and Rick opened his mouth to tell him so. But Collins was talking again.

"Smitty's been acting so strange lately that I should have realized that he wasn't himself. But I had no idea that he'd go this far. Jesus! Suicide!"

"Suicide?" Rick's reaction was instantaneous. "Surely you don't think Smitty committed suicide! He isn't the type—"

"What else is there to think? The police—"

"To hell with the police. They won't find his body." Susan's words echoed in his ears. *"They've* done something with him, but I pray to God that they haven't killed him."

"They? Who are 'they'? What the hell are you talking about?"

"Hunter. And Gorman."

"Hunter and Gorman? Good God, Rick, you're out of your mind. I knew you didn't like the new set-up, that you didn't get along with Gorman, but I didn't know you'd become paranoid—"

"I'm not paranoid, Jay. I'm more lucid than I've ever been in my life. Things are going on that you can hardly believe. I couldn't believe them, either, until—" Rick stopped, then drew a deep breath and plunged forth. "Until someone tried to kill me last Thursday evening."

". . . that's all that I know." Rick had poured out the whole fantastic story to a silent Jay Collins, and he was still talking. "Part of it is factual—I can prove it. But a lot of it can't be proved. At least not yet. But, Jay, I know they're behind Smitty's disappearance. I know it. We've got to go to the police and tell them—"

"Go to the police? With *that* story? God*damn,* Rick, you're crazier than I thought you were. You haven't got a shred of proof, except that someone hit Joe Greenberg and hospitalized him. And that somebody totally different—probably some drunk—came close to hitting you. All the rest of it sounds like something out of a bad suspense novel."

"Maybe. I can't prove anything, as I said. But we can at least slow them down. We can let them know that we're on top of their plot. We can get them out of the agency and own our own souls again. And maybe—*maybe*—we can find Smitty before they do anything. I can't fight them alone, Jay. I need your help. What do you say?"

Collins sat in the darkness without answering. The silence dragged on until the moments seemed interminable to Rick and finally he repeated his question.

"Well, Jay, what do you say?"

Collins spoke at last, in a measured, controlled voice. "If you had a shred of evidence, if you knew anything factual about Smitty's disappearance, I'd do anything to help him. But you don't. And, frankly, Rick, I don't believe a word of what you're saying. No. I won't go to the police with you. And I hope you won't go to them alone. Because they'll think you're crazier than a loon."

He fell silent a moment before speaking again. "It's getting late, Rick. I'd better be going." He turned the key in the ignition and the engine sprang to life.

Without a word, Rick Craig opened the door and started to step to the curb. But Jay Collins' voice stopped him.

"One more thing, Rick. You said something a moment ago about getting them out of the agency, about owning our own souls again. Make no mistake about it,

Rick. *I don't want them out of the agency.* I like what I have and I intend to keep it. To get even more if I can. And neither you nor anyone else is going to screw it up. Do you understand, Rick? Don't try to screw up my deal."

The car pulled away with a screech and Rick stared at the taillights as they disappeared around a corner. A flood of bitterness came over him.

Goodbye, Jay, he said silently.

Inside the apartment building Rick made his way through the lobby, stopping by habit at the lobby mailbox to pick up his mail. As he swung the door of the box open, he saw a solitary envelope awaiting him. Reaching into the box he pulled it out to inspect it. A local postmark, he noted—and his name and address written in a neat, formal script. He puzzled over it for a moment before he realized that the handwriting was a form that he customarily saw on financial documents at the agency.

The envelope was from Logan Smith.

His natural impulse was to rip it open, but he contained himself until he was in the privacy of his own apartment. There he dropped his luggage inside the front door and walked quickly to a chair, flicking on a lamp beside him. He tore open the envelope and pulled out the contents: a sheet of yellow legal paper wrapped around a small cassette tape.

"Dear Rick," Smitty's meticulous handwriting began. "It's critical that I get this cassette into your hands before they find me. If I don't, Gorman will destroy it—destroy the evidence. So I'm doing the only thing I can think of that's safe. I'm dropping it in the post office. It'll be safe there.

"Gorman is out to get me because I discovered this tape in Diana Malloy's recorder, and I listened to it. Gorman heard it, too, and I had to fight him to get away. Because now I know too much.

"Actually, I don't *know* anything. Nothing specific. Just that something is wrong at the agency—something that we don't know about. Something involving Anthony Hapworth. And Gorman, and Mac Hunter, too. And I don't know who else. They're doing it behind our backs, and they're playing for keeps. I've known that ever since that night on the island, but I've been afraid to cross them.

"You saw me with Steve Gorman that night, but you didn't know what was going on. You thought Gorman bribed me, but actually he blackmailed me. It was all very carefully planned. I realize that, now. He set me up on New Year's, when we were in New York. I went to a groupie bar in the Village. I was looking for a little action, and this guy at the bar said he knew some girls and we could all go to his apartment for a group-sex thing. But somehow, after the action started, the girls moved out of sight long enough for someone to take a picture of me—with the man. Honest to God, I'm not that way—but the pictures made it look awful. And that night in the beach house, Gorman showed me the prints. Told me that unless I sold my stock he'd make prints and send them to all of our clients. At first I didn't believe him. Then I realized he was dead serious. *To our clients*—think about it! That was the insidious thing about it—not show them to Susan, or to you and Jay, but to every client of Collins & Craig. He wouldn't ruin me alone, he'd ruin the entire agency. The whole thing was sick—but Gorman *is* sick. Really sick, Rick.

"Well, that's the story. All of it that I know. I'm going to go up to my cabin at the lake, lie low up there for a day or two. Maybe it will all blow over. Maybe not. I can take care of myself in a fair fight—I'm not worried about that. But Gorman doesn't fight fair. Whatever happens, I want you to have the tape. And I want you to find out what's going on.

"Good luck—to both of us. I'm sure everything will be all right, but if something *should* happen to me, tell my girls that their father wasn't ever a coward."

Rick Craig exhaled an enormous breath as he finished reading the words in front of him. His brows were crimped together in a frown and he started again at the beginning, reading Smitty's confession one more time. Then, with a shake of his head, he stood and moved to his desk to remove a tape recorder. Plugging it into the wall, he inserted the cassette and pushed the "on" switch. Diana Malloy's voice spoke to him clearly through the amplifier.

"Diana Malloy . . ."

Rick leaned forward to adjust the volume as a man's voice joined the conversation—Anthony Hapworth, obviously—and he settled back to listen to the words being exchanged by the Congressman and his mistress.

He was about to touch the "forward" button, anxious to reach the meat of the tape, when a phrase of Hapworth's caught his attention.

". . . I'm going to be President of the United States, Diana. President! First, I'm going to win all the primaries and gain control of the delegates. Then I'm going to get the nomination at the convention this summer. *And then I'm going to be elected.* And the voters are never going to know what happened. They're never going to know that we've meddled with their minds . . ."

Rick listened intently, anxious for Hapworth to spell out the details of the scheme, to outline the mechanics of how they intended to accomplish their mission. He heard Hapworth begin.

". . . we'll do it with advertising. Funny advertising—advertising that tells you to do something, but you're not even aware that you've been told. With the regular campaign advertising, sure. But with secret advertising, too. Invisible ads. Ads for other products . . . like the new Phoenix Press campaign." Hapworth chuckled. "And the new television spots for FRESH! That'd blow their minds if they knew—"

The Press. That didn't surprise him, Rick realized. In the back of his mind he'd known that something was amiss, had been since the very beginning. But FRESH! He knew Hunter had taken control of the company, but until now he hadn't realized the full ramifications.

FRESH! And The Press. Those bastards were meddling, somehow, with the creative messages he'd worked so hard to produce. He felt his temper rising, his anger beginning to blot out the words on the tape.

But then his own name brought him back to the voices on the tape.

". . . Rick Craig's causing a problem. Craig asks too many questions. He's no pushover, like Jay Collins has been. Hell, all we needed was a respectable front. How else do you think Collins & Craig got The Press? And FRESH!? Because Hunter wanted them to have it—"

There was a pause, punctuated by Hapworth's sudden exclamation. "Jesus! What am I doing? I'm letting you sweet-talk all of the high-level secrets out of me. I shouldn't have told you any of this . . ."

The fool, Rick thought. The absolute fool, spilling his guts to Diana. Discussing such unbelievably sensitive information on the telephone. But then Diana's words, her petulant tone soaked through to his consciousness and he realized: Hapworth was weak. Whether it be for Diana's sexual favors or the grandiose promises of Maxwell Hunter, Anthony Hapworth was weak. He had to be weak, weak enough to be completely controlled by Hunter. By Gorman, even. If he wasn't, if he wasn't controllable, they wouldn't have chosen him.

He focused back on the tape and heard Diana again, her voice wheedling, demanding.

"Hap, when were you in Los Angeles?"
"Three weeks ago. Why?"
"Do you have another girlfriend there?"
"Hell, no. I haven't got the time."
"Then how do you explain this note you left on my dresser the last time you stayed with me?"
"What note?"
"Oh, don't act so innocent, Hap. You know which note. It had a girl's name on it. And a phone number in Los Angeles."
"Diana, what in the hell are you talking about?"
"You ought to know!"
"I swear to God that I don't know what you're talking about. What girl? What number?"
"Minerva. That's her name. And the note had a Los Angeles phone number. And some initials . . . VTR . . . something like that. What are you up to, Hap? Maybe I don't want to see you tonight if you've got another girl . . ."
There was a pause in the conversation, and when Hapworth's voice came into the room again it was obvious that it was strained.
"It's nothing, Diana."
"Like hell it's nothing—"
"It's *nothing,* Diana! Forget it. Drop the subject. It's none of your business . . . I've got to go. They're calling my flight."
"Who is Minerva, Hap? Who is she?"
"Forget it, Diana."
"I won't forget it. Who is she? What are you up to?"
"Diana, you've stumbled on something that you shouldn't know. For your own good."
"I want to know. If it has to do with business, maybe I should ask Steve Gorman. Maybe he'll know—"
"No! For God's sake, Diana, keep your mouth shut about it. It could cause you big trouble. For God's sake

don't mention it to Gorman."

"Then tell me who she is."

Hapworth's voice became more urgent. "Minerva is a woman—but it's also a code name. It's a code name that I use in Los Angeles, sometimes. That others use. To identify members of the team. It's used to gain admittance to a motion picture studio. I need to know that name, but you don't. You don't ever need to know that name. You ought to forget it. And for God's sake, never use it around the office. *Never.*" He paused. "Oh my God, there's the final call on my flight. I'll see you in a couple of hours." Again he paused. His final comment was terse and insistent. *"Diana, forget about Minerva."*

Rick rewound the tape and played it again. And again. And then he sat in the solitude of his apartment and sorted out the message.

Congressman Anthony Hapworth, the darling of the conservatives. President of the United States. Collins & Craig tied to his campaign. Assured of election because of advertising. Mac Hunter controlling his campaign, pulling the strings. And Gorman.

And Smitty had stumbled onto it, had uncovered it. Rick reflected. Funny advertising, Hapworth had called it. Paul Prescott, Rick realized, would have called it subliminal advertising.

Rick shook his head in dismay as other threads of the conversation replayed themselves in his mind . . *FRESH! . . . The Phoenix Press . . . how do you think Collins & Craig got that account? . . . a respectable front.*

While the elements of the scheme began to take form in his mind, his dismay slowly turned into anger. They were making a fool of him, trying to pull off a massive con job, trying to do it through Collins & Craig—

Suddenly his mind turned away from the voices on the tape, returned to the yellow sheet of paper beside the recorder. Smitty. What had happened to him? And he realized that he knew nothing more than he had known earlier.

Gorman had, in fact, apprehended Smitty. That much seemed certain. But nothing in the handwritten note, nothing on the tape lent a clue as to his whereabouts, his condition.

What was it Jay Collins had just said? "If you had a shred of evidence." And now there was proof to back up supposition. Rick started for the telephone, ready to tell Collins the latest development, to enlist his aid.

But he stopped. Would Collins really assist him? Or would his lust for power emasculate him? Rick shook his head.

The police. All he could do was go to the police, and again he started for the phone. But again he stopped. If Smitty *is* alive, he told himself, they have him stashed away somewhere. And if I blow the whistle, I could be forcing their hand.

He sank back into the chair, absorbed in his thoughts. At last he stood and walked across the room to his desk, switching on the small lamp and searching through his address book. He picked up the phone and dialed a number and, amazingly, heard Dan Osborne's voice at the other end of the line.

"Dan? I guess the third time is a charm. I need you again. How soon can you be in Atlanta?"

Part IV

Chapter 1

Dan Osborne sprawled on the couch in Rick Craig's living room. He leaned forward to take a drink of coffee, his broad forearm straining uncomfortably against the white dress shirt. One finger tugged unconsciously against the tie that circled his neck, but he made no further move to loosen it. His attention was riveted to the tape recorder that sat before them.

But finally, with a grunt of irritation, he jumped to his feet, tearing away the tie and unbuttoning the confining shirt. As he attacked the sleeves, rolling each to a point past his elbows, he kicked off his shoes and threw himself back into a corner of the couch.

"Well, ol' buddy, I guess you've got your answer." His voice was soft and thoughtful, but the words spilled into the silence of the room and brought a puzzled look from Rick Craig. "You wanted to know why Mac Hunter wanted to buy your agency. Now you know."

"Goddamnit, Dan, I don't know *anything.* I've just got a vague idea of what they're doing—"

"You know a helluva lot more than you *did.*" He held up a clenched fist extending a blunt finger. "First, you know why they needed Collins & Craig. Second, you know that Paul Prescott is involved in the whole mess, and Paul Prescott's a *very* smart man—not a half-assed photographer or writer like you or me, but a real brain man. And he's got Hunter's money behind him. And a whole team of people."

"Including Minerva." Rick shook his head bitterly. "One of the 'women in my life' has played me for a fool. And when I find out which one . . ."

Osborne looked at him in silence for a moment, a troubled look on his face. He finally spoke, softly, almost gently. "You're missing the point, Rick." Rick looked at him, a question mirrored on his face, and Osborne continued. "You're taking this personally, Rick. You're too close to the forest. They're not playing *you* for a fool. Don't you see? They're playing America for a fool. They're going after the Presidency—*after the Presidency,* Rick! Granted, in the last few years we've had some real losers, but they're trying to foist *Anthony Hapworth* off on us." Osborne's voice was incredulous. "A two-bit rightwinger with a goddamn communications czar pulling the strings. *Damn!*"

A growing anger had filled Osborne's voice, but he suddenly lapsed back into a thoughtful mood. "And no matter how absurd it sounds—using soft drink television commercials to implant a subliminal message—no matter how silly it sounds, *they wouldn't be this far into it if they didn't know it would work.*

"Hell, Paul Prescott *knows* it will work. I saw him in Aspen, Rick, talked with him. And I heard him address a group of other professional men—men who understood him, men who didn't question him. And he said that he knew, beyond a shadow of a doubt, that the human mind can be motivated with subconscious messages."

Anger began to light up Osborne's eyes again. "Goddamn! I wish we knew how they do it. I wish that broad Minerva hadn't stolen the book—"

"And it's the *only* book," Rick interrupted. "At least

the only copy I can find. That was the first thing I thought of. I've tried the library, talked to a couple of professors at the medical school. Even called Johns Hopkins. They remember the book, remember the incident. The book was recalled. Recalled by the author, by Paul Prescott. One of the guys I talked with—a neurosurgeon at Johns Hopkins—told me that Prescott made quite a scene when they couldn't find their copy. Prescott wrote them, called, finally appeared in person to demand that they find the book and return it."

Rick paused a moment, then directed a question to Osborne. "If he made such a big thing about getting all of the copies back, how the hell did he let you keep your copy?"

Osborne chuckled. "Because he didn't know he gave it to me. He was dead drunk. Gave me the copy after a cocktail party one evening and left Aspen the next day before I ever saw him again."

Rick pondered the matter. "The only other copy that I've ever seen was in Steve Gorman's desk. But I have the feeling that it's been locked in Mac Hunter's vault by now." A frown came over his face. "The most unfortunate thing about the whole situation is that I never got a chance to finish it. Dan, do you remember—"

"Not much of it," Osborne replied. "It's very heavy. Scholarly. Hard to follow. All I remember is that they can plant a subliminal image that the naked eye can't see. It's invisible. But the subconscious can see it, and if it's repeated often enough, the subconscious will act on it. They can use almost any medium—radio, newspaper, magazines—"

Rick snapped his fingers. "The FRESH! proof. It was for newspapers in New Hampshire. Something must have been wrong with it, something that could be detected. That's why they damned near killed Joe Greenberg to get it back."

Osborne nodded and went on. "But it's most effective in motion pictures or television. They use trigger words and the viewer associates those words with the regular message he sees on the screen. Or they can produce an entirely different commercial—an erotic scene, for example—and they can play it *under* the regular message. And the bitch of it is that since you can't ever see it, you can't ever prove it. The subliminal film is invisible to the naked eye, even under ultraviolet light."

Rick sighed. "Then Hapworth was right. There's absolutely no way to prove it." He shook his head in anger. "And who in the hell would believe you without proof? The police? The FBI? The other candidates? The opposition party? Hell, their own skirts aren't so clean. They'd probably be more interested in how to copy the technique than in putting a stop to it."

"The press?" Osborne tossed out tentatively.

Rick thought a moment. "Maybe. So long as you weren't stepping on *their* toes. So long as you weren't exposing one of their darlings. But you'd have to offer proof positive before they'd believe you. And there's no way to prove it."

"Not unless you catch 'em in the act," Osborne retorted. He fell silent a moment, lost in thought. Then he repeated himself slowly, thoughtfully. "Not unless you catch 'em in the act. Not unless you catch an engraver etching a plate—"

Rick picked up the line of thought. "The engraver. It's a firm called Fine Arts Engraving in New York. Gorman demanded that we use Fine Arts. That's why Joe Greenberg was fired—" He stopped suddenly, the excitement drained from him. "But after all the furor over the FRESH! proof, you can rest assured they've got top security in New York."

Osborne tried another approach. "What about the TV spots? Or the new spots for The Press?"

"They're done in LA," Rick answered. "That's the VTR that Hapworth mentions—VTR Studios. They're probably not so sensitive out there." He stopped, remembering. "That's where Laura and I were, working with Brett Stanley. She went back there, while I was in Aspen. Maybe she set the whole thing up—"

"Or maybe it's Brett Stanley or somebody inside his studio. It's interesting, though, that Laura has a close connection with Stanley." He paused, thinking. "What about Suzanne? Does she have any connection with Stanley?"

"Not that I know of, but I'll damned sure find out."

The two men lapsed into silence as the first rays of the early morning sun crept through the windows into the apartment. Finally Osborne broke the silence. "What are you going to do about Smitty?" he asked quietly.

"I'd like to go to the police. Tell them what I know. Prefer charges against Steve Gorman for kidnapping, for attempted murder, whatever." Rick spoke matter-of-factly, his voice not reflecting the intensity of his feelings for Gorman.

"I don't believe I'd do that, ol' buddy."

Rick looked at him sharply. "I don't intend to. I told you what I'd *like* to do. But if I did that I might force them to do something to Smitty. And I can't risk doing that."

Osborne was watching him, waiting for him to continue.

"It's not likely that they've done anything to Smitty," Rick went on, "other than rough him up, keep him locked up somewhere until they can figure out a more permanent solution. I don't think Hunter is into murder. Gorman might be, but Hunter calls the shots. But if I stir up the water, it might push Gorman off the edge. He might try another hit-and-run. This time on Smitty. But even if it didn't force them to do anything violent, it would force them to go underground and make it totally impossible for us to catch them with any evidence."

"You're right," Osborne said after a moment. "Let's don't tip our hand. Do everything you can to locate Smitty, but keep it business as usual. I've got another plan. It wouldn't do any good for me to hang around Atlanta, so I think I'll take myself a little trip."

He sprang up and walked to his bedraggled suitcase, still standing in the middle of the room. Opening it, he began to throw faded denims on the floor followed by a disreputable pair of boots. He stood again and turned to face Rick, unbuttoning the white shirt and stripping it from his lean torso. Unbuckling his belt, he stepped out of his pants and stood there in his shorts and socks.

"What the hell are you doing?" Rick demanded.

Grabbing a toilet kit from the bag, Osborne grinned at him. "I'm getting out my hippie clothes. If you'll lead me to the shower, I'll be on my way."

"What are you talking about, Dan? Where are you going?"

Osborne's grin broadened. "I'm going on what may be the biggest flyer in my life. I'm going to Los Angeles," he answered. "And I'm going to tell 'em that Minerva sent me."

Chapter 2

Later that morning Rick sat at his desk looking over a layout, scanning the copy sheet that accompanied it. He realized that his eyes had moved over a page of typewritten words, but he hadn't the slightest comprehension of what the words said. With a frustrated sigh, he pushed the advertisement aside and turned to stare out the window.

"Business as usual," Dan had said, but it was proving an impossibility. It had ever since his arrival at the office after dropping Dan back at the terminal.

Smitty's disappearance had cast a gloom over the entire office. More than a gloom, he analyzed. More like a shroud of sorrow. It hung over the heads of all of them, each employee and every associate. From the receptionist to the delivery boy, from Jay Collins to Laura Talbott.

Laura. His mind went back to their encounter earlier that morning. She had entered his office announcing her concern over Smitty but covering it with her tiresome professional veneer. Rick had studied her face intently, searching for some indication of duplicity, listening for any telltale sound in her voice. Later he had watched fruitlessly for a trace of emotion when he had told her the police verdict: no body had been found and Logan

Smith was officially listed as a Missing Person.

With a sigh Rick pushed himself away from the desk and stood. He wandered out his office door into the hall, walking aimlessly, trying to mentally untangle the threads of the cobweb that was enmeshing him.

He walked into Smitty's office, still lost in his thoughts. There was the tape recorder—the one Smitty had been using when Gorman happened on him. What a turn of events, Rick thought. It was fate, he supposed, fate that caused Diana to leave the tape—

Diana. Diana Malloy, he thought with a start. He had forgotten about Diana. He whirled around and strode to the door to her office, whipping it open. But like Smitty's office, hers was dark and empty.

He stared at her vacant desk a moment, his mind beginning to function again, to push away the despondency that had settled over him. Diana. The missing link. She didn't know much: the tape told him that. But she might know something—

"Martha!" He was back at his secretary's desk. "Martha, where is Diana?"

"Sick again, I suppose," Martha sniffed. "Like she was on Thursday and Friday."

Thursday and Friday. And again today. Rick heard Hapworth's taped voice in his mind. *I'm coming home tonight, baby.* That would have been Wednesday. *Tell them you're sick . . . I'm taking you back to Miami for the weekend.* For the weekend. She should have been back at work this morning—

But of course not. Diana was as great a threat to Gorman as Logan Smith, as the tape itself. A feeling of dread came over Rick as he walked to his desk and flipped open his Personnel Directory, hastily dialing the number listed beside her name. Finally he slammed down the receiver.

Maybe she's still all right, he told himself as he hurried from the office. Maybe I can get to her before Gorman finds her.

"No, Mr. Craig, they didn't say where they were going. Miss Malloy was awful sick and the big guy—her brother, he said—was taking her home to recuperate."

"What did her brother look like?"

"Oh, he was a nice enough looking man," the apartment manager answered. "Big and tall. Real husky, you know. And blond. Kinda reddish hair. A big man. But I didn't see much resemblance between him and Miss Malloy—"

"Did he give you a name?"

"Why sure. Malloy. John Malloy. And I asked for a forwarding address—so I could send her deposit to her. But he said he'd write me when he knew which hospital she'd be in. They were in a big hurry, you know. Waiting for the ambulance and all. Matter of fact, I have the feeling that he hadn't even intended to tell me if I hadn't gone up there to check on a disturbance report. Lots of loud noises, sounds like furniture being broken. But Mr. Malloy, he said she had fainted and he had to drag her to her bed. And she was there, all right, I could hear her kind of moaning—"

"Did you see her?"

"Nope, not then. But later when I took the ambulance men up there, I sort of hung around. And when they carried her out on the stretcher, she was out like a light. Looked pretty sick to me."

"Mr. Hogan, do you remember the name of the ambulance company?"

"The name? Why, I don't think I noticed—"

"Think, Mr. Hogan," Rick persisted. It's very important."

"Well . . ." The old man's brows knit together as he concentrated. Finally he spoke again. "I'm sorry, Mr.

Craig. I just can't remember. They all look alike, you know. And they sound alike, too—wait a minute. Sure. I don't know what I was thinking of. They left me a card just in case I ever needed to call 'em again. Let's see if I can find it . . ."

The old man shuffled away. Rick Craig silently cursed to himself. He'd missed her, missed an encounter with Gorman, the chance to catch him in the act—

"Here you are. Primrose Ambulance Service. Funny name for an ambulance, isn't it? I ought to have remembered . . ."

"This is highly unusual, Craig." The man glared at him across the desktop. "We aren't required to divulge this kind of information without a court order." His eyes fell to the roll of bills in Rick Craig's hands, and he relaxed and leaned forward. "However, since it's an emergency and you're trying to locate a missing employee . . ."

He reached out to take a file folder from a stack on his desk. He opened and studied it for a moment.

"Yes, I remember now. We picked up two patients—at different locations—and took them to the Midtown Air Park—"

"Two patients?" Rick sat erect, surprise reflected in his face and his voice.

"That's right. A man and a woman—"

"A man? What was his name? Do you have the name?"

"Yeah. A Mr. John Smith." The man pursed his lips and looked at Rick. "Sounds phony, doesn't it?"

Rick nodded, thinking ahead. "Do you have a description of him?"

The man shook his head. "That's not part of our procedure." His eyes again fell to Rick's hands, and Rick peeled another bill from the others. "But Mike is here now—he was the driver. Let me see if he remembers."

Rick waited. It must have been Smitty. And it had only happened last night. Maybe Smitty was all right, maybe—

"OK. Mike picked up the woman first. Name listed as Jane Smith. She was an attractive redhead. Early twenties. Picked her up on Euclid Boulevard, the Plaza Towers. Her brother rode with her and then asked for a second pick-up." He consulted the folder. "On Homestead Way. The Homestead Court apartment complex."

Rick stared at him. Laura Talbott lived at the Homestead Court. Then with a rush of memory, he realized that Gorman had taken an apartment in the same complex when he moved to Atlanta.

"And the man—what did he look like?"

"Nondescript. Late twenties, early thirties. Dark brown hair. Had a stubble of a beard. He was unconscious. That's all Mike remembers."

Rick sighed. Nothing definite. The description fit Smitty, but it fit a thousand others, too. "And where did he take them?"

"I told you. To the Midtown Air Park. Right out on the runway. To a plane that was waiting. Mike and his assistant loaded the stretchers on the plane, strapped them down, and left. They must have been in a hurry. He said the plane was already taxiing out for takeoff before they got past the control tower."

Rick sighed again, more audibly. He stood, pressing the bills into the man's willing hand. "Thank you. If Mike remembers anything else, here's my card. I'd appreciate it if you would—"

His words were interrupted by the buzz of the intercom, and the man across from him took the receiver, listening. Finally he hung up. He looked Rick in the eye. "One more thing. It might help. The man—the patient —didn't have a shirt on. And Mike remembers a tattoo on his upper arm. On the biceps. USMC. That's all it said."

Rick Craig left the office with a feeling of jubilation. Smitty's tattoo. The one that had caused him so much embarrassment, the one he and a Marine buddy had recklessly, drunkenly inscribed on themselves the night they finished Boot Camp at Quantico.

Smitty was alive. But where was he?

A few hours later he still pondered that same question. He had spent a grueling session at the air park, begging and coercing them into a search of the previous evening's flight plans.

A Cessna, registered to The Miramar Corporation, had taken off at 9:28 P.M., its destination, Brunswick, Georgia.

Funny, he thought to himself. I wonder why I didn't think of it earlier. If I were Gorman, that's exactly where I would have taken him. To the island.

Then a feeling of dread settled over him. Now that I know where they've taken him, what am I going to do about it?

Chapter 3

"Shut up!"

Steve Gorman's voice shot through the room, stilling the volley of abusive words that Mac Hunter was heaping upon him, leaving in their wake a look of shock on the other man's face.

"Shut up!" Gorman cried out again, not even aware that he was speaking, not conscious that the pressures that pounded in his brain had caused him to involuntarily rise and call out in protest.

Hunter's immediate reaction was one of fury. He started to lash out at Gorman, but then he recognized for the first time Gorman's uncontrollable blinking, heard the younger man gasping for air in noisy spasms. Gorman's hands drew into fists, relaxed, and then compulsively clutched back into tightened balls. His arms moved aimlessly upward, then his hands gripped the lapels of his jacket, squeezing the fabric, wadding it into wrinkled lumps. He stepped toward Hunter, his eyes widening as he stared blankly into the other face, his breath still coming in short gasps.

Paul Prescott watched the scene in fascination for a moment and then, noting the look of fury that was beginning to reappear on Hunter's face, he signaled Hunter, shaking his head in warning.

Gorman was oblivious to it all. He was talking again, his voice reflecting the emotional pressure he felt.

"Shut up, goddamnit, shut up. You don't have any reason to be so upset." His voice became more shrill. "Everything's all right." He whirled around and his face sought the others. His eyes were focusing again, and he had released his grip on the jacket.

"Everything's all right—do you understand? I've handled the deal. I've *handled* it. It's taken care of. There's no harm done."

Hunter could no longer contain himself, despite Prescott's warning signal. "No harm done? *No harm done?*" His voice held a combination of anger and disbelief at the words he was hearing. "First, the FRESH! proof and now a tape. A *tape,* Gorman. Just like the tapes from the White House. And a spree of violence from one end of Atlanta to the other. And then, of all the stupid things to do, you kidnapped two people. At least you had the good sense to take them to the island. And after all of that, you have the sheer gall to stand there and tell me that there's no harm done?"

"Goddamnit, there *was* no harm done—by *me.*" Gorman's voice had a healthier sound now, the sound of righteous indignation, the sound of a person unjustly accused. "There may have been harm done, but not by me. It wasn't Steve Gorman."

His words spilled over themselves as he continued. "Sure, there's been harm done. Immeasurable harm. To put it more bluntly, everything is all screwed up. But I'm not the screw-up, Mac. All I've done is take care of the problems some of the others have caused. Like Anthony Hapworth. Why don't you have Hapworth in here on the carpet instead of me?"

Hunter's face was black. "He's on the way."

Gorman ignored his answer. "Hapworth is the screw-up. Your hand-picked choice for President! He sneaked off to get a little piece of ass from his in-house whore. That's OK for Hap, I guess, but not for Steve. 'Watch yourself, Steve. Get control of yourself, Steve.' On top of that, the stupid bastard left the code name lying around her bedroom. And then he spilled his guts—*over the telephone,* by God—to a dumb broad who didn't have enough sense to stop the goddamn tape recorder."

Gorman paused. The angry outburst had calmed him.

"No, Mr. Hunter, *I* haven't screwed up. All I've done is to handle the situation in Atlanta while all the rest of you were playing games in New York. I've put the security leaks out of commission."

"Yes," Hunter said grimly, "you've done that, all right. You've put them out of commission—almost permanently. You damned near killed Joe Greenberg. There were other ways to retrieve that proof."

Gorman swallowed and blinked his eyes again. So they knew about Greenberg. He had hoped they wouldn't find out. And then another thought went through his tormented mind. The incident with Rick Craig in the parking garage. He'd been drunk, he realized now. But he hoped they didn't know. It wouldn't be easy to explain it away.

He answered defensively. "So what the hell difference is Joe Greenberg? I got the proof back, didn't I? What did you expect me to do? Burglarize his house? Just so he could report that someone stole a FRESH! proof?

"And what about the others? Did you expect me to let Logan Smith run loose after he had heard the tape? Or let Diana spill her guts to the next guy she slept with? I did all I could do. I removed the security risks. And put them both on ice. Out of it. I used the same stuff we used on that college kid from Utah. Smith is out of commission. And I'll take care of Diana. She won't talk." A smirk crossed his face as he remembered the look on Diana's face when he had pushed into her apartment

Sunday night, the fear in her eyes as he had pulled her into the bedroom and torn her clothes from her. But he hadn't lied to Hunter. There had been no harm, not after his initial attack. In fact, he thought now, she'd liked it. Later, when he had tied her with ropes, she'd come around easier. Maybe it was the coke . . .

Suddenly he became aware of the silence in the room and he pulled his thoughts back to Hunter and Prescott.

"When you analyze the situation, you'll see that I did what had to be done. And that's what you expect from me, isn't it?" Gorman looked from face to face and he could see, to his amazement, that he had temporarily outwitted them.

The throbbing sensation in his head had begun to subside. "If there's nothing more, gentlemen," he said, "I have work to do in Atlanta. And in Miami." He turned, ready to leave the room, but Paul Prescott's quiet question stopped him in his flight for the door.

"What happened to the tape, Steve?"

Almost instantly the pounding returned, but Gorman kept his composure. "I burned it," he lied, taking care to keep his voice level. "It's gone. Forever. The same as I did with the FRESH! proof. Isn't that SOP? Destroy incriminating evidence?"

Nodding his head curtly, he again turned and completed his exit, closing the door firmly behind him.

Outside he stopped, his body sagging. He leaned helplessly against the wall, one arm extended to support his weight. The other arm moved upward, the hand spread over his face, his fingers attempting to rub away the pounding pressure he felt in his brain.

Where *was* that goddamned tape? he asked himself. Smitty had lied to him about dropping it accidentally in the lake. Automatically his mind turned to Rick Craig. Perhaps Smitty had found some way to get it to Craig. But, his logic told him, Rick Craig had been in New York.

* * *

Inside Hunter's office, the two men looked at each other in silence for a moment. Prescott was the first to speak, mirroring the thoughts in the other man's mind.

"He's right, you know. He didn't screw up. This time. But he will, Mac. He's standing on the brink of a breakdown. You'd better remove him from the Project."

Chapter 4

Dan Osborne brought the bottle of beer to his lips and took a long, relaxed swallow, then addressed himself to the automated shuffleboard. He took aim, and his arm propelled the steel puck forward.

He watched it shoot down the surface of the board and heard with satisfaction the metallic clicking sound as his opponent's puck flew off into the gutter.

"Too bad, ol' buddy," he said, taking another draw from the bottle and approaching the man at the other end of the table. "That's ten bucks." One hand reached out to receive payment for the wager, and his face wore no expression other than the practiced boredom of the regulars at the tavern.

Pocketing the money, he walked toward the bar with a studied nonchalance and slid onto a barstool next to the man he had quietly followed from bar to bar for the past two hours.

The man didn't look up, didn't acknowledge his presence. Nor had he paid attention to Osborne at the other bars. He merely stared ahead, occasionally glancing down at the highball glass before him.

Osborne broke the silence. "Goddamn," he said loudly, addressing everyone in general. "I'm getting as good at a frame of shuffleboard as I am with a frame of film."

His comment went unnoticed at first. And then it

caught the attention of the unkempt character next to him.

"You in the film business?" The man spoke without interest, his voice muffled by the sounds of the tavern.

Thank God, Osborne thought silently. I'm about to get his attention. "Hell, yes. I'm a big film man from the East Coast." His voice was arrogant, with just a trace of a drunken slur in it. "I'm one of the best goddamn lab men in the business. Back in New York, they say I can work miracles in editing. That's why this VTR outfit is paying me a bundle to come to the West Coast."

Osborne stared at his beer bottle, keeping his eyes averted from the figure next to him, but he was aware that the man had jerked his head sharply around, studying Dan, appraising him.

Osborne responded with indifference, draining his beer from the bottle and sliding the bottle forward. "Bartender!" he called.

The man broke the silence. His voice held more animation than before. "You going to work for VTR Studios?" he inquired.

"That's right," Osborne said offhandedly, but his mind was intent on pursuing the subject. "Don't tell me you've ever heard of the place. It's not the biggest one in Hollywood, but—"

"I work there," the man cut in.

I know, Osborne thought silently. I've been following you since you got off at five o'clock. I've spent two hours setting you up, trying to get you into a conversation. I *know* you work at VTR.

But his response was casual. "That right?" he said. "Small world, huh."

"You just in from New York?"

Osborne nodded. "Yeah, just today. Going to work in the lab." The man fell silent again, and he played his final card.

"Yeah, I'm one of the sons of Minerva."

The reaction was instantaneous. His companion turned and stared at Osborne. He spoke, his voice alert and guarded. "Listen, buddy, you better not throw that name around."

Osborne looked at him in surprise. "You're on the project, too?" he asked.

"Hell, no. I'm just a goddamned grip. But I know better than to use that word in public. And you better not use it either." The man studied his drink for a minute, then shrugged his shoulders. "Hell, it's no skin off my ass. It's just that that's a no-no at VTR."

He dismissed his fleeting concern for Osborne and continued. "Hell, this must be a big day for the project. Lots of work coming up." He turned to Osborne. "You're the second new man today."

It took a moment for the significance of his words to penetrate Osborne's comprehension. The *second* man today. His mind raced ahead, his instincts fully attuned to this remarkable stroke of good luck.

"Yeah," he answered, choosing his words carefully, probing for more information. "Yeah, I guess there's a lot of activity about to begin." Receiving no reaction, he took it a step further. "Who was the guy who showed up today? It wasn't my good friend Charlie Jones, was it?"

The other man shook his head. "Naw, it was somebody named Davis, Davies, something like that. I didn't meet him. I heard him talking to one of the VP's—the boss is out of town 'til Wednesday. But I guess you know that, don't you?"

Osborne nodded. "Yeah, all I can do is wait," he chanced, and when the other man nodded, he knew he had guessed the procedure. "What's the big man's name? Brett Stanley?"

He was rewarded with a nod, and again proceeded with another question. "Davis? Davies?" He paused, as if in thought, then shook his head. "Guess I don't know him, but by God, I'd like to have a drink with him."

Osborne waited a minute and then tried the longest shot of all. If this works, he told himself, I'll be the luckiest son of a bitch in Los Angeles.

"You don't know where he's staying, do you?"

The man looked at him strangely, as though he had asked too obvious a question. "I guess he's at the Holiday Inn down the street from the studio. That's where they usually put up all the new men until they can find an apartment. How come you aren't staying there?"

Osborne shrugged. "I haven't checked in yet," he said quickly, and then his voice picked up the arrogance it had held earlier. "Besides, if I have any luck maybe I'll find a good-looking chick who'd like to take me home. That's better than the Holiday Inn, right?"

Realizing he had pushed his luck far enough, Osborne stood. "Well, ol' buddy, see you around the studio. I think I'll look for greener pastures."

As he stepped outside the front door of the bar, his swaggering gait changed to a fast pace, and shortly he slid behind the wheel of the car he had rented.

The Holiday Inn, he thought. A new man in from New York. Assigned to the special project. And, Dan'l, my boy, you've got until Wednesday to figure out a way to take his place.

Chapter 5

Rick Craig studied the printed page before him, assimilating the political analysis of *U.S. News*. The circumstances of his life made him intensely interested in the developing presidential primaries, and as he read the article he occasionally underlined a passage with a yellow marking pen.

On the seat beside him was a litter of other news magazines and periodicals, each of them bearing the markings of his felt-tip: underlined passages, notes scrawled in the margin, asterisks highlighting points of particular significance.

He started to underline another passage when a sudden lurch of the small chartered aircraft forced his hand awry, leaving a jagged yellow line to mark the course of the brief air disturbance.

He looked up at the pilot in front of him and saw the young man grinning over his shoulder. "Sorry about that," he apologized.

"How much farther to Brunswick?" Rick asked him.

"Twenty, twenty-five minutes," he was told and he let his mind wander to the absurdity of the mission on which he had embarked. It's probably the most foolhardy thing I've ever done, Rick told himself. And I'll probably never even get to see Smitty—much less rescue him. But I couldn't just sit at home and wait. I had to do something.

He shrugged the nagging doubts away and turned his attention back to the magazine and the closing words of the analysis he had been reading.

> It was in New Hampshire that this election year's biggest political mystery began to unfold, when Congressman Anthony Hapworth of Ohio, one of the darlings of the far Right, pulled off a major upset and finished in the money.
>
> Polls indicate the same thing is happening in Florida. If his showing there is as strong as in New Hampshire, he will become recognized, even by a myopic president, as a serious contender for the nomination. Hapworth's political fortunes have never looked better.
>
> The big ones are still coming up: Illinois, California, Texas, his home state of Ohio, and scores of others. And if the dark horse pulls ahead in those races, he may well ride into the White House. He's hardly a thoroughbred, but scuttlebutt has it that he'll be ridden by Steve Gorman, a political jockey who rode into the Winner's Circle before, only to be thrown from his horse by more experienced Washington riders who were better trained at jockeying for position.
>
> There's an old saying in the South: Politics is always a horse race. We couldn't agree more wholeheartedly.

Rick lit a cigarette and pondered the political analysis. He went back to place an asterisk beside the reference to the New Hampshire primary. New Hampshire. One of the test markets for FRESH! And Florida. Another primary, another test market.

Tossing the magazine with the others beside him, he took a pad from his attache case and drew a line down the middle of the page. On the left side he wrote "Presidential Primaries" and meticulously constructed a timetable of all primary election dates. On the right side he wrote another caption: "Test Market Campaigns/ FRESH!"

A short while later the pattern became clear. For every primary election there was an exact correlation to a FRESH! advertising campaign. A campaign created and placed by Collins & Craig. A campaign that, if he were to believe the theories of Paul Prescott, sold both the soft drink and the hard-nosed conservative.

He continued throughout the list of primaries, and the pattern held. A massive introductory campaign for FRESH! in Los Angeles and San Francisco and San Diego coincided exactly with the California primary. And in Ohio, test campaigns for the beverage in Cleveland and Columbus and Cincinnati culminated on the day of the Ohio primary election.

He sat lost in thought. There was little question about it. Someone connected with Collins & Craig was involved with the subliminal effort—totally involved. And had been for months.

Laura Talbott was the obvious answer. She had helped conceive the FRESH! campaign, had produced the television spots, had been involved in planning the marketing strategy and test effort. And now she was doing the same thing with The Phoenix Press.

But it wasn't necessarily Laura. Not necessarily. She could have been as oblivious to the plot as he had been. The subliminal messages—whatever they were, however they were executed—could have been inserted by Brett Stanley in Hollywood. And Brett Stanley had gotten his job with VTR through Suzanne Carmichael's personnel agency.

Suzanne's link went far beyond Brett Stanley, however. Rick had had to resort to subterfuge to get the information, but when her secretary had finally dug up all of the data, it had formed an impressive link between Suzanne and Miramar. And Collins & Craig.

Suzanne had placed Brett Stanley as president of VTR after Mac Hunter had bought the film studio, and she had placed six other employees there. Suzanne had obtained jobs for three different craftsmen with Fine Arts Engraving in New York. Suzanne had recruited the marketing director at FRESH!—the marketing hotshot who had planned the test market strategy and had dictated the states where the test campaigns would appear.

And so, although his emotions wanted to deny it, he was forced to admit that Suzanne Carmichael could be the link between the advertising agency and the plot to elect Anthony Hapworth.

But not necessarily. Not necessarily Suzanne. Not necessarily Laura. But almost certainly one of them.

The pilot's voice interrupted his thoughts. "Brunswick's coming up. We'll be on the ground in five minutes. Can I radio ahead for a taxi?"

"Right," Rick answered. "I want to go to the harbor area. I need to charter a boat."

Rick stood across the street from the waterfront cafe, preparing himself, mentally rehearsing the plan that he hoped would gain access for him to the island.

He glanced at his reflection in a plateglass window and, satisfied that he looked every inch the professional man, he strode across the street and entered the café.

It was obviously the peak of the morning coffee hour on the waterfront. The smoke-filled room was alive with men of all ages and sizes and descriptions, their voices and laughter blending into a raucous hubbub.

Rick walked to the counter, setting his attaché case

down briefly and addressing a plain-looking waitress imperiously. "Jonathan Chadwick. I want Jonathan Chadwick," he announced in a voice loud enough to cut through the noise. "I was told he was here."

His manner, his demanding tone took the attention of several of the rough-cut patrons at the counter and the waitress studied him in silence for a moment. Then she jerked her head toward the rear.

Rick turned and walked arrogantly through the crowded room, his eyes searching for the wrinkled face of Old John. And then he saw him, sitting with two other old men at the rear of the restaurant.

He walked directly up to the table and stood before the elderly employee of Mac Hunter. "John," he inquired loudly, unpleasantly. "Where the hell have you been? I've been waiting at the airport for half an hour. Mr. Hunter told me you would meet me, but I finally had to take a cab into town and try to find you." He stared down at the gnarled old face in obvious irritation. "Didn't you get Mr. Hunter's message about my arrival? Dr. Prescott is expecting me this morning. I'm sure that he will be as unhappy as I am that you forgot to pick me up." Rick paused, awaiting the reaction.

The ruse worked. Old John was already struggling to his feet, mumbling his apologies. He hadn't received any message, but the boat was at the dock and it would only take a moment . . .

John grabbed a visored cap from his hip pocket and slapped it on his head, starting toward the front door. He continued in his efforts to absolve himself with Rick. There must be some sort of mistake, he mumbled in a weathered voice, because Dr. Prescott wasn't even on the island today—

Rick breathed a sigh of relief when he heard that Prescott was absent. His plan wouldn't have worked well at all if Paul had been present. Not at all.

"I'm well aware that Dr. Prescott is not on the island," he told John in a condescending tone. "But I told him that I would be here today and he expects me to keep my word. Just as I expect to be met at the airport and taken to St. Sebastian's when I've been told that you would meet me."

Annie Parkinson opened the heavy wooden door and stood planted there, arms akimbo, a forbidding look on her face. "Yes?" It was more of a challenge than a question.

For a moment, Rick Craig lost his carefully planned resolve, but then he pulled himself erect and carried on. "Good morning," he said briskly, brushing past her into the dark entryhall. He turned back to face her and saw her still standing in the doorway, staring after him. You are Miss—er . . ."

"Miss Parkinson. Annie Parkinson," she mumbled in her shock.

"Ah yes. Miss Parkinson. Dr. Prescott has spoken of you." Rick set his attaché case on a bench in the hall and began to strip off his trench coat.

"Are you ready for the examination? Do you have the patient prepared?" He thrust the coat at her and turned away, down the hall. Without waiting for her reply, he moved down the long corridor. "Which examining room do you wish me to use? I'm sorry that Dr. Prescott was unable to be here, but—" Rick left the sentence hanging and turned back to face the befuddled woman. "Well, which room do you want me to use? Perhaps you'd better lead the way."

Suddenly Annie Parkinson regained her senses. "Just a minute," she said. "Just who *are* you? And what are you doing here?"

Irritation spread over Rick's face. "*Who am I?* I'm Dr. Christianson. From the Neurological Clinic in

Montreal. Surely you were aware of my visit? Unless, like that poor old man, you forgot—"

"I didn't forget anything," she shot back. "I've never heard of you or anything about your being here. Dr. Prescott didn't tell me anything about this before he left —"

Rick saw an opening and took it. He allowed indignation to fill his voice. "I'm not surprised. I'm not here at Dr. Prescott's invitation. I'm here because Maxwell Hunter asked me to do an independent evaluation on Logan Smith. And on Miss—" he pulled a small black notebook from a coat pocket and pretended to consult it "—er, Miss Malloy. They *are* still here, aren't they?"

Rick held his breath. In a moment he would know if Smitty were on the island, if he were alive and well—

"Yes, of course they're still here. But I'm not authorized to let you see them."

"Perhaps I should call New York and speak with Mr. Hunter. Perhaps I should tell him that you're not being cooperative—"

"No! Don't do that." The threatened confrontation with Hunter made the woman more cooperative. "You say Mr. Hunter made the arrangements for you to come here?" Her tone had become almost solicitous as she probed for more information.

"Not Mr. Hunter personally." Rick was about to play his final card. "A woman. Not his secretary—an associate. She called herself—" He consulted the black notebook again, then turned it for her to observe a name scrawled on a page. "She called herself Minerva."

Miss Parkinson's face relaxed. "Why didn't you tell me that earlier?" she demanded, walking past him down the corridor. "Come this way. Logan Smith is heavily tranquilized, but I'll get him ready for you to see him. You can wait in Dr. Prescott's study."

The door closed behind him and Rick sank into a

chair, his whole body suddenly trembling in reaction to his audacious entry into Prescott's private domain.

What am I doing here? his mind kept asking him. What in God's name am I doing playing cloak-and-dagger on this godforsaken island like some cheap melodrama? And now that I'm here, how in hell am I going to get off? And how am I going to get Smitty off with me?

Rick's thoughts turned to Logan Smith. What kind of shape would he be in? Heavily tranquilized, the nurse said. But how heavily? Could he walk and talk and think rationally? Could he help himself? Could he move quickly enough to evade the guards? Rick had seen only John and an old black man at the dock, who had helped John make port and then had driven him here to Prescott's laboratory. But his common sense told him that there would be other guards. Gorman would have seen to that. Guards more formidable than Old John or Miss Parkinson or the household servants at the Manor House.

Anxiously he looked at his watch. It was taking Parkinson longer than he had anticipated. If she didn't reappear shortly he'd have to seek her out. Perhaps she hadn't accepted his story as readily as it seemed. Perhaps the magic name "Minerva" had not satisfied her as to his credentials.

He stood and began pacing back and forth in the small sitting room where she had left him. The room was tastefully appointed, but nondescript. Nothing about it indicated that it was Prescott's private office. On a far wall Rick saw another door, closed, and he walked to it and quietly pulled it open.

He was looking into Paul Prescott's study. A huge desk and leather armchairs dominated the center of the room and beyond them Rick saw a massive stone fireplace lined on either side by bookcases that stretched from floor to ceiling. The shelves were filled to the overflowing with heavy leatherbound volumes. Academic journals, textbooks, research volumes, Rick surmised, and turned to study another part of the room.

But suddenly the enormity of what he had seen struck him. Paul Prescott's private library. He advanced into the room, walking past Prescott's desk directly to the bookcases. He scanned shelf after shelf, looking for a telltale splotch of color, and finally he was rewarded with the glint of a thin-spined magenta volume. And on the spine he saw the words he had searched for: *Mind Control.*

His hand shot out to take the volume and he was about to turn to leave. But another volume caught his eye, a volume bound in a similar fabric and bearing the legend *Mind Control II.* He reached for it and flipped open the cover to the title page. "Mind Control II;" he read, "the Utah Experiment: A Continuing Scientific Exploration of Subconscious Perception."

At that moment a sound from the hallway beyond the sitting room startled him, and he ran lightly across the room, pulling the door to Prescott's office closed behind him. Hurriedly he slipped both volumes into his attaché case. He was snapping the latch closed as the door opened.

Annie Parkinson walked into the room. "Logan Smith is ready for you to examine," she told Rick, and he studied her face intently, looking for any sign of distrust. But he saw only a look of professionalism that matched the tone of her voice. "You'll have to wait awhile to see Diana Malloy," she went on. "She's so heavily sedated that she can't be aroused."

Miss Parkinson nodded her head toward the open door behind her. "Macomb will take you to his room." Rick followed her gesture and, for the first time, noticed the man standing there. He was young and his broad shoulders strained against the fabric of the white clinical jacket he wore. He towered over Miss Parkinson.

Taking his attaché case in preparation for accompanying the young man, Rick silently nodded to himself. Indeed, Macomb was a more formidable guard than the others. But perhaps, if all went well, he could avoid a physical confrontation.

Rick stepped into the small room without a sound, pulling the door closed behind him and leaning against it as he surveyed the room before him. It was plain, but comfortably furnished, and its look was more of a dormitory room than of a hospital.

An overstuffed chair was placed by a window and sitting there, silhouetted against the bright sunlight, was Logan Smith. His back was to the room. He sat motionless, staring out the window.

Rick watched him for a long moment before speaking. Finally, his voice soft and muffled, he spoke the other man's name.

"Smitty."

There was no response and Rick repeated the word, his voice louder, more urgent.

The figure stirred, shifted its position in the chair slightly. Rick spoke again. "Smitty. It's me. Rick. Rick Craig."

The words brought a stronger reaction than before. Logan Smith turned his head, the motion abrupt, almost choppy. He stared at Rick for a moment, his brows drawn together in a look of confusion, intently studying Rick's countenance as if he suspected an imposter.

"Rick?" He spoke, and his voice was tremulous. "Rick? Is it you?"

Rick walked across the room and knelt beside the chair. "Yes, Smitty, it's me. I've come to get you. To take you home."

"Thank God." Smitty stood, his movements more agitated but his body apparently strong and coordinated. "Thank God you've finally come. I knew someone would come. Sometime. You. Or Susan. Or someone. I knew that somebody would find out that I was in the hospital. But—" The look of confusion returned to his face and it was reflected in his voice. "But, Rick, I can't remember anything. I don't know why I'm here. I don't even know where I am. The last thing I remember is leaving the house for work one morning. That's the last that I remember. The next thing I knew, I woke up in this room, and I've been here ever since."

Rick sat on the edge of the bed, leaning forward so that he could quietly emphasize every word that he spoke.

"Listen to me, Smitty. We're going to get you out of here. But you'll have to do exactly what I tell you. Tonight, after it's dark, an old man is bringing a boat out here to pick me up and take me back to the mainland. And you're going to be with me."

Jonathan Chadwick steered toward the single light at the end of the dock, directing the boat toward the quieter waters inside the inlet. He searched the dock for signs of Ben, who was always on hand to help him tie up, but he caught no sign of movement.

He pulled closer. Still no sign of Ben. Confound that nigger. Probably up at the kitchen, trying to warm up the cook for some extra vittles. Done forgot all about Old John and his pick-up of that Dr. Christianson fellow.

Suddenly a movement caught his eye and he called out, "Ahoy," and he heard a call in reply. But it wasn't Ben's voice. It was a strange voice. He called out again. "Who is it?" And he heard the voice again. "It's Dr. Christianson. I'm here alone. The dockman is sick.

They've put him to bed. Throw me your line and I'll secure you until we can load and leave."

In a short while he was docked. The doctor had tied up—done a sloppy job, all right, but tied up nevertheless. And it didn't matter too much. They'd be leaving in just a moment, as quick as the doctor could get on board.

John walked over to offer the younger man his hand for boarding.

"Oh yes," Dr. Christianson said. "There's a load of boxes in the boathouse over there that have to go back to the mainland. Miss Parkinson said that Dr. Prescott wants them shipped to Atlanta. Come on. I'll give you a hand in loading them and then we can be on our way."

John shuffled over the wooden planking toward the boathouse. Funny there wasn't a light on in the boathouse, but maybe the doctor didn't know where the switch was. And since Ben was sick and all.

John stepped over the threshold of the small structure and automatically felt for the switch, flooding the room with light. He looked over the room, searching for the materials that were to be loaded on his boat.

"What boxes?" he asked. "I don't see any boxes. Did you say they were here, in the boathouse?"

His only reply was the sound of the door behind him being slammed, the heavy bolt being slid into place. And a few moments later he heard the boat's engine thrown into reverse. And then accelerated in forward. And gradually its sound faded into the night and was gone.

Chapter 6

"This isn't at all customary, Davis."

Brett Stanley looked across his desk at Dan Osborne. His handsome, tanned face wore a perplexed look, his hands toyed idly with the résumé that rested on the desk before him.

"What's not customary?" Osborne asked him in surprise.

"This résumé form isn't enough. It's customary for new men to bring the approved application form from Carmichael. I tell them what I need, they find the bodies and send them to me. But they always follow procedure. And *this* doesn't follow procedure." Stanley pushed the résumé back toward the man opposite him.

Dan Osborne reached forward to take the form, his heart pounding. For the past two days he had been treading delicately on eggshells and now he saw his entire intricate charade about to collapse. He knew that his next words were vital in gaining admittance to the special projects division of VTR Studio.

"I don't know what the hell kind of procedure you're talking about," he said loudly, affecting the tone of bravado that had served him so well. He put his blunt forefinger on the document before him, stabbing at the printed words on the page. "My name's Tom Davis and

I'm a damned good lab man. Everything it says on this résumé is correct. You can check it out. *They* already have. I don't know what else you need—"

Suddenly Osborne stopped, as if a thought had struck him. "Wait a minute. You said something about an approved application form. You mean like a printed form with my name on it, and other stuff about me?"

Stanley nodded tersely. *"And* your photograph."

"Hell," Osborne lied. "I didn't know that was important. I didn't think I needed that anymore. I think I've still got it somewhere. In my car. Or in my room." Memory seemed to flood his mind, and he added brightly, "Yeah, that's where it is. I've still got it. You want me to go get it?"

Stanley glanced at his watch and shook his head. The look of distrust was beginning to fade from his face, and was replaced by one of irritation. "Hell, no," he snapped at his new employee. "It's quitting time now, and I've got a meeting at five o'clock. Have it here first thing in the morning. And Davis, remember one thing. Be here on time."

"If you're referring to my coming in so late today, let's get one thing straight." Osborne's tone was somewhat belligerent, pushing Stanley to see how the other man would react. "I was here on Monday. *You* were out of the office. And I was told to report to you. It's not my fault—"

"That's all, Davis," Stanley said quickly. It seemed obvious, Osborne thought, that the man wanted to avoid any further confrontation.

He left the office, using the muscular swagger that he had adopted since he arrived in Los Angeles, and it was only when he was driving down the tree-lined boulevard that he dropped the pose and expelled a long sigh of relief.

His eyes darting to the rearview mirror, Osborne

began a circuitous series of turns and cut-backs. When he was satisfied that no one was following him, he drove to a Western Union office and went inside.

"I want to pick up a money order from Atlanta," he said. Offering identification, he took the missive from Rick Craig and looked for a drive-in bank. Soon he had $3,000 in cash in his pocket and he drove toward another part of Los Angeles.

The graceful palm trees dissolved into a neon jungle. The cocktail lounges and bistros became bars and short-order cafés, the smart clothing shops and gilded boutiques turned into adult movie houses and pornographic newsstands. And everywhere there were head shops.

Osborne's mind turned to the real Tom Davis. He thought of the man regretfully, not because he felt any compunction for what he had done and not because he was sorry that Davis had been a victim. He regretted only his duplicity in the matter.

Tom Davis had brought him here, to this same street, for an evening on the town. He remembered how easily he had established a camaraderie with the other man, gradually gaining his confidence as they proceeded from bar to bar. Osborne had hinted at his desire for a stronger trip than the liquor was producing and finally Davis suggested that they go back to his room where he had the good stuff.

Even before Davis had displayed his personal cache of drugs, Osborne had suspected that he had found a key that would unlock the doors of VTR Studios. But when he had seen the accumulation of paraphernalia, had observed the massive quantities of sophisticated mind-bending narcotics, he realized that he had stumbled on far more than a man with a habit. Tom Davis was a pusher who, in just a couple of days, had already started to establish himself on the West Coast.

The rest had been easy. Not for the average man, but for Dan Osborne. Because Osborne had produced a photographic essay on the Los Angeles Police Department and had kept alive the contacts in the months that had passed.

A telephone call to Lt. Joe Fletcher of Narcotics, a brief meeting early the following morning, and the hit was set up. It was executed flawlessly, before Davis was due to report to VTR. And shortly after, Tom Davis was too concerned with his own misfortune to even consider the consequences of his prospective job.

Now Osborne saw a sign ahead of him and he pulled the car into the slower lane, looking for a parking place at the curb. As he approached the dingy storefront, his eyes noted the sign over the door: "The Paper Trip."

He pushed open the door, feeling the anger return. "Davis," he said abruptly to the fat man behind the counter. "Three documents. You get 'em ready?"

Little, furtive eyes looked out at Osborne from eyelids almost swollen shut, but the face wore no expression. He spoke in more of a wheeze than a voice, and when his lips began to move an ash cascaded from the drooping cigarette and fell across his massive belly.

"I had them ready earlier, mister," he said tonelessly. "But you didn't have the money." Their eyes locked, and the man stood motionless, seemingly the victim of his own inertia. Finally he wheezed two more words at Osborne. "The money."

Osborne took the roll of bills from his pocket and peeled off several hundreds, throwing them on the counter in front of him. As the fat man reached to grab them, Osborne brought his fist down on the bloated hand and pulled the bills away with his other.

"You see the money, you cheap son of a bitch," he snarled. "But you don't get it until I see the documents."

The man looked at him for a moment, then shrugged and turned away to pick up an envelope on the counter behind him.

Osborne continued. "You damned near screwed up

my whole deal," he said bitterly. "I told you I was good for the money, and it almost cost me my job because I didn't have these earlier in the day."

The man shrugged off the comment and opened a brown envelope, spilling plastic-encased cards on the counter. Osborne studied them. The driver's license would work, so would the ID card. The Social Security card, too, passed his scrutiny.

"Is this the same Social Security number as on the application form?" The man nodded. Osborne went on. "Let me check it. Where's the application form with the photograph? That's all that I needed earlier." The man produced it from the envelope, holding it away from Osborne's reach.

"The money," he said.

Osborne threw the bills back on the counter, grabbed the envelope, and stalked out of the shop. In his car, he stripped his billfold of every vestige of Dan Osborne and, with the new documents tucked into place, drove away, ready to begin his shadow life.

A smile crossed his face as he drove out of the neighborhood. I wonder if Rick will accept a collect call from Tom Davis? he thought.

Rick Craig sat in his empty apartment reflecting on the events of the past two days, awaiting the prearranged phone call from Dan Osborne.

He thought back to the night on the island, to his and Smitty's escape in Hunter's yacht. Somehow the two of them had steered the massive boat back into the harbor at Brunswick, ramming the dock in their clumsy efforts and haste. But they had made it, had found a cab on the deserted streets, and had finally got back to the airstrip and the waiting pilot.

And despite his anxiety to get airborne, to get away from John and Annie and the burly Macomb, he had delayed their departure long enough to get to a telephone and place a call to Atlanta to Susan Smith.

When he heard her voice on the line, he shoved the receiver into Smitty's hands and left them alone for a few minutes. And then he had talked with Susan again, giving her explicit instructions. Pack a suitcase, he had told her. Pack warm clothes, enough for her and the girls, and for Smitty, too. Tell her friends she was going to her parents' home, to get away for a few days. And then get on the next available flight to Denver, and then to Aspen. She'd be met there by a woman named Ginny York. And Smitty would be there, too, as soon as Rick could manage it.

Ginny had called to report their arrival. And now they were safe in Dan's house. And together again.

How pleased Dan will be, Rick thought. When he calls. *If* he calls, he thought impatiently, looking at his watch. And as though Osborne could read his mind, all of those thousands of miles away, the telephone rang.

Rick intercepted the call after the first ring, grabbing the receiver and jamming it to his ear.

"Dan, is that you?" When he heard the familiar voice at the other end of the line, he settled back in relief, but he spoke again before Osborne could begin a conversation.

"What's going on out there? Did you get the money? Are you all right?"

Osborne led him, step by step, through all of his activities since he had left Atlanta, from his meeting with the technician from VTR through his encounter with Tom Davis and his assumption of his identity.

When he finished, Rick spoke. "You've been busy," he commented. "But so have I. I found Smitty, Dan." He heard an explosion of excitement on the other end of the line, and he continued. "They were holding him prisoner on St. Sebastian's—Hunter's island. Prescott's got a complete lab set-up out there—nurses, technicians, film studios, the whole works. Everything they need to produce experimental advertising.

"But that's not the important thing. Smitty is." Rick's voice became more serious. "They've tampered with his mind, Dan. I don't know how Prescott did it, but they've erased a portion of his memory. He's all right—" Rick hastened to assure him. "Physically, he seems to be in pretty good shape. But he can't remember the tape, his encounter with Gorman, not anything about how they got him to the island. Prescott has actually erased four or five days out of Smitty's life."

Rick drew from the knowledge he had gathered from Prescott's books. "He does it by isolating a memory neurone in the brain. That's where a particular event or occurrence is stored. And through a medical process—I don't really understand how—he destroys the neurone and erases the event."

He paused before launching into the details of the experiment in Utah. "Dan, does the name Drew Martin ring a bell in your mind? Or a college riot in Utah about a year and half ago?"

They talked, then, for more than an hour, Rick meticulously outlining all of the data he had read and absorbed from Prescott's medical reports.

He finally ended his narrative on Project Jupiter, as he had come to call it. "Knowing the facts doesn't help us, though. It wouldn't stand up in court, wouldn't stop them. We've still got to catch them in the act, and you're the only one who can do that. I'm too well known at VTR, so it's up to you. Good luck, Dan."

As Rick fell silent, preparing to end their conversation, Osborne spoke again. This time he was less direct, his voice holding a note of sympathy.

"Rick, there's one other thing you ought to know. This guy Tom Davis that I'm impersonating—he was hired for this job by Suzanne Carmichael's personnel agency. The key to his admittance to the inner sanctum is the Carmichael application form. It looks like Suzanne may be the mystery woman—"

"Not necessarily." Rick cut him off, and he was surprised at the defensive feeling that came over him when he thought of Suzanne Carmichael.

He started again, more logically. "Not necessarily, Dan. I found out the same thing—Suzanne's agency is the exclusive agency for all of Mac Hunter's companies. I didn't know anything about this guy Tom Davis, but she's been working with Hunter for years. A long-time client, her secretary says. She's placed half of the people who are involved in this thing.

"Suzanne helped establish Brett Stanley with VTR, after Hunter had bought the studio. The firm has placed six other employees with VTR. And she's helped get jobs for three top engravers with Fine Arts in New York. She was responsible for placing the new advertising director with FRESH! and he's the guy who dictated which states would be used for the FRESH! campaigns, who told us the dates for the campaigns. He's the one who made the FRESH! campaigns jibe with the primaries. And by now she's placed ten or twelve new employees with Collins & Craig."

He sighed and was silent for a moment. When he continued, his voice was flat. "There's no question that Suzanne's been involved—maybe in a big way. But the evidence doesn't point to her any more than Laura Talbott. Laura's been creating the material that has the subliminal embeds." He paused again and then said softly, "At least, I'm not ready to admit that Suzanne is any further involved than Laura."

"I'm sorry, Rick. Just be careful." His voice returned to normal. "I've got to get off this phone. Tomorrow's my first day on the job. But for God's sake, don't ever call me there. In fact, you'd better not call me 'til I have my own apartment. I'll call you every evening just to check signals. Nine or nine-thirty, your time. I don't want any slip-ups in my cloak-and-dagger act. Something tells me that Mac Hunter wouldn't like my being on the inside of his mind factory. Ol' Dan'l's ass would be mud. I'll talk to you tomorrow, Rick. Hang in there!"

Chapter 7

Dan Osborne walked down the hallway toward the executive offices of VTR Studios. In the two weeks that he had been masquerading as Tom Davis, he hadn't discovered anything of great importance. But, he thought to himself wryly, he *had* made certain inroads.

He paused before an open doorway and stood there a moment until the young woman inside looked up. He waved casually at her, punctuating his gesture with an exaggerated wink.

"Come on in," she said, beckoning him into the room.

He entered, a curious look on his face. "I thought you told me that you were off-limits during working hours?"

"I did. But Mr. Stanley's out of town today and tomorrow." She nodded her head toward the closed door behind her.

"When the cat's away, huh?" Osborne said insolently.

"The mice will play," she finished the sentence for him. "Want a cup of coffee?"

"Sure," he replied, watching her body undulate across the room, her hips switching provocatively.

She stood at the coffee bar and without looking up said, "I enjoyed being with you last night."

Dan walked over to her and slipped his arm around

her waist. "I enjoyed it, too." His hand dropped to gently caress her body.

She pulled away. "Not here!" she said in a sharp whisper, but as she handed him the coffee mug, she kissed him lightly on the lips, then walked away.

He sidled up to the desk and sat on its edge, watching her sort Stanley's morning mail. He was about to ask her when he could expect a repeat performance when he saw something among the letters and pamphlets that lay before her.

"What's this?" he asked, pulling out a tan folder addressed to Stanley. The words on the cover had caught his attention: Design Institute of Southern California. The woman glanced up.

"Oh, that's an invitation for Mr. Stanley for the Design Institute next month." She looked back to the other correspondence.

Son of a bitch, Osborne thought to himself as he turned the page to study the announcement folder. *Son of a bitch!* I'm a featured speaker. Surely they didn't use my picture! His hands turned another page and then he stopped, his eyes riveted to the likeness that stared out at him. And the words below the photograph: Featured Speaker, Daniel Osborne, Aspen, Colorado.

Son of a bitch! His hands began to shake slightly. He rose and turned away from the desk, his manner still casual, but his mind racing.

"The Design Institute, huh? I've always wanted to attend one of those conferences. Mind if I take this with me? I'll get it back to you—after I copy off the address and dates."

"Go ahead," she replied easily. "He'll get another one at home. He's invited to a lot of stuff like this, but he'll probably go to this one. They're featuring a big-name photographer from Aspen."

Osborne's heart sank. He slipped the folder into his

hip pocket and turned to go. "Thanks for the coffee," he said, and when she looked up he winked at her again. He fought to keep his voice natural. "When did you say the boss is due back? Maybe we could get away for a long lunch?"

She smiled at him. "Tomorrow night, the next morning. So it would have to be today or tomorrow . . ."

"I'll stop by later in the day." He grinned and sauntered from the room, desperately trying to devise a plan.

A short while later, he reappeared at her door. He wore a look of concern on his face, and he barged in without an invitation.

"I've got a problem," he said, a note of urgency in his voice. "I've got to run an errand—an important errand—and my battery's dead. Can I borrow your car for a few minutes?"

"Sure." She smiled, taking her handbag from beneath the desk and fumbling through it. She pulled out a ring crammed with keys of all shapes and sizes and extended it to him. "Be careful with these keys," she cautioned him. "They're to my car—" she selected one and gave it to him "—and to my apartment. But I have all the office keys here, too. To the front door and to the laboratories. Mr. Stanley wouldn't like it if I let them out of my hands."

You don't need to tell me about the keys, Osborne thought. He had watched her use them on the laboratory doors, seen her lock the front door when she left. But he only winked and said, "Thanks, sweetheart."

He drove until he found a hardware store and approached the young man who stood behind the counter. "I want a duplicate key made for every key on this key-ring. Rush order!"

The young man took the ring and began to inspect the number of keys. Osborne again addressed him. "Is there a pay phone around here?"

The clerk looked up from his work and pointed toward the front door. "Outside," he muttered. "On the street."

Osborne peeled off several bills and threw them on the counter. "I need some change. Quarters."

In the phone booth he silently cursed the noisy traffic sounds that penetrated the sagging doors as he waited for the operator to complete the call. Finally a woman's voice told him that Rick Craig was out of the office. Out of Atlanta. He would return to the city tonight, be in the office tomorrow.

Shit, he murmured to himself. He had agreed never to call the agency, but he had no other choice. He spoke into the mouthpiece.

"Operator, I'll talk to Mr. Craig's secretary."

He was speaking to Martha Tyler, his voice terse and clipped. "I have an urgent message for Rick Craig," he told her. "Wherever he is, find him and get this message to him. Tell him that his Ol' Buddy called. Use those words—he'll know who it is. Tell him his Ol' Buddy called. Tell him I said it's too hot to work today, but that I'm going to work tonight—*alone*. Tell him I can't call him tonight, for him to be by his phone in the morning. You got that?"

He received an affirmative answer and started to hang up. But he turned back to the receiver.

"Sweetheart," he told her, "this is very important. And very confidential. Make sure that Rick gets that message tonight—but make sure that *no one else* gets it. Do you understand? *No one else.*"

That damned photograph, he told himself as he was driving away. The duplicate keys to the VTR front door and workrooms rested on the seat beside him. That damned photograph will blow my whole cover. He pondered the matter. Stanley would be home tomorrow evening, would see his mail when he got home. It had to be tonight or never. And although he didn't know much, yet, he knew where to look. And if he could work alone all night, maybe he could find what he was looking for. *If* he could work undisturbed. *If* the keys opened all the doors. *If*.

Osborne shrugged his shoulders. There were too many "ifs" to worry about. This was the time to put worries aside. To act.

VTR's massive studio loomed on his left, but he drove past the building and finally pulled into the Holiday Inn. He packed his belongings quickly and tossed them into the back seat of the borrowed car.

"I'm checking out," he told the desk clerk when he reached the lobby. His fingers drummed the counter in impatience as she prepared his bill, and then another thought struck him.

He moved to the bank of telephones off the lobby and studied the listings under "Hotels," searching for a hotel near the airport. Finally he spied an address in the vicinity and he searched his pockets for a slip of paper. He found the incriminating conference announcement in his hip pocket and scribbled the name and address of the hotel on its wrinkled cover.

An hour later, after checking in at the disreputable motel, he pulled back into the parking lot of the studio. Dan'l, he told himself as he slid out of the car, you're pretty good at this cloak-and-dagger stuff—for a beginner.

His movement dislodged the wrinkled folder from where it had precariously been suspended in his hip pocket, and it fell onto the seat of the car. Without a backward glance, Osborne headed jauntily into the building.

"Goddamnit, Mr. Hunter, I don't want him in Los

Angeles. I don't need him in Los Angeles."

"But you're going to *have* him in Los Angeles, Stanley, because I can't have him in Atlanta any longer. Or in New York. Or in Miami or Chicago. Gorman will be all right out on the Coast. Find him a couple of starlets—"

"The last time I did that, he damned near killed one of them. That son of a bitch is crazy, Mr. Hunter—"

"Then find him some girls who don't care. There are plenty of them around. And pay them well. Whatever it takes. But I want him as far away as possible, and I want somebody to keep an eye on him. And that someone is you, Brett. Christine has the tickets. For both of you. Tonight."

Hunter turned in his chair and looked out of the window. His hand unconsciously went to his ring and he fingered it thoughtfully.

He heard a noise behind him and glanced in that direction. He found Stanley still standing there, a look of discomfort on his face.

"That's all, Stanley. You're dismissed."

The look on his face was so forboding that Stanley turned at once and left the room.

Rick Craig stared at the telephone in his apartment, as if by his concentration he could make it ring.

But the phone remained silent, as it had since his return to Atlanta the night before. Martha's presence at the airport had been a surprise. Her message—delivered exactly as she had been instructed—had jolted Rick.

The urgency of it worried him. The man's voice, Martha had said, seemed so serious that she had driven to the airport to personally tell Rick of the conversation.

It's too hot to work today. Dan was in trouble, obviously. *I'm going to work tonight—alone*. He must mean at VTR. But that was too dangerous, too risky. Why was he taking such chances? For something that didn't concern him directly.

When the phone finally rang, Rick was in the kitchen puring another cup of coffee, and the shrill sound in the silence of his apartment caused him to jump. Coffee spilled across the counter. He was across the room and caught it on the second ring.

He breathed a sigh of relief when he heard Osborne's voice. He started to talk quickly, to question Osborne about the events of the previous day and night, but Osborne shut him off.

"I can't talk long, Rick, and I've got a lot to tell you. Just listen. I've got everything we need. I know how they're transmitting the subliminal message, and I've got the proof of what they're doing—work prints of the TV spots, the campaign film, plus a schedule of the spots, the strategy, the whole thing."

Rick cut in. "Where are you, Dan? What are you going to do?"

"I've changed hotels. I'm at the Sarasota Springs Motel. A real flophouse. The Sarasota Springs. Got that? But I won't be here long. I'm talking from a pay booth in the lobby. I'm catching a flight to Atlanta in an hour. Meet my flight. It's on Delta—you'll have to call to get the flight number."

"Will you have the film with you?"

"Hell no. If they catch on to what I've done, they'll be out looking for me. I'm sending the film to you, Rick."

Rick started to protest, but Osborne again cut him off.

"It's the safest way, Rick. I've put it on a *bus.*" Osborne laughed aloud at his ingenuity. "On a bus, Rick! They'll never think of that! It'll take a couple of days, but it'll be safe. Here's the waybill number: three-eight-four-nine-two-ATL. Write it down. And meet that goddamned bus when it gets to Atlanta.

"There's one big cannister of film. It's got a new batch of FRESH! spots—then some new Phoenix Press spots—and the rest of the film on the spool is a new Hapworth campaign film. And man, it's the hottest little bit of subliminal pornography either of us has ever seen.

"Now here's the strategy. The new FRESH! spots are purely defensive. They'll be used to tear down the opposition in every primary campaign throughout the spring. The Press spots go on the offense, intended to make Hapworth look like a goddamned savior. But a virile savior. And the film emphasizes the virility. It's obviously intended to make the female voter—or the female delegate to the convention—throw her support to Hapworth by sexually arousing her. I don't have time now to go into the whole technique.

"This film is all the proof we'll ever need. It shows the subliminal messages clearly. After they produce the work print, they keep it under lock and key until the finished product. Then they burn it. If I hadn't been able to get my hands on this, we couldn't prove a thing. But it's all there, on that little ol' bus heading for Atlanta. And I'll be there soon. I can hardly wait to see the look on Minerva's face when you call her hand."

"Minerva!" Rick's voice was sharp. "Did you find out which one—"

"I found out—oh, my God!" Osborne's voice was quick, the distress obvious in his tone.

"What's wrong?"

"They're here."

"Who's there?"

"Brett Stanley just walked in the lobby. Along with another guy. A big bastard. They're at the desk right now. Oh shit. They're showing the desk clerk that goddamned photo."

"What photo? Dan, what in the hell is going on?"

"They're leaving. I've gotta go. I'm going to make

that plane or die trying. Gotta go, ol' buddy. They're after my ass and I don't want them to have it. Remember I'll be on Delta. See you in Atlanta."

The two men left the motel lobby and approached the car. They paused there a moment, studying the nondescript string of rooms that encircled the dingy lobby building. Finally Brett Stanley's hand shot out and he pointed toward a room.

"There it is. There's the room."

Together they started over the graveled parking area. When they reached the door, Stanley rapped briskly. He knocked again, louder, the sound reverberating down the corridor formed by the wall of doors and the cars parked in front of them.

Finally Stanley stepped back and moved to the window. The curtains were pulled back slightly, and he pressed his face against the glass, shielding his eyes from the bright morning sun.

"There's no one in the room," he announced, turning to Steve Gorman. "The bed hasn't been slept in. But there's luggage sitting in the middle of the floor." He waited for Gorman to speak, but the other man only looked at him.

"What are we going to do?" Stanley asked, fumbling in his jacket for a cigarette.

His only answer was a contemptuous sneer.

Stanley pulled a lighter from his pocket and flicked his thumb across it. His hand was trembling a little, his voice more plaintive, almost pleading for a reply.

"What are we going to do, Steve?"

"We? What are *we* going to do?" Gorman spat out. "It's not *my* problem, Stanley. You're the one who's fucked up. Just like all the others. And just like all of them, you want me to get you out of trouble."

Suddenly Gorman pulled the cigarette from Brett

Stanley's mouth. He inserted the filtered tip in his own lips and took a long draw of smoke. When Stanley made no move to counter the insult, Gorman's sneer broke into a barking laugh.

"It's not so bad having old Steve in California, is it, Brett, now that you're in trouble? No more lectures on how I'm going to have to watch my step, or take it easy with the girls. Now you're talking out of the other side of your mouth."

Stanley ignored his derisive remarks. "We've got to find him, Steve. We know his name—"

"You stupid son of a bitch. You wouldn't have known that if your secretary hadn't told you. You wouldn't even have realized that he'd broken your security. *She* found your desk had been tampered with, *she* gave you the program with his real name on it, *she* found the name of this crappy motel. *She* did it—you didn't. You'd rather spend your time lecturing me on keeping out of trouble."

Gorman inhaled from the cigarette, his eyes fastened on Stanley. "I'll help you . . . I'll help you, Stanley. Not because I give a shit about *you.* But I'll find that son of a bitch and *get* him, so I can show Mac Hunter that he made a big mistake kicking me out of Atlanta. He's going to eat his goddamned words."

He flicked the cigarette with force against the walk, and the live embers shot up. Stanley moved his foot, brushing defensively at his trouser leg, and opened his mouth to speak. But Gorman was already walking away.

"Go on back to your office," he called out to Stanley over his shoulder.

Stanley ran to catch up with him. "I'll wait here with you."

Gorman looked at him with contempt. "I don't need you here, Stanley. I don't *want* you. I can handle Osborne, or Davis, or whatever his name is—and I'll handle it my own way." He gestured across the busy street to the taxi stand. "Catch a cab and get back to the office. Find out why he's here, how he broke through your security. Do anything. But don't hang around here. *I don't need you.*" His voice was cold and commanding, and Stanley obeyed.

"And don't call Hunter!" Gorman yelled after him. "Not yet. I'll call him when I have something to report."

Gorman watched him leave. Then he opened the door of the small compact car Brett Stanley had rented for him at the airport and slid behind the wheel. He started the motor, racing it, listening to it respond. A compact was always best, he thought. Lots of maneuverability and still enough power to get the job done.

He turned and flipped open his briefcase on the back seat. Rifling through the business papers, he took a mailing envelope and carelessly dumped the contents into the case. With the brown envelope in hand he got out and went to the rear of the car, kneeling and carefully fitting the large envelope over the license tag. Satisfied with the results, he walked back to the open door.

It works better at night, he thought to himself—less chance of being identified. But there's no choice. And by God I'm going to get that son of a bitch.

He knew that Osborne was still in the lobby. He'd seen him trying to hide in the phone booth while Stanley had talked to the man behind the desk, had recognized him from the shaggy moustache. He knew Osborne would have to come out, have to go to his room. And so he waited, his eyes riveted on the lobby door.

In a moment his vigil was rewarded. Dan Osborne pushed the door open and peered cautiously around the entrance. Seeing no trace of the figures he had spotted earlier, he walked quickly out of the lobby and turned the corner of the building toward the room where he had left his luggage.

Steve Gorman threw the car into low gear and shot

forth, throwing gravel in a spray behind him. He rounded the corner and gained momentum. Ahead of him he saw Osborne exposed in the middle of the drive. Osborne looked over his shoulder and, as he realized what was happening, a look of fear came over his face.

Maybe daytime *is* best, Gorman thought with growing excitement. You can see their faces so much more clearly. His foot shot down on the accelerator and the helpless figure loomed up before him.

Chapter 8

As Rick Craig approached the passenger lounge, people were already deplaning from the Los Angeles flight. He stood expectantly, watching the faces bobbing along, trying to spot Dan's familiar shaggy head among the others.

On and on they came, spilling into the lounge to greet family and friends, hurriedly going on their way. Eventually the bodies began to thin, and finally the long deplaning corridor was empty.

Rick continued to stand there, awaiting Dan's appearance at the end of the tunnel, his attitude still expectant.

It was not until he saw four stewardesses leave the plane that he realized Dan was not on the flight, and the nervousness returned, the aching, helpless feeling that had been with him since Dan's hurried goodbye early that morning.

He approached one of the stewardesses. "Are there any other passengers on the flight?" he inquired abruptly.

"No, sir," she answered.

"But there must be. I'm expecting a friend. He's about medium height, has blond hair, a big moustache. He's supposed to be on this flight."

"I'm *sorry,* sir." Her voice was becoming impatient. "There's no one else on the plane. Now, if you'll excuse me—"

Only then did Rick realize that he held the young woman by the arm, his grip so tight that she could not pull away.

He released her, absently mumbling his apology, and turned back toward the terminal. After a few steps he stopped and sank into a seat in the lounge. There, oblivious to the constantly changing scene about him, he tried to piece together the next course of action.

Finally his eyes focused again, and when they did he saw the sign behind the passenger counter.

Atlanta to Los Angeles. Nonstop.

He stood and approached the ticket agent. "Can I get a ticket for LA here?" he asked.

The California landscape flashed past his eyes and he was vaguely conscious of the green and white overhead marker that spelled out the exit from the freeway.

"I'm sorry, Craig," the man beside him was saying. "Dan Osborne is almost as good a friend of mine as he is of yours. Of the whole department, in fact. Hell, he was like a member of the force. He even shared my apartment for a couple of weeks." Lt. Joe Fletcher sighed. "But I've already told you that, haven't I?" he finished lamely.

Rick nodded. There was nothing else to say. He had done everything possible to locate Dan Osborne. Joe Fletcher had almost literally turned the entire Los Angeles Police Department over to him. With no results.

Fletcher was speaking again, almost apologetically. "I don't know anything else we can do except keep on the lookout." He began to tick off their activities during the two days Rick had been in Los Angeles. "No reports at headquarters, no record of hit and runs. No homicide, nothing at the morgue. We've checked at the hospitals. Nothing at private clinics. Nothing at VTR Studios—just that Tom Davis didn't show up for work on Friday morning. And we can't hang 'em for that—not without something more to go on. Nothing at the motel. No luggage. Somebody checked him out, paid his bill—"

"Steve Gorman," Rick said bitterly.

"Yeah, the guy at the motel fits your description of this man Gorman. But hell, we can't even find any trace of Gorman. Stanley says he hasn't been here."

"Stanley's lying," Rick said. "I know—you can't do anything without proof. But Stanley's lying."

"You're probably right. And we'll keep our eye out for him. But damnit, Craig, trying to find one man in *this* goddamned town—" He gestured widely, his arm covering the wide circle of humanity that was Los Angeles. He shook his head in frustration as he pulled into the departure area of the terminal, his eyes searching for the airline name. They rode on in silence until Fletcher pulled his car to the curb.

"Well, here we are." Fletcher's hand was out and Rick took it, their eyes sharing the same concern. "I'm terribly sorry, Rick—"

"Thanks, Joe. Thanks for everything. And keep on it, will you? You have my phone number, my address." Rick got out of the car to leave, and then slid back onto the seat for a moment. "Joe, I don't know what's ahead for me. Maybe the same thing that happened to Dan." And Smitty, he thought, and Diana. And Joe Greenberg. And God only knows who else.

Joe Fletcher was waiting for him to continue, his face expectant.

"Well, what I'm trying to say is this: if anything should happen to me, if you should hear that I'm missing, it'll be up to you. You're the only other person who has heard the whole story. And I'm still not sure that even *you* believe it. But back in Atlanta, in my apartment, you'll find the tape of the conversation between Hapworth and Diana Malloy. And at the bus terminal, you'll find a cannister of film, addressed to me. It will be up to you to expose this thing. That's a tall order, Joe. But it's important. Don't let me down. OK?"

Joe Fletcher nodded his head without comment, his eyes serious.

Again the men clasped hands, and Rick Craig slammed the door behind him and walked through the sliding glass doors. Back to Atlanta, back to the bus station. Back to the final piece of string in the tangled, knotted ball that he alone must now unravel. He squared his shoulders and pushed through the crowds that were already beginning to clog the terminal.

The projection room in Collins & Craig's Atlanta office was dark except for the small splash of light that encircled the tiny high-intensity projectionist's lamp and fell on the dull surface of the work table. The only sound was a whirring noise that came from the projector as it laboriously rewound the large reel of film.

Suddenly Rick Craig stopped the machine and plunged the room into soundless darkness. He sat in the black void, his ears straining against the silence. But he could hear only the sound of his own breathing.

He sat in the darkness for several moments, awaiting a recurrence of the noise he thought he had heard, but there was nothing. Not satisfied, he rose and began to creep across the darkened room into the larger viewing room and toward the door. He moved slowly, steathily, straining to remember the position of tables and chairs, his body inching its way silently, step by step.

Finally he reached the wall and his hand groped on the flat surface searching for the doorknob. His fingers touched metal and his hand closed gently over the knob, turning it slowly and noiselessly. After interminable seconds, it swung quietly inward toward him and he stared into the dark hallway beyond.

The pale light of the moon, seeping into the corridor from the adjoining office, offered a slight degree of relief from the tomblike blackness of the viewing room, but Rick's eyes welcomed it. When he had sequestered himself in the isolation of the projection room, it had been late afternoon. Now, after scrutinizing time and again all of the film Dan Osborne had stolen, the minutes had turned into hours and the twilight had turned into night.

Rick could discern shapes and angles as he stared up and down the hallway. But nothing more. No movement. No further sounds.

With relief he closed the door again. He took a cigarette lighter from his pocket, and with its flickering assistance returned to the projector on the workbench. He flicked on the tiny lamp, pushed down almost level with the tabletop to keep the reflection at a minimum. He reached out to touch the projector's rewind switch and the Anthony Hapworth campaign film wound back through the projector and coiled itself around its original spool.

Perhaps he had been wrong, he thought, to come to the agency offices to view the film. But the obviousness of it offered the greatest security. It was the last place they would look, he had told himself.

And he was sure they were looking for him. On the long flight back from Los Angeles Rick had realized that, knowing Dan Osborne's true identity, it would be relatively easy for their long-time relationship to be discovered. And he had realized with regret that he had taken no steps to keep his impromptu trip to Los Angeles secret. He had called Martha before he left on Friday to tell her where he would be. But she was out and he had carelessly left word with the receptionist. And his

Porsche still sat where he had left it in the airport parking lot, a bright green beacon that would instantly identify him the moment he drove it away.

And so he had taken precautions. Finally. As he left the plane, he had surrounded himself with crowds of people. Instead of going to the parking lot, he had thrown himself into the first available taxi. He had rented a car then, and had driven in relative anonymity to the bus station where, luckily, the film had awaited him.

Only then did he realize that he had no place to go. His apartment wouldn't be safe. He couldn't trust anyone from the office. And so, feeling more comfortable in crowds, he had followed a stream of cars to the Braves Stadium, where they were playing an exhibition game. There, parked among thousands of other cars he had sat until dusk began to fall, engrossed in the research documentation of Dr. Paul Prescott.

Then he had driven to the office. He avoided the underground parking lot, choosing instead a deserted side street. And when he entered the building, the security guard had fortunately been absent on inspection rounds.

The television commercials and the campaign film, he had come to find out, embodied every subliminal technique that Prescott's manuscript described. The entire project—Project Jupiter, the label on the cannister called it—had been a product of months, maybe years, of effort and planning. It had been devised by a brilliant scientific mind and executed with flawless marketing expertise.

Its first objective: destroy the opposition. Not through customary campaign rhetoric, but through an unseen message on a commercial for a carbonated beverage, a message that pounded home again and again the most devastating weakness that each of the frontrunners had sought to overcome.

The disco scene with Barry Starr was the best example. Ostensibly it introduced FRESH! to the youth market. But subliminally, it appealed to the youth market by destroying the credibility of the senator from Texas. Though he had been cleared, years earlier, of bribery charges, the suggestion was repeated afresh, planting the seeds of suspicion across the nation.

Next they sought to create the image of leadership through subliminal messages concealed in the new spots for The Phoenix Press' blockbuster saturation campaign. The techniques were almost textbook examples of the Prescott premise. Implantation of words and images. And accompanying the words, a sickening display of erotic scenes and pictures, all calculated to arouse the viewer, to stimulate and excite the subconscious.

And finally an in-depth approach to the subconscious to be delivered under controlled circumstances: the campaign film. And the campaign song. A twenty-minute barrage of eroticism combined with positive words and repeated over and over again to elaborate on the brief messages already established by the television commercials.

But for what purpose? Why?

Rick pondered that final question. Now he knew what and when and where. But why? Why had Mac Hunter gone to such lengths to elect a president? His money alone could have done it.

And who was responsible?

Certainly, he knew that Hunter and Prescott and Gorman were behind it. And Anthony Hapworth, obviously. But who was the woman? Who was Minerva? He realized that he was no closer to the answer than he had been before.

Rick sighed and rose from the stool where he had been sitting. He began to collect his evidence, to prepare to leave as secretly as he had entered.

It was at that moment that he heard the sound. It was muffled, barely discernible. But in the silence of the empty room there was no mistake about it. Rick stood, his ears straining, his mind trying to connect the dull thumping noise with an everyday office sound. He had heard it before. Repeatedly.

And then he realized it was the muffled noise of the elevator doors down the corridor.

He quickly shut off the small light and grasped the cannister of film to his chest in a protective gesture. His mind feverishly searched for hiding places, for a secure place where the documentation of the Jupiter plot would be safe. But he realized there was none.

He stood in blackness, waiting. A tiny sliver of light appeared under the door to the hallway, and he knew they had turned on the overhead lights in the corridor.

And then he could hear the movements outside the door: vague sounds of footsteps down the hall, an occasional door being slammed.

Slowly the sounds of a methodical search came closer to him. He could hear heavy steps punctuated with the clack of high heels; the low rumble of a man's voice, the higher-pitched tones of a woman.

Rick stood there, his mind still seeking a hiding place for the film, and for himself as well. In desperation, he pulled at the door that separated the small projectionist's alcove and the viewing room. Letting it stand slightly ajar, he moved behind it and attempted as best he could to conceal himself there. Silently he crouched down and placed the film on the floor, leaving his hands free to do whatever he might be called upon to do.

Suddenly the door to the hall swung open and he heard the voices distinctly. A man asked, "Is he in there?" The voice was familiar to Rick, but there was no time to connect it in his memory.

"I don't see him." A woman's voice answered.

Rick edged closer to the wall, pushing toward the hinged surface and the slender vertical crack between the door and jamb. And seconds later he *could* see—could see a shaft of light pouring into the darkened viewing room, see a woman's body silhouetted against the light.

The woman spoke again. "I don't see him, but let me find the light." Her words were punctuated with a burst of light as she found the wall switch.

Standing there, one hand casually resting on the handle of the open door to the hallway, was Suzanne Carmichael.

For a moment his mind deadened. His lips silently repeated, again and again, a single word. Minerva. Minerva. But then, as she walked across the viewing room toward the tiny projectionist's booth where he hid, his mind accepted the fact and he prepared himself for action.

Suzanne walked directly to the doorway and pushed the door farther open to gain a better vantage of the room. Rick flattened himself against the wall and stood rigid, without breating. Only the thickness of the door itself stood between them.

Then miraculously she turned and walked away.

"He's not here," she called out. "But he's been here. I can smell his cigarette smoke."

She moved out of the viewing room, into the hallway, and her hand again sent the room into darkness. As she turned back to pull the door closed, he heard her parting words. "He's already left the agency. I'll have to try his apartment."

And then they were gone, the dull thump of the elevator doors finally signaling their departure.

Rick stood for long minutes, his back still pressing against the wall. Finally he relaxed and closed the door that had hidden him.

He thought quickly now. They were gone. But they

might come back, he reasoned. Time to get the hell out of there. He again flicked on the small lamp, and he stooped to retrieve the cannister of film that he had so precipitously deposited on the floor when Suzanne had entered the viewing room.

Suzanne. Minerva. The pain of his discovery swept over him again and he stood there for a moment motionless, the film in his hand. And then abruptly he swung back into motion.

He bent down to take his battered attaché case off the floor and, flipping it open, he put the film on top of the other documentation they had collected: the two books he had stolen from Paul Prescott's study on the island, the diminutive cassette that carried a taped admission of guilt in the unmistakable voice of Anthony Hapworth.

It was a neat package of evidence, proof positive. And no matter how bizarre, it would stand up in any court. Rick shook his head at the thought. Not in a court. That wasn't the way he would expose them. Hell, he wasn't even certain that any law had been broken.

It was a crime against the public, the American voter. And it was up to him, Rick Craig, to tell them about it. With a nod of determination, he closed the case and locked it. For the final time he extinguished the light and walked through the now familiar darkness to the hall door. He moved quietly down the corridor, past Laura Talbott's office, past the door to his own office and on toward the elevator.

But his better judgment again stopped him. Better take the stairs, regardless of the time and effort it might require.

He found a cigarette lighter in his coat pocket and as he held the flickering light up to help him find the exit sign to the stairway, he was conscious of a vague movement to his left, of a form barely discernible to his line of sight.

At the same moment he felt a hand on his throat and then his neck was locked in the viselike grip of a powerful arm. A moist cloth covered his mouth and a strong odor assaulted his nose.

In a moment his body went limp, supported only by the arms of the man who now held him.

Part V

Chapter 1

Colors swirled before his eyes, but Rick Craig's mind refused to give them definition. He heard muted voices and felt a violent pounding in his head, a sensation that gave way to a throbbing pain. His throat contracted with nausea as he tried to sit up, and the colors still swam before his eyes. He fell back into unconsciousness.

When he finally opened his eyes and focused them, he found himself staring at the brilliant hues of Kathy's painting on the wall of his office.

He stayed motionless a moment, his head still throbbing from the anesthetic that had overpowered him, his mind resisting coherent thought.

He moved his head to one side. Another wave of nausea. He fought it down, then allowed only his eyes to move over the familiar scene before him. What was he doing in his office? What had happened out there in the hallway? He struggled to sit up on the sofa where he lay, but the movement sent a starburst of pain through his skull. He fell back against the cushion, both hands pressing against his temples, trying to rub away the ache.

Suddenly a sound filled the room, a short machine-gun burst of laughter. It rang out, then repeated itself, and it was so unexpected that Rick's mind, as well as his body, jerked involuntarily. Despite the throbbing, he pulled himself up on an elbow and turned his head toward the sound.

Steve Gorman was propped against Rick's desk, half sitting, half leaning, his feet crossed casually in front of him. His arms were carelessly crossed over his chest and in one hand he loosely gripped a pistol.

"What's the matter, Craig? Can't you take it? This cloak-and-dagger stuff getting a little rough for you?"

The shock was evident on Rick's face. "Gorman!" His voice was thickened and awkward, the word little more than a croak. He blinked his eyes, trying to assimilate the facts. He spoke again. "Gorman. I thought you were in Los Angeles—"

The snort of a laugh was repeated. "I was," Gorman answered.

Rick struggled to sit up. Despite the pain, he swung his legs over the side of the sofa and sat forward. A searing pain shot through his skull again, but he disregarded it and fought to get to his feet.

Gorman was beside him in an instant, a hand roughly shoving Rick back against the leather of the sofa, the pistol in his face, its barrel just inches from his forehead. "Keep still, Craig. Don't move a goddamned muscle or I'll blow your fucking head off and tell them I did it in self-defense."

Rick sat there, every muscle tensed, his body stiffened, watching Gorman's face. A strange look was on it. Nervousness, his facial muscles twitching, his eyes blinking uncontrollably. But with the nervousness, a look of anticipation. A brightness about his eyes, a faint smile on his lips.

Suddenly Rick let his body go limp. He closed his eyes submissively and sat there, his head against the back of the sofa. Finally Gorman relaxed his grip on Rick's shoulder and moved away. Rick remained silent for another moment before he opened his eyes and spoke again.

"What do you want with me?"

"That. That's what I want." Gorman motioned toward the desk and Rick followed his eyes. His attaché case sat there, its lock sprung, the cover opened. The contents were a jumble, but Rick could see the film canister and one of the magenta volumes extending over the top of the case.

"That's what I came to get. And you made my job easier for me. You had everything all neat and tidy and together. I didn't even have to look."

"If that's what you want, then why don't you take it and get out? Without it, I don't have any proof. I can't do anything. Why don't you leave me alone? You've got what you came for—"

"Oh, that's not all that I want. I want you, too. And Mac Hunter wants you. Wants you put away where you won't cause any more trouble. And he doesn't care, anymore, how I do it." Gorman paused a moment, then continued, his tone almost conversational. "Jesus, Craig, you *have* been a pain in the ass. Hopping around from one coast to another, rescuing people off islands, setting up undercover agents in our film studios—"

"What have you done with Dan Osborne?" Rick interrupted.

Gorman snorted out a laugh. "And what did you do with Logan Smith?" He let the question hang there on the air, not really expecting an answer. "You were pretty clever, weren't you, Craig? Or should I say Dr. Christianson? Pretty clever. And pretty gutsy. I'm surprised you had it in you." He looked at Rick a moment, then repeated his question. "What did you do with Smitty?" Finally he shrugged and turned away. "Not that it makes any difference. Smitty doesn't remember a damned thing. You've probably already found that out. Nothing. Nothing about Diana or Anthony Hapworth or Minerva or any of the rest of it."

Rick repeated his original question. "Where's Dan

Osborne? What did you do to him?"

"I put him on ice." Gorman glared at him. "I took care of him, the same way I did that son of a bitch who stole the proof. The way I did Diana. And Smitty." His eyes narrowed to slits. "And the same way I damned near put *you* on ice. But I missed. That time."

The thought seemed to provoke something in Gorman's emotions and he began to move slowly toward Rick. "I've waited a long time to do this, Craig. Ever since that day, right here in this office when I told you that I'd get you. And I almost did in the parking lot that night. But you got away. And now I'm glad that you did. It's going to be better this way. Because I can see your face. I can see how much I hurt you."

Gorman began to move forward, slowly, menacingly. Rick got to his feet, inching backward, commanding his body to react, to shake away the lingering effects of the anesthetic.

Gorman's eyes focused only on Rick's face and he took another step forward. He paused a moment, tossing aside the pistol and stripping off his coat, letting it fall to the floor. Anticipating his lunge, Rick crouched and continued to inch his way backward until finally he felt the wall.

But Gorman stood fast. His hand plunged into a pocket and reappeared holding a dark object. With a flick, he exposed the long blade of a knife.

"The gun is too quick," he murmured. He crouched and came forward slowly, one hand weaving, the knife blade cutting through the air before him.

"I'm going to get you this time, Craig. I'm going to carve up that pretty face of yours."

Another step nearer, another flash of the blade.

"The next time maybe you'll stay out of things that don't concern you."

Rick looked about for a means of escape, for a weapon, for some form of protection against the blade. In desperation his fingers clutched at his belt, pulling the leather from his waist in a single motion and coiling it around his hand. He crouched again, the leather-wrapped hand before him, ready to parry, as best he could, the rushing strokes of Gorman's knife.

"Steve!" A woman's voice called out and then, with greater agitation, repeated the single word she had spoken. "Steve! What are you doing? Stop it!"

The sound pierced through Gorman's neurotic determination and he allowed his eyes to leave Rick for the moment, seeking the source of the command.

Rick Craig's eyes had already flickered to the doorway, to the woman standing there, and now, as Gorman stopped his advance, Rick looked back at Laura Talbott.

Thank God, Rick thought to himself. Thank God it's Laura. Maybe she can help, if only it's to divert him. His mind leaped ahead, trying to formulate a plan.

Gorman eyed Laura briefly, acknowledging her presence with a grunt, then dismissing her. His eyes focused again on Rick and again his knife blade swished through the air.

"Laura!" It was Rick's voice. His eyes were on Gorman's, his hand still extended to ward off the impending thrusts. He realized that moments mattered. Gorman had been playing with him. Teasing him with fear. But Laura's presence would change that. "Laura, thank God it's you. His gun, Laura. He dropped it on the leather chair. Get it!"

"Steve, stop it. Leave him alone!" Her voice was intense, high pitched with excitement.

"Don't try to reason with him, Laura," Rick urged. "Can't you see that he's gone off the deep end? Get the gun—"

Laura sprang into motion. She ran into the office, exploring the leather chairs beside the sofa. Finding the pistol, she took it in her hand and aimed it at Gorman.

"Steve! Stop it!" Once again she demanded his compliance. But again he ignored her. Steadying one hand with the other, she raised the gun, aimed it at the wall beside Gorman's head. A thunderous blast exploded in the small room and, in shock and surprise, Steve Gorman at last stopped his deadly advance.

One hand went to his ear and a look of pain spread over his face. He shook his head, trying to shake the ringing from his ears, and a dazed look slowly formed itself.

"Drop the knife, Steve." Laura's command assaulted Gorman's mind and he looked at her, confused, not understanding.

"Drop the knife, Steve."

He did nothing.

With the gun still aimed at him, Laura walked forward and drew back her hand, bringing it against his face with staggering force. "Drop the knife, Steve." Her voice was deeper, more commanding, and gradually the words seeped into Steve Gorman's inner consciousness. He let the knife slip from his fingers to the floor and stood there, dazed looking, staring alternately at Laura and then at Rick.

Relief flooded Rick Craig's mind and body, an enormous, overpowering relief. He stepped forward and scooped the weapon off the floor, collapsing the blade and dropping the heavy switchblade into his pocket. Suddenly he felt the delayed reaction. His knees began to shake almost uncontrollably. He sank into a chair, breathing heavily, trying to restore his physical and emotional equilibrium. It was a moment before he was able to talk.

"Laura." His tongue was still thickened and his voice unsure, but his words came in a torrent. "Thank God, I know—thank God that I know I can trust you. Laura, there's a terrible thing happening. Right here at the agency. Right under our noses. You've got to help me stop it. Stop *them.* We've got Gorman now, but Hunter is behind it. And Paul Prescott is involved. And Suzanne Carmichael and—oh God, Laura, it seems like the whole world is in on it."

"Rick, what are you talking about?" Laura's voice was calm, probing.

"Mac Hunter is using Collins & Craig as a front. They're trying to use subliminal advertising to elect a president. And I've got the evidence to prove it." Rick stood, testing his legs, and found them to be steady. He walked toward Laura, holding out his hand. "Here, I'll take the gun. You telephone the police and we'll let them handle Gorman."

Rick's hand remained outstretched. Laura did not offer him the gun, and when he moved to take it she backed away.

"Give me the gun, Laura, and get on the phone to the police." There was an edge of urgency in his voice. "Let's get Gorman locked up and then I'll tell you the whole story. And then I'm going to blow this whole thing sky high."

Laura backed up another step. Her gaze had been fastened on Gorman, but now she turned it on Rick, a strange smile on her lips.

"That wouldn't fit my plan, Rick. I don't want Gorman locked up. I want *you* locked up, instead. Locked up and out of trouble. But I don't want you hurt." The pistol had been pointed at Gorman, but now she slowly moved her hand toward Rick so that the gun was pointing at his chest.

Rick smiled, trying to cover the confusion that was encompassing him, and again reached for the gun. "What are you talking about, Laura? Give me the—"

"Listen to what I'm saying, Rick. I *don't* want to hurt you. But I will if I have to, because neither you nor anyone else is going to endanger this project—"

"That's enough!" Rick heard Gorman's voice, felt himself being pushed roughly out of the way and the other man, too, reached out toward the woman. "I'll take the gun back, Laura."

Her eyes snapped and she took another step backward, motioning both men away with the gun. Her voice was hard. "No, you *won't* take the gun, Gorman. *No one is going to endanger this project.* And that goes for you and that insane streak of violence in you. From here on out, you're not going to do anything unless I tell you to—"

"You're crazy. I don't take my orders from you. I take my orders from Mac Hunter and—"

"These *are* Hunter's orders!" Seeing the incredulous look on his face, she laughed at him. "Don't believe me? Why not check it out with the man himself? He's in his office in Manhattan right now. He's just put Paul Prescott on the Gulfstream headed for Atlanta and then the island. Go ahead, Gorman," she taunted. "Call him. Let him tell you where you stand. And while you're at it, tell him that you *didn't* destroy the Hapworth tape. That you let it fall into Rick Craig's hands."

Rick stood transfixed, staring dumbly at the scene in front of him. Laura giving orders to Gorman? Laura involved in the plot? But no. It was Suzanne. He had seen Suzanne earlier. She had almost discovered him.

His confusion mounted. If Suzanne had been looking for him—but now Laura was holding a gun on him, threatening him, talking about the project. His mind was numbed, and involuntarily he mumbled a single word aloud.

"Minerva . . ."

Laura had turned away from him momentarily,

watching Gorman as he spoke into the telephone. But when she heard his voice, she turned around and looked at him.

"What did you say, Rick? Minerva?" She laughed lightly. "Yes, Rick. I'm Minerva. Not Suzanne. But I confused you, didn't I? You thought Suzanne might be one of the bad guys."

Rick nodded. "But she was here, earlier. What was she—"

"She was looking for you, too. But for different reasons. She wanted to help you, to warn you. She and the security guard—" Rick's face registered surprise and Laura smiled. "Who did you think it was? Gorman? No, it was just old Charlie from the security desk downstairs. And after the two of them searched the offices, all we had to do was wait for you to appear."

The abrupt sound of a telephone being slammed against its cradle drew Laura's attention and she looked over to see Gorman seated at Rick's desk, his hand still on the telephone, a dark, belligerent expression spreading over his face.

"Congratulations," he said to Laura, his voice bitter. "You've moved to the head of the class in back-stabbing. Not only have you done a number on me, but on Prescott, too. You've convinced Hunter that neither one of us can be trusted."

"I haven't done a number on anyone." Laura's voice was cold with anger at the charge Gorman had leveled against her. "You did the number yourself, Gorman. You're a sadistic son of a bitch, and you can't keep it under control. And Paul drinks too much. Far too much. Neither one of you can be trusted with major responsibilities any longer. Hunter realized it, and I realized it. And we've done something about it."

"Does Prescott know he's been demoted?"

"Hunter told him this afternoon in New York."

"I'd like to be around when Prescott tells you what he thinks of you. He was your teacher, wasn't he? Taught you everything you know. Introduced you to Hunter, to the project." Gorman paused a moment, then continued. "Like I said, you've moved to the head of the class in back-stabbing. Well," he shrugged, "apparently I don't have any choice. You're the boss. For the time being anyway. But I'll come out on top, Laura. And when I do, I'll get you—"

"Shut up, Gorman. I'm tired of your threats." Laura's voice was hard and cold, and she walked over to stand facing him. "What time is the Gulfstream due here?" she asked crisply.

"Within the hour."

"Good. We've got work to do. Now listen to me . . ." Her voice dropped to a soft murmur.

Rick Craig stood across the room, watching the two of them. But instead of apprehension, instead of concern over his own safety, he experienced an altogether different emotion—an exhilaration that Suzanne was guiltless, that she had nothing to do with the plot. That she had not betrayed him. And coupled with the exhilaration was a feeling of relief that Suzanne was safely out of the building, free from Gorman's grasp.

He was drawn back to the present by Gorman. The look of belligerence had been displaced by a smile, then a twisted grin. He walked across the room to retrieve his jacket, still lying on the floor where it had dropped. He slipped into it, then moved back to the desk to snap the cover of the attaché case closed and grasp it by the handle. He was at the door, about to leave, when he looked back at Laura.

"And what about him?" he asked gruffly, nodding in Rick's direction.

"I can handle Rick," she said, waving the gun toward him, and then she laughed. "I have been ever since I met him. One way or another. Haven't I, Rick?"

Steve Gorman stepped from the elevator and approached the security desk. "Good evening, Charlie," he said, his voice and his manner direct and businesslike.

"Mr. Gorman!" Surprise was in the older man's voice. "I didn't know you were here. I didn't see you come in—"

Gorman allowed a sheepish tone to come into his voice. "I forgot to sign in, Charlie," he admitted. "Sorry about that. I'll take care of it now," he said, reaching over for the register. Matter-of-factly, he continued. "Oh, by the way. I don't suppose Suzanne Carmichael is still around. It looks like she's signed out—"

"Miss Carmichael? Yes sir, she's gone. She was awful anxious to find Mr. Craig, but we couldn't locate him nowhere upstairs—"

"Actually she just wanted his briefcase," Gorman said, patting the case that now sat on the desk in front of them. "And Rick wanted me to give it to her. She didn't say where she was going, did she?"

"She sure did. Said if Mr. Craig should show up to tell him she'd be waiting at his apartment."

"Good." Gorman's casual smile concealed the pleasure Charlie's announcement brought him. "I'll stop off on my way home and see if she's still there."

"I'm sure she will be. I've never seen one of Mr. Craig's ladies so anxious to see him." Charlie winked at Gorman, sharing this private joke with him.

Gorman smiled. "She's in for a disappointment then. She may be expecting Rick Craig, but she's going to get me."

Chapter 2

They sat in the car Rick had rented, the lights from the private airstrip and the parking lot casting shadows over their faces. The sound of a jet obscured their voices for a moment.

Rick sat in the driver's seat, staring dully from the window. When the jet sound had subsided, he again phrased the question he had asked Laura earlier.

"How long has this whole thing been going on?"

"How long?" Laura reflected a moment, her eyes locked on him, the pistol firmly pointed at his chest. "How long has Prescott's research into subconscious perception been going on? Forever, maybe. For years, at least. The Miramar Corporation has been supporting Dr. Prescott's research efforts for ten, twelve, maybe fifteen years. Since long before he gave up his practice.

"But if you're asking about Project Jupiter, I can be more specific. The seeds were planted about the time Mac Hunter lost control of the White House. At that time he pressured Paul to begin to convert scientific assumptions into working facts. To develop the techniques to utilize subliminal stimuli to help the voter make up his mind. That's when they started recruiting the specialists on the team."

"Why?" Rick pursued the subject. "Why does Mac

Hunter want to get Hapworth elected in *this* way? Why not just buy the election?"

Laura laughed. "He doesn't just want the presidency—he wants the people. He started with the primaries, and he's winning those. Next come the delegates to the Convention. And by July he'll control enough delegates. And then comes the election. And control of the voters. And it will work. We already know it will.

"And when Hap is in the White House, he'll control him. Hunter will make every decision, call every shot. And he'll continue to make the people like it. He'll make Anthony Hapworth the most popular president in the history of the United States.

"And when Hapworth has outlived his usefulness, he'll put another man in office, and start the same game all over again." She paused for a moment and continued in a more thoughtful voice. "Hunter wants absolute control, total power. Not just over the president and the executive branch. But over the people, too. He wants to own America, to control the minds of the people. That's just for openers, Rick. Tomorrow he'll control the world."

Rick grunted, a mixed sound of disbelief and shock, and Laura quickly continued.

"You don't believe it could happen, Rick? Of course it can—and will. It will take time and money. And foreign connections. And Hunter has all three. He can elect the president, then control him. And if he controls the people, then he can control the Congress. Or Parliament or the Common Market. Or perhaps even the Presidium, given the right circumstances. He'll be able to provoke riots in South America, or quell them. He can dictate the world's energy policy or control the price of gold. And all because he's learned how to *manipulate minds*." She paused, then added somewhat ruefully, "With our help."

Rick was silent, but he studied her, watched the gun waver carelessly as she became involved in the conversation.

"And what's your goal, Laura? First Lady of the World?"

She jerked her head toward him with a flare of anger. "Of course not."

"Then what *are* you up to, Laura? If it's not power you're seeking, then what—"

"I'm a professional, Rick. Oh, not a professional communicator, like I've always made you believe. I have my doctorate in psychology." She laughed. "I'm a doctor, Rick. *Doctor Talbott.* And all of those months, you thought you were sleeping with just a plain advertising woman, didn't you?" She became more serious. "I studied at the University of Montreal—one of the best neurological centers in the world. Then I interned with Paul Prescott. He's one of the best in the world, too. My major field has always been subliminal perception, and when I learned about Paul's research efforts for Miramar I wanted to be a part of it. I joined the project team very early and I've been involved in everything that's happened.

"My job was to become the advertising specialist. Hunter set me up with an agency in New York, then he sent me to San Francisco to learn the business, to master the mechanics of creativity. Brett Stanley and Ron Spence came on board—oh yes, they're a part of the team. But not Barry Starr. He's not smart enough to do anything but sing. He thinks that talent got him where he is today. He's right. It was talent, but it was Ron Spence's talent. Ron and I masterminded 'Puppet in Love.' And it worked. It was responsible for the religious riots at Brigham Young, responsible for Drew Martin's assault on that kid in the dorm—"

"Assault? Don't you mean murder? I've read

Prescott's journal, remember? On the Utah Experiment."

Laura shifted her position in her discomfort, and Rick saw her grasp of the pistol become looser for a moment. But then she again tightened her control of the gun.

"Call it whatever you want, Rick. It was never intended to go that far. I regret that the boy was killed, regret that Drew Martin had to go to trial. But I personally hired the best criminal lawyer in America and we got him off. And Drew is no worse for wear—"

"Like Smitty?"

"Like Smitty. Smitty just learned a little too much. And we just erased a couple of the neurones in his brain, where certain memories were stored."

"Is that what you intend to do, Laura? To erase a part of the brain of the whole world, like you did to Martin and Smitty?"

Laura stared at him, then glanced out the window of the car. Again the gun wavered.

"I couldn't expect you to understand. You're not trained in the behavioral sciences."

"I'm not trained in behavioral science, but I'm not stupid. Try me. Try explaining it to me and see if I can understand." If I can just keep her talking, Rick thought to himself, if I can get her distracted . . .

"Rick, we're not going to do any harm by electing Anthony Hapworth president. *Someone* has to be president, and someone always pulls their strings. And Hapworth's not so bad. But that's beside the point. Hapworth has been necessary. To get Hunter's support. To get Miramar funding. And while Hunter is playing around with the presidency, think of the good that *we* can accomplish with subliminal advertising—"

"The good?" Rick Craig was genuinely astonished. "*The good?* How can you ever accomplish good by meddling with someone's mind?"

"Why couldn't it influence the course of human behavior for the *good* of mankind instead of its *detriment?* Have you considered what might be done subliminally to erase years of racial bigotry, to make nations friendly, bring peace to the world? The subconscious could eradicate crime and violence—or seriously curtail it. That wouldn't be bad, would it?"

"No," Rick answered tentatively, drawn intellectually into the conversation. He turned the idea over in his mind. Then he reversed himself. "Yes. Yes, it would. Those are honorable goals. If they're in the hands of honorable men. But they're not Mac Hunter's goals. And even if they were, that kind of thing should be done to the rational mind, not the subconscious. People have to have a free choice, to do something because they believe in what they're doing. Good men *might* use it for the good. But Mac Hunter would use it to make fools out of the American people."

"The American people *are* fools," Laura retorted. "They've become soft and gullible. They can be manipulated like puppets—"

"I don't want anyone manipulating my mind, pulling my strings. Sneaking thoughts past my rational mind into my subconscious."

"Oh, come now, Rick." Laura's voice was soft, her tone persuasive. "Isn't that what advertising people do every day? Persuade people that they want something they don't need or can't afford? That's been its goal for decades, hasn't it—to mold the consumer's mind?"

"Of course not." Rick's voice was louder than he had intended. "Advertising doesn't mold anyone's mind. It just tells the public what's available. The public makes up its own mind. All that advertising does is to communicate—"

Rick stopped in midsentence. Good God, he thought

to himself. I'm being held at gunpoint by a woman I almost loved, I'm waiting to be taken to an island where they'll do brain surgery on me—if I'm lucky. And despite all that, I'm sitting here and defending advertising. He shook his head at the idiocy of the situation, shrugging his shoulders to signify an end to the conversation.

The two of them fell silent, Laura apparently lost in her own thoughts while Rick searched his mind for a way to distract her attention long enough to overpower her and escape.

And then she supplied the answer that he sought: she unveiled her own emotions.

"I'm sorry, Rick."

He looked intently at her profile, illuminated by the reflected lights around them. "Sorry?" he asked. "What do you mean, Laura?"

"Sorry that it had to turn out this way. Sorry that it had to be Collins & Craig instead of one of those smartass New York agencies who are already on the make. Sorry that we had to discover Jay's weak spot and break up the beautiful thing the two of you had going. But most of all, I'm sorry that you had to be so damned honest and forthright, that you couldn't have bent a little, couldn't have gone along with Hunter's acquisition of Collins & Craig.

"Because that would have been such a wonderfully easy way for me, a way to have my cake and eat it too —to have the man I loved and carry out a scientific project that I've devoted my professional career to.

"Yes, Rick, I did love you. I never intended to, never wanted to. All of those evenings we spent together, all of the times we made love—I wasn't acting, Rick. Even last January, in Los Angeles on New Year's Eve, I tried to get you to accept The Press, to accept Miramar. But you fought it.

"And then I tried to get you to accept me. I asked you

to give up a memory. And if you had, I might have given the project up. But you didn't. Or couldn't. Whatever the reason, you rejected me. You rejected me, offered me no hope."

Throughout her recitation her voice had grown softer, more introspective, and now she looked at Rick in the shadowy light. "I'm sorry, Rick. I'm sorry it didn't work out." One hand flicked to her face, brushing at her eyes, and she was silent for a moment.

But only for a moment. She spoke again, and Rick heard the determination, the professionalism, the strength surging back into her tone. "And so," she completed her emotional soliloquy, "you'll have to be dealt with."

She paused and looked away. Again Rick had seen the pistol falter and he shifted his position on the seat away from the steering column and closer to Laura. His hand began to edge toward the gun.

He felt the emotionalism of her mood begin to slip away and he sought to rekindle her feelings.

"What's going to happen to me, Laura?"

She responded with a sigh. "I don't honestly know, Rick. That's not my department. I stopped Gorman from killing you, but he won't be satisfied until you're dead. And Paul Prescott wants you alive. He wants you involved, he wants you hurt, he wants you embarrassed." Laura shook her head. "He hates you, Rick. He has ever since your wife was killed. He blames you for her death—"

"Then why does he want me alive? Why doesn't he let Gorman get rid of me?"

"He'd rather do it his way—kill you emotionally. He saw you recover once before, after you hit the skids. He wants to see you hit the skids again, and do away with yourself. Slowly, bit by bit."

"And Hunter? How does he feel?"

"Hunter just wants you on the island. Out of the way . . ."

She kept talking, but Rick did not hear her. His hand continued to slide toward her, toward the hand that now held the pistol in a rather listless grip. And suddenly he lunged forward, his right hand seizing the barrel of the pistol and turning it away from him, his left hand pushing against her head to keep her off balance. She struggled to free the hand, fought with all her might. Her startled cry became a scream, and still they fought for control of the gun. And finally, by accident, Rick's hand slipped away from the gun barrel.

Without the pressure of his grip to counteract her own force, the suddenly freed hand involuntarily flew upward and struck her face. Her head snapped back against the side window and the gun slipped from her hand.

Rick studied her inert body for a moment and then drew back his fist to release his pent-up fury on the woman who had quite literally seduced him—first his body and then, gradually, his mind. But his tensed arm relaxed, his clenched fist fell back to his lap. He looked at her a moment, and then his mind repeated a phrase she had so recently spoken to him.

I'm sorry, too, Laura.

Rick shook the thought from his mind and fell into action. Bending over her he picked up the gun. As his arm brushed against her, her unconscious body collapsed against the door in a heap.

He sat staring at her, trying to determine a course of action. Gorman was on his way to the airport. The Gulfstream carrying Paul Prescott would be arriving within the hour. And all of them would likely be heading for St. Sebastian's.

And with them they had the one thing that was essential to his plan: his attaché case, and in it, all of the evidence to expose Project Jupiter.

Time. That was what he needed. Time to slow them down until he could gain possession of the case. He sat thinking, wasting precious moments, until the framework of a plan began to suggest itself.

He flicked the key in the ignition and felt a surge of power from the powerful engine. Throwing it into reverse, he pulled from the parking lot amidst an earsplitting screech of rubber.

Moments later he roared to a halt in front of the Operations Tower of the sprawling air park, his eyes searching for the taxi stand. He saw it finally, and with it a single taxicab. He pulled up beside it, driving now at a more restrained speed.

He got out and walked to the driver's window, addressing the taxi driver. "Are you available to . . . uh . . . can you take a lady back into town . . ." He feigned an embarrassed smile. "I don't hardly know how to ask you this," he told the driver with a shrug. "My date—over there in my car—has had a little too much to drink. In fact, she's had a *lot* too much to drink. And I just got word her husband's on his way out here to look for her. I'm going to load her in the back seat of your cab and give you her address in Atlanta and pay you in advance. And then I want you to take off and get her the hell out of here. You know what I mean?"

The driver stared at him in disbelief, trying to grasp the tale of marital infidelity that he was hearing and suddenly burst out in loud laughter. "Hell yes, buddy," he told Rick. "That's a helluva idea. One helluva idea. I might use it myself, some day. Load her in and I'll get her out of your hair."

Rick already had Laura placed in the back seat of the cab, and he peeled a twenty off the roll in his pocket and stuffed it into the driver's hand. "Here's her address," he said, scribbling a street number on a piece of paper.

"And much obliged for the favor," he said as the driver started the engine.

As the other man was about to pull away, Rick called out to him as if in afterthought. "Oh, by the way. When she comes to, she'll be mad as hell, but don't pay any attention to her. She'll probably want to come back out here, but just tell her that her husband is raising hell, trying to find her. Remember, just don't pay any attention to her. No matter how mad she gets."

Rick smiled as the cab drove away. She *will* be mad as hell, he told himself. Then he jumped back in the car and pulled out in the opposite direction.

First, he thought, I have to stash this car away. Then, a telephone. And finally, a lot of luck.

He dropped a coin into the pay phone and dialed the number. Funny, he thought to himself. When you live alone, you're not accustomed to calling your own number.

The phone was ringing now, and he could imagine the shrill sound resounding through his apartment. Five rings. Six. With each successive ring he became more anxious. Be there, he silently implored. Please, Suzanne. *Be there!*

The last words he had heard her speak, when she left him hiding behind the door at the office, indicated that she would wait for him at his apartment. Then, he had looked on it as a threat. But now . . .

Nine rings. Ten. He was about to hang up the instrument when he heard Suzanne's voice.

"Hello?"

Her tone was tentative, questioning. Maybe a little frightened. But in that moment, Rick realized how grateful he was that his suspicions and fears had been proved wrong. Suzanne was Suzanne. Laura was Minerva.

"Suzanne—"

"Rick!" She cut him off. "Rick, where are you? I've been all over this town looking for you, to warn you, to tell you to watch out for Laura Talbott. And Steve Gorman. He's back from Los Angeles. Rick, where are you? Are you all right?"

"Wait a minute, wait a minute." He stilled the torrent of words, and then the enormity of what she had said sunk into his mind.

"Wait a minute." His voice was more stern and deliberate. "How did *you* know about Laura? Why are you in Atlanta?"

"Dan Osborne asked me to come. He called me—"

"Dan Osborne? When? When did he call you?" Rick's voice was terse, his mind centered on Dan.

"This afternoon. He asked me to—"

"This afternoon?" Rick's voice was incredulous. "Sunday afternoon? Then he's alive! I was in Los Angeles this morning. I thought he was dead—"

"Steve Gorman almost killed him, Rick—ran him down in a car. And Dan was hurt, badly hurt—a concussion. Apparently Gorman loaded him in the car after hitting him and took him to Brett Stanley's apartment. They've been holding him there, but today he got to a phone and called a friend of his with the police department—a Lt. Fletcher. The two of them tried to reach you at your apartment, but they couldn't get an answer. Finally Dan called me in New York and I caught a plane—"

"Suzanne, are you all right?"

There was a slight pause before the answered. "Yes . . ."

"Suzanne, what's wrong? Why did it take you so long to answer the phone?"

"Someone knows I'm here. I don't know who—Steve Gorman, probably. He started calling about a half hour ago. Just calling, breathing into the telephone. He never said anything. And then someone came to the door, rang the bell, but I wouldn't answer—"

"For God's sake, Suzanne, *don't!* Don't open that door for anyone."

"Don't worry. I've got it locked. But he's been back. Ringing. Finally knocking, pounding on the door. It's a man. It sounds like Gorman, but I can't be sure."

"Suzanne, don't open that door. Wait a minute—how did you get in?"

"The building manager. But he's gone. He left for the evening. Only the right key will open that door now. Don't worry about me, Rick. I'll be all right. They can't get in—"

"Suzanne, you've got to get out of there. I'm going to call the police, explain the situation. They'll come over, give you an escort away from there. They'll even provide protection when I tell them what's going on—"

"Rick!" Her voice was almost a whisper, a terrible urgency to it. "Rick, be quiet. Let me listen. I hear something." There was a pause, and Rick held his breath as he waited for her to speak again. And finally he heard her in that same soft, secretive tone. "Rick, they're at the front door again. It sounds like a key in the lock—"

"Suzanne, listen to me—"

"Ssh! Let me listen . . . *Oh, my God—"* And then silence. And finally a thumping noise, the sound of the telephone hitting the carpeted floor.

"Suzanne! Suzanne!" Rick was screaming the words into the phone, but he was met with a dead silence at the other end of the line. And then a sound.

He listened intently, the tension so completely enveloping his body that his ears began to pound, his skull throbbed with pressure. But still nothing. Nothing identifiable.

And then he heard the voice. A woman's voice. But not Suzanne's.

"Rick?" she said, and instantly he recognized the voice. "This is Laura." She laughed lightly, dramatically. "How fortunate that you sent me back into town. The cab driver was positively adamant, but he finally agreed to drop me by your place instead of mine. I thought Steve might still be here and that I could catch a ride back to the airport with him."

She paused, then repeated her earlier statement. "Yes, how fortunate that you sent me back into town. Because if you hadn't, Steve would never have been able to get into your apartment and we would have never been able to persuade Suzanne to join us on the Gulfstream."

Rick was stricken by her words, by the turn of events. He mumbled out a few words. "But how did you—"

"How did we get into your apartment? It was simple, darling. You gave me a key months ago, remember? When we were still lovers."

Rick's shoulders drooped in defeat. He leaned his head against the cold metal of the telephone station and stood for a long moment in silence. Finally, his voice flat, his mind numb, he spoke.

"What do you want me to do?"

"Meet us in Lounge C of the Operations Building at the airpark. You realize, of course, that we'll take whatever action is necessary with Suzanne, so it wouldn't be advisable to bring the police with you." She repeated the instructions. "Lounge C. The Operations Building. Within thirty minutes."

Rick started to hang up when Laura's voice called out once again for him.

"Rick!" He put the receiver back to his ear and let her words soak through his deadened consciousness. "Rick, we have Suzanne. We have the film, the tape, all of the evidence you've collected. We'd like to have you, too.

But that really isn't essential. Without the evidence, without Suzanne, you'll only be a nuisance. But you won't slow down our project."

He heard a click and the line went dead.

Chapter 3

"Where's Gorman?" Laura Talbott snapped as she whirled around from the window where she had been watching the swarm of men servicing the Gulfstream. Her hand moved to the discolored area of her jaw, soothing the swollen and bruised flesh and her anger flared anew.

"Where's Gorman?" she demanded, repeating her question a second time.

Across the room, Paul Prescott studied her disinterestedly. After a moment he shrugged and directed his attention to the glass of vodka he held in his hand. "I have no idea," he muttered. His words slurred themselves together.

"You must have an idea. I heard him tell you something before he left—"

"I have no idea *where* he is. He's out *there* somewhere." With a grand gesture, Prescott threw his arm dramatically toward the window and the runways beyond. *"Out there somewhere, looking for Rick Craig."* Liquid from the glass sloshed over his lap and onto the floor. "Rick Craig. Looking for Rick Craig."

Prescott laughed as the thought took hold. "Rick Craig. Everyone's looking for Rick Craig. Gorman wants to find Rick Craig, Laura wants to find Rick

Craig, Mac Hunter wants to find Rick Craig. Even *she* wants to find Rick Craig." He nodded at the motionless form of Suzanne Carmichael lying on a couch. "Everyone wants to find Rick Craig." He repeated himself, his voice almost singsong in its repetitiveness. "Everyone wants to find Rick Craig, everyone wants to find Rick Craig."

Suddenly he sat erect. The drunken mood seemed to drop away, to be replaced by an intensity that came from the depths of his emotions.

"But why?" He said it again, pounding the highball glass on the long table before him, emphasizing every word. *"Everyone wants to find Rick Craig. But why?* Why in God's name would anyone want him? Why would anyone want to be associated with the vicious son of a—"

"Please, Paul." Laura cut him off, her voice sharp and commanding.

"No, my dear, tell me. You want Rick Craig. You've wanted him for months now. Despite what I've told you about him, despite—"

"Oh shut up, Paul. I'm tired of it all. I'm tired of hearing about it, about what he did to your daughter—"

"Tired of it? I'm sure you're tired of it. Especially after tonight. Tell me, dear, how did it feel? How did it feel when he beat you and bruised you, when he—"

"Paul, please be quiet. I told you. He didn't hit me. It was an accident. I was holding a gun on him, he was trying to escape." She shook her head, dismissing the idea of any further explanation.

They were silent for a moment, and then Laura reverted to her original question. "Where's Gorman?" It was more a reflection of her thoughts than an honest question. "The Gulfstream is ready for the flight to the island. I want to leave for the island in ten minutes."

"If you find Craig."

She shrugged her shoulders. "Regardless of whether we find Craig. It really doesn't matter. So long as we have the evidence that he so carefully collected—" she nodded at the case on the table in front of Prescott "—and so long as we have Suzanne Carmichael, we'll eventually have him, too. And in the meantime, he wouldn't risk doing anything foolish, anything that might endanger Suzanne."

She was silent for a moment, then added a conversational postcript. "But I do wish Gorman could find him. I'd feel more comfortable if we had him with us . . ."

Prescott laughed. He stood and walked to the portable bar the steward had brought in from the plane, still laughing. "I'll bet that you would, my dear. I'll just bet that you would. Now that you've taken command of the project, it was unfortunate that your first act was to let Craig overpower you and escape, wasn't it? I'll bet that Mr. Hunter won't like that, when he finds out.

"Does he know yet?" Prescott continued. "Have you told him, Laura? Or perhaps you'd like me to do that? Perhaps one good turn deserves another.

"You told him some terrible things about me, Laura. You lied. And you did it simply to bring yourself more glory. How dare you tell him that you're afraid to trust me? That my judgment isn't sound? *And how dare you say that I drink too much?*"

"You *are* drinking too much, Paul. You're drinking too much at this very moment—"

"Nonsense." He poured more vodka over ice cubes and turned back to face her. "Nonsense. I may take a drink every now and then, to relieve the pressures, to relax myself, but it's certainly not the way you pictured it to Hunter. I'm certainly not putting the project in jeopardy—"

"Oh? You're not putting the project in jeopardy?" She flipped open the attaché case and held up Prescott's two medical dissertations. "What about these? How do you account for these books being in Rick Craig's possession? He might never have suspected anything if his photographer friend in Aspen hadn't given him *Mind Control.*" She saw the look of shock come over the old man's face. "Oh, yes, Paul. I know about that. And I know how Osborne got it. You got drunk one night in Aspen and gave him the book. And when Hunter forced you to recall all copies, you couldn't even remember doing it. So Osborne kept a copy and Craig got it. I tried to salvage your carelessness in New York during the personnel interviews at The Press. I stole the book from Rick's case during lunch. I even made him think Suzanne might have done it.

"But that's not all, Paul. At a time when you could almost be assured he would try to rescue Smitty, you relaxed security measures on the island. And Rick came. And found your office unlocked. So he stole *Mind Control* along with your journal about the Utah Experiment. So now he knows about that, too, and if we don't stop him, he'll expose that along with everything else.

"I don't understand you anymore, Paul. I don't know what you're trying to do. *It's almost as though you want the Jupiter Project exposed.*"

Laura paused a moment, considering. "Do you really want to elect a president, Paul? Do you really want to successfully complete the total experiment? Or do you just crave the adulation of your peers? Is that it, Paul? Is that what you're up to? Let Rick Craig expose the whole thing, *allow it to happen.* So that you'll be recognized from one coast to the other. Not just in neurological circles, but by the medical profession as a whole. Even by the man on the street."

She had walked up to him and now she stood with her face just inches from his own. Realization was on her face, a challenge in her voice.

"That's it, isn't it, Paul? That would accomplish both of your purposes, wouldn't it? Let Rick Craig destroy himself at the same time that he's exposing your academic brilliance.

"Despite what you say about him, you know that Rick is an honorable man. And you've maneuvered him into a position that, in order to do the honorable thing, he has to destroy himself. Destroy his advertising agency, destroy his career. For the second time.

"And because he has to expose the plot, he'll expose your role in it, your academic brilliance, and you'll be lionized among your medical colleagues."

Laura studied his florid face, listened as he sputtered words of denial. Then she spoke again. "You're sick, Paul. Granted, I'm dedicated to the project's success. I'll do almost anything to insure our contribution to neurological research. But at least I'm not out for personal glory.

"Thank God Hunter has relieved you. And he did it just in time. Thank God you're no longer a part of the Jupiter Project."

"I am a part of the project. I'm a viable part of the team, of the effort." Laura tried to move around him but he blocked her way. His voice was becoming more strident. "Do you understand? I'm still a viable part of—"

She pushed him out of the way. "The only thing you're a viable part of is the *bottle,* Doctor Prescott. It took me a long time to realize it, but thank God I figured it out before it was too late. Your name will never be associated with the project, Paul. You'll never gain the credit you want so badly."

He stood there looking after her, his eyes hardly able to focus. But her words sank into his consciousness and he became uncontrollably furious. He followed her, seizing her by the arm and whirling her around. He drew back his hand and released it with such force that it staggered her, almost knocking her down.

"I'll never forgive you for this," he told her coldly. "And I'll never forget it. And someday, somehow, I'll make you pay for it."

Steve Gorman paced back and forth at the foot of the boarding steps to the Gulfstream. His eyes searched the darkness in vain for the figure he so desperately wanted to find.

When the crew started descending the steps of the plane, he challenged them. "Where the hell do you think you're going?"

"They want us inside. We're leaving in ten minutes."

Gorman swore silently to himself. Ten minutes. And then he'd be gone. Without Rick Craig. Without paying him back.

Again he scanned the landing area for a sign of his enemy, but he saw only the normal airport activity. Another of the small electric ground carts was scooting across the apron, and he watched it as it came nearer, but when he saw that the driver was wearing the rumpled coveralls of a mechanic, he diverted his attention.

The cart came closer, obviously headed toward the Gulfstream and Gorman watched it absently. Suddenly a voice called out from beneath the soiled mechanics cap.

"You Mr. Gorman?"

"That's right," Gorman answered.

"They want you inside. In Lounge C. They sent me to tell you." The cart activated itself again, starting to move away.

Gorman cursed to himself and started to move toward the bright lights of the building. But suddenly something stopped him. The voice. That was it. Something in the voice struck a chord of memory—

"Hey, wait a minute!" Gorman called to the figure on the cart. But the figure did not respond and the cart moved away from him with an increasing speed.

And then Gorman knew. The voice had sounded different, but something about it was familiar, a voice he had come to hate. The man on the cart was Rick Craig.

With a scream of anger, he took off across the field, trying to catch the figure on the departing cart.

"Craig!" he screamed. "I know it's you." He ran faster, but he saw the vehicle getting farther and farther ahead of him.

The cart skirted by a fuel truck and passed it. As Gorman came abreast of the truck an idea raced into his mind and he stopped short beside the vehicle, pulling open the door and reaching inside. A feeling of jubilation overcame him as he discovered the keys in the ignition. In a moment he experienced the throb of power as the heavy truck sprang to life under his hands.

He pulled out with a screech of the tires, and in the beam from the truck's headlights he saw the cart clearly in the distance ahead of him.

He watched the cart veer from the congestion of the hangar area to the open spaces of the landing strip, and he gunned the motor to catch it. The gap was narrowing now and soon he was close enough to see the dark hair of the driver beneath the cap, and excitement welled up in him. He gunned the motor even faster, his eyes locked on Rick Craig's back.

The cart began swerving, first to the left and then to the right, but the truck's superior power overcame its maneuverability, and Steve Gorman moved closer to his prey.

They were on a straightaway now, on the open runway. Gorman could see nothing but the cart, could pay attention to nothing but the figure driving it. The vision of Rick Craig in the parking garage played in his mind and he knew that this time he would be successful. He was within yards now—

Suddenly a massive bulk loomed before him and, too late, he realized that the small cart could easily maneuver under the wing of a private jet moored there in front of him. He threw his foot on the brake, put the weight of his body against it, but it was too late. With a screeching of rubber the fuel truck ground into a wing of the deserted jet, and then, its momentum hardly stopped, it slid sideways into the fuselage.

The cabin of the truck was crushed on first impact, and with it Steve Gorman. But even before the sound of crushing metal had subsided, another sound of massive intensity supplanted it.

With the explosion came an enormous flash of light, and flames from the jet fuel leaped high into the night air.

On the other side of the field, the mechanic's cart again approached the Gulfstream. A solitary figure, still clad in grease-stained coveralls, left the cart and stealthily climbed the deserted stairs to the cabin.

Inside, the toilet door locked in safety, Rick Craig stood and waited. They should be in the air shortly, he guessed. He gave way to the trembling sensation that was beginning to shake his entire body. Comfortingly his hand slipped into the pocket of the baggy coveralls and clasped the grip of the pistol.

Chapter 4

Laura Talbott led her ragtag band from the Operations Building to the Gulfstream. Cochran, the pilot, stood at the bottom of the entry steps.

He touched the edge of his cap. "Let's get going, Miss Talbott." The flickering shadows of the distant flames played on his face. "There's been a bad accident over there. I've still got clearance, but we'd better be on our way. They're liable to shut the field down before long."

The group boarded the plane, its state of disarray accentuated by its haste. Suzanne Carmichael was dumped unceremoniously onto the long couch, a seat belt hastily strapped about her. Paul Prescott, stumbling and weaving, was assisted—almost pushed—into a seat by the steward. He slumped there, lost in a haze of drunken emotion. Laura took a seat at the rear, the seat usually reserved for Mac Hunter himself.

The plane was already taxiing toward the runway when the steward stuck his head into the cockpit. "The door to the john is locked," he reported. "What should I do?"

"Forget it," snapped the pilot. "It's probably stuck. Hunter's not on board and he's the only one who cares about his goddamned security checks. Let's get this baby in the air."

The steward shrugged and closed the door, moving back toward the passenger area.

"Steward! Another drink, if you will." Paul Prescott's voice carried above the noise of the jets.

The attendant shook his head as he responded. This is going to be a helluva flight, he thought to himself. I wish I was staying in Atlanta. Better still, he concluded, I wish I had never come.

They had been airborne for a long while. Rick stood in the cramped cubicle, stretching his long frame.

So far, so good. Except for the moment before takeoff when the handle to the toilet had been jiggled insistently. He'd held his breath and withdrawn the pistol from his pocket, but whoever it was had abandoned the attempt.

So far, so good. But he knew it was time for the next step and as he reached out to open the door, he found that his body was not willing to cooperate. Fear is like that, he realized. Debilitating. Paralyzing. But fear is only a state of mind, he assured himself. And there's no other way, no other way to save myself, to save Suzanne. And he found his body responding once again.

He silently released the lock and slowly pushed the door open. Outside he could see half darkness. He stepped into the cabin, cautiously closing the door behind him and leaning his weight against it.

He studied the cabin in silence. Far ahead, near the galley, the steward was absorbed in a magazine, the reading light above him reflecting dully against the black of his uniform.

The figure across from him was obscured by the high back of the swivel chair, but a man's leg extended into the aisle and occasional snores broke through the air. Paul Prescott.

And then he saw Suzanne, lying on the couch across from the two men. She was silent and still, but as he watched her, he could see the slight motions of her breathing. She's alive, he thought to himself with relief. For now.

And then his thoughts turned to the final occupant of the cabin, and he searched for Laura Talbott. He saw her hand first, illuminated by the reading light over her seat, and it was so near to him that he almost gasped. She was only a few feet away, her body obscured by the high back of the swivel chair. Rick stepped forward quietly, holding the pistol firmly in his right hand. With a quick motion he pressed the barrel against Laura's temple and leaned forward, speaking in a whisper.

"It's Rick, Laura. And this time I'm holding the gun. Sorry that I had to be so rough—but we're playing the game by your rules."

She moved only slightly, twitching as she understood the feel of metal against her head.

Rick leaned closer. "That's right, Laura. It's a gun. Your gun. Or Gorman's. It's the same one you held on me down there in the parking lot."

Laura's hand on the armrest had tensed, but now it relaxed slightly. Then Rick saw her move it, extending itself to the seat opposite, inviting him to be seated.

Rick considered the idea, then rejected it. Instead he moved quickly to the high-backed chair across from her. He was virtually invisible there from the front of the cabin, from the other occupants. Not safe, he realized, but invisible. For the time being.

Now Laura looked at him, a curious mixture of emotions playing over her face. For a long moment they stared at each other, each reliving thoughts from the past, two lovers suddenly become adversaries, separated by a pistol held between them.

Finally Laura opened her mouth. "May I speak?" she asked softly.

Rick answered in a whisper. "In a moment. But first turn off your light."

Laura's hand reached up, and the aft section of the cabin suddenly fell into a deeper gloom.

Rick spoke again, this time more audibly. "Now, put both of your hands on the armrest." She obeyed him.

"Is your seat belt fastened?" he asked, anxious to prevent any sudden movement on her part. Laura nodded, and in proof she ran an enameled thumb under the heavy webbing to show that it was securely in place.

"OK. You can talk. But hold your voice down. I'm not ready to alert the rest of the plane that I'm here."

Laura's voice was low and controlled. "Really, Rick. Aren't you being a little melodramatic? You're treating me like I'm some kind of dangerous desperado or something. I'm just one woman, you know—"

A sound of sarcastic amusement escaped Rick's lips. "Just one woman? Maybe so. But you're tough, Laura. A lot tougher than I ever thought possible. And you're cold. You'll do anything in your power to protect your blessed project. Including kidnapping Suzanne." His voice became bitter. "Until you did that, I thought we were playing fair. But now I know what I'm facing. And maybe I am being a little melodramatic, but I'm not going to take any chances. As you told me earlier, 'I don't want to hurt you, but . . .' " His voice trailed off.

As he had spoken, he had seen a troubled look come over Laura's face. "Yes, I can see that taking Suzanne from your apartment would make you angry." She shrugged. "And maybe I don't blame you. But it was necessary. She knew too much. I couldn't allow her to talk."

They were silent for a moment until finally Laura spoke again. "What do you want? What do you expect of me?"

"That shouldn't be too hard to figure, Laura. I want what I wanted earlier. The cannister of film. Paul Prescott's dissertation on mind control. Plus his journal about the experiment at Brigham Young. Oh yes, and the cassette. Hapworth's admission about Project Jupiter.

"And I want Suzanne Carmichael. I want to see this plane set down in Washington and I want to walk away from it with Suzanne. I want Diana Malloy released, plus any others you may be holding. And I want you and Maxwell Hunter and The Miramar Corporation and The Phoenix Press and FRESH!—" He spoke with such ferocity that his voice was a hoarse whisper and he stopped for breath. *"I want all of you out of my life—forever."*

"Those are the things I want, Laura. But while I'm at it, let me tell you something that I *don't* want. I don't want to have to hurt anyone. I don't want to have to kill anyone in order to protect Suzanne or to save my own life. I didn't want to see Steve Gorman run that gasoline truck into the jet. But Steve saw me and he was determined to kill me. Just like he has been all along. But this time I outsmarted him. I kept the upper hand. And I have the upper hand over you, too, Laura. And I'm going to keep it.

"Now, let's start out with my attaché case. Where is it?"

"Just a moment," Laura countered, and when Rick stirred restlessly she spoke to calm him. "I just want to talk a moment. After all, you have me totally under control. You can give me a minute, can't you?"

Rick grunted his assent.

And then she began. *"Rick, it's still not too late."* Her voice was intense, insistent. "We'll cancel Project Jupiter. We'll pull our support away from Hapworth and let him go down the tube where he belongs. We'll do whatever you say, so long as you don't expose the whole concept. Let us continue with it, Rick. Let us use it for the good of the world—"

"That's ridiculous, Laura. You know as well as I that Maxwell Hunter isn't interested in the 'good of the world.' He wants power, control over America, maybe even the world. And you can't control Hunter. Sorry, Laura, I can't buy that. Where's my attaché case?"

"Wait a minute, Rick." Her voice became harder, more calculating. "Rick, you can be a wealthy man—"

"Laura! No!" He couldn't believe that she would try such a ploy.

"Rick, wait. I don't mean just a few hundred thousand. I mean a lot. A million. Maybe more. You and Suzanne could go away, wherever you wanted. Back to Aspen, maybe. You could write again—"

His voice was flat as he interrupted her. "I'm not interested, Laura. There's not enough money in the world for me to see Mac Hunter control the country—"

"You could help, Rick. You could help control the country. I can arrange it so you sit on the Committee. You can be in on all the President's decisions, maybe on the White House staff, or a cabinet position—"

"Laura, this is ridiculous—"

"Rick, you can't do this. You can't expose the project. I've worked too hard. And now you want to just blow your whistle and bring an end to years of research and planning—"

"It's wrong, Laura. I can't let you go through with it."

"Rick, please! Please!" Her voice was becoming louder, more vehement, and he knew that the others would hear her.

"Laura, keep your voice down—"

"No, Rick, I'm not going to let you do it . . ." He had never seen her so agitated. She was squirming, almost writhing in the seat. Her hands twisted and wrenched against each other. And suddenly, uncharacteristically, she was crying. At first it was almost a whimpering sound, mixed with unintelligible words, but then the sound grew in intensity to great gasps. For a moment her hands covered her face, then she fumbled in her coat pocket for a handkerchief and, not finding one, began to search in her handbag.

And suddenly Rick knew what was happening and he moved instantly to save his life.

"Stop it, Laura!" He thrust the pistol at her, shoved it in her face, and with his other hand he snatched the purse from her clawing hands. And he found it. A small pistol. A ladies' gun. Tiny, but deadly.

Now she sat facing him, her ruse set aside, her composure regained totally. Her face was cold and calculating in the half-light.

"You would have killed me, wouldn't you?" he asked.

She shrugged and continued to stare at him in icy calm. "What are you going to do about it?" she asked dispassionately.

He jumped to his feet. "Steward!" he shouted. "Steward, get the overhead lights on. Get them on now!"

Laura's voice joined him in a scream. "Help! Steward, help me. This man has attacked me, he's trying to skyjack this plane—"

"Damn you." Rick poked the gun at Laura's neck. "On your feet, Laura. And hold your hands in the air."

The overhead lights flickered on, then brought their full brilliance to the cabin. The steward stood at the front of the plane, his eyes opened wide in his total shock at the actions behind him.

"Steward," Laura began again, but he cut her off.

"Shut up, Laura. And get on your feet." She slowly unbuckled the seat belt and rose to her feet, extending her hands to the ceiling. "Don't move," Rick cautioned her.

He addressed the steward again. "Get the copilot back here." The man turned to go forward and Rick called after him. "And don't try anything—" the man stopped and whirled around, his face masked with fright "—don't try anything unless you want to be responsible for someone's death."

Rick turned back to the woman beside him. "Turn around, Laura."

She turned slowly, fastening him in a cold, malevolent glare, her mouth a thin line of anger. "You son of a bitch," she muttered, never loosing him from her icy stare. "I'm sorry that I didn't let Gorman kill you."

"Where's my attaché case, Laura?"

She didn't answer, and Rick was about to repeat his demand when the steward appeared with the copilot.

"Are you the copilot?" he questioned, and without waiting for an answer, he continued. "What's your name?"

"Jurgens." The reply came in a clear, hard voice, a voice not accustomed to violence but capable of dealing with it.

"OK, Jurgens. Let me tell you what's happening. The young woman lying on the couch has been kidnapped. She's obviously been drugged. I'm here trying to get her off the plane. That tells you what's going on. Miss Talbott has just tried to kill me. That tells you why I have this gun. And this one, too." He produced the miniature pistol. "That's the one she tried to use on me." He went on. "And Jurgens, I'm not used to guns. They make me nervous. And anything you do to make me more nervous might make me pull the trigger. Get me?"

"I get you," came a grudging reply.

"OK, I'll tell you what we're going to do. First, ask the steward to try to revive Miss Carmichael. She's stirring now. It shouldn't be too hard to do. Second, go back to report to your pilot. Tell him exactly what's going on. And tell him I want him to set this plane down at Washington National Airport. He'll want to alert the airport police, and that's fine with me. As a matter of fact, *instruct* him to alert the police. The FBI, too. They're interested in kidnappings. I'd like them to take me into custody. I'd like them to take us all into custody. Do you understand all of that, Jurgens?"

"Yes, sir." The reply was more cooperative. The request for the police had lent credence to the situation.

"OK, Jurgens. Take off up front. And give me a report as soon as you've talked to the captain."

Laura suddenly made a movement, as though to turn toward the front of the cabin.

"Stay here, Laura."

She eyed him coldly. "Why? You have the situation well in hand. I may as well join the other hostages in this skyjacking attempt—"

"We'll see, Laura, when we talk to the police. But for now, stay here." Rick paused, and then he added softly, "And believe what I told Jurgens. I *am* nervous. I'm *not* used to guns. And since I know you wouldn't hesitate to shoot me—" His inference was unmistakable. "Sit down —right here. And buckle your seat belt again."

He directed himself to the steward. "How's Miss Carmichael?"

"She's coming around."

Suzanne was leaning on an elbow, rubbing her forehead.

"Get her some coffee," he said, and the steward moved to the galley.

Suzanne was fully awake now, sitting on the couch and shaking her head to clear it. At the sound of his voice, she looked back at him and gave a cry of emotion.

"Come back here, Suzanne," Rick said as calmly as possible. "I want you back here. With me."

She stood, but immediately sank back into her seat again, one hand at her head. She took the coffee and sipped at it. In a moment she rose shakily to her feet. She looked at him and smiled, and then moved uncertainly toward him.

As she approached Laura's seat, Rick stepped forward. "Let her pass, Laura. Don't try any more rough stuff on her." Suzanne walked past the other woman and for a moment their eyes met, but no word, no emotion passed between them.

When she reached his side, Rick spoke to her in an undertone. "Are you all right?"

She nodded. "I'm still a little woozy, but I'm all right."

"Stay here, beside me. And if anything happens, get to the rear. To the toilet. Get inside it and lock the door."

He pushed her behind him and called out to the steward again. "There's a brown leather attaché case somewhere on board. It's monogrammed with the initials *RJC.* Find it and bring it to me."

The man departed and, after several moments, returned with the battered case in his hands. The copilot was with him.

"We've radioed the National tower. They've cleared us for landing. We'll be down in twenty minutes. And the police will be there in force."

The steward made his way to the rear, and Rick extended his hand to take the case from him. The man remained for a moment, eyeing Rick, and then Laura, and shaking his head. Then he was gone, sinking back into his seat in bewilderment.

Rick motioned Suzanne into a seat, then eased himself against the rear wall of the cabin to keep his vigil. Only twenty minutes, he told himself. Maybe less. And then it will all be over. At least the rough part. Another twenty minutes and he and Suzanne could walk away from the plane, away from the nightmare—

He was jolted back to reality by another voice—a strange voice, yet oddly familiar.

"Steward, get me another drink."

Rick pulled himself erect again and turned toward the sound. The steward was staring at the seat opposite him in disbelief, and slowly the rumpled figure of Paul Prescott unfolded, blinking his eyes and looking about in confusion.

Good God, Rick thought, I'd forgotten about Paul.

A muffled groan escaped Laura's lips.

Prescott's eyes focused on the steward, and then on the rear of the cabin. He blinked again, his gaze resting on the figure in the mechanic's greasy coveralls standing in the rear of the cabin with a gun in his hand.

"What's going on here?" he questioned, and when he received no response he repeated the question, his eyes seeking the answer first from Laura, then from the steward.

"What's going on here?"

"You'd better sit down, Dr. Prescott," the steward told him. "This guy claims we've kidnapped the lady—"

"Kidnapped!" Prescott's voice was loud and disbelieving. "Kidnapped? Why that's absurd. She's—"

He stopped. He was studying Rick's features and slowly the light of recognition appeared on his face.

"Well." He uttered the phrase with a combination of meanings. Surprise. Realization. And then acceptance. "Well, well," he repeated. "Rick Craig. With a gun in his hand. It appears the tables have been turned."

Prescott drew himself up, buttoning his jacket, smoothing the wrinkles from the fabric. He addressed the steward, this time more deliberately. The short sleep had refreshed and sobered him and his slurred words were replaced with more polished diction, the drunken stare replaced with an alert gaze. "Steward, I really do need another drink. If you will."

Prescott stood there in silence until the steward returned, placing the heavy crystal highball glass in his outstretched hand.

He looked steadily at Rick for a moment, then he turned to look at Laura Talbott. "Indeed, it seems that the tables have been turned. Only a short while ago, Dr. Talbott was in complete control of the situation. In control of the project, she told me. Our new leader, with Mr. Hunter's blessings. But now she sits there, cowering from the gun he holds on her."

He addressed Laura. "How did he do it, my dear? Did he overpower you? Did he hit you again?" His words were solicitous, but his eyes were cold and they bored into her with their intensity.

She returned the look of hatred. "Shut up, Paul. This is no time to—"

He ignored her, switching his eyes back to Rick. He looked at him, a look of distaste forming on his face. Prescott raised the glass to his lips and drank slowly, almost luxuriously. He stepped into the aisle and slowly began to walk to the rear of the cabin.

"Rick has always had a weakness for hitting women, haven't you, Rick? The way you hit Laura earlier, in the parking lot—"

"I didn't hit Laura. It was an—"

"—and the way you hit Kathy, all those years ago and drove her to her death." He was standing in front of Rick now, and he moved his hand as if to touch him.

"Get back, Paul. Don't come any closer."

"Why don't you hit me, too? Why don't you hit me the way you hit women. Old men and women. What about children? Do you hit them, too?" he taunted. But he kept his place, no longer approaching the outstretched gun.

"Or maybe you'd rather shoot me. Then you'd have

the blood of two members of the Prescott family on your hands. You can kill me, the same way you killed my daughter."

"I didn't kill your daughter. I didn't kill Kathy." Rick's voice was tight, the pain apparent on his face. "A hit-and-run driver killed Kathy. A drunk."

"You're right. A drunk killed her. A drunken author. You hit her, you beat her, there on the street. And then you pushed her in front of that car—"

"Paul, that's not true. I *didn't* push her. Where did you get such an idea?"

"The police. They told me. They said you hit her—"

"We fought. She was leaving me. I was drunk. But God knows that I didn't push her. She did it herself. I tried to stop her, tried to catch her—"

"You pushed her. The police said—"

"The police didn't know. They weren't there. No one was there."

"But the accident report said—"

"The accident report said we fought. Only that. And that was the statement that I gave them. Surely you haven't believed that I willfully pushed my wife—"

"You pushed her. You did it to her. She wanted to go home. Home. Home to me." His eyes were wide, almost hypnotic in their fixation on Rick. "And I'm going to make you pay . . ."

Home . . . I want to go home. A burst of red splotches exploded in Rick's mind. *I want to go home.* Prescott's words recalled those isolated phrases that had haunted him through the years and suddenly the scene that night by the Hotel Carlyle that had shrouded itself in an alcoholic blackout lit up in brilliance and he remembered it all clearly.

They were standing there. He had drawn his arm back to hit her. But Kathy stood solidly before him, defying him. And he had wavered, had dropped his arm, had felt the resolve leave him as reason took hold. She had turned then and walked into the street, calling "Taxi!" And he had followed her, and now he remembered his words clearly. His words, not hers. "Kathy. I want to go home. Take me home, Kathy, take me away from all of this. I want to go home, Kathy. With you." And she had turned, joy on her face, to come to him, to take him back to the earlier times, to the good times. But it had been too late. Out of the dark, the car had come . . .

The memory, the realization had come over him like a flood, obscuring the action in the cabin of the Gulfstream, obscuring Prescott's threats. But the old man saw the blank look on Rick's face and acted.

With a speed that Rick would have thought impossible, Prescott threw the glass of liquor squarely in his face. The shock was enormous and he lowered the gun involuntarily, raising one hand to wipe the whiskey from his burning eyes.

He felt a strong grip on his arm, stronger than he would have imagined, felt his arm hammered against the back of the seat, felt the gun slip from his fingers.

And, as suddenly as it had begun, it was over—before Rick could recover himself, before Laura or Suzanne could get to their feet.

A look of elation was on Laura Talbott's face and the laugh of victory came from her throat. She stood and started to go to Prescott, but Prescott motioned her back, confronting both of them, the pistol in his hand. Slowly he edged his way back to his seat, swinging the gun in a wide arc as he ordered the steward to the back of the plane with the others.

His eyes fell first on Rick. "I hate you, Rick Craig. And I'm going to make you pay. I've already taken your advertising agency from you, destroyed the new life you so carefully built for yourself. And now I'll fix it so you'll never be able to go back to that life. The world must know that you were responsible for this gigantic plot against their minds—you and Laura Talbott and Mac Hunter."

Laura was walking slowly toward the silver-haired man, speaking. "You're right, Paul," she said, her voice conciliatory. "We must make him pay. Give me the gun, Paul, and we'll—"

"No! *We* won't do anything. I hate him, but I hate you almost as much. You turned on me. You turned Hunter against me."

"Don't get excited, Paul. Just give me the gun. Hunter was just angry when he relieved you from the project. I'll talk to him, get him to reinstate you." A smile was on her face as she took another step toward him.

"Oh no, Laura. Stay where you are." Prescott waved the gun around wildly, an irrational look of hatred on his face, and Laura stopped. "I just decided which one of you I hate the most. You, Laura. Rick Craig was a real bastard, but at least he was drunk when he hurt Kathy. But you—*you!* You've taken advantage of me. You've used me. And now you're willing to throw me away like yesterday's newspaper." Prescott's eyes were wild now, and he stared at her with a demonic look.

"Come on, Paul. Give me the gun. Everything will be all right—"

"No. It won't ever be all right again. You flattered me, encouraged my research, helped me, learned from me. You drained me for your own purposes. You convinced me that the subconscious could bring real good into the world. You convinced me that Anthony Hapworth was a necessary conclusion to the entire experiment. And then you discarded me, got me thrown out. And you aren't even going to let me have credit with my associates. Credit that I deserve."

"That's enough!" Laura screamed, her control gone. "Give me the gun. I'm not going to stand here and play games with you. Do you realize that Rick Craig did away with Steve Gorman? And he'll do away with us, too. This plane is about to land in Washington. He's going to expose the whole thing, the thing we spent years trying to bring about. He's got all the evidence in his attaché case, there. We can't let him do that—"

Prescott studied her, then his eyes drifted to Rick, to the case on the floor beside him. "We can't? Oh come now, Laura. Indeed we can. And I will." Prescott's voice had a dreamlike quality to it, and he went on. "I'll let him expose it. I want him to expose it. I've thought about it since you mentioned it earlier. This way I can prove the thesis, but I won't have to allow that ass Hapworth to be elected. Perhaps one or two more primaries would have strengthened the final report. But we have proof now. Irrefutable proof. It will make my name go down in medical history." His mind seemed to wander. "Perhaps even the Nobel committee . . ."

"Paul, you're drunk. Stop talking nonsense. Stop this plane before it's too late!" She took a step, testing his reaction, and then another. And then she ran toward him, her hand outstretched to grab the gun. "You goddamned fool!" she screamed. "I'll kill you for this—"

Rick could see the figure of Jurgens sneaking silently up behind Prescott, his arms spread to grab him. And suddenly he remembered Laura's miniature pistol in his coverall pocket, and he grappled in the pocket to get it.

But he was too late. A deafening sound shattered through the cabin, and then another. A searing pain tore through his shoulder, and he was aware that Jurgens was grappling with Prescott, could see Laura throw herself against the two men, her hand reaching out for

Prescott's flailing arm, for the gun.

Rick stepped forward, but before he could move any closer the pistol fired again and Laura Talbott staggered backward against a seat.

She balanced there a moment, one hand clasped to her chest, a red ooze of blood beginning to seep through her fingers. A strange look was on her face. She spoke, her voice little more than a whisper, but Rick could hear her words.

"Paul . . . how could you, Paul? . . . The project . . . go on with it, Paul . . . don't let . . . Jupiter . . . fail."

Her legs gave way beneath her and Laura Talbott's body slipped to the floor.

The Gulfstream was nearing Washington now, and the cabin had regained a semblance of normalcy. Jurgens and the steward had put a blanket over Laura's body and retired to the cockpit, the gun safely removed from Prescott's hand.

Paul Prescott sat on the forward couch. At first he had sat there staring dully into space. But as his senses returned he had dropped his face to his hands and his body had shaken uncontrollably. Gradually the shaking had subsided, but now he still sat there, his face covered from sight.

Rick stood, the temporary bandage Jurgens had applied restricting his movement, the pain from the random shot still shooting through his shoulder. He patted Suzanne gently on the shoulder, moving his head toward the front of the cabin, and she nodded her understanding.

He walked slowly forward until he stood before Prescott. Then he spoke.

"I'm sorry, Paul."

At first Prescott did not move. Then he gradually raised his head and dropped his hands. The old man stared blankly at Rick for a moment, his face pale and drawn and strangely gray.

"Sorry?" he murmured.

"Sorry that you've lived with the memories, with the pain. For all these years. I'm sorry for you because I've lived with them too. But tonight, while you were talking, while you were blaming me, I suddenly saw something. I really didn't kill Kathy. And now I think I can put the memories away."

Chapter 5

I *want to walk away from this plane,* he remembered telling Laura Talbott that night in the darkened cabin of the Miramar plane. *I want you out of my life forever.*

And now she *was* out of his life. Forever. Laura and Paul Prescott and Steve Gorman. Just three pawns in Mac Hunter's insane scheme for power.

Rick thought about Laura. Not unkindly, now. He had come very close to loving her. But something had always been there, an unseen barrier between them. He had always blamed it on his own guilt, but now he knew that it was more. Laura could never have given herself completely to him or any other man. Project Jupiter would have stood between them.

With Rick, she had tried. But she had wanted it both ways. She had wanted him, but she had wanted him to acquiesce. To become a partner in the scheme. An unknowing partner, perhaps, but nevertheless a partner.

And he had been unable to do so. Thank God, he told himself, as he dismissed the thoughts from his mind and turned to the present.

The past forty-eight hours. The aftermath. The clean-up period. The time for doing things that had to be done, for laying it all to rest.

The press conference had been grueling. But necessary. He'd known that from the moment he had tried to explain the circumstances of Laura's death to the airport police. And to the two skeptical reporters who had appeared on the scene that night.

And so he had demanded a press conference and had painstakingly laid bare the unbelievable details of the Jupiter Project to the cynical eyes and ears of the Washington press corps. They had been tough, suspicious at first. Only when he had run the film that Dan Osborne had stolen from the VTR Studios, only when he had played the tape containing Hapworth's unwitting confession—only then did they believe. And then they had fought like a pack of jackals for the single copies of Prescott's books.

And only then did it hit the front pages of America's newspapers and the screens of its television sets.

And finally, Project Jupiter had been exposed.

Maybe today, Rick told himself as he wiped the last smudge of lather from his face, I can finally walk away from it.

Awkwardly he tried to wrap the bath towel around his waist. The wound in his shoulder wasn't really painful, just a nuisance. The doctor had insisted that he keep his arm in a sling, and he'd probably been right. But it made it difficult to function.

He finally abandoned his efforts and let the towel drop to the floor as he pulled open the door of the bathroom and walked across the room to the dressing table.

Suzanne looked up at him as he bent over her, kissing her gently on the neck. "You'll have to help me dress," he murmured. "My arm . . ." he shrugged helplessly.

She laughed, pushing him away. "Your arm is the only part of you that's been immobilized." She looked back at her reflection in the mirror, pulling the brush again through her long dark hair. "And you'd better get a move on. Dan is waiting for us downstairs—"

"Dan is waiting for us downstairs *in the bar,"* Rick completed her thought. "And if there's anything Dan Osborne likes any better than waiting in a bar, it's starring in press conferences." Rick turned away and sank down on the bed, picking up a copy of the *Washington Post* and pointing at one of the headlines on the page. "NOTED PHOTOGRAPHER HELPS UNCOVER PLOT," he read aloud. "Daniel Osborne, one of America's foremost commercial photographers, was a key figure in uncovering the bizarre plot to manipulate the minds of the American voter . . ."

Rick's voice trailed off as his eyes scanned the other headlines on the page, the headlines on the front pages of the *Star* and the *Times* and the other papers scattered over the bed. They told the story. MYSTERY WOMAN DEAD OF GUNSHOT WOUNDS . . . NEUROSURGEON CHARGED WITH MANSLAUGHTER . . . HAPWORTH WITHDRAWS FROM CAMPAIGN . . . FCC LAUNCHES INVESTIGATION.

Rick's face clouded as his eyes fell on another headline on the page. COMMUNICATIONS CZAR DENIES IMPLICATION IN MIND CONTROL PLOT. He went on to read the story again.

"R. Maxwell Hunter, chairman of one of America's largest and most powerful communications empires, today denied all knowledge of charges brought against him in the plot to control the minds of the American voter.

"In a statement released by his New York office, Hunter placed the blame at the feet of subordinates employed by one or the other of the companies owned by The Miramar Corporation.

" 'It is inconceivable that such a thing could have happened,' Hunter said, 'but The Miramar Corporation disclaims any knowledge or participation in this scheme.

It is totally impossible for the chief executive officer of a major corporation to be personally aware of the misdeeds that may occur in one of his subsidiary companies . . .' "

Rick brought his hand down on the newspaper with anger. "Goddamn him," he told Suzanne. "God *will* damn him, damn his soul. But God is the only one. The rest of the world will believe the son of a bitch, will think it was the demented scheme of poor Paul Prescott. It's not fair, it's not right—I've got to do something—"

Suzanne was beside him on the bed and she took his hands in hers and looked into his eyes for a moment.

"There's nothing you can do, Rick. You've done all that you can. And there's no evidence to prove that Hunter was personally involved. It's his word against yours. And his word carries more weight," she said bitterly. "More weight than yours, or mine, or Dan Osborne's. But don't you see, Rick? In reality, you've won. You've stopped him. You've opened people's eyes to what might have happened. You've kept this dreadful thing from happening."

"Thank God for that," Rick murmured. "Thank God there'll never be another Project Jupiter." With a sigh hc stood and walked to the suitcase that someone had packed and brought to him. He took a pair of shorts from the bag and began to pull them on.

The telephone in the room jangled and he looked around as Suzanne answered its ring. She looked at him, her face wreathed in a smile. "Rick, it's Smitty. He wants to talk to you."

Rick strode across the room and took the instrument. "Smitty! Are you home? How was Aspen? Is Susan with you? Are you all right?"

Smitty laughed at the torrent of questions. "We're home, Rick. And I'm all right. I still don't remember those things, but I guess I'm fortunate that that's all that they did to me. I'm just glad that it's all over."

"So am I, Smitty." Rick's voice was lower, more serious. "Thank God it's all over." He forced a note of enthusiasm into the conversation. "And now, it's business as usual. I'll expect you back at the office bright and early tomorrow morning. We've got a lot of work ahead of us—"

"That's one of the things I wanted to talk to you about, Rick. Jay Collins is here with me, and he wants to talk to you. He says that you haven't returned his phone calls—"

"I don't want to talk to him, Smitty. Not yet."

"He wants to know about the future of the agency, wants to know where he stands."

"I don't know where he stands," Rick answered. "I haven't thought everything out yet. It's too bad Jay sold all of his stock to Hunter. But that was his decision. And it was his decision to turn his back on the whole business. He wanted the bigtime, and he got it." Despite the emotion he felt, his voice was businesslike. "It won't come as a surprise to you that Mac Hunter no longer is interested in ownership of Collins & Craig. I received a telegram here this morning from one of his attorneys. By the terms of our contract, he is obligated to offer the stock he owns to me first, before he can sell it to anyone else. He's tendered an offer of the stock to me, and I've accepted it. As of today, I own all of Collins & Craig. I want Jay to stay around, of course. He's a good ad man, if nothing else. But the relationship will be different in the future. It will have to be."

There was a silence before Rick continued. "Right now, all I can tell you is that Collins & Craig will go on, that we'll still be the hottest shop in the South. But we'll do it the right way."

Rick replaced the receiver in the cradle and looked up to find Suzanne staring at him.

"Collins & Craig will go on?" she asked. "I'm sort of surprised. I thought you might want to write another novel . . ."

"I do," he answered her. "And I think I'll be able to. With your help. But in the meantime, Collins & Craig will go on."

He turned to pull a shirt from his suitcase. "And now, if you'll help me get this shirt on we'd better get down to the bar. Ol' Dan'l has probably already absconded with one of the cocktail waitresses."

Epilogue

Maxwell Hunter sat in the spacious anteroom, his manner relaxed, his face devoid of any emotion.

He reached out to take a newspaper from the pile on the table before him. He scanned the front page, his eye coming to rest on a headline. CONGRESS TO PROBE MIRAMAR'S INVOLVEMENT. Without interest, he tossed the paper back on the table and diverted his gaze toward the window where the darkness was broken by the glow of a single grounds light below.

A young woman entered the room and walked up to him. "You may go in now," she said softly. "The office is this way—"

"I know where the office is, thank you," he told her and walked down a corridor.

As he entered the room, he saw a man sitting behind the large desk. His eyes swept the room. He's changed things around, he thought to himself. But that's not unusual. Each one of them tries to turn the office into his own.

He approached the desk and extended his hand.

"I'm delighted that you could fly down to Washington tonight, Mr. Hunter, to meet with me personally. Your telephone call was most provocative."

Hunter settled himself in one of the chairs, a cold

smile coming to his lips. "We've been on the opposite sides of the political fence for too long, Mr. President," he said. "I think my proposition will be of great interest to you."